ALSO BY MICHAEL PALMER

From Bantam Books

The Sisterhood

Side Effects

Flashback

Extreme Measures

Natural Causes

Silent Treatment

Miracle Cure

And coming soon

The Patient

THE
SISTERHOOD

Michael Palmer

BANTAM BOOKS
NEW YORK · TORONTO · LONDON · SYDNEY · AUCKLAND

THE SISTERHOOD
A Bantam Book

PUBLISHING HISTORY
Bantam edition published September 1982
Bantam reissue/January 1995

ISBN 0-553-27570-4

Published simultaneously in the United States and Canada

Bantam Books are published by Bantam Books, a division of Random House, Inc. Its trademark, consisting of the words "Bantam Books" and the portrayal of a rooster, is Registered in U.S. Patent and Trademark Office and in other countries. Marca Registrada. Bantam Books, 1540 Broadway, New York, New York 10036.

PRINTED IN THE UNITED STATES OF AMERICA

OPM   34   33   32   31   30   29   28

Dedicated with Love
to my sons, Matthew and Daniel
and
to my parents

ACKNOWLEDGMENTS

The Sisterhood is the godchild of the very special people listed below. My gratitude to them goes much deeper than the words on this page could express.

- —To Jane Rotrosen Berkey, my agent and friend, for knowing I could long before I knew
- —To my editors, Linda Grey and Jeanne Bernkopf, for the style, wit, and wisdom they have injected into this work
- —To Donna Prince and Dr. Richard Dugas for critical reading after critical reading
- —To Attorney Mitchell Benjoya of Boston and Dr. Steven I. Cohen of Providence, Rhode Island for technical assistance
- —To Clara and Fred Jewett and the others who have taught me to live—and to write—one day at a time.

Finally a special thanks to Jim Landis, without whom, quite truthfully, none of this would have happened.

M.S.P.
Boston, 1982

PROLOGUE

"It's all right, Mama . . . I'm here, Mama . . ."

Fine fingers reached across the starched hospital sheet.
Slowly, they closed about the puffy, white hand,
restrained by adhesive tape and a leather strap to the
side of the bed.

The patient, her other arm and both legs similarly
bound, stared unblinking at the chipped ceiling. The
rhythmic rise and fall of the sheet over her chest and
sweep of her tongue across cracked lips were the only
outward signs of life. Her gnarled, gray-black hair framed
a face that had once been thought quite beautiful.

Now, skin clung tightly to bone, and dark circles of
pain obscured her eyes. Although one could easily have
placed her age at sixty-five, the woman was, in fact,
only five months past her forty-fifth birthday—the day
on which her terminal illness had first been diagnosed.

The girl seated to one side of the brass bed tightened
her grip, but turned her head away as a tear broke free
and glided over her cheek. She wore a heavy, navy
blue coat and winter boots that dripped melting snow
into a small pool on the linoleum floor.

Five motionless minutes passed; the only sounds came

1

from other patients in other rooms. Finally, the girl slipped off her coat, moved her chair close to the head of the bed, and spoke again. "Mama, can you hear me? Does it still hurt as much? Mama, please. Tell me what I can do to help?"

Another minute passed before the woman answered. Her voice, though soft and hoarse, filled the room. "Kill me! For God's sake, please kill me."

"Mama, stop that. You don't know what you're saying. I'll get the nurse. She'll give you something."

"No, baby. It doesn't help. Nothing has helped the pain for days. You can help me. You must help me."

The girl, more confused and frightened than at any time in her fifteen years, looked up at the bottle draining clear fluid into her mother's arm. She rose and made several tentative steps toward the door before the older woman's renewed pleas stopped her short.

Haltingly, she returned to the bedside, stopping a few feet away. An agonized cry came from a room somewhere down the hall. Then another. The girl closed her eyes and clenched her teeth against the hatred she felt for the place.

"Please come over here and help me," her mother begged. "Help me end this pain. Only you can do it. The pillow, baby. Just set it down over my face and lean on it as hard as you can. It won't take long."

"Mama, I . . ."

"Please! I love you. If you love me, too, you won't let me hurt so anymore. They all say it's hopeless . . . don't let your mama hurt so anymore . . ."

"I . . . I love you, Mama. I love you."

The girl continued to whisper the words as she gently lifted her mother's head and removed the thin, firm pillow.

"I love you, Mama . . ." she said again and again as she placed the pillow over the narrow face and leaned on it with all the strength she could manage. She forced

2

her mind back to the warm and happy times—long spring walks, baking lessons, steamy mugs of hot chocolate on snowy afternoons.

Her body was thin and light, with only hints at the fullness of a woman. Struggling for leverage, she grasped the pillow case and drew her knees up. With each passing scene she pressed herself more firmly against the pillow. Bumpy rides to the lake, picnics on the water's edge, races to the raft. . . .

The movement beneath the sheet lessened then stopped.

Her sobs mixing with the rattle of sleet against the window, the girl lay there, unaware of the fragment of pillow case which had ripped free and was now clutched in her hand.

After nearly half an hour, she rose, replaced the pillow, and kissed her dead mother's lips. Then she turned and walked resolutely down the hall, out of the hospital, into the raw winter evening.

The day was February seventeenth. The year, 1932.

CHAPTER I

BOSTON
OCTOBER 1

Morning sun splashed into the room moments before the first notes came from the clock radio. David Shelton, eyes still closed, listened for a few seconds before silently guessing Vivaldi, *The Four Seasons,* probably the *Summer* concerto. It was a game he had played nearly every morning for years. Still, the occasions on which he identified a piece correctly were rare enough to warrant a small celebration.

A soothing male voice, chosen by the station to blend with the dawn, identified the music as a Haydn symphony. David smiled to himself. You're getting sharper. The right continent—even the right century.

He turned his head toward the window and opened his eyes a slit, preparing for the next guessing game in his morning ritual. Hazy rainbows of sunlight filtered through his lashes. "No contest," he said, squinting to make the colors flicker.

"What did you say?" the woman next to him mumbled sleepily, drawing her body tightly against his.

"Sparkling autumn day. Fifty, no, fifty-five degrees. Nary a cloud." David opened his eyes fully, confirmed his prediction, then rolled over, slipping his arm beneath

5

her smooth back. "Happy October," he said, kissing her forehead, at the same time running his free hand down her neck and across her breasts.

David studied her face as she awoke, marveling at her uncluttered beauty. Ebony hair. High cheek bones. Full, sensuous mouth. Lauren Nichols was by all standards a stunning woman. Even at 6:00 A.M. For a moment, another woman's face flashed in his thoughts. In her own special way Ginny, too, had always looked beautiful in the early morning. The image faded as he drew his fingers over Lauren's flat stomach and gently massaged the mound beneath her soft hair.

"Roll over, David, and I'll give you a back rub," Lauren said, sitting up suddenly.

Disappointment crossed his face, but was instantly replaced by a broad grin. "Ladies' choice," he sang, rolling over and bunching the pillow beneath his head. "Last night was really wonderful," he added, feeling the thick muscles at the base of his neck relax to her touch. "You are something else, Nichols, do you know that?"

Out of David's field of vision, Lauren forced the smile of an adult trying to share a youthful enthusiasm she had long outgrown. "David," she said, increasing the vigor of her massage, "do you think you might be able to get a haircut before the Art Society dinner dance next week?"

He flipped to his back, staring at her with a mixture of confusion and dismay. "What has my hair got to do with our lovemaking?"

"Honey, I'm sorry," she said earnestly, "I really am. I guess I have a thousand things hopping around in my head today. It was beautiful for me, too. Honest."

"Beautiful? You really mean that?" David said, immediately regaining his élan.

"There's still a hell of a lot of tension in your body,

6

doc, but less each time. Last night was definitely the best yet."

The best yet. David cocked his head to one side, evaluating her words. Progress, not perfection. That was all he could ask for, he decided. And certainly, over the six months since they had met, progress there had been.

Their life together was often an emotional roller coaster, quite unlike the easy, free-flowing years with Ginny. Still, their differences had not been insurmountable—her judgmental friends, his cynicism, the differing demands of their careers. As each crisis arose, was dealt with, and passed, David sensed their caring grow. Although there were things he wished were different, he was grateful just to feel the caring, and the willingness to try.

It was willingness David thought had died for him eight years before in screams and glass and twisted metal.

Realizing that Lauren had said all she was going to on the subject of their physical relationship, David flipped over once again. The back rub continued. Maybe you're finally ready, he thought. Maybe it's time. But for God's sake, Shelton, don't rush it. Don't push her away, but try not to smother her either. As he played the feelings through in his mind, the apprehension surrounding them faded.

"You know," he said after a while, "of all the bets and guesses I've ever made with myself, you've been the most striking loss."

"How's that?"

"Well, I think it's safe to tell you now. On our first date I bet myself a jumbo Luigi's special-with-everything-except-anchovies pizza that we would run out of things to say in a week."

"David!"

"I just couldn't imagine what an unsophisticated,

7

stripes-with-plaids surgeon was going to find to talk about with a chic, jet-set newspaper reporter, that's all."

"And now you know, right?"

"What I know is that my body turned you on so much you couldn't resist trying to play 'enry 'iggins with the rest of me." He laughed, spinning around to give her a bear hug, a maneuver that usually led to an out-and-out wrestling match. When Lauren showed no inclination to join in, he released her and leaned back on his hands.

"Something the matter?" he asked.

"David, you started crying out in your sleep last night. Was it another nightmare?"

"I . . . I guess so." David answered uncertainly, testing the muscles in his jaw. Only then did he realize they were aching. "My face hurts, and that usually means I spent most of the night with my teeth clenched."

"Can you remember what it was this time?"

"One I've had before, I think. Fuzzier than other nights, but the same one. It doesn't happen so often anymore."

"Which one?"

David felt the concern in her voice, but her expression held something more. Impatience? Irritation? He looked away. "The highway," he said softly. "It was the highway." The tone and cadence of his words took on an eerie, detached quality as he drifted back into the nightmare. "All I see for a while is the windshield . . . the wipers are thrashing back and forth . . . faster and faster, fighting to keep pace with the rain. The center line keeps trying to snake under the car. I keep forcing it back with the wheel. Ginny's face is there for a moment . . . and Becky's, too . . . both asleep . . . both so peaceful. . . ." David's eyes had closed. His words stopped, but the memory of the dream was unrelenting. Out of the darkness and the rain, the headlights began coming. Two at a time. Heading straight

8

for him, then splitting apart and flashing past, one on either side. Wave after blurry wave. Then, above the lights, he saw the face. The crazy drunken face, twisted and red with fire, eyes glowing golden in the flames. His hands locked as he prayed the oncoming lights would split apart like all the others. But he knew they wouldn't. They never did. Then he heard the brakes screeching. He saw Ginny's eyes open and widen in terror. Finally, he heard the scream. Hers? His? He could never tell.

"David?"

Lauren's voice cut the scream short. He shuddered, then turned to her. Droplets of sweat had appeared on his forehead. His hands were shaking. He took a deep breath, then slowly exhaled. The shaking stopped. "Guess I got lost there for a moment, huh?" He smiled sheepishly.

"David, have you seen your doctor lately? Maybe you should get in touch with him," Lauren said.

"Ol' Brinker the Shrinker? He tapped me dry—head *and* pocketbook—about three months ago and told me I had graduated. What are you worried about? It's only a nightmare. Brinker told me they're normal in situations like mine."

"I'm worried, that's all."

"Lauren Nichols, you're frightened that I might come apart in the middle of the Art Society banquet and get your life membership canceled!"

Lauren's laugh lacked conviction. After a few seconds, she stopped trying to pay homage to his sense of humor. "David, is there anything at all that you take seriously? In just one sentence you manage to poke fun at me for being concerned about your health and for caring enough about art to be active in the Society. What is with you?"

David started to apologize, but swallowed the words. The look in her eyes told him that some very basic

9

issues were suddenly on the griddle. Something more than a simple "I'm sorry" was needed. For several interminably silent seconds their eyes locked.

Finally, he shrugged and said, "There I go again, huh? An ounce of flippancy is worth a pound of facing up to real feelings. I know I do it, but sometimes even knowing isn't enough. Look, Lauren, what I said wasn't meant maliciously. Truly it wasn't. The nightmares still scare me. It's hard for me to face that. Okay?"

Lauren was not yet placated. "You haven't answered my question, David. Is anything significant enough to keep you from joking about it?"

"As a matter of fact," he said, "most things are significant to me. Shit, you should know that by now."

"But only you know for sure which is which, right?"

"Dammit, Lauren, I'm a doctor—a surgeon—and a damn good one. Of course things are important to me. Of course I care. I care about people and pain, about suffering, about life. My world is full of injury and disease and no-win decisions. The day I lose my ability to laugh is the day I lose my ability to cope." He fought back the impulse to continue, sensing he was already guilty of attacking their morning spat with a sledge-hammer.

"I'm going to take a shower," Lauren said after a few moments. She was already out of bed, pulling on a blue velour dressing gown.

"Want company?"

"I think it's the right time for a little space and some hot, soapy water. Go make some breakfast. I'll get myself squeaky clean and we'll give this day a fresh start over a cup of coffee."

David sat staring out at the glittering new day until he heard the sound of water against tile. The day, possibly the most important one for him in years, was not starting out the way he had planned. By now he was to have told Lauren about the exciting turn of

10

events at the hospital. Events that might well mark the beginning of the end to so much of the frustration and disappointment that had colored his life. By now he was to have reaffirmed his desire to have her move in with him, and she was to have at last agreed that it was time.

"Just calm down, Shelton, and let things happen," he said, clenching his hands, then consciously relaxing them. "Everything is finally coming together. Nothing, no one, can mess them up again except you."

He selected a frayed, green surgical scrub suit from the half-dozen stuffed in a bureau drawer, dressed, and walked to the window. Four stories below, a few early risers were crossing the still-shaded islands of Commonwealth Avenue. He wondered how many of them were feeling the same sense of anticipation he was—the excitement of facing a new beginning. Beginnings. The thought brought a wistful smile. How many times had he, himself, felt that way? High school, college, medical school. Ginny, Becky. So many beginnings. Beginnings as promising as this one. David sighed. Was the morning the start of a page, of a chapter, or perhaps of a whole new story? Whatever it was to be, he felt ready. For of all the bright beginnings in his life since the accident and the nightmare year that had followed the deaths of his wife and daughter, this was the first one he completely trusted.

The apartment, though small, gave the illusion of roominess, born largely of tall windows and ten-foot ceilings—trademarks of many dwellings in the Back Bay section of the city. A long, narrow corridor connected the bedroom to a living room cluttered with near-antique furniture, a dining alcove, and a tiny kitchen that faced an alleyway at the rear of the building. The front and bathroom doors faced one another midway down the hall.

Humming an off-key rendition of the Haydn symphony, David shuffled to the kitchen. Usually, he would

11

exercise and run before eating, but this morning, he decided, could be an exception. He was a muscular man, with broad shoulders and powerful arms that made him appear heavier than his 175 pounds. There were slivers of gray throughout his black, bushy hair. His wide, youthful eyes ran the spectrum from bright blue to pale green, depending on the light. Fine creases, once transient and now indelible, traversed his forehead and the bridge of his nose.

He stood in the center of the kitchen rubbing his hands together with mock professionalism. "Zo, ve crrreate ze brrreakfast." He swung open the refrigerator door. "Ze choices, zey are many, yes?" His voice echoed back from near-empty shelves.

Once, after hopelessly blackening two steaks, he had announced to Lauren, "I think I'll write a culinary arts book for the single man. I'm going to call it *Cooking for None*."

Selecting breakfast fare was not difficult. "Let us zee . . . ve could haf tomato juice or . . . tomato juice. Ze English muffin, eet looks nice, non? . . . And zee five ecks, zey beg to be scrrrambled, yes?"

Lauren breezed into the dining alcove as he was setting their meal on the table. "Nicely done," she said, surveying his work. "You'll make a wonderful wife for someone someday." A few strands of glistening hair fell from beneath the towel she had wrapped around her head. Her smile announced that, as advertised, she was starting the morning over again.

"So," David said deliberately, "what are your plans for this day?" He was pleased at having fought back the impulse to blurt out his good news. He would disclose it casually, in the same matter-of-fact way Lauren so often told him about the luncheon she had been to at the White House or the assignment she had won to cover thus-or-so senator's campaign.

"David, do you have something you want to tell me?" she said.

"Pardon?" He stretched for one last bit of insouciance.

Lauren smiled. "My college roommate once had a surprise party for me. Just before everyone jumped out and yelled, she had the same expression on her face as you do now."

"Well, I guess I do have a little good news," he said, his nonchalance now a parody. "Dr. Wallace Huttner— *the* Dr. Wallace Huttner—is leaving town tomorrow for a few days."

"And?"

"And . . . he's asked me to make rounds with him this evening and to take over his patients until he gets back."

"Oh, David, that's wonderful," Lauren said. "Wallace Huttner! I'm impressed. The most widely acclaimed pair of hands to come out of Boston since Arthur Fiedler."

"Well, now we know that he's smart enough to recognize true surgical talent when he sees it. I'm covering his practice until he gets back from a three-day conference on the Cape."

"And there you sit, trying to impress me with how blasé you can act about the whole thing. What a funny duck you are, David."

The scrambled eggs, none too appetizing to begin with, remained on her plate as Lauren fired one question after another at him.

"Huttner was written up in *Time*, do you know that?"

"So he's operated on a few sheiks and prime ministers. He still puts his scrub suit on one leg at a time, just like the rest of us."

"Be serious for once, will you? Could this mean more money for you?"

David's eyes narrowed. He studied her face for a few seconds, looking for more than superficial interest behind her question. Although his lack of a typical surgeon's

13

salary came up infrequently, a battle of some sort was sure to follow whenever it did. Lauren seemed unable or unwilling to accept the fickle economic realities of a medical specialty that was dependent on referrals from other physicians, especially in a city like Boston with its surfeit of doctors.

Even after two years at Boston Doctors Hospital he realized that many of his colleagues still had reservations about him. Word had filtered back. "Shelton? Oh, yes, I suppose I could refer this woman to him. But she's not the easiest person to deal with and, frankly, I'm just not sure he could handle her. I mean that trouble he got into, going to pieces after his wife and kid died. I'd like to help him out, I really would. But what would *I* look like to my patient if I send her to a surgeon and he up and comes unglued?"

It wasn't easy. He had never expected it would be. Lauren's concern over his financial situation was understandable, albeit somewhat discouraging. It would take time, he tried to explain. That's all—just some time.

Her expression appeared nonjudgmental. Still, David tiptoed around the issue. "Well, Huttner is chief of the department. It should mean more acceptance from the doctors who refer patients to surgeons." Any acceptance from most of them would be an improvement, he reflected ruefully. He still appeared in the operating room so infrequently that the nurses sometimes stood around after he entered, waiting for the surgeon to arrive.

"Is he grooming you to be his partner?"

"Lauren, the man hardly knows me! He just saw the chance to throw a few crumbs in the direction of a doc who's struggling some, that's all."

"Well, Mr. Ice Water," she said, smiling, "you can act any way you want to. I'll stay excited enough for both of us. What time do you take over for him?"

"I'm meeting him at the hospital at six. We should be

14

done by eight or nine and . . . God, that reminds me. The Rosettis invited us for dinner, either tonight or tomorrow. I told them we'd—"

"I can't make it," Lauren said. "I mean I have to work."

"You don't like them, do you?"

"David, please, we've been over this before. I think the Rosettis are very nice people." Her words were hollow. David's unsuccessful attempts to draw her into his long-standing friendship with the tavern owner and his wife remained a source of tension.

"Okay, I'll phone Joey and get a raincheck," David said, relieved that he was able to put the matter to rest without a major confrontation.

"That would be fine. Really." It was Lauren's way of thanking him for his restraint. "I do have to work. In fact, I'm flying to Washington this morning. The President's going to announce details of his latest economic program and the service wants me to cover it from the personal, human side. I'll probably be there for a couple of days."

"In that case, you'll need all the nourishment you can get." He nodded at her untouched breakfast. "Want seconds on the eggs?"

Lauren glanced at her watch, stood up, and stretched as high as she could reach. "Just leave them there until I get back from Washington." She walked halfway toward the bedroom before adding, "They can only improve with age." She giggled and dashed down the corridor as David sprang up to give chase. She waited until he had nearly reached the bedroom door before pushing it closed and flipping the lock.

"You'll live to regret this," David called out through the door. "Someday I'm going to become a famous chef and marry the Countess of Lusitania. Then I'll be lost to you forever."

Twenty minutes later, Lauren emerged from the bed-

15

room, breathtaking in a burgundy suit and beige blouse. A silk scarf was draped loosely about her neck. "No caveman stuff, David," she said, anticipating his hug and blocking it with an outstretched hand. "This outfit has to last me at least a day. Listen, I almost forgot. You might be able to help me out."

"Only in exchange for caveman stuff."

"David, this is serious."

"Okay." He motioned that he was ready to listen.

"Senator Cormier's office announced that he's entering your hospital in the next day or two for an operation. Gall bladder, I think."

"You sure? Cormier seems more the White Memorial than the Boston Doctors type."

Lauren nodded. "Could he be coming in as Huttner's patient?"

"No chance. Huttner would never go away with that kind of prestige coming in on his service."

"Do you think you could get in to see him? Or even better, get me in to see him? His campaign for a stiff windfall profits tax against the oil companies has made him really big stuff. An exclusive interview would be an ostrich-sized feather in my cap."

"I'll try, but I can't guarantee any—"

"Thanks, you're a dear."

Lauren wished him luck with his new responsibilities, squeezed his hands, and kissed him lightly on the mouth. Then, with a final, "Be a good boy, now," she walked out of the apartment and down the hall to the elevator.

For several minutes David stood silently by the door, breathing in her perfume, but feeling only a strange emptiness. "At least she could have tasted them," he said as he began to clear the table. "In spite of what they looked like."

* * *

The night watchman was fat. Fat and agonizingly slow. From a recessed doorway, the nurse, a fragile-looking woman with hair the color of pale sun, watched and waited as he lumbered down the hallway. Now and again he stopped to poke at the door of a storage room or to check one of the bank of staff lockers lining the wall. B-2 West, the subbasement of the west wing of Boston Doctors Hospital, was, but for the two of them, deserted.

The nurse looked about at the grime, illuminated by bare ceiling light bulbs, and her skin began to itch. She was a petite woman, impeccably groomed, with makeup so meticulously applied it was almost invisible. Impatiently, she rubbed her thumbs across her fingertips. The watchman was taking forever. She glanced at her watch. Forty-five, maybe fifty minutes of safe time—more than enough, provided she could get moving and avoid any other unanticipated delays. A roach crawled over the tip of her shoe and for a moment she thought she was going to be sick. She forced herself to relax and waited.

Finally, the watchman was done. He keyed the security box, began whistling the "Colonel Bogey March," and, after a few in-place steps, strutted off to his own accompaniment. To some the man might have looked silly, or jovial, or even cute. To the delicate woman observing him he was, quite simply, repulsive.

She waited an extra few seconds, moved quickly down the row of lockers to number 178, then dialed the combination printed on the card Dahlia had sent her. The thin, half-filled syringe was right where she had been told it would be. She briefly held it to the light, then dropped it into the front pocket of her spotless uniform. Another check of the time and she headed for the tunnel leading to the south wing. She rode the elevator to Two South, then slipped into the rear stairwell and hurried up two more flights. Ducking into

17

Room 438, she stopped, regaining her breath in soundless gulps. Through the gloom she could see John Chapman. The man was asleep, tucked in a fetal position, his face toward her. From beneath the sheet a catheter drained clear urine into a plastic collecting system.

Chapman's recovery following kidney surgery had been uneventful. The woman smiled at the thought. Uneventful . . . until now.

She checked the corridor. A nurse's aide—the first arrival of her day shift—had just stepped off the elevator. The fragile night peace was holding, but the nurse knew that within half an hour it would yield to the chaos of day. The time was now. Her pulse quickened. Anaphylactic shock! Almost fifteen years in hospital nursing and she had never even seen a full-blown case, let alone watched one from start to finish.

She moved to the bedside. There, on the nightstand, were the flowers. A glorious spray of lilies. Taped to the vase was the card.

"Best Wishes, Lily." She whispered the words without actually reading them. There was no need. They were her words.

On the table next to the vase lay Chapman's silver necklace and medic-alert tag. She illuminated the disc with her penlight. Again she smiled. It said:

DIABETIC
ALLERGIC TO PENICILLIN
ALLERGIC TO BEE STINGS

The small syringe in her hand held the bee venom concentrate used by allergists to desensitize their high-risk patients. Although practically speaking the dose was enormous, it was still minute enough to escape detection during a conventional autopsy.

John Chapman's cocoa face was loose and relaxed. Even asleep he seemed to be smiling. The nurse pulled

18

over a straight-backed chair and sat. With one hand, she slipped the needle through the rubber stopper of his I.V. tubing. With the other, she gently shook him by the shoulder.

"Mr. Chapman, John, wake up," she cooed. "It's morning."

Chapman's eyes eased open. "Little Angel? Zat you?" His voice was a rich bass. A boyhood in Jamaica twenty-five years before still tinged the edges of his words. He focused on her and smiled. "My, but you are somethin' to gaze upon," he said. "Is it really morning or are you just one of my dreams?"

"No dream," she answered. "But I am a little early. My shift doesn't start for another half hour or so." She depressed the plunger, emptying the venom into the intravenous line. "I came in early just to see you."

"What?"

She didn't answer. Instead, she watched intently as a quizzical expression crossed Chapman's face, which quickly gave way to apprehension.

"I . . . I feel funny, Angel," he said. "Real funny." Panic crept into his voice. "I'm starting to tingle all over. . . . Angela, somethin's happening to me. Somethin' awful. I feel like I am going to die."

The woman looked at him blandly. You are, she thought. You are. At that instant the full force of the anaphylactic reaction hit. The lining of John Chapman's nose and throat swelled nearly shut. The muscles surrounding his bronchial tubes went into spasm. The nurse spun around to be certain the room door was closed. The reaction was more rapid, more spectacular than she had ever imagined it would be. In fact, she decided, it was more spectacular than anything she had ever witnessed.

"An . . . gel . . . please. . . ." Chapman's words were barely audible. His eyes had swollen shut.

Instinctively, she checked for a pulse, but she knew

that vascular collapse had already occurred. A second later, the last sliver of air space in Chapman's respiratory passage closed. He rolled to his back and was still.

The nurse with pale sun hair held her breath during the final moments, then exhaled. Her faultless face glowed with a beatific smile, acknowledging that once again she had done her job well.

The Seth Thomas wall clock in his living room showed seven thirty when David finished stacking the dishes in the sink and changed into a navy blue sweat suit. He made a deliberate study of his small record collection before selecting Copeland's *Rodeo* and then began a series of slow-motion stretching exercises and calisthenics.

The Copeland was a perfect choice, he thought as he dragged a set of weights out from behind the couch. For ten minutes he lifted in various positions and angles, pushing himself harder than usual until the tension of Lauren's unemotional departure left him.

The weights had come to be as much mental as physical therapy—a morning ritual for almost five years, begun the day David had decided to return to surgery by repeating the last two grueling years of residency. That same day he smoked his last cigarette and ran his first mile. Within a few months he had more than regained the stamina lost during three years away from the operating room.

Glistening from the workout, he grabbed his stopwatch and keys, stuffing them into the pocket of his sweatpants as he stepped out the door.

He bypassed the narrow, rickety elevator in favor of the stairs at the end of the hall. Trotting down four flights and across the dimly lit foyer of the building, he pushed through the front doors and out onto Commonwealth Avenue.

The sunlight hit his eyes like a flashbulb. It was one of those days New Englanders boast about when they tell outsiders that there is nowhere else on earth to live. One of those days that renders February little more than a distant memory, and helps them forget the muddy drizzle of April and the oppressive, steamy heat of mid-August, at least for a while.

Stiffly at first, but with rapidly developing fluidness, he jogged the few blocks toward the esplanade. Elms and oaks flashed by, heavy now with reds and oranges and golds. The air, unwilling this day to succumb to commuters' exhaust fumes, tasted like mountain water.

David crossed over Storrow Drive and picked up his pace as he turned onto the tarmac path paralleling the river. For a time he ran with his eyes nearly closed, breathing in the day and taking increasing delight in the responsiveness of each muscle in his body.

He watched a lone oarsman sculling the Charles like some giant water bug. Even at such an early hour there were people scattered along the grassy bank reading, sketching, or just soaking in the morning. Cyclists glided silently past him in both directions. Dogs tugged their masters along. Intense-faced students, wearing their books on their backs like hair shirts, shuffled reluctantly toward classrooms where sterile fluorescence would replace the autumn sun.

David checked his stopwatch and glanced around him. Under six minutes to the bridge. He had won his first bet of the run. Sooner or later a Rolls Royce and an A-frame in the Berkshires would be his. Wiping sweat from around his eyes, he picked up his tempo a bit.

To his right a barefoot girl wearing jeans and a bright red T-shirt sent a Frisbee spinning toward her boyfriend. "Two Twinkies and a Big Mac says he catches it," David panted just before the disc spun sharply toward the river, hit the ground, and rolled down the bank. "Thank goodness," he laughed out loud.

At the three-mile mark he turned and headed back.

21

"Everything is getting better," he said out loud, matching each syllable to the slap of his Nikes on the pavement. "Better and better and better."

Christ, it felt good to be alive again.

CHAPTER II

Christine Beall eased her light blue Mustang past the guard at Parking Lot C, forcing a thin smile in response to his wave. She cruised past several empty spaces without noticing them, then spotted one in the corner farthest from the gate and pulled in. Stepping onto the gravel, she adjusted her carefully tailored nurse's uniform and squinted up at the afternoon sun, but quickly gave up trying to absorb any of the magic of the brilliant autumn day. Her preoccupation with other thoughts, other issues, made it impossible.

Lot C was one of three satellite parking areas appropriated by Doctors Hospital to meet the needs of an ever-expanding staff. Christine started toward the minibus stop, then decided she needed the time and the three blocks' walk as a bridge between her outside world and the hospital. Up ahead, two other evening shift nurses waved her to join them, but after a few quick steps, she stopped and motioned them to go on. Pausing by the window of a secondhand furniture store, she studied her image in the dusty glass.

You look tired, she thought. Tired and worried . . . and scared.

She was not a tall woman, barely five foot four. Her sandy hair was tied back in a ponytail that she would pin up beneath her nurse's cap before starting work. Scattered freckles, still darkened by the summer sun, dotted the tops of both cheeks and the bridge of her nose.

"What are you going to do, kid?" she asked her reflection softly. "Are you really ready to start this whole thing in motion? Peg-whoever-she-is may be ready. Charlotte Thomas may be ready. But are you?" She pressed her lips together and stared at the sidewalk. Finally, with an indecisive shrug, she turned and headed down the block.

Boston Doctors Hospital was a massive glass and brick hydra with three tentacles probing north and west into Roxbury and another three south and east toward the downtown area. Over the one hundred and five years of its existence several wings had grown, decayed, and died, only to be replaced by larger and higher ones. Ongoing construction was as much a part of its being as the white uniforms scurrying in and out of its maw.

Never able to snare a benefactor generous enough to endow an entire building, the hospital's trustees had adopted the unimaginative policy of identifying the tentacles by the direction of their thrust. The sliding doors through which Christine entered the main lobby were located between Southeast and South.

She glanced at the large gold clock set in a marble slab above the information desk. Two thirty. It would be another twenty or twenty-five minutes before the day shift on Four South would sign out to her three-to-eleven group.

Christine leaned against a stone column and surveyed the activity around her. Patients and visitors filled every available seat, while dozens more crowded around the information desk or weaved their way across from one

24

wing to another. Scattered wheelchairs punctuated rows of molded plastic chairs. The scene, one she had viewed hundreds of times over the past five years, still filled her with fascination and awe. There were days, certain special days, when she actually felt a physical merging of her body with the fiber of the hospital. Days when she felt its pulse as surely as if it were her own. Slowly, she crossed the lobby and joined the flow heading down the main artery of the South wing.

Christine's floor, Four South, like most of the other floors in the seven-story wing, housed a mixture of medical and surgical patients, each with a private doctor. A few residents, widely scattered throughout the hospital, served as emergency backup. On Four South, as on all other private floors in all other hospitals, nurses were the sole medical presence for most of each day.

Stepping off the elevator, Christine scanned the corridor, checking for an emergency "crash" cart or other equipment that might suggest trouble in one of the rooms. The floor seemed normally busy, but an instinct, developed over five years, whispered that something was wrong.

She was nearing the nurses' station when the cries began—pitiful, piercing wails from the far end of the hall. Christine raced toward the sound. As she passed Room 412, she glanced in at Charlotte Thomas, who was sleeping, though restlessly, through the commotion.

The cries were coming from 438—John Chapman's room. At the doorway Christine stopped short. The room was a shambles. Candy, books, flowers, and shattered vases covered the floor. Seated in a chair, her face buried in her hands, was John Chapman's wife, a proud, stocky woman Christine had met at the time of his admission. The bed was stripped and empty.

"Oh my God," Christine murmured. She crossed the

25

room and knelt by the woman, whose cries had given way to helpless whimpers. "Mrs. Chapman?"

"My Johnny's dead. Gone. They all said he would be fine, and now he's dead." She was staring through her hands at the floor, talking more to herself than to Christine.

"Mrs. Chapman, I'm Christine Beall, one of the evening nurses. Can I do anything for you? Get you anything?" Christine ached at the thought of John Chapman's death. The near-legendary fighter for blacks and other minorities had been up and doing well when she had left the hospital just sixteen hours before.

"No, no, I'll be all right," the woman finally managed. "I . . . I just can't believe my Johnny's dead."

Christine looked about. A few vases of flowers were intact, but most had been thrown to the floor or shattered against a wall. "Mrs. Chapman, who did this?"

The woman looked up. Her eyes were red and glassy, her features distorted by grief. "Me. I did," she said. "I came up to clean out Johnny's room. All of a sudden it hit me that he was gone. He's never coming back. The next thing I remember, the nurse was trying to keep me from smashing any more of Johnny's gifts. He even got a card and a book from the governor, you know. My God, I hope I haven't ruined it. I—"

"You didn't ruin it, Mrs. Chapman. I have it right here. And here's the orange juice you wanted."

Christine turned toward the voice.

Angela Martin nodded a greeting, then brought over the book and the juice. "I called your pastor, Mrs. Chapman," she said. "He'll be right over."

At the sight of Angela, immaculate and unruffled despite a difficult eight-hour shift, the woman calmed perceptibly. "Thank you, child. You've been so kind to me. And you were to my Johnny, too." She gestured at the mess. "I . . . I'm sorry about this."

"Nonsense," Angela said, "I've called Housekeeping.

They'll take care of it. Come, let's wait in the quiet room until your pastor comes." She put a slender arm around the grieving woman's shoulders and led her out.

Christine stood alone amid the wreckage, remembering her initial surprise at John Chapman's humor and erudite gentleness. Was there anything else she could do now for the man's widow? Not really, she decided. As long as Angela Martin was with her, the woman was in exceptionally compassionate and skilled hands.

Christine started toward the door, then stopped and returned for the two undamaged vases of flowers. Mrs. Chapman might want to bring them home, she thought. She glanced at the note taped to the green glass vase. Lilies . . . from Lily? Good grief, what next? She shook her head. An unexpected death and bizarre namesake flowers. It all felt quite in keeping with a day that from its very beginning had seemed beyond her control.

Her roommates, Lisa and Carole, had both left for work when the phone began ringing. Christine had made a quick thrust at her alarm clock, then identified the true source of the insistent jangle. She had tried burying her head under the pillow. Eventually she had stumbled to the kitchen, certain that the ringing would stop as soon as she reached for the receiver. It did not.

"My name is Peg," the caller had said in a voice that was at once both soft and strong. "I am one of the directors of your Sisterhood. There is a patient on your floor in Doctors Hospital whom I would like you to evaluate and, if you see fit, present for consideration to your Regional Screening Committee. It is not possible for me to do so myself without an awkwardness that might well be noticed, since I no longer actively practice nursing."

Christine had put her hand under the faucet, then rubbed cold water over her face. Although mention of The Sisterhood had awakened her like a slap, she wanted

27

to be sure. She stammered, "Well, no one has ever called and asked me to . . . what I mean is . . ."

The woman had anticipated Christine's concern. "Please, Christine, just hear me out," she said. "As is always the rule in our movement, you are under no obligation to do anything other than that which you believe in your heart to be right. I have known the woman about whom I am calling for many years. I feel certain that she would not want to survive the situation in which she now exists. She is in great pain and her condition, from what I have been able to learn, is without hope."

At that moment Christine knew, without being told, whom she was being asked to evaluate. "It's Charlotte, isn't it?" she said. "Charlotte Thomas."

"Yes, Christine, it is."

"I . . . I've thought about her a great deal lately, especially with the agony she's been going through these past few days."

"Were you planning to report her case yourself?" the caller asked.

"Last night. I almost called her in last night. Something stopped me from doing it. I don't know what it was. She is such a remarkable woman, I . . ." Christine's voice trailed away.

"The path we have chosen to follow will never be an easy one," the woman said. "Should it ever become easy, you will know that somehow you have lost your way."

"I understand," Christine said grimly. "My shift begins at three this afternoon. If it feels right to me then, I'll call in her case report and let the Screening Committee decide."

"That is as much as I could possibly ask or expect, Christine. Perhaps sometime in the future circumstances will allow us to meet. Good-bye."

28

"Good-bye," she said, but the woman had already hung up.

Before falling asleep the previous night, Christine had drawn up an ambitious list of projects for the day. Suddenly, with a single phone call, none of them mattered. She carried a pot of tea to the living room and sank into an easy chair, totally absorbed in thoughts of The Sisterhood of Life. Over the ten months following her initiation into the movement a new meaning and purpose had entered her life. Now she was being asked to test that purpose. With Charlotte's life at stake, the test would not be easy.

Engrossed in thoughts of Charlotte Thomas and John Chapman, Christine wandered into the lounge to hang up her coat. Two of the day nurses had put aside the shift notes they were writing and were, instead, arguing about which of John Chapman's medications had most likely caused his fatal reaction. Christine had no inclination to join in. She greeted them with a nod, then said, "I'm going to see Charlotte for a few minutes. Send someone to get me in four-twelve if I'm not back by the time report is ready to start. Okay?" The women waved her off and resumed their conversation.

It had been nearly two weeks since Charlotte Thomas's surgery, two weeks during which Christine had walked into Room 412 dozens of times. In spite of the frequent visits, as she approached the door a strange image appeared in her mind. It was an image that came to her almost every time she was about to enter 412. Well, not exactly an image, Christine realized—more an expectation. It was quite vivid despite what she knew in the practical, professional part of her. Charlotte would be sitting in the vinyl chair next to her bed writing a letter. Her light brown hair would be piled carelessly on the back of her head, held in place by a floppy bow of pink yarn. The thin lines at the corners of her eyes and along the edge of her lips would crinkle upward in pleasure at the appearance of her "super-nurse." She would look as healthy and radiant and alive at age sixty as she had probably looked at sixteen. A woman totally at peace with herself.

That was the way she had looked each day during her stay in August for diagnostic tests. The moment before she entered the room Christine imagined her voice, as clear and free as a forest brook, saying, "Ah, sweet Christine. My one-woman pep squad, come to bring some cheer to the sick ol' lady . . ."

At the foot of the bed Christine stopped and closed her eyes, shaking her head as if trying to dislodge what little remained of her imaginings and hope.

Charlotte lay on her right side, propped in that position by several pillows. White-lipped, Christine tiptoed to her bedside. Charlotte seemed asleep. Her coarse breathing, nearly a snore, was labored and unnatural. The oxygen prongs designed to fit in her nostrils had slipped to one cheek, exposing an angry redness caused by their continuous pressure. Her face was puffed and pasty yellow. Hanging from the poles on either side of the bed, plastic bags dripped their fluid into her through clear plastic tubes.

Christine was close to tears as she reached down and gently smoothed Charlotte's hair away from her face. The woman's eyes fluttered for a second, then opened.

"Another day." Christine said with cheer in her voice but sadness in her smile.

"Another day," Charlotte echoed weakly. "How's my girl?"

How typical, Christine thought. Lying there like that and she asks how *I* am. "A little tired, but otherwise all right," she managed. "How's *my* girl?"

Charlotte's lips twisted in a half-smile that said, "You should know better than to ask." She brought a bruised hand up and tugged lightly at the red rubber tube taped to the bridge of her nose and looping down into one nostril. "I don't like this," she whispered.

Christine shook her head. The tube had not been there when she had left last night. Her words were forced. "You . . . must have had some trouble with your stomach. . . . The tube is keeping it from swelling with fluid. It's attached to a suction machine. That's the hissing sound you keep hearing." She looked away. The tubes, the bruises, the pain—Christine felt them as if they were her own. She knew that with Charlotte more than with any patient she had ever cared for her perspective had gone awry. Many times she had wanted to run from the room—from her own feelings. To turn Charlotte Thomas's care over to another nurse. But always she had stayed.

"How's that boyfriend of yours?" Charlotte asked.

The change in subject was her way of saying she understood. There was nothing that could be done about the tube. Christine knelt down and with accentuated girlish embarrassment said, "Charlotte, if you're talking about Jerry, he's not my boyfriend. In fact, I don't think I even like the man very much." This time Charlotte did manage a thin smile—and a wink. "Charlotte, it's true. I'll have none of your sly winks. The man is a . . . a conceited, self-centered . . . prig."

Charlotte reached out and silently stroked her cheek. All at once, through the dim light, Christine fixed on her eyes. They held a strange, wonderful glow that she had never seen in them before. There was a force, a power in Charlotte's voice that Christine could almost feel. "The answers are all within you, my darling Christine. Just listen to your heart. Whenever you must really know, listen to your heart." Her hand dropped away. Her eyes closed. In seconds Charlotte was in exhausted sleep.

Christine stared down at her, straining for the mean-

31

ing behind her words. She isn't talking about Jerry, she thought. I just know she isn't. Trancelike, she walked down the hall to shift report.

The lounge was filling up. Eight nurses—six from the outgoing group and two from Christine's shift—were seated around a table covered with papers, charts, coffee cups, ashtrays, and several squeeze bottles of hand lotion. One of the women, Gloria Webster, was still writing notes. Gloria was Christine's age, had bleached platinum hair, and wore thick, iridescent eye make-up. She looked up, took a sip of coffee, then returned to her writing. At the same time, she spoke. "Hi, Beall."

"Hi, Gloria, busy day?"

The blonde continued writing. "Not too bad. The same old shit. Just more of it than usual, if ya know what I mean." She put down her coffee.

"Report soon?" Christine asked.

"In a minute. As usual, I'm the last one to start these damn shift notes. I think what we should do is just mimeograph one set and paste 'em in each chart. They all say the same thing anyway, if ya know what I mean."

Christine's brief laugh was purely for the sake of the other woman. One of the other nurses had summed up Gloria's skills when she quipped, "She may be careless as hell doing meds and notes and things, but just the same she doesn't give a shit about thè patients."

The last two nurses arrived and took their places at the table. Report began with a discussion of the new patients who had come onto the floor during the two shifts since the evening crew had last been on. They were discussed in more detail than the rest of the patients would be. Even so, most of the remarks from around the table were not about the patients, but about their doctors.

"Sam Engles, patient of Dr. Bertram . . ."

". . . Uh-oh, Jack the Ripper strikes again."

"Bert the Flirt, ten thumbs in the operating room but a dozen hands around the nurses."

"Stella Vecchione, patient of Dr. Malchman . . ."

"Good luck, Stella."

"Donald McGregor, patient of Dr. Armstrong . . ."

"She's nice, don'cha think?"

"Nice, but senile. She writes like my grandmother."

"Edwina Burroughs, patient of Dr. Shelton . . ."

"Who?"

"Shelton, the cute one with the frizzy hair."

"Oh, I know who you mean. Is he on drugs or something?"

"What?"

"Drugs. Penny Schmidt on three said she heard from one of the O.R. nurses that Shelton was on drugs."

"Good ol' Penny. Always a kind word for everybody. I'll bet she could find dirt in a sterilizer."

They went through the rest of the patients on the floor room by room. As she listened, Christine predicted to herself which of the nurses would limit her report to facts, lab reports, and vital signs, and which would make some comment on the appearance and activities of her patients. Three stressed the numbers, and three the people. Christine scored 100 percent, noting with some satisfaction that the human-oriented reports were given by the nurses whose work she admired the most. Gloria Webster was not among that group.

"Beall, I guess you're gonna take four-twelve again, like always," Gloria said as she doused a half-smoked cigarette in the bottom of a Styrofoam cup. She addressed all the floor nurses at her level by their last names, more out of a sense of camaraderie than any effort to display toughness. "Well, there's not much to report except that things are even worse than they were yesterday, and that includes the bedsore, if ya know what

I mean. Her temp and B.P. keep bouncing up and down. Nasotracheal suction is ordered every two hours. I did the bedsore, so you won't have to do it again for four hours. Christ, does that thing smell. Nothin' much else, I guess. Any questions?"

Christine fought back the impulse to say, "Yeah, one. How can you talk like that about a woman who has more wonder, more magic in one cell than you have in your whole body?" Instead she bit back her feelings of disgust and anger and merely shook her head.

The remainder of the report took ten minutes. Then the six day nurses put on their coats and left. The torch of care had been passed.

After the lounge had emptied out, Christine sat with Charlotte's chart and began reviewing it a page at a time. The process was painful. Page after page of notes, reports, and procedures. The chronology of a medical nightmare. As she jotted significant items on a small pad, Christine's sense of resolve grew. It *was* enough. Just as Peg had said on the phone. Enough. She would present Charlotte's case to The Sisterhood.

She spent several minutes rewriting her notes and double-checking to insure she had omitted no important information. Satisfied, she opened her address book and copied a phone number on a scrap of paper. Then she hesitated. Her mouth grew dry. She sat, picking absently at a fingernail. Come on, lady, she urged herself. If you're going to do it, then do it. In the moment before she stood up, her mind saw Charlotte's eyes. The glow of peace, of infinite peace, was even clearer than before. ". . . Whenever you must really know, listen to your heart."

There was a pay phone at one end of the floor, partially shielded by a glass partition. The nearby corridor was deserted. Christine hesitated once more, sensing her resolve begin to crumble. Maybe the Committee won't even return the call. Maybe when they review the case they won't approve. Maybe . . .

With every muscle tensed, she set the scrap of paper in front of her and dialed. After two rings, a click sounded, then a short beep. A female voice, nearly neuter on the recording, said, "Good day. Ten seconds after my voice goes off, you will hear a tone. There will then be thirty seconds for you to leave your message, the time of your call, and a number where you can be reached. Your call will be returned as soon as possible. Thank you."

Christine waited for the tone. "This is Christine Beall, evening shift, Four South, Boston Doctors Hospital. I would like to submit a patient for evaluation. The number at this pay phone is five, five, five-seven, one, eight, one. It is now three fifty P.M. I'll be available at this number until eleven o'clock tonight. After that I can . . ." Before she could leave her home number there was a sharp click as the recording machine shut off. She moved to place the call again and finish her message. Then, overcome by renewed uncertainty, she returned the receiver to its cradle. If it's supposed to happen, it will happen, she thought.

Harrison Weller stared vacantly at the ceiling, unaware of Christine's entrance. The tiny Sony television suspended over his bed by a metal arm flashed the logo and closing music of "The Guiding Light." He took no obvious notice of it. He was seventy-five, but his narrow, craggy face had a serene, ageless quality.

"Mr. Weller, how are you doing?" Christine asked, crossing over to him. "Why do you have the drapes closed? It's just beautiful outside. The sunlight will do you good."

He looked at her and forced a smile. "Charlene, isn't it?" he asked.

"Mr. Weller, you know my name. I've been in here nearly every day since you arrived. It's Christine."

"Sunny out, you say?" Weller's creaking voice reminded Christine of a high school actor trying to imitate an old man. He had arrived on the floor following repair of a fractured hip and immediately had become a pet of the nurses. Although he never seemed to mind their endearments, neither had he responded to them. He often appeared confused or withdrawn, behavior that had led his orthopedic surgeon to label him senile.

Christine opened the drapes, flooding the room with late afternoon sun. She raised Weller to a sitting position and set herself down next to him so that he could see her face. The old man squinted at her for a moment, then broke out in a grin.

"Well, aren't you a pretty one," he said, reaching up and lightly pinching her cheek.

Christine smiled and took his hand in hers. "How's your hip feeling, Mr. Weller?" she asked.

"My what?"

"Your hip," she said more deliberately in a voice that was nearly a shout. "You had an operation on your hip. I want to know if you are having any pain."

"Pain? In my hip?"

She was about to try again when Weller added, "Nope. Not a twinge, 'cept sometimes when I move my foot over to the left."

Christine gasped. It was by far the most complicated response he had made to any question since she had met him. All at once realization sparkled across her face.

"Mr. Weller," she shouted. "Do you have a hearing aid?"

"Hearing aid?" Weller creaked. "Of course I have a hearing aid. Had one for years."

"Why aren't you wearing it?"

"Can't very well wear something that's in a drawer at

home, now, can I?" he said, as if the conclusion should have been obvious to her.

"What about your wife? Can't she bring it in for you?"

"Who, Sarah? Her arthritis has acted up so bad, she hasn't even been able to get out of the house to come see me."

"Mr. Weller, I can send someone out to your house to get your hearing aid. Would you like that?"

"Why sure I would, Charlene," he said, squeezing her hand. "And while they're at it, tell 'em to fetch my glasses too. Sarah knows where they are. Can't see past the tip a my nose without 'em."

Christine's glow had blossomed to an excited smile. "Mr. Weller, who's helping Sarah at home while *she's* sick?" she asked.

"Don't know for certain. Annie Grissom next door helps out some when she can."

"I can send a nurse to your house, Mr. Weller. If she thinks your wife needs one, she'll arrange for her to have a homemaker."

"A what?"

She started to repeat herself, but stopped in mid-sentence and threw her arms around him. "Don't worry, I'll take care of everything," she said in a voice that was half shout and half laugh.

Suddenly, Christine shuddered, then slowly loosened her embrace. She felt the eerie sensation of eyes watching her from behind. She spun around. Standing there, filling the doorway, was Dorothy Dalrymple, director of nursing for the hospital. She was in her mid-fifties, with close-cropped hair and a cherubic face. Her uniform stretched like a snowy tundra, enclosing a bulk of nearly two hundred pounds. Puffy ankles hung over the tops of her low white clinic shoes. The fleshy folds around her eyes deepened as she appraised the scene.

Christine hopped off the bed, tugging her uniform

straight. Although she had come to know Dalrymple professionally over the years, she had never felt completely at ease around the woman. Perhaps it was her imposing size, perhaps her lofty position. She had certainly been kind and open enough.

The director moved toward her, stopping a few feet away, hands on hips. "Well, Miss Beall," she said reprovingly, but unable to completely conceal a wry smile, "is this some new nursing technique, or have I walked in on a budding May-December romance?"

Christine smiled sheepishly and turned back to Weller. "Harrison," she said softly, "I told you we'd be discovered. We simply cannot go on meeting like this." Christine squeezed his hands reassuringly, then followed Dalrymple out of the room.

Over the decade and a half she had headed the service at Boston Doctors Dotty Dalrymple had become something of a legend for her fierce protection of "her nurses." Never considered a brilliant thinker, she was nevertheless well known throughout the medical community not only because of her bearlike charisma, but also because her identical twin, Dora, was the nursing director at Suburban Hospital, located some fifteen miles west of the city.

The two were called Tweedledum and Tweedledee—though never to their faces. They were, to the best of anyone's knowledge, the only nursing directors in the area who still faithfully wore their uniforms to work. It was a gesture, however unaesthetic, that contributed to their popularity.

Dalrymple put a motherly paw on Christine's shoulder. "So, Christine, what was that all about?" she asked.

Briefly, Christine recounted her discovery of the likely causes of Harrison Weller's "senility." The nursing director shared her excitement.

"You know," she said, "I spend so much of my time buried in paperwork, labor negotiations, and hospital politics tht sometimes I actually forget what nursing is all about." Christine nodded modestly. "The flair you show for your work reminds me that no matter how little respect physicians show us, no matter how much they demean our intelligence or our judgment, we are still the ones who care for the patients. The ones who really know them as people. I honestly believe that most patients who recover from their illnesses are nursing saves, not doctor saves."

What about those who don't recover? Christine wanted to ask.

They walked down the hall in silence for a bit, then Dalrymple stopped and turned to her. "Christine, you are a very special nurse. This hospital needs you and more like you. Always feel free to talk with me about anything that troubles you. Anything."

Her words should have been reassuring, but something about her expression did not seem to fit with them. Christine felt suddenly cold and uncomfortable. She was searching for a response when the pay phone at the end of the hallway began ringing. She whirled to the sound as if it had been a gunshot.

"Well, it doesn't look like that telephone is going to answer itself, Christine," Dalrymple said, starting toward it.

"I'll get it," she blurted out, racing past the bewildered director and down the corridor.

Christine slowed as she approached the phone, half hoping it would stop ringing before she could answer it, yet at teh same time worried that it might. She hesitated, then grabbed the receiver, reaching into her pocket for the pages of notes on Charlotte Thomas. Somehow she knew with total certainty that the call was for her.

The voice was a woman's, stern with perhaps that hint of an accent. "I am calling Miss Christine Beall, a nurse on this floor."

"This is Christine Beall," she said, swallowing against the dryness that had reappeared in her mouth.

"Miss Beall, my name is Evelyn. I am calling in answer to your message of earlier this afternoon. I represent the New England Regional Screening Committee."

With darting, fawnlike eyes, Christine scanned the corridor. Dalrymple had gone. There were people, staff and visitors, but none within earshot. "I . . . I have a case I wish to present for evaluation and recommendation," she stammered, not quite certain she remembered the prescribed order in which their conversation was to proceed.

"Very well," the woman said. "I shall be taking notes, so please speak slowly and clearly. I won't interrupt unless I feel it is absolutely essential to do so. Please begin."

Christine's hands were shaking as she set the notes in front of her. Thirty seconds passed during which her thoughts and emotions were racing so fast she was unable to speak. *Charlotte wants so much to have it end,* she reasoned, *it must be right. It has to be right.* Somewhere deep inside her, though, a kernel of doubt lingered. She was able to begin only after convincing herself that, even if the case were approved, she could always change her mind.

"The patient in question is Mrs. Charlotte Thomas," she said in a slow, factual monotone that she hoped would mask the quiver in her voice. "She is a sixty-year-old white woman, a registered nurse. On September eighteenth she had a Miles's resection and colostomy for cancer of the colon. Since her surgery, she has not done well at all. I have known Mrs. Thomas since her diagnostic admission in August and have spent many hours talking with her both before and after her operation. She has always been a vigorous, active, athletic woman and has told me on several occasions that she could never face life as an invalid or crippled by pain.

40

As recently as this past July, she was working full time for a home health agency."

Christine sensed that she was rambling. Her hands were wet and cold. She had known it wouldn't be easy. Peg had told her this morning that it shouldn't be. Still, she had not expected this kind of tension. And this was only the initial case report. What if they approved? What if she actually had to . . .

"Miss Beall, you may continue," Evelyn said. At that instant Christine heard footsteps close by. Panicked, she whirled to face the noise. "Miss Beall? Are you there?" Evelyn asked.

Dotty Dalrymple was standing a few feet away. My God, what's happening, Christine thought. Has she heard?

"Miss Beall, *are you there?*" The voice was more insistent.

Her knuckles whitened around the receiver. "Oh, ah, yes, Aunt Evelyn," she managed, "hold on for a minute, can you? My nursing director is here." She set her arm down on the counter of the booth. Even then she could feel it shaking.

"Christine, are you all right?" Dalrymple said in a tone that seemed too bland, too matter-of-fact. "You look a little pale."

How much explanation does she want? Christine wondered. How much of a lie? "Oh, no, I'm fine, Miss Dalrymple. It's my aunt. My Aunt Evelyn."

Dalrymple shrugged. "As long as you're all right. You nearly jumped out of your skin when the phone rang before. Then, when you didn't come back, I became concerned that perhaps something had . . ."

Christine cut her off with a laugh that felt far too forced. "No, everything is fine. It's . . . my uncle. He had an operation today and I was waiting to hear. Everything's fine." Lies, one after another. She couldn't remember the last time she had lied.

"Tell your aunt I'm glad everything is okay."

"I'll just be another couple of minutes, Miss Dalrymple." She could barely speak.

"No problem, take your time." Dalrymple gave her a perfunctory smile and headed down the hall. Christine felt as though she were going to be sick. The notes on Charlotte Thomas were a crumpled ball in her fist.

"Evelyn, are you still there?" she said weakly.

"Yes, Miss Beall. Can you continue now?"

Christine thought, No, but said, "Yes . . . yes, I'm okay. I mean, just a second while I arrange my notes." Her fingers felt stiff, unwilling to respond. First Peg's phone call, then the agony of John Chapman's wife, then Charlotte, and now Miss Dalrymple showing up on this, of all days, and seeming to be watching her more than any of the other nurses. Barely connected or unconnected events, yet suddenly she was nearly paralyzed, her imagination braiding a cord of panic that tightened around her chest and throat. Awkwardly she smoothed the notes on the counter, fighting to regain control.

"The . . . the home health agency. Did I tell you about the home health agency?" The sound of her own voice began to loosen the fear.

"Yes, you did," Evelyn said patiently.

"Oh, okay. Let's see. Oh, yes, I was here." The words blurred in and out of focus. "Mrs. Thomas has been on hyperalimentation through an in-dwelling subclavian line for nearly two weeks and is still on intravenous antibiotics, hourly pulmonary therapy, and continuous oxygen." At that moment she realized that she had skipped a whole page. In fact, she was not certain what she had already covered. "Evelyn, I . . . I seem to have passed over some things. Is it all right to go back?"

"It's all right to do anything, dear. We'll be able to

42

figure things out. Now just relax and give me what other information you have."

The woman's first warm words had an immediate effect. Christine took a deep breath and felt much of her tension vanish. "Thank you," she said softly. Evelyn's reassurance had reminded her: she was not functioning in isolation. She was part of a team, a movement committed to the highest good. If her role was difficult, at times frightening, so were those of the rest of her sisters. For the first time a note of calm appeared in her voice. "What I left out was that shortly after her surgery she had to be operated on again for drainage of an extensive pelvic abscess. One week ago she developed pneumonia, and last night a nasogastric tube was inserted because of the possibility of an intestinal obstruction."

She was still shaking, but now the words came more easily.

"Recently she developed a large, painful sacral pressure sore and is now requiring around-the-clock Demerol as well as the usual local therapies. The physician's notes in her chart as of yesterday state that her pneumonia is worsening. Despite all her problems, she has been designated a full resuscitation should she arrest." Almost done, she thought. Thank God. "Mrs. Thomas is married, has two children and several grandchildren. That is the end of my presentation." She sighed deeply.

"Miss Beall," Evelyn asked, "could you please tell me if there is documented evidence in her record of the spread of her tumor to other organs?"

"Oh, yes, I'm sorry. I missed part of a page. There was one thing. An X-ray report. It's a liver scan dated last week. The report from the radiologist says, 'Multiple filling defects consistent with tumor.' "

"When was the last case that you handled?"

"The *only* case. Nearly a year ago. Mrs. Thomas would be my second." It wasn't like this the last time,

43

she thought. That was beautiful, not an ordeal. Her legs felt boneless. Instinctively she looked about for a chair.

"Thank you for your call," Evelyn said, "and for your excellent case presentation. The Sisterhood of Life Regional Screening Committee will evaluate this patient and contact you within twenty-four hours. In the meantime, as you know, you are to take no action on your own."

"I understand." It was almost over.

"Oh, one more thing, Miss Beall," Evelyn added. "The name of this patient's physician?"

"Her physician?"

"Yes."

"It's Dr. Huttner. Wallace Huttner, the chief of surgery here."

"Thank you," Evelyn said. "We'll be in touch."

CHAPTER III

David Shelton drummed impatiently on the arm of his chair and leafed through a three-month-old issue of *The American Journal of Surgery*. His excitement and anticipation at making evening rounds with Wallace Huttner had been dulled by a wait that had now grown to nearly three quarters of an hour. Huttner must have encountered unexpected difficulty in the operating room.

For a time David paced through the deserted surgeons' lounge, closing locker doors—a gesture that seemed, inexplicably, to restore some order to the situation. Forty-five minutes in an empty locker room had hardly been part of his scenario for the evening.

With mounting concern that Huttner might have forgotten their appointment altogether, he took off the suit he had resurrected from the recesses of his closet for the occasion and changed into a set of scrub greens, then slipped paper shoe covers over his scuffed loafers and tucked the black electrical grounding strip in at the back. He considered putting on his own green canvas O.R. shoes, but rejected the notion, fearing that the shoes, a clean, new pair, might give the impression, however accurate, that he had not spent much time in the operating room of late.

The ritual of dressing for the O.R. had an immediate buoying effect on his flagging morale. Donning a paper mask and hair guard, he began absently humming the opening bars of "La Virgen de Macarena," a melody he had first heard years before, heralding the arrival of the matador at a Mexico City bullfight.

Suddenly he realized what he was singing and laughed out loud. "Shelton, you are really off the wall. Next thing you'll do is demand two ears and a tail for a successful appendectomy." Stopping before a mirror, he stuffed several protruding tufts under his cap, then stepped onto the surgical floor.

The Dickenson Surgical Suite, named after the first chief of surgery at the hospital, consisted of twenty-six rooms, devoid of windows, and occupied the entire seventh and eighth floors of the East building. Ubiquitous wall clocks provided the only hint of what life might be doing outside the hospital. In atmosphere, politics, social order, even language, the surgical suite was a world within a world within a world.

From his earliest days as a medical student, and even before, David had dreamed of being a part of that world. He loved the sounds of machines and hushed voices echoing down the gleaming hallways, the tension in hours of meticulous surgery, the seconds of frantic action in a life-or-death crisis. Now, for the second time in his life, the dream was becoming reality.

Scanning the lime-tiled corridor, he saw signs of activity in only two of the operating rooms. The others had been scrubbed down and set up for the first cases of the next morning, then darkened for the night.

He bet himself that Huttner would be working in the room on the right and lost a weekend in Acapulco with Meryl Streep.

"Can I help you?" The circulating nurse met David at

the doorway. She wore a wraparound green scrub dress that fell short of concealing her linebacker's build. Turquoise eyes appraised him from between a paper mask and a cloth, flower-print hair cover.

Assert yourself, David thought. Show some nice, crisp consternation at not being recognized. He was trying to formulate an intimidating response when Huttner looked over from his place at the right side of the table.

"Ah, David, welcome," he called out. "Edna, that's Dr. Shelton. Will you get him a riser, please. Put it, ah . . . over there behind Dr. Brewster." He nodded toward the resident who was assisting from across the table.

David stepped onto the riser and looked down into the incision.

"Started as a simple oversew of a bleeding ulcer," Huttner explained, unaware—or, at least, not acknowledging—that he was late for their rounds. "We encountered a little trouble when we got in, though, and I decided to go ahead with a hemigastrectomy and Bilroth anastomosis." David took note of Huttner's choice of pronouns and filed the insight away in the back of his mind.

Within a few seconds the rhythm in the room, disrupted by David's arrival, was reestablished. It became rapidly apparent to him that Huttner's concentration, deftness, and control were extraordinary. No wasted words or motion. No outward evidence of indecisiveness. Although others in the room were playing their parts, he was clearly both conductor and principal soloist.

Suddenly a pair of scissors slipped off the side of Huttner's hand as the scrub nurse passed them to him. They hit the floor with a clatter that might have been a small explosion. The surgeon's gray-blue eyes flashed. "Goddammit, Jeannie," he snapped, "will you pay attention!"

The nurse stiffened, then muttered an apology and

carefully handed over another pair. David's eyes narrowed a fraction. From his vantage point the pass had seemed quite adequate. He glanced at the wall clock. Seven thirty. Huttner, he realized, had probably been operating for the better part of twelve straight hours.

A minute later, Huttner surveyed his results then rotated his head to relieve the tightness in his neck. "Okay, Rick, she's all yours. Go ahead and close," he said to the resident. "Standard post-op orders. I don't think she'll need the unit, but use your judgment when she's ready to come out of the recovery room. If there are any problems, contact Dr. Shelton. He'll be covering for me while I'm down at the vascular conference on the Cape. Any questions?"

David thought he saw a flicker of heightened respect and interest appear in the eyes of the scrub nurse. Real or imagined, the look immediately rekindled his excitement about what the next three days held in store for him.

Huttner stepped back from the table, stripping off his bloodstained gown and gloves in a single motion, and headed for the lounge with David close behind. Rather than collapsing in the nearest easy chair, as David expected, Huttner walked casually to his locker, withdrawing his pipe and tobacco pouch. He filled, packed, and lit the elegant meerschaum before settling into a thick leather couch. With a wave of his pipe, he motioned David to join him on the sofa.

"Turnbull should have referred that woman for surgery two days ago," he said, commenting on the internist who had failed to stop the bleeding ulcer. "I'll bet I wouldn't have had to take her stomach if he had." Huttner closed his eyes and massaged the bridge of his nose with carefully manicured, porcelain fingers.

In his early sixties, a tall, angular man an inch or two over six feet with dark hair appropriately gray at the temples, Huttner appeared every bit the patrician depicted by his press clippings.

"I've been hearing some nice things about your work from the nurses in the O.R., David," Huttner said in his well-cultivated New England accent.

Nice things. David spent several seconds evaluating the compliment. It was a reflex reaction, born of nearly eight years of condescending interviewers and pseudo-solicitous colleagues. David disliked the trait, but had come to expect it. Huttner's flattery was genuine, he was sure.

"Thanks," he said. "As you saw tonight, some of them don't even know me yet. I mean, one major case every week or two is hardly the best basis for judging." His words were not bitter—merely a statement of fact. David knew that Huttner might perform fifteen or more major operations for each one of his own.

"Patience, David, patience," Huttner said. "I recall telling you that when you first came to see me about applying for staff privileges. You must remember that, just as physicians are constantly hoisted up on pedestals, so are they also under continuous, magnified scrutiny." He tapped his fingertips together, carefully selecting his words. "Problems such as . . . ah . . . have befallen you are not quickly forgotten by the medical community. They are a threat, pointing up a vulnerability that most doctors don't want to admit they have. Just keep doing good, conscientious work the way you have been, and the cases will come." He sat back pontifically and folded his hands around the meerschaum.

"I hope so," David said, his smile a bit forced. "I want you to know how grateful I am for your trust and acceptance. It really means a lot to me personally."

Huttner brushed the compliment off with his pipe, although his expression suggested that it was expected and would have been missed. "Nonsense, I'm the one who is grateful. It's a relief to know that my patients

49

will have a bright young Turk like you looking after them while I'm gone. As I recall, you trained at White Memorial, didn't you?"

"Yes, sir, I was chief resident there once upon a time."

"I never could seem to get accepted into that program," Huttner said, shaking his head in what might have been wistfulness. "And it's 'Wally.' I get enough 'sirs' every day to fill King Arthur's Court."

David nodded, smiled, and stopped himself at the last possible instant from saying, "Yes, sir."

Huttner bounced to his feet. "A quick shower, then I'll sign out to you on the floors." He tossed his scrub suit into a canvas hamper, then took a journal from his locker and handed it to David. "Take a look at this article of mine on radical surgery for metastatic breast disease. I'll be interested in what you think."

With that, he strode into the shower room, calling out just before he turned on the water, "You play tennis, David? We have to get together and hit a few before the weather closes in on us."

"It's often hard to distinguish between my tennis and my weight lifting," David said softly enough to be certain Huttner couldn't possibly have heard. He thumbed through the article. Printed in a rather obscure journal, it advocated radical breast, ovarian, and adrenal surgery for patients with widespread breast cancer. The concept was nothing revolutionary. In certain instances it was accepted. However, as horrible as the disease was, seeing the radical surgical approach laid out in print, scanning the tables of survival, brought a tinge of acid to David's throat. Survival. Was that really the bottom line? He slapped the journal shut and shoved it back in Huttner's locker.

The page operator was announcing the eight o'clock end to visiting hours when the two surgeons started making rounds on the floors in the West building. Earlier David had seen the patients he had in the hospital—a ten-year-old boy in for repair of a hernia and Edwina Burroughs, a forty-year-old woman whose factory job and four pregnancies had given her severe varicose veins, gnarled and twisted as the roots of a Banyan tree.

Wallace Huttner had more than twenty-five patients scattered over three different buildings. Almost all of them were recovering from major surgery. On every floor Huttner's arrival had immediate impact. Horseplay around the nurses' station stopped. Voices lowered. The charge nurse materialized, charts in hand, to accompany them on their rounds. Replies to Huttner's occasional questions were either stammered monosyllables or nervous outpourings of excess information. Throughout Huttner maintained an urbane politeness, moving briskly from one bedside to the next without so much as a hint of the fatigue David knew he must be feeling. The man was absolutely one of a kind, he acknowledged to himself. A phenomenon.

Before long, a comfortable pattern had evolved to their rounds. Huttner allowed the charge nurse to lead them to the doorway of a room. Then he took the patient's chart from her and proceeded to the bedside. David, the charge nurse, and often the staff nurse on the case followed. Next, Huttner handed the unopened chart to David, introduced him to the patient, and gave a capsule history of the initial problem, operative procedure, and subsequent course of treatment, couching details in medical jargon that no one except a physician or nurse could possibly have understood.

Finally he conducted a brief physical examination while David flipped through the record, using a spiral-bound pad to record pertinent lab data as well as Huttner's overall approach and plan for the case. For the most part, he tried to remain inconspicuous, speaking when addressed, but keeping his questions to what seemed like an intelligent minimum.

From time to time he glanced at Huttner. As far as he could tell, the man seemed satisfied that his charges were being left in capable hands. Before long, though, David began feeling uneasy. Despite the legends, the backup residents, and the unquestionable—perhaps unparalleled—surgical skills, Wallace Huttner was sloppy: progress notes were brief and often lacking some piece of information; some abnormal laboratory results went undetected for several days before they were noticed and a recheck ordered. Small things. Subtle things. But the pattern was there, unmistakable. It was not the kind of carelessness that would affect every case, but inevitably it would be manifest somewhere—in a prolonged hospital stay, a second operation, even a death.

He must know, David thought to himself. He knows, but so far he just hasn't found any way of dealing with the problems. It wasn't lack of pride or caring or skill— Huttner clearly possessed all three. The man was simply spread too thin, David decided. Too many cases. Too many committees, panels, and teaching obligations. How much could a man do in one day? Sooner or later he must either draw lines or make compromises or . . . get help. Maybe Lauren was right, he realized excitedly. Maybe Huttner *was* looking for a partner. Or maybe, David laughed to himself, Huttner had chosen him to cover the practice believing that of all the surgeons in the hospital he was the least likely to notice these inadequacies. No matter. The oversights and omissions were small ones. He would go through the charts the next day and fix it all up.

Just keep your mouth shut, he told himself. Only a few cases to go, then you're on your own.

Minutes later, David's decision to keep silent was challenged. The patient was a man in his late fifties, a

commercial fisherman named Anton Merchado. He had
been admitted to the hospital several weeks earlier for
an abdominal mass. Huttner had drained and excised a
cyst on the pancreas and Merchado was recovering
nicely when he developed symptoms of an upper respiratory infection. In a telephoned order, Huttner had
put the man on tetracycline, a widely used antibiotic.

The condition must have improved, David thought,
because there was no further mention of it in Huttner's
brief notes. However, the tetracycline order had never
been rescinded. It had been in effect for nearly two
weeks.

Anxious to speed up rounds, Huttner was giving his
capsule review of the man's history while he examined
his heart, lungs, and abdomen. David stood off to one
side, his attention focused more on the chart than on
what the older surgeon was saying.

On the day before Merchado was to be discharged
from the hospital, he had developed severe diarrhea.
Huttner's initial impression was viral enteritis, but over
a few days the condition worsened beyond what a simple viral infection would cause. The early signs of dehy-
dration began to appear.

David flipped from the progress notes to the laboratory reports and back. Huttner's mounting concern was
mirrored each day in an increasing number of orders for
laboratory tests and diagnostic procedures, all unrevealing.
Efforts intensified to keep pace with Merchado's dete-
riorating condition, but there could be no doubt that
the man was on a downhill slide.

As David read, the germ of an idea took root. He
scanned page after page of laboratory reports, looking
for the results of the stool cultures that had been ordered
on several successive days.

"Well, what do you think?" Huttner said, turning to
David. "David? . . ."

"Oh, sorry." David looked up. "I noticed the man

was still on tetracycline and was just looking to see if he might have somehow developed staph colitis secondary to the treatment. It doesn't happen often, but . . ."

"Tetracycline?" Huttner interrupted. "I called in a stop on that order days ago. They're still giving it to him?"

Behind Huttner, in David's line of vision, the charge nurse nodded her head in vigorous confirmation.

"Well, no matter," Huttner said, hesitating slightly. David could almost hear him asking himself whether he had actually called in the stop order or had just meant to. "The culture reports have all been negative. Why don't you write an order to take him off tetra. Go ahead and get another culture if you want to."

David was about to comply when he noticed a culture report at the bottom of the lengthy computer printout that listed all results obtained on the patient to date. It read

"9/24, STOOL SPEC:
MODERATE GROWTH, S. AUREUS,
SENSITIVITIES TO FOLLOW."

Staph aureus, the most virulent form of the bacteria. David closed his eyes for a moment, hoping that when he looked at the sheet again the words would be gone. He took several seconds in making the decision to say nothing about his discovery and to correct the problem later. The hesitation was too long.

"What is it, David?" Huttner asked. "Have you found something?"

"Dammit," David cursed to himself. A dozen possible responses poured through his mind, were evaluated and rejected. There was going to be no comfortable way around it. No place to hide. Out of the corner of one eye he saw the two nurses standing motionless at the end of the bed. Did they know that in the next few moments the success of the evening and possibly of David's career might vanish?

The whole scene became strangely dreamlike for him. The hand slowly passing Merchado's chart to Huttner, the finger pointing at the offensively impersonal line of type—they were someone else's, not his.

The look David had last seen directed at the O.R. scrub nurse sparked in Huttner's eyes. They locked with his for a fraction of a second, then turned on the nurses. He thrust the chart at the charge nurse.

"Mrs. Baird," he growled, "I want you to find out who is responsible for failing to call my attention to this report. Whoever it is, nurse or secretary, I want to see her in my office first thing Monday morning. Is that clear?"

The nurse, a stout veteran who had engaged in her share of hospital wars, looked at the page, then shrugged and nodded her head. David wondered if Huttner would actually follow through with what seemed so obvious an attempt to produce a scapegoat.

"Come along, Dr. Shelton," Huttner said curtly. "It's getting late and we still have several more patients to see."

It was nearly ten o'clock when they arrived on Four South to see the last of Huttner's patients, Charlotte Thomas. For the first time all evening Huttner deviated from the routine he had established. Taking the chart from the charge nurse, he said, "Come and sit down in the nurses' lounge for a bit, David. This next patient is by far my most complicated. I want to take a few minutes to go over her with you in some detail before we see her. Perhaps someone could bring us each a cup of coffee." The last remark was transparently addressed to the nurse, who managed a faint smile of acquiescence. "Light, no sugar for me, and for Dr. Shelton . . . ?"

"Black," David answered. For a split second he had almost said "bleak."

"Here you go, Doctor," Huttner said, sliding the chart across to David. "Leaf through it while we're waiting for coffee."

Before reading a word, David could tell that Charlotte Thomas was in trouble. Her hospital record was voluminous. He thought back to his residency and a tall, gangly New Yorker named Gerald Fox, who was one year ahead of him. Fox had achieved immortality, at least in White Memorial Hospital, by Xeroxing a three-page list of cynical maxims and definitions entitled, "Fox's Golden Laws of Medicine." Among his axioms were the definition of Complicated Case ("When the combined diameters of all the tubes going into a patient's body exceeds his hat size"), Gynecologist ("A spreader of old wives' tails"), and Fatal Illness ("A hospital chart more than an inch thick").

Coffee arrived just as David had begun to scan the admission history and physical examination. He heard Huttner say, "Ah, Miss Beall, thank you. You're an angel of mercy."

He looked up from the chart. It was not the nurse with whom Huttner had placed their order, but a far younger woman David had never seen, or at least had never noticed before. For several seconds his entire world consisted only of two large, oval, burnt umber eyes. He felt his body flush with warmth. The eyes met his and smiled.

"So, are you with our lady Charlotte again?" Huttner asked, oblivious to the silent meeting that was taking place.

"Huh? Oh, yes." Christine broke the connection and turned to Huttner. "She's not looking too well. I asked to bring the coffee in because I wanted to talk to you about . . ."

"How rude of me," Huttner interrupted. "Miss Beall, this is Dr. David Shelton. Perhaps you two have met?"

"No," Christine said icily. She was well acquainted with Huttner's lack of regard for the insights and suggestions of nurses. Over the years she had given up even attempting to share hers with him. But Charlotte's situation was distressing enough for her to try. If Huttner would only agree to let up on his aggressive treatment, to cancel the resuscitation order, she might not intervene even if the Screening Committee approved her proposal. So she had tried, and predictably the man had cut her off—this time with an inane social amenity. Still, she felt determined to speak her mind. It was *his* tube that was sticking into Charlotte's nose. *His* order to prolong her suffering no matter what. He could play puppet-master with his other patients, but not with Charlotte. He would listen or . . . or have his strings to her cut. Christine swallowed the bone of anger that had begun sticking in her throat.

Huttner took no note of the chill in her voice. "Dr. Shelton will be covering all my patients, including Mrs. Thomas, for a few days," he said.

Christine nodded at David and wondered whether he might have the authority to back off on Huttner's overzealous approach to Charlotte, then realized there was no chance the surgical chief would permit that. "Dr. Huttner," she said flatly, "I would like to talk to you about Charlotte for a few minutes."

Huttner glanced at his watch. "That would be fine, Miss Beall," he said. "Why don't you let us finish reviewing Charlotte's case and examining her. Then you can go over things with Dr. Shelton here. He'll know exactly what I want for this woman." Huttner looked away before the first of the daggers from her eyes reached him. David shrugged his embarrassment, but Christine had already turned on one heel and left the room.

Huttner took a sip of coffee, then began speaking without so much as a word or gesture toward the nurse who had just left. "Mrs. Thomas is a registered nurse. In her late fifties, I think." David glanced at the birth-date on the chart. She was nearly sixty-one. "Her husband, Peter, is a professor at Harvard. Economics. She was referred to me by an internist because of a suspected cancer of the rectum. Several weeks ago, I performed a Miles's resection on the woman. The tumor was an adenocarcinoma extending just through the bowel wall.

"However, all the nodes I took were negative. I feel there's a very good chance that my clean-out may have gotten the whole thing."

David looked up from the coffee stain he was absently erasing with his thumb. The five-year survival rate after removal of a rectal cancer with such extension was under 20 percent. A chance? Certainly. A "very good chance"? He leaned back and wondered if it was worth asking Huttner to clarify the reasons for his optimism. It would not, he decided, be wise to question him about anything.

Comfortable in the blanket of his own words, Huttner continued his presentation. "As always seems to happen when we work on nurses or doctors, everything that could have gone sour postoperatively seems to have done so. First, a pelvic abscess—I had to go back in and drain it. Next, a pneumonia. And then a nasty decubitus ulcer over her sacrum. Yesterday she developed signs of a bowel obstruction and I had to slip down a tube. That seems to be correcting the problem, and I have a feeling that she may have turned the corner."

Huttner folded his hands on the table in front of him, indicating that his presentation was done. An almost imperceptible tic had developed at the corner of his right eye. He must be absolutely exhausted, David thought. Uncomfortable and anxious to do anything other than stare, David returned to the chart. "If she needs to be operated on for the obstruction?" he asked, already praying it would not happen.

"Then you go ahead and do it if that's your judgment. I'm leaving you in complete charge," Huttner said somewhat testily.

No more questions, David resolved. Whatever you want to know, figure it out for yourself. Just get through this night.

But already another potential problem was becoming obvious. He tried to reason it through, but quickly realized that only Huttner could supply the answer. His resolve stretched, then snapped.

"If she should arrest?" he asked softly.

"Dammit, man, she's not going to arrest," Huttner snapped with startling vehemence. Then, sensing the inappropriateness of his outburst, he took a deep breath, exhaled slowly, and added, "At least, I hope she doesn't arrest. If she should, I want a full Code Ninety-nine called on her, including tracheal intubation and a respirator if need be. Clear?"

"Clear," David said. He looked down at the chart again. Whatever criticisms might be leveled at Wallace Huttner, undertreating Charlotte Thomas certainly could not be one of them. Thousands of dollars in laboratory work, hospital care, and radiologic studies had already been done. Still, at least on paper, the woman appeared far from "turning the corner."

"Shall we go see the patient?" Huttner's tone was more order than request.

David was about to comply when he noticed the report of Charlotte's liver scan. The words burst from the page: "Multiple filling defects consistent with tumor." Numbness crept over him as he stared at the reading. Rarely had he heard of a patient surviving long with the spread of rectal cancer to the liver. Certainly, with this kind of disseminated disease, there could be no way to justify the aggressive therapy being given Charlotte Thomas. If, as in the Merchado case, this report had somehow been overlooked, whatever remained of his relationship with Huttner was about to disappear with the finality of a nuclear explosion.

"What is it this time, doctor?" Huttner asked acidly.

"Oh . . . probably nothing," David said, wishing he were anyplace else. "I . . . ah . . . I was just reading this liver scan report."

"Hah!" Huttner's exclamation cut him short. "Multiple defects consistent with tumor, right?" He suddenly looked happier than he had all evening. "Look at the name of the radiologist who gave us that report. G. Rybicki, M.D., the living Polish joke of radiologic medicine. He read the same thing on a scan that we did preoperatively, so I checked her liver out carefully in the O.R. Even sent off a biopsy. They are cysts, David. Multiple, congenital, totally benign cysts.

"I even went to the trouble of sending Rybicki a copy of the pathology report," Huttner continued. "He probably never even looked at it, as witnessed by this repetition of his initial misreading. Maybe we'd better just tear the report out of the chart." He crumpled the sheet in a ball and tossed it into the wastebasket. "Now, if you have no further questions, shall we go in to see the woman?"

"No further questions, your honor." David shook his head in amazement and smiled, grateful to be allowed off the hook. There was something about Huttner's broad grin that went far toward dispelling the misgivings David had developed about the man.

Shoulder to shoulder, they walked down the corridor of Four South and into Room 412.

CHAPTER IV

The only light in Room 412 came from a gooseneck treatment lamp directed at an area just above Charlotte Thomas's exposed buttocks. Huttner strode to that side of the bed with David close behind and moved the lamp back a foot. He stiffened, then forced a more relaxed pose. Bewildered and somewhat amused, David stifled a smile at the man's reaction; then he looked down at the reason for it. The bedsore Huttner had described as "nasty" was far worse than that. It was a gaping hole six inches wide. The walls of the cavity were raw muscle, stained white by a drying poultice. A quarter-sized eye of sacral bone stared sightlessly outward from the center.

Huttner gave the kind of shrug that said, "Nothing worse than other things we've dealt with, right?"

David tried to respond, but could manage only a shake of his head. He had seen sores and wounds countless times from every conceivable source. But this . . .

"It's Dr. Huttner, Charlotte," Huttner announced as he flicked off the lamp and turned on the dim fluorescent light set in a cornice over her bed. He drew the sheet up above her waist and stepped to the other side of the bed. David followed, glancing at the I.V. bags and the restraints that held her on her side, at the urinary catheter snaking from beneath the sheet, at the oxygen and suction tubes. He understood the need for them and accepted their presence without a second thought. They were all as much tools of his trade as were the giant saucer lights and variegated steel instruments of the operating room.

However, in those first few seconds the one thing he noticed most about Mrs. Thomas was the emptiness in her face—a static soulless aura centering about her eyes, which were watching him through the dim light with a moist flatness. Even the sound of her breathing—soft, rhythmic cries—was empty.

Charlotte Thomas had The Look, as David had come to label it. She had lost the will to live, lost that extra bit of energy essential to surviving a life-threatening illness. The spark that was often the single difference between a medical miracle and a mortality statistic was gone.

David wondered if Huttner saw the same things he did, felt the same emptiness. Then, as if in answer to his question, the tall surgeon knelt by the bed, slipping his hand under Charlotte's head and cradling it to one side so that she could look directly at his face. For nearly a minute they remained that way, doctor and patient frozen in a silent tableau. David stood several feet away, swallowing against the heaviness that was building in his throat. Huttner's tenderness was as genuine as it was surprising—another facet had shown itself in this strange kaleidoscope of a man.

"Not exactly feeling on top of the world, huh?" Huttner said finally.

Charlotte forced her lips together—an unsuccessful attempt at a smile—and shook her head. Huttner smoothed the hair from her forehead and ran his hand over her cheek.

"Well, your temperature is down near normal today for the first time in a while. I think we might be getting on top of that infection in your chest." He went on, carefully mixing encouraging news with questions that he knew would be answered negatively. "Is the pain in your back any less?" Another shake. "Well, if things settle down the way I expect them to, we should be able to get that tube out of your nose in a day or two. I know what an annoyance it is. While I have you rolled over like this, let me take a listen to your chest, then I'll put you on your back and see if there are any new noises in your belly."

He examined her briefly, then glanced at the fluid levels in the intravenous bags and catheter drainage cylinder before kneeling beside her again. "You're going to make it, Charlotte. You must believe that," he said with gentle intensity.

This time Charlotte did manage a rueful smile to accompany her negative response.

"Please, just be patient, have faith and hang on a little longer," Huttner implored. "I know the pain you're going through. In many ways it's as awful for me as it is for you. But I also know that bit by bit you're turning the corner. Before you know it, you'll be putting on lipstick and getting ready to see those beautiful grand-children you've told me so much about." He paused. In the silence David studied the man's face. His brows were drawn inward, his jaw taut as a bow string. He seemed to be trying, through sheer will, to transfuse the energy of his words and hope. The woman showed no reaction. "My goodness, I almost forgot," Huttner said at last. "Charlotte, you are in for a treat. I know how tired you must be getting of seeing my smiling mug every day. Well, you're going to get a break from that.

"I'm going off to a conference on the Cape for a few days. This handsome young doctor will be covering for me. He was the chief resident a few years ago at White Memorial. I couldn't even get accepted for an internship there. His name's David Shelton." Huttner motioned David over to the head of the bed.

David took Huttner's place, setting his arms on the sheet and resting his chin on them, six inches away from Charlotte's face. It seemed to take several seconds for her to focus on him.

"I'm David, Mrs. Thomas. How do you do?" he said, realizing at the same instant that she had already answered his ill-conceived greeting several times. "Is there anything you need right now? Anything I can get for you?" He waited until he felt certain no response was forthcoming, then made a move to stand up. Suddenly Charlotte Thomas reached out a spongy, bruised hand and grasped his with surprising force.

"Dr. Shelton, please listen to me," she said in a husky, halting voice that had its own unexpected strength. "Dr. Huttner is a wonderful man and a wonderful doctor. He wants so much to help me. You must make him understand. I do not want to be helped anymore. All I want is to have these tubes taken out and to be kept comfortable until I go to sleep. You must make him understand that. Please. This is torture for me. A nightmare. Make him understand."

Her eyes flashed for an instant, then closed. She took several deep breaths and settled heavily back on the pillow. Her breathing slowed. It seemed to David that it might stop altogether, but within a minute a coarse, rhythmic stertor developed and held.

All David could manage was a whispered, "You're going to be all right, Mrs. Thomas," as Huttner took him by the arm and led him out of the room.

In the hallway the two men faced one another. Huttner was first to break the silence.

"Quite some night we've had for ourselves, yes?" he said, smiling his understanding.

"Yeah," David answered. He pawed at the floor with one foot. He would have said more but for a persistent sliver of fear that he was about to come apart in front of the man.

Huttner scrutinized his face, then said, "David, never forget that many times patients with serious illness express the wish to die when they're in a stage of weakness and pain. I've been around for a long time. I've seen many patients as sick or sicker than Charlotte Thomas recover. This woman is going to make it. She is to get total, aggressive treatment and, if necessary, a full-scale Code Ninety-nine resuscitation. Understand?"

"Yes, sir . . . I mean, yes, Wally," David said mechanically, although he was searching his memory for the last time he had seen a sixty-year-old patient recover from the sort of severe, multisystem disease that beset Charlotte Thomas.

"We're in agreement, then," Huttner said, beaming with pleasure at having successfully made his point. "Let's go write a few orders on this woman, then we can call it a day."

As they approached the nurses' station, David bet himself a guitar and six months of introductory lessons that the last critical moment of the hectic evening had passed.

An instant later, a portly man dressed in a turtleneck sweater and tweed sportcoat emerged from the visitors' lounge at the far end of the hall and headed toward them. He was still thirty feet away when David knew with certainty that another wager had been lost. The anger in the man's jaw-forward stride was mirrored in his reddened face and tight, bloodless lips. His fists were suspended several inches away from his body on rigid arms.

David glanced over at Huttner, who showed a flicker of recognition but no other emotion.

"Professor Thomas?" David whispered.

Huttner nodded his head a fraction, then moved forward. David slowed and watched as the two men closed on one another like combatants at a medieval joust. The grandstand for their confrontation was the nurses' station, where several nurses, an aide, and the ward secretary fell silent, fascinated spectators.

"Dr. Huttner, what the hell is going on here?" Thomas lashed out. "You told me there would be no more tubes and I get here to find a red rubber hose coming out of my wife's nose attached to some goddamn machine."

"Now, Professor Thomas, just calm down for a minute," Huttner said evenly. "I tried to call you last night to let you know what was going on, but there was no answer. Let's go down to the visitors' lounge, and I'll be happy to go over the whole thing with you."

Thomas was not a bit mollified. "No, we'll have this whole business out here and now with these people as witnesses." He gestured at the gallery. "I came to you with Charlotte because our family doctor told us you were the best. To me the best meant not only that you would be the best in the operating room, but that you would be the best at treating my wife—as a human being, not just as some unfeeling piece of . . . of *carrion*."

The intensity and pain in Peter Thomas's voice was startling. Behind the nurses' station, Christine Beall cautiously turned her head toward Janet Poulos, the evening nursing supervisor. Poulos met her gaze impassively, then responded with an almost imperceptible nod. She was a slender woman, a decade older than Christine. Her coal-black hair was coiled in a tight bun, accentuating her narrow features and dark, feline eyes. A thin scar paralleling her nose gave even her warmest smile a slight sneer and undoubtedly contributed to her reputation among the nursing staff as being uncompromising and humorless.

Christine saw her in a far different light, for it was

Janet who had supervised her initiation into The Sisterhood of Life. The secrecy of the movement was such that Janet remained the only Sisterhood member whom she knew by name and face. The nod acknowledged that Poulos, too, was assessing the drama unfolding before them.

"All right, Professor," Huttner said, a thin edge appearing in his voice. "If it is what you wish, we shall discuss matters right here. Do you have more to say or do you want to know exactly what is happening with Charlotte?"

"Go on," Thomas said, relaxing his fists and leaning one elbow on the high counter in front of a totally bewildered ward secretary.

With the condescending patience of one who has learned that sooner or later he will carry the day, Huttner systematically reviewed the developments that had led to his decision to insert an intestinal drainage tube in Charlotte Thomas. Then, more gently, he said, "It may not be obvious to you right now, but I believe that our treatments are starting to take hold. Charlotte could turn the corner any time now."

Peter Thomas looked down and retreated half a step. At that moment it seemed to David as if Huttner had, in fact, won the man over. Then, as though in slow motion, Thomas brought his head up, shaking it back and forth as he spoke. "Dr. Huttner, I believe my wife is dying. I believe it and I even accept it. I also believe that because of what you call *treatment*, she is dying by inches, without so much as a flicker of dignity. I want those tubes pulled out."

Behind the counter, a nurse whispered something to the woman next to her. Huttner silenced her with a look that could have frozen a volcano.

With an instantaneous, almost theatrical change in expression, he turned back, smiling calmly, to Peter Thomas. "Professor, please know that I understand how you're feeling, I really do," he reasoned. "But you must

67

understand my position and my responsibility in this thing. We talked about it when you first brought Charlotte into my office, and you agreed that I was to be in complete charge. I offered to arrange for a second opinion, but you felt back then that none was necessary. Now here you are questioning my judgment. I'll tell you what. We have a built-in second opinion right here." Huttner motioned David over. "This is Dr. Shelton. He's an excellent young surgeon who was chief resident in surgery at White Memorial. We've just examined Charlotte in great detail because Dr. Shelton will be covering my patients for the next few days. David, this is Peter Thomas. Tell him what our feelings are about Charlotte."

David reached out his hand and Thomas shook it uncertainly. During the seconds they stood appraising one another, Thomas seemed perceptibly to calm down.

"Well, Dr. Shelton," he said finally, "what *do* you think of my wife's chances?"

David looked down momentarily and closed his eyes. Somewhere in a remote corner of his mind a voice kept telling him that if he could just stall for a few minutes his clock radio would go off, waking him up. With consummate effort he brought his eyes up until they connected once more with Thomas's.

"Mr. Thomas, I just reviewed your wife's hospital record and met her for the first time," he said deliberately. "It really is impossible at this time for me to assess her whole situation accurately."

Thomas opened his mouth to object to what he considered an inadequate answer, but David stopped him with a raised hand. "However," he continued, hoping that his tone would not give away the fact that he had no desire to continue at all, "I will tell you that I see her as a critically ill woman whose chance of surviving this illness rests not only with receiving the best possible medical and nursing care—which, incidentally, she has been receiving—but also in having the will to make it through. This is the part I cannot assess yet. That strength comes not only from inside her, but from you, from Dr. Huttner, and from the rest of those who love and care for her.

"I know you'd like to hear a more clinical evaluation of her prospects, but right now I'm just not in a position to give you that."

Out of the corner of his eyes he saw Huttner beaming his approval. Holy shit, I got out of it! was all David could think. Then, even before Thomas responded, he felt a spark of anger at himself. He had not given even a hint of his true, bleak feelings about Charlotte's chances. As Thomas spoke, the spark grew white hot.

"You really don't see it, do you?" Thomas said, looking wildly around him. "None of you do. Charlotte and I have been married for over thirty years. Thirty full and happy years. Don't you feel we should have some say as to what kind of tortures she must be put through to prolong the agony of what has until now been a totally rich and fulfilling life?"

This time David did not look away. For several seconds a painful silence held. Finally he spoke. There was anguish in his voice, but also the power of conviction. "Dammit, I do feel that way. Exactly as you do, Mr. Thomas. I feel that very strongly."

Again there was an agonizing silence. David felt Huttner's eyes and sensed the world sinking beneath him. His tone mellowed. "But you must understand," he said. "I am not your wife's primary physician, Dr. Huttner is. And he is more experienced than I am in every aspect of medicine and surgery. It is his final say as to what kind of treatment your wife will or will not receive. I intend to carry on his therapies to the absolute best of my abilities."

Thomas glared at Huttner, then snapped, "I understand, all right. I understand completely." Spinning so fast that he nearly lost his balance, he stalked down the corridor toward his wife's room.

His outburst was the last straw for Huttner. It had been a long and trying day. He stepped back so that David and everyone at the nurses' station was included in his gaze. "I am going to say this one time and one time only." His voice was dry ice. "Charlotte Thomas is to be treated as aggressively as necessary to save her life. Have I made myself clear? Good. Now all of you get back to your jobs. Dr. Shelton, perhaps you had better go home and get some rest. Straightening out my practice could prove an exhausting experience for you."

With that, he marched down the hall and followed Peter Thomas into Room 412.

David stood alone in the center of the corridor. The group behind the nurses' station some fifteen feet away was frozen and silent. He glanced about with the sheepishness of a janitor sweeping center stage when the curtain suddenly opens before a packed house. For an instant he had the impulse to break and run. Then, out of the corner of his eye, he saw Christine Beall push herself off the counter and head in his direction. It was hardly the triumphant moment he would have picked for a second encounter with the woman.

As she neared, he looked away, inspecting a heel-mark by his shoe. He sensed her eyes measuring him. When they first met, he had been captivated by their gentle power and determination. Now, before their umber stare, he felt vaguely discomforted.

Moments before she spoke he breathed in her perfume—a muted suggestion of spring. "Dr. Shelton, we're all very proud of the way you stood up for what you believe in," she said softly. "Don't worry. Things have a way of working out."

Her words. The way she spoke them. Not at all what

David had expected. He repeated them in his mind but could not seem to grasp the feelings behind them. "Thanks . . . thanks a lot," he managed, preparing himself for the eyes before he looked up. By the time he did, Christine was gone. Activity behind the nurses' station had returned to normal, but she was not there.

David elected to go and write new orders on Anton Merchado before putting the whole ghastly evening to rest. In the morning he would be on his own. As he shuffled away, thoughts of the day to come, of regaining control of his life, sweetened the distasteful events of the past five hours.

"Things have a way of working out." He said Christine's words out loud as he pushed through the door to the stairway.

CHAPTER V

Hidden in a doorway, Christine watched David leave Four South. She waited until she was certain he would not return before stepping into the dimly lit corridor. Her shift was nearly over. In the nurses' lounge, as in similar rooms on every floor in the hospital, the evening staff was compiling notes in preparation for the 11 P.M. to 7 A.M. crew—the graveyard shift.

In less than an hour 263 nurses would leave the hospital and head for diners or bars or home to mates who would, as often as not, be too tired to respond as lovers. They would be replaced by 154 others, each struggling to maintain biologic equilibrium in an occupation that demanded life-and-death decisions during hours when most of the world was sleeping.

For a time Christine stood in the deserted hallway listening to the clamorous silence of night in the hospital. The sighs and coughs. The moans and labored, sonorous respirations. Oxygen gurgling through half a dozen safety bottles. The obedient beep of a monitor in duet with the mindless hiss-click of a respirator. And in the darkened rooms, the patients, thirty-six of them on Four South, locked in their own struggle—a struggle not for riches or power or even happiness, but merely to return to the outside world. To return to their lives.

At night more than any time Christine felt the awesome responsibility of her profession. Like any job, nursing had its routine. But beyond the drudgery and the complaints, beyond the scut work and the deprecating attitude of many physicians, there were, above all, the patients. At times, it seemed, a silent conspiracy existed among physicians, administrators, and nursing organizations whose sole purpose was to expunge from nurses any notion that their primary purpose was the care of those patients. It even included the nurses themselves, many totally drained of the sense of caring and kindness that had first brought them into the profession.

Christine gazed down the corridor toward Room 412. Silently she renewed a vow that she would never give in to the confusion and the negativism. She would never stop caring. If a commitment to The Sisterhood of Life was the only way to honor that vow, so be it. Somehow she knew that as long as she was part of The Sisterhood, she was safe from the frustrations and heartache that had driven so many out of hospital nursing.

For Christine the commitment had begun on a Sunday. Outside Doctors Hospital a winter storm raged. Inside the nurses' lounge on Four South another kind of storm was brewing. Much of its fury emanated from Christine and all of it was directed against a physician named Corkins who had just ordered an emergency tracheotomy on an eighty-year-old woman, the victim of a massive stroke that had left her paralyzed, partially blind, and unable to speak. Christine had spent countless hours caring for her. Although the old woman was unable to move or talk, she had communicated with her eyes. To Christine the message was clear: "Please, let me go to sleep. Let this living hell end." Now, with the operation, hell would continue indefinitely.

For nearly an hour Christine had sat in the nurses' lounge sharing her tears and her anger with Janet Poulos. Carefully, gradually, Janet had introduced her to knowledge of The Sisterhood of Life.

Over the two days following the old woman's tracheotomy, Christine had spent many hours discussing her dismal condition with Janet, while at the same time learning more and more about The Sisterhood. Throughout her nursing career she had been able to find joy in even the most distasteful aspects of daily patient care. But with each minute spent helping to prolong the agony of the old woman, Christine's frustration grew. Disconnecting the respirator to suction the tube each hour. Frequent turnings. Urinary catheter changes. Deep intramuscular injections. Frantically trying to keep abreast of one incipient bedsore after another. And always the eyes looking at her, looking through her, their message even more desperate than before.

Finally the commitment was there. Christine followed the direction given to her by Janet Poulos and reported the old woman's case to the Regional Screening Committee. A day later, she received their approval and instructions.

Toward the end of her shift she slipped quietly into the woman's room. The drone of the respirator blended eerily with the howling winter wind outside. In the darkness she felt the woman watching her. She bent over the bed, pressing the tears on her cheek against the woman's temple. After a few moments, she felt her nod—once and then again. She knew! Somehow she knew. Christine gently kissed her forehead.

She brought her lips close to one ear and whispered, "I love you."

Reaching up, she disconnected the respirator, then waited in the darkness for five minutes before reconnecting it.

Nearly four hours into the next shift a nurse reported

74

that she was unable to feel a pulse or obtain a blood pressure on the woman. A resident was called and, after finding a straight line on her electrocardiogram, pronounced the woman dead. Later that morning her two sons, much relieved at the end of their mother's suffering, had the body brought to a local funeral home. By 11 A.M. her bed was filled by a young divorcée in for elective breast augmentation. Like the waters of a pond, disturbed momentarily by a pebble, the hospital appeared as it always had, the last ripples of the old woman's existence gone from its surface.

"Christine?"

She spun toward the voice. It was Janet Poulos.

"You okay?"

Christine nodded.

"It looked like you were posing for the cover of *Nurse Beautiful*."

"More like *Nurse Troubled*."

"That scene with Huttner and the Professor?"

"Uh-huh."

"Want to talk about it?"

"No. I mean maybe a little. I mean you're the only one who . . ."

Janet silenced her with a raised hand. "The visitors' lounge is empty." She nodded toward the nurses' lounge. "From the looks of things in there, you've got about ten minutes before report. It's been sort of crazy up here tonight, hasn't it? I heard there were some problems after that Mr. Chapman was found dead," Janet added.

As they walked to the small visitors' lounge, Christine described the reaction of John Chapman's grief-stricken widow. Janet shook her head in disbelief.

"Why do you think she picked on the flowers to throw around the room?" she asked.

"Oh, she threw other things, too. Not just flowers."

75

Christine dropped onto a sofa and Janet took the chair across from her.

"So she wrecked everything?"

"Almost. We managed to salvage two vases."

"Oh?" Janet shifted in her chair.

"Yes, and even one of those was a little strange."

"How do you mean?" The question was asked matter-of-factly, but Janet's posture and expression suggested more than passing interest.

Christine glanced at her watch impatiently. They had only five minutes before report. "Oh, it was nothing, really. Just that the flowers in the last vase were lilies, and the card attached to them said something like 'Best Wishes from Lily,' that's all."

"Oh," Janet said with a flatness not mirrored in her eyes. She scratched absently at the scar beside her nose, then suddenly changed the subject. "Are you thinking about submitting this Thomas's wife to the Screening Committee?"

"I've already done it." Christine felt off balance.

"And?"

"And nothing, Janet. I haven't heard yet whether she's been approved. You see, Charlotte and I have grown very very close to one another—"

"Well, I say, 'Bravo for you,' " Janet broke in.

"What?"

"I hope she's approved."

"Janet, you don't even know the woman . . . or the situation. How can you possibly say . . ."

"I may not know her, but I know Huttner. Of all the pompous, conceited, self-righteous bastards who ever hid behind a goddamn M.D., Huttner is the worst."

Janet's outburst was totally unexpected. For a time Christine was speechless. Certainly it was the over-zealous, at times ego-based aggressiveness of physicians that had spawned The Sisterhood, but to Christine it had always been a conflict of philosophies, not personal-

76

ities. "Wh . . . what has Huttner's conceit got to do with Charlotte?" She felt confused and strangely apprehensive.

Janet calmed her with a wide smile. "Whoa, slow down," she said, patting her on the knee. "I'm on your side. Remember?" Christine nodded, but uncertainty remained. "I believe in The Sisterhood and what we're doing the same way you do. Why else would I have recruited you? All I was trying to say is that in cases like this Mrs. Thomas we get a . . . double benefit. We get to honor the wishes of the woman and her husband by reestablishing some dignity in her life, and at the same time we get to remind a person like Huttner that he's not God. Yes?"

Christine evaluated the notion, then relaxed and returned the smile. "Yes, I . . . guess we do." She rose to leave.

"If support is what you need," Janet said, "you've got mine. I think you did the right thing in presenting this woman, and now it's up to the Screening Committee to do its part."

Christine nodded her acknowledgment.

Janet continued as she reached the door. "You know, Christine," she said, pausing to study the younger woman's face, "it's quite all right to benefit from doing something you believe in. The goodness of any work isn't diminished by the fact that you might, in some way, profit from it. Do you understand?"

"I . . . I think so," Christine lied. "Thanks for talking with me. I'll let you know what the Committee decides."

"Do that, please. And Chris? I'm here if you need me."

Still uneasy, Christine hurried to the nurses' lounge. She paused outside the door, trying to compose herself. Janet's explosion on the subject of Wallace Huttner had been startling, but it wasn't as disturbing as it had at

77

first seemed. Janet had been part of The Sisterhood for years; surely she had handled a number of cases. Proposing and carrying out a death, even a euthanasia death, was an emotionally charged, gut-wrenching business. Over the years the necessity of facing the same decisions again and again was bound to take its toll in some way. In Janet's case, Christine decided, it was a bitterness toward those who made such awesome choices necessary.

She glanced down the hall in time to see Janet step into the elevator. The woman was an excellent supervisor and, even more important, a nurse dedicated to the truest ideals of the profession. In the moment before she entered the nurses' lounge, Christine felt a resurgence of pride at the secrets she shared with her "sister."

CHAPTER VI

Carl Perry steeled himself against the pain he knew would knife through his throat, then, as gingerly as possible, swallowed. Pain, almost any pain, was better than the goddamn drooling he had been doing since the polyps or growths or whatever they were had been snipped off his vocal cords. It would be two more days of bed rest, intravenous fluids, and writing notes in order to communicate before the danger of his vocal cords swelling shut would be passed. At least, that's what Dr. Curtis had told him.

He reached over and tugged at the band of adhesive tape that held the intravenous line in place on his right forearm. Several hairs popped free from his skin and he hissed a curse at the I.V. nurse who had neglected to shave the area clean.

"I.V. tape—complain to Drs. Hosp. Admin.," he scribbled on a pad, tearing the note off and stuffing it in a drawer that was rapidly filling with other, similar reminders.

He flipped up the small mirror in his Formica hospital tray and took stock of himself. Even with the scratches Curtis's instruments had made on the corners of his mouth, he liked what he saw. Deep blue eyes, tanned skin just leathery enough, square jaw, perfect teeth. He looked the way most other men of forty-eight could only dream of looking. The women saw it, too— even the young ones. They fought for the chance to spend a few hours with him in the suite he kept at the Ritz. They all went home satisfied, too.

What a perfect idea it had been to start the rumor around the singles bars that each year the girl who gave him the best lay would get a free Porsche courtesy of Perry's Foreign Motors. He might actually do it too, if the day ever came when his looks gave out on him.

Bored and uncomfortable on the sweaty sheets, he flipped on the television, then just as quickly turned it off. Nothing but the eleven o'clock news starting on every channel. He massaged the front of his blue silk pajama pants and felt the stirrings of an erection. No, not yet, he decided. Wait until you're really ready to go to sleep, then have at it.

At that moment a nurse stepped into his room, closing the door carefully behind her. She was the same one who had sat on his bed and talked to him the night before the operation. A little old, maybe forty, he thought, but with a body that just wouldn't quit. Perry felt an immediate surge in the limp organ beneath his hand and again began massaging himself under the sheets, picturing the shapely nurse lying nude on his hotel suite bed, waiting for him.

"How are you doing, Mr. Perry?" she asked softly. She was standing less than a foot from him. Inviting him, he just knew it.

For a moment Perry was torn by the dilemma of having to release himself in order to write a note. Finally, he scribbled. "Fine, sweetheart, how're you?"

"Is there anything I can get for you before I call it quits for the night?" she asked, moving an inch closer.

Perry checked her left hand for a wedding ring.

80

There was none, but that added little to his already mushroomed fantasy. "That depends . . ." he wrote.

"On what?"

Teasing him, tantalizing—that's what she was doing. He decided to chance it. "Whether we make it now or after I get out!"

He debated writing about the free Porsche, but rejected the notion as unnecessary.

"Do we do it alone or invite your wife along with us?"

His new, giddy abstraction had her legs stretched upward, heels resting on the wall over his bed. "Wife doesn't understand me," he wrote, playing along and adding a little smile face to the bottom of the page.

"Well, we'll see about everything when you're a little better," she said. "I'll admit that the idea of spending some nice time with you had crossed my mind." She toyed with the top button of her uniform and for a moment Perry thought she actually might undo it for him.

"You say when," he scribbled, slipping his free hand around her thigh.

"Soon." She smiled and stepped out of his grasp. "First, I have two presents for you. One is from your doctor and one is from me. Which do you want first?"

Perry deliberated, then wrote "Yours."

The woman left the room and returned holding something behind her back. Perry inhaled sharply at the way her uniform pulled tightly across her breasts. A C for sure, he thought. Absolutely. Thirty-four C. He looked up at her beaming face and noticed, for the first time, a thin scar running almost parallel to one side of her nose. A minor flaw, he decided. Candlelight, a little makeup, and, *poof*, no more scar.

After giving him what seemed like a deliberately prolonged look at her, the nurse theatrically drew her hands from behind her back. She held a bouquet of flowers. Bright, purple flowers.

"Beautiful," he wrote.

"They're hyacinths," she said.

After a brief search for a vase, she set the flowers in the empty urinal that rested on his bedside table. Perry winced at her somewhat crude break with the romantic mood of the moment. Maybe she's into kinky sex, he thought, not at all certain he was ready to play someone else's game.

"Second present?" he wrote.

"Just some new medicine." She moved inches from his face as she produced a syringe full of clear liquid from her pocket and injected it in the tubing of his intravenous line.

He reached out and again grabbed her by the back of the thigh. This time she made no attempt to move away. Suddenly he felt a strange tightness in his chest. His grip weakened, then, in less than a minute, disappeared all together. With difficulty and mounting panic, he turned his head upward and looked at the nurse. She was standing motionless, smiling benevolently down at him. He tried to scream, but only a soft hiss emerged from beneath his swollen, paralyzed vocal cords.

The air became as thick and heavy as molasses. No matter how hard he tried, he could not force it down into his lungs. His left arm dangled uselessly over the side of the bed.

"It's called pancuronium," the nurse said pleasantly. "A rapid-acting form of curare. Just like on poison darts. You see, your wife understands you much better than you realized, Mr. Perry. She understands you so well that she is willing to share a large portion of your insurance with us in order to eliminate you from her life."

Perry tried to respond, but could no longer manage even a blink. A dull film seemed to cover all the objects in the room, as gradually his panic yielded to a detached sense of euphoria. Through now immovable eyes and the mounting film, he watched the nurse carefully unbutton the top two buttons of her uniform, exposing the deep cleft between her breasts.

"Don't worry about the flowers, Mr. Perry. I'll see to it that they get some water," were the last words that he heard.

Janet Poulos set Perry's arm on the bed, checked the darkened corridor of Three West, and calmly left the floor. As the stairway door closed behind her, she gave in to the smile that had been tugging at her mouth from the moment the last of the pancuronium was injected. It had been an incredibly profitable day for The Garden. Just as Dahlia had promised it would be. First, a masterful performance by Lily, and now she, Hyacinth, had done at least as well. She laughed, and listened to her echo reverberate throughout the empty stairwell.

In her office on One North, Janet settled behind her desk, then closed her eyes and relived the scene in Carl Perry's room. The sense of power—of ultimate control—was at least as thrilling as it had been at the bedside. It was an excitement that she, like all the others in The Garden, had first discovered through The Sisterhood of Life. The Sisterhood, with its high-flown nobility, was fine for some, Janet reflected, but Dahlia's creation of the Garden had been sheer inspiration. That they could be paid, and paid well, for their efforts only sweetened the game. Janet blessed Dahlia for bringing Hyacinth to life.

Then, as so often happened after she handled a Sisterhood or Garden case, Janet began thinking about the man—the first man who had ever taken her, the only man she had ever loved. Was he a professor of surgery now as he had planned? Why had he never called again after that night? Well, he would certainly see her in a different light now. She had power, too. As much as the most powerful surgeon in the world. If he could only see her he would . . . Janet shrugged. "Who cares," she said out loud. "Who the hell cares anyhow."

She picked up the telephone. It was time to share the excitement of the day with Dahlia.

CHAPTER VII

It was after eleven thirty when the evening shift on Four South completed their report and the eleven-to-seven group took over for the night. Christine Beall rode the Pinkerton minibus to Parking Lot C. Exhausted, she declined an invitation for a nightcap from the four nurses riding with her and headed home.

Twenty miles away, in the bedroom suburb of Wellesley, Dr. George Curtis downed two fingers of brandy and shuffled back to bed from his oak-paneled study. His wife, who had turned on the bedside lamp and propped herself up on several pillows, looked at him anxiously.

"Well, how did it go with Mrs. Perry?" she asked.

Curtis sank down on the edge of the bed and sighed his relief. "She's pretty shaken up, but all things considered, she seems to be holding together all right. I offered to go over there and talk with her, but she said it wouldn't be necessary, that she had people. Best of all, she didn't say anything about wanting an autopsy."

His wife was concerned. "What do you mean 'best of all'? George, is something the matter?"

"Well, from what the resident on duty told me, Perry

must either have had a coronary or bled into his vocal cords where I did the surgery. Either way, his wife could try and make a case for negligence by saying he should have been cared for in the I.C.U. Without an autopsy, she's got no definite findings, so she's got no grounds for a suit, and I say 'Amen' to that."

"Amen," his wife echoed as she turned off the light and rolled over next to him.

Christine drove slowly, steering by rote, unaware of the traffic around her. On the gaslit sidewalks the night world of the inner city was in full cry. The hookers and the hustlers, the junkies and the winos, and the clusters of young men milling outside tavern doorways. It was a world that usually fascinated her, but this night the people and the action went unnoticed. Her mind had begun playing out a far different scene.

It was a tennis match. Two women on a grassy emerald court. Or perhaps it was only one, for she never saw them both at the same time. Just a bouncing figure in a white dress, swinging out with energetic, perfect strokes.

Totally immersed in the vision, she cruised through a red light, then onto a wide boulevard leading out of the city.

All at once, Christine realized why it seemed like a match. With each swing, each stroke, the woman's face changed. First it was Charlotte Thomas, radiant, laughing excitedly at every hit; then it was the drawn, sallow face of her own mother, a stern Dutch woman whose devotion to her five children had eventually worn her to a premature death.

The strokes came faster and faster, and with each of them a flashing change in the competitor's face until it was little more than a blur.

Suddenly Christine glanced at the speedometer. She was going nearly eighty. Seconds later, a route sign

86

shot past. She was traveling in a direction nearly opposite to her house.

Shaking almost uncontrollably, she screeched to a stop on the shoulder and sat, gasping as if she had just finished a marathon. Several minutes passed before she was able to turn around and resume the drive home.

It was after midnight when she reached the quiet, treelined street where she and her roommates had lived for two years. The decision to search for an apartment in Brookline had been unanimous. "An old town with a young heart," Carole D'Elia had called it, referring to the thousands of students and young working people who inhabited the quaint duplexes and apartment buildings. After a three-week search, they found—and immediately fell in love with—the first-floor apartment of a brown and white two family. Their landlady, a blue-haired widow named Ida Fine, lived upstairs. The day after they moved in, a large pot of soup outside their door heralded Ida's intention to adopt the three of them. Christine had resented her intrusion in their lives at first, but Ida was irrepressible—and usually wise enough to sense when she had overstayed her welcome.

Christine, Carole, and Lisa Heller were quite different from one another, but tailor made for living together. Carole, an up-and-coming criminal lawyer, handled the bills, while Christine took care of the shopping and other day-to-day essentials of cooperative living. Lisa, a buyer for Filene's, was the social chairman.

With a groan of relief and fatigue, Christine eased her Mustang up the driveway and into its customary spot next to Lisa's battered VW. The two-car garage was so full of the "treasures" Ida was constantly promising to throw out that there had never been room inside for more than their bicycles. As she walked around to the front, Christine noticed for the first time that lights were blaring from every room. A party. The last thing in the world she wanted to deal with. "Lisa strikes again," she muttered, shaking her head.

The unmistakable odor of marijuana hit her as soon as she opened the door. From the living room the music of an old Eagles album mixed with the clinking of glasses and a half-dozen simultaneous conversations. She was searching her thoughts for somewhere else to sneak off to for the night when Lisa Heller popped out from the living room.

Three years younger than Christine and six inches taller, Lisa was dressed in what had become the unofficial uniform of the house—well-worn jeans and a baggy man's shirt pirated from some past lover. Her face had a perpetually intellectual, almost pious look to it that seemed invariably to attract men who were "into" Mahler and organic food, both of which Lisa abhorred.

"Aha! The prodigal daughter returneth to the fold." She giggled.

There was something disarming about Lisa that had always made even Christine's blackest moments seem more manageable. "Lisa," she said, smiling around clenched teeth, "how many people are in there?"

"Oh, eight or ten or twelve or so. It's hard to count because some of them aren't really people, you know."

"Do me a favor, please," Christine pleaded, "Go get some rope and your raccoon coat and see if you can sneak me past the door as your pet Irish wolfhound or something. I just want to go to bed."

"Ah, bed," Lisa said wistfully, steadying herself against the wall. "Soon all that Gallo Chablis and fine Colombian dope in there will have us all in bed. The only question remaining is who will be bedded down with whom. Speaking of which . . ."

"Lisa, is *he* in there?"

"Big as life. It's his dope, doncha know."

Christine grimaced. Jerry Crosswaite was hanging on like a bad cold. She shook her head. "It's my fault," she

88

added with theatrical woe. "My cardinal rule, and I broke it."

"What rule is that?" Lisa punctuated the question with a hiccup.

"Never date a man more than once who has vanity plates on his car with *his* name on them." The two friends laughed and embraced.

Although seeing Jerry still had its pleasant moments, they were becoming fewer and farther between. Ever since his unilateral decision that they were "made for each other," Jerry had mounted an all-out campaign to make Christine "The Wife of the Youngest Senior Loan Officer in Boston Bank and Trust History." For weeks he had barraged her with roses, gifts, and phone calls. To Christine's mounting chagrin, Lisa and Carole had become so swept up in the romantic adventure that they had undermined her efforts to discourage his ardor.

"Chrissy, will you stop complaining." Lisa said now. "I mean you're past thirty, and he's a nice man with an Alfa. What more could a girl want?"

Christine wasn't totally certain she was being teased. "Lisa, he has fewer sides than a sheet of paper . . ."

"Well, babe, I wouldn't kick 'im out of bed," Lisa said.

"Stick around, Heller, you may get the chance to find out if you mean that." Christine brushed past her and into the living room.

Jerry Crosswaite set down his wine and began a piecemeal effort to rise from the couch and greet her. Christine forced a grin and waved for him to stay where he was. There were twelve others in the room, many of them looking even more gelatinous than Jerry.

"Brutal," Christine muttered, at the same time smiling irrepressibly at Carole D'Elia, who was engrossed in a game of her own creation called 'Scrabble For Dopers.' In this version, to be played only with the aid of marijuana, any word, real or invented, would be

89

counted as long as it could be satisfactorily defined for the other players.

Carole called her over. "Hey, Chrissy, you're the only one with any sense around here. Come and arbitrate this. Is or is not Z-O-T-L the noun for a decorative arrangement of dead salamanders?"

"Absolutely," Christine said, giving her a hug from behind. None of the women sharing the house smoked marijuana regularly, but from time to time parties simply materialized, and as often as not, pot was a part of them. Despite the relative inactivity around the room, there was a sense of vitality that Christine felt every time she was around her roommates. She decided that their company might be just the tonic for her trying day. Even if it meant dealing with Jerry Crosswaite.

"By the way," Carole said. "You had a call a little while ago. Some woman. Said she'd call back. No other message."

"Old woman? Young?" Christine asked anxiously.

"Yes." Carole nodded definitively, polished off the rest of her wine, and wrote down her thirteen points.

Crosswaite had negotiated his way across the room and come up behind Christine, putting his hands on her shoulders. She whirled around as if struck with meat hooks.

"Hey, easy does it, Christine, it's only me," he said. He had discarded the jacket of his Brooks Brothers suit and had unbuttoned his vest—a move that for him was tantamount to total relaxation. Only the fine, red road maps in his eyes detracted from the Playboy image he liked to project.

"Hi, Jerry," she said. "Sorry I missed the party."

His gesture swept the room. "Missed it, hell. It's been waiting for you. Lisa said you like the necklace. I'm glad."

Christine glanced around for Lisa so that she could

glare at her. "Jerry, I really wish you would stop sending me things. I . . . I just don't feel right accepting them."

"But Lisa told me . . ."

She cut him off, trying at the same time to keep her voice calm. "Jerry, I know what Lisa told you, and Carole, too. But neither of them is me. Look, you're a really nice man. They think a lot of you, so do I, but I'm getting very uncomfortable with some of the gifts you've been sending and with a lot of the assumptions you've been making."

"Such as what?" Crosswaite said, an edge of hostility appearing in his voice.

She bit at her lower lip and decided that she was simply not up to a confrontation. "Look, just forget it," she said. "We can work the whole thing through another time when we have a little more privacy and a little less wine."

"No, Chris, I want to discuss it now." Crosswaite's control disappeared completely. "I don't know what your game is, but you've led me along to the point where this relationship is really important to me. Now, all of a sudden, you've gone frigid." His tone was loud enough to break through to even the most somnolent in the room. Embarrassed looks began to flash from one to another as Carole and Lisa rose to intervene. The banker continued. "I mean you were never any tiger in bed to begin with, but at least you were there. Now, all of a sudden, you're a fucking glacier around me. I want an explanation!" The room froze.

Christine took a step backward and brought her hands, fists clenched, tightly in against her sides.

The ring of the telephone shattered the silence.

Carole rushed to the kitchen. "Chrissy, it's for you," she called out after a few seconds. "It's the woman who called before."

91

Christine loosened her fists and lowered her arms before breaking her gaze away from Crosswaite.

There were three people in the kitchen. With a single look Christine sent them scurrying to the living room. Then she picked up the receiver.

"This is Christine Beall," she said, sharpness still in her voice.

"Christine, this is Evelyn, from the Regional Screening Committee. Are you in a position where you can talk uninterrupted?"

"I am." Christine settled onto a high rock maple stool she had found at a Gloucester flea market and later refinished.

"The Sisterhood of Life praises your deep concern and your professionalism," the woman said solemnly. "Your proposal regarding Mrs. Charlotte Thomas has been approved."

In the quiet kitchen, Christine began, ever so slightly, to tremble, as each word fell like a drop of water on hard, dry ground.

The woman continued. "The method selected will be intravenous morphine sulfate, administered at an appropriate time during your shift tomorrow evening. An ampule of morphine and the necessary syringe will be beneath the front seat of your car tomorrow morning. Please be certain the passenger side door is left open tonight. We shall lock it after the package has been delivered.

"We request that you administer the medication as a single rapid injection. There will be no need to wait in the room afterward. Please dispose of the vial and the syringe in a safe, secure manner. As is our policy, after your shift at the hospital is completed, you will please call the telephone recording machine and tape your case report. We all share the hope and the belief that the day will arrive when our work can become public knowledge. At that time reports such as yours—already nearly forty years' worth from nurses throughout the country—can be properly honored and receive their due praise. In transmitting your report there will be no need to repeat the patient's clinical history. Have you any questions?"

"No," Christine said softly, her fingers blanched around the receiver. "No questions."

"Very well, then," the woman said. "Miss Beall, you can feel most proud of the dedication you show to your principles and your profession. Good night."

"Thank you. Good night," Christine replied. She was speaking to a dial tone.

With a glance at the closed door to the living room Christine pulled on a green cardigan of Lisa's that had been draped over a chair. Quietly she slipped out of the back door of the apartment.

The night sky was endless. Christine shivered against the autumn chill and pulled the sweater tightly about her. On the next street a car roared around a corner. As the engine noise faded, a silence as deep as the night settled in around her. She looked at the stars—countless suns, each one a mother of worlds. She was a speck, less than a moment, yet the decision she had made seemed so enormous. Pressure through her chest and throat made it difficult to swallow. Panic, uncertainty, and a profound sense of isolation tightened the vise as she moved slowly to her car and unlocked the passenger side door.

Christine walked around the deserted block once, and then again. Hidden, she sat on a low rock wall across the street from her apartment and watched until the last of the partygoers finally left and the lights in the windows winked off. With a prolonged, parting gaze at the jeweled sky, she sighed and headed home. All that remained in the living room were a few half-filled glasses and a single, dim light, left for her by her roommates.

Christine flipped off the lamp. She was undressed even before reaching her room. Standing by the bureau, she unpinned her long, sandy hair, shook it free, and began slow passes with her brush, softly counting each one.

"Whenever you must really know . . ." Charlotte's words dominated her thoughts as she stepped across to her bed.

It was not until she turned the covers that she saw the envelope resting on her pillow.

She read the note inside, stiffened, then crumpled it into a tiny ball and threw it on the floor.

It said, "Christine, I've left. Maybe for good. Feel free to call, but only when you have something significant to say. Jerry."

CHAPTER VIII

David began his first day as Wallace Huttner's replacement by identifying a Berlioz piece as Mendelssohn, but bounced back moments later by correctly sensing that outside his window a day of change was developing.

There was a dry chill in the air that kept him from working up the heavy sweat he liked during his run by the river. To the east an anemic sun was gradually losing its battle for control of the morning to an advancing army of heavy, dark clouds, each with a glossy white border. The day mirrored his mood: the difficult evening rounds with Huttner had left him with a vague sense of discomfort and foreboding that neither a night of fitful sleep nor his morning workout had totally dispelled.

He had planned to make morning rounds along the same route he and Huttner had taken the previous night, but once in the hospital, he succumbed to a growing impatience to see how Anton Merchado was doing on his new treatment regimen.

The fisherman's bronzed, weathered face broke into a wide grin as soon as David entered his room. With that single smile David's apprehension about the day evaporated.

"I had a turd, Doc!" Merchado's gravelly voice held all the pride of a mother who had just given birth. "This morning. One beautiful, plop-in-the-water turd. Doc, I can't thank you enough. I never thought I'd ever have one again."

"Well, don't get too excited yet, Mr. Merchado," David said, barely able to control his own enthusiasm. "You certainly look better than you did last night, but I don't think the diarrhea is gone for good. At least, not just yet."

"My fever is down, too, and the cramps are almost gone," Merchado added as David probed his abdomen for areas of tenderness and listened for a minute with his stethoscope.

"Sounds good," David said, placing the instrument back in his jacket pocket, "but still no solid food. Just sips of liquids and several more days of the new antibiotic and intravenous fluids. You can tell your family that you'll be in the hospital for another week if things keep going well. Maybe even a little longer than that."

"Will you be my doctor when I get out?" he asked.

"No, only for a few days, then Dr. Huttner will be back. You're fortunate to have him, Mr. Merchado. He's one of the finest surgeons I've ever seen."

"Maybe . . . and then again, maybe not." Merchado's squint and wise smile said that he would push the matter no further. "But you leave your card with me just the same. I have a bunch of relatives that are gonna be beating down your door to get you to do some kind of operation on them. Even if they got nothing wrong."

With a grin that understated his delight, David left the room, then looked at the list of patients he had to see that morning. The names filled both sides of the file card on which he had printed them. Joy sparkled through him. For so many years he had not allowed himself even to daydream of having such a case load. As he neared the end of the hallway, he gave a gleeful yip and danced through the stairway door. Behind him, two plump, dowager nurses watched his performance, then exchanged disapproving expressions and several "tsks" before heading pompously to their charges.

David's rounds were more exhilarating than anything he had done in medicine in years. Even Charlotte Thomas seemed to have brightened up a small notch, although simply seeing her with the benefit of daylight may have had something to do with that impression. Her bed was cranked to a forty-five-degree angle and an aide was spoon-feeding her tiny chips of ice, one at a time. David tried several ways to determine how she was feeling, but her only response was a weak smile and a nod. He examined her abdomen, wincing inwardly at the total absence of bowel sounds. No cause for panic yet, but each day without sounds made the possibility of yet another operation more likely. For a moment David toyed with the notion of stopping even the ice chip feedings, then, with one last look at Charlotte, he decided to leave things as they were.

At the nurses' station he wrote a lengthy progress note and some orders for maneuvers he hoped might improve her situation. By the time he finished it was nearly one o'clock. He had twenty minutes for coffee and a sandwich before he was due in his own office. Five and a half hours had passed in what seemed almost no time at all. He tried to remember the last time it had been like this and realized it had probably been eight years. Not, he reflected ruefully, since the accident.

Even his afternoon office hours, at times embarrassingly slow, were made pleasantly hectic today by frequent phone calls from the hospital nurses to clarify orders or discuss problems.

At precisely five o'clock, as the door closed behind the last patient, David's office nurse, Mrs. Houlihan, yelled, "Dr. Shelton, there's a call for you from Dr. Armstrong. Her secretary is putting her on. You can pick up on three."

"Very funny," David shouted back from his office. He had only one telephone: its number happened to end in three. It was good to see Houlihan enjoying the unaccustomed busy day as much as he was.

"I'm off to cook up some hash for my brood. Good night, Doctor," she called out.

"Good night, Houlihan," David answered.

Moments later, Dr. Margaret Armstrong came on the line. As the first female chief of cardiology at a major hospital, Armstrong had earned nearly as much of a reputation in her field as had Wallace Huttner in his. Of all those on the medical staff of Doctors Hospital, she had been the most cordial and helpful to David, especially during his first year. Although she referred her patients to cardiac surgeons almost exclusively, or, where appropriate, to Huttner, she had, on several occasions, sent a case to David, taking pains each time to send him a thank-you note for the excellent care he delivered.

"David? How are things going?" she asked now.

"Busy today, but enjoying every minute, Dr. Armstrong." Perhaps it was the regal bearing, the aristocratic air that surrounded the woman, perhaps it was the twenty or so years difference in their ages—whatever the reason, David had never once had the impulse to address Margaret Armstrong by her first name. Nor had he ever been encouraged to.

"Well, I'm calling to see if I can make it busier for you," Armstrong said. "To be perfectly honest, I called Wally Huttner's office first, but I was pleased to hear that you're covering for him."

"Thanks. Fire away."

"It's an elderly gentleman named Butterworth—Aldous Butterworth, if you will. He's seventy-seven, but bright and spry as a puppy. He was doing fine for a week following a minor coronary until just a little while ago, when he suddenly started complaining about tingling and pain in his right leg. His pulses have disappeared from the groin on down."

"Embolus?" David asked, more out of courtesy than any uncertainty about the diagnosis.

"I would think so, David. The leg is already developing some pallor. Are you in the mood to fish us out a clot?"

"Happy to." David beamed. "Have you gone over the risks with him?"

"Yes, but it wouldn't hurt for you to do it again. David, I'm a bit worried about general anesthesia in this man. Do you think it might be possible to . . ."

David was so excited about capping his day with a major case that he actually cut her short. "Do him under local? Absolutely. It's the only way to fly."

"I knew I could count on you," Armstrong said. "I am most anxious to hear how things go. Aldous is a dear old friend as well as a patient. Listen, there's an Executive Committee meeting in an hour, and as chief of staff in this madhouse I have to attend. Could I meet you somewhere later this evening?"

"Sure," David said. "I have several patients to see before I head home. How about Four South? I've got a woman to see there with total body failure. Maybe you can even come up with some ideas."

"Glad to try," Armstrong said. "Eight o'clock?"

"Eight o'clock," David echoed.

Hands scrubbed and clasped protectively in front of him, David backed into Operating Room 10, then slipped into a surgical gown and began making preparations to orchestrate and conduct his own symphony. Aldous Butterworth seemed small and vulnerable stretched out on the narrow operating table.

David ordered Butterworth's right foot placed in a clear, plastic bag to keep it visible without contaminating his operative field. The foot was the color of white marble.

Using small injections, he deadened an area of the man's right groin. With no pulse to guide him, he knew that the femoral artery could be an inch or more away from his incision. A miscalculation, and he faced an operation so difficult that a second incision might be the only solution. Focus in, he thought. See it. Hidden beneath his mask, the corners of his mouth turned up in a thin, knowing smile. He was ready.

"Scalpel, please," he said, taking the instrument from the scrub nurse. He paused, closed his eyes, and breathed in the electricity of the moment. Then he opened them and surveyed the expectant faces watching him, waiting for him. With a slight nod to the anesthesiologist and a final glance at Butterworth's bloodless foot, he made his incision. The taut skin parted, immediately exposing the femoral artery. "Bull's-eye," he whispered.

In minutes the artery, stiff and heavy with clot, was isolated and controlled with two thin strips of cloth tape placed two inches apart. David made a small incision in the vessel wall between the tapes. Gently he eased a long, thin tube with a deflated balloon at the tip down the inside of the artery toward the foot. When he determined that the tip was in position, he blew up the balloon and carefully drew it back through the incision. Two feet of stringy, dark clot pushed out before David lifted the balloon free. Repeating the procedure in the opposite direction, he removed the thicker clot that had caused the obstruction in the first place. An irrigation with blood thinner, and he was ready to close. He tightened the cloth tapes to prevent blood flow through the artery, then closed his incision in the vessel with a series of tiny sutures.

For the second time in less than twenty minutes David shared a momentary gaze with each person in the room. He then took a silent, deep breath, held it, and released the tapes. Instantly, Butterworth's foot flushed with life-giving color. A cheer burst out from the team. Textbook perfect. The whole case, textbook perfect. In absolute exhilaration, he called out the good news to Butterworth, who had slept through the entire procedure.

"That was *really* fine work, Dr. Shelton. That was really *fine* work, Dr. Shelton. That *was* really fine work, Dr. Shelton." David repeated the words of the veteran scrub nurse over and over, trying to reproduce her inflection exactly. "Maybe you should give her a call and ask her to say it again so you can get it just right," he advised himself. He had dictated an operative note, showered, and dressed. Now he was headed down the corridor of Four South to share the news of Butterworth's successful operation with Dr. Armstrong.

He glanced at his watch. Ten of eight. His second straight late evening in the hospital. A first for him since joining the surgical staff more than eighteen months before.

Margaret Armstrong had already arrived on the floor and was seated at the nurses' station sharing coffee and relaxed conversation with Christine Beall and the charge nurse, Winnie Edgerly. As David approached the group, his eyes were drawn to Christine. Her eyes and her smile seemed to be saying a thousand different things to him at the same time. Or maybe they were his words, his thoughts, not hers. Lauren's jewel-perfect face flashed in his mind, but faded as the tawny eyes tightened their hold.

Dr. Armstrong's voice pulled him free. "Yo, David," she called out merrily. "Word is sweeping the hospital about my little man's new foot. Bravo to you. Come, we shall toast your successful operation with a cup of this coffee." She glanced in her cup, grimaced, then added, "If, in fact, that is what this is."

She wore a black skirt and light blue cashmere sweater. A simple gold butterfly pin was her only jewelry. Her white clinic coat, unbuttoned, was knee length—the type reserved unofficially only for professors or those with sufficient seniority in the teaching community. Her dark wavy hair was cut short in a style perfect for her bright blue eyes and finely carved features. There was an air about her, an energy, that commanded immediate attention and respect. An article written six years before about her contributions to her field had dubbed her the Grande Dame of American Cardiology; she had been only fifty-eight years old at the time.

As David took in the scene at the nurses' station, he couldn't help but reflect on the easy, animated relationship that existed between Armstrong and the two nurses. Quite the opposite from Dr. Wallace Huttner, even allowing for the fact that Dr. Armstrong was a woman. The contrast became even more striking when she got up and poured him a cup of coffee.

She introduced him to the nurses as the "hero of the day," and, with a mischievous wink at Christine, added that David was, to the best of her knowledge, single. He blushed and covered his eyes in genuine embarrassment, but realized at the same time that he was carefully avoiding any further eye contact with Christine. Seconds later, Armstrong had him describing Butterworth's operation in detail. For the moment the danger had passed.

Rona Gold, a practical nurse, joined the group as David used red and blue pens to sketch pictures of the procedure he had done.

It seemed clear to David that Armstrong already knew the details, probably from one of the O.R. nurses. Still, she encouraged him at every chance to continue.

"Well," she said finally, "I stopped by the recovery room to see Aldous and he doesn't remember a thing. Snoozed his way through the whole ordeal. Here he is in danger of losing a leg or worse and he sleeps through the procedure. That is my idea of good local anesthesia, what?"

"I think I put him to sleep while I was trying to explain what I was going to do to him," David said.

Armstrong shared an appreciative laugh with the three nurses, then said, "David, you mentioned something about having a complicated patient here on Four South. Charlotte Thomas?"

"Why, as a matter of fact, yes," David said. "Are you a mind reader as well as a cardiologist?"

"Nothing that exotic. The nurses and I deduced that she was the only one on the floor who fit the bill, so I took the chance and went over her chart."

"And?"

"And you're right. She is rapidly developing total body failure. In fact, I have only one observation to add to the excellent note you wrote this morning outlining her many problems. Your Mrs. Thomas has, on top of everything else, definite signs of coronary artery disease on her electrocardiogram. At least, in my interpretation of her electrocardiogram," she added modestly. "I really have nothing dramatic to contribute to what is already being done. Does it seem as though the bowel obstruction will require reexploration?"

"God, I hope not," David said. "It would mean her third major operation in less than three weeks."

"Dr. Shelton, I have a question," Christine said.

He responded quickly. "It's five, five, five-two, oh, one, six."

"What is?"

"My phone number!" David said, immediately realizing that he should have learned more about Christine Beall before exposing her to his sense of humor.

103

Gold and Edgerly laughed briefly, but Christine did not crack the slightest smile. "That's not funny," she said. "Neither is a woman as sick and in as much pain as Charlotte Thomas."

David muttered an apology, but she ignored it.

"What concerns me," Christine continued, "is why, if she has so many seemingly incurable problems, Dr. Huttner has made her a full Code Ninety-nine. Especially after what happened last night."

"Last night?" Armstrong asked. "What happened last night?"

David paused, uncertain which of them she was addressing. Christine sat back, looking expectantly at him for his version.

"Well," he said finally, "Mrs. Thomas's husband and Dr. Huttner got into a discussion about the aggressive approach Huttner has elected to take in her treatment. The husband was frustrated and more than a little angry. Understandable, I guess, and certainly something we're all used to encountering."

"How did Wally handle it?" Armstrong leaned forward with interest, absently rolling her coffee cup back and forth between her hands.

"As well as could be expected under the circumstances, I think," David said. "He may have overreacted a bit. He stuck by his philosophical guns. Refused to alter his treatment plan regardless of what Thomas, who was under obvious strain and pressure, demanded him to do. Finally Huttner drew me into the whole thing. I'm afraid that my opinion and the way I expressed it were not quite what he wanted to hear in that situation." David managed a rueful grin at his own understatement.

"And how do you feel about the whole thing, David?"

Dr. Armstrong's voice was soft. There was an openness in her expression that made him certain there would be no recrimination from her.

"I think it's a bitch of a situation, if you'll pardon the

104

expression," he said. "I mean it's always harder to decide *not* to use treatment on a patient than it is to just go ahead and employ every medicine, machine, and operation you can think of. That's why we end up with so many patients who drag on as little more than vegetables.

"Personally," he continued, "having watched several of my own family members die prolonged, painful deaths, I think there are times when a doctor must make the decision to hold off and let nature take its course. Don't you agree?"

Hold off . . . Let nature take its course. . . . There was something about the words, the way they were said. Margaret Armstrong closed her eyes as they echoed in her mind, then yielded to other words. Other words and the voice of a young girl.

"It's all right, Mama. . . . I'm here, Mama."

"Don't you agree, Dr. Armstrong?"

"Mama, tell me what I can do to help. . . . Does it still hurt as much? Tell me what I can do to help. . . . Please, tell me what I can do. . . ."

"Dr. Armstrong?"

"Oh, yes," she said. "Well, David, I'm afraid I agree much more with Dr. Huttner's approach than with yours." How long had she drifted off? Were they expecting an explanation?

"How do you mean?"

No, she decided. No explanations. "The way I see it, following your philosophy, a physician would constantly be confronted with the need to play God. To decide who is to live and who is to die. A medical Nero. Thumbs up, we put in an intravenous. Thumbs down, we don't."

David responded with an emotion and forcefulness that momentarily startled even him. "I believe that the major responsibility of a physician is not constantly to do battle against death, but to do what he can to lessen

105

pain and improve the quality of patients' lives. I mean," he went on, less vehemently now, "should every treatment, every operation possible be used on every patient, even though we know there's only a one-in-a-million or even a one-in-ten-thousand chance that it will help?" In the silence that followed, he sensed that once again he'd used a verbal cannon where a slingshot or perhaps even a velvet glove had been called for.

At this point, Winnie Edgerly, a straightforward if somewhat plodding woman of about fifty, felt moved to enter the discussion. "I cast my vote with Dr. Armstrong," she said earnestly. "I wouldn't want any tubes pulled out of me if there was even the slightest chance. I mean, who knows what might happen or what might come along at the last minute to help. Right?"

"Now don't get me wrong, Mrs. Edgerly," David said, carefully minimizing the intensity in his voice. "I am not advocating pulling out any tubes from anyone. I'm arguing that we should all think twice—or more than twice—before putting the tubes down someone in the first place. Sure they can help, but they also can prolong hopeless agony. Does that help make my feelings any clearer?"

Edgerly nodded, but her expression suggested that she did not agree.

Finally Dr. Armstrong said, "So, David, how does all this apply to your Mrs. Thomas?"

"It doesn't," he said shortly. "The treatment program for Mrs. Thomas has been clearly spelled out by Dr. Huttner. It's my responsibility to carry those plans out to the best of my ability. That's all there is to that."

Armstrong seemed about to say something further when the overhead page sounded, summoning David to the emergency ward. "When it rains, it pours." He smiled expectantly at Dr. Armstrong.

"But I'll bet you don't mind getting wet like this at all," she said. "I'm very happy for you, David."

"Thank you, Dr. Armstrong." He swallowed the last of his coffee. "Thank you for everything."

With a nod to Edgerly and Gold, and a longer look at Christine, David headed off toward the emergency ward.

Christine sat silently behind the nurses' station as the others dispersed to go about their business. There was a puzzled, ironic expression on her face. She slipped her right hand into the pocket of her sweater and, for a minute or two, fingered the syringe and ampule of morphine that she had wrapped in a handkerchief and stuffed inside. Then she rose and walked with forced nonchalance down the hall toward Room 412.

CHAPTER IX

"Do you do hands, Dr. Shelton?" Harry Weiss, the hawk-nosed resident who had called David to the emergency ward, could easily have won the role of Ichabod Crane in a production of *The Legend of Sleepy Hollow*.

"Show me what you have," David said.

The emergency ward was in its usual state of mid-evening chaos. Two dozen patients in various stages of discomfort and anger at the hospital sat in the crowded waiting room. Litters glided past like freighters in a busy port, bearing their human cargo to X ray or the short-term observation ward or an in-patient room. Telephones jangled. A dozen different conversations competed with one another. David caught snatches of several of them as the resident led him to Trauma Room 8. "What do you mean you can't have the results for an hour? This man is bleeding out. We need them now . . ." "Mrs. Ramirez, I understand how you feel, but I can't help you. There is simply no Juan Ramirez on the emergency ward at this time . . ." "Now, you're going to feel a little pinprick . . ."

The patient David had been called about was a forty-year-old laborer who had lost a brief but unmistakably furious encounter with his power saw. The top halves of two fingers were gone completely, and a third was held together at the first knuckle by a sliver of tendon. Another no-win situation, David thought to himself as he evaluated the damaged hand. He spoke briefly with the man, who had stopped his profuse sweating but was still the color of sun-bleached bone. Then he guided the overwrought young resident into the hallway. It was David's decision whether to do the repair himself or to spend the extra time to take the resident through it. He chose to take the time, remembering the many late nights when other surgeons had made the extra effort to teach him. It was nearly half an hour before he felt confident that Weiss could complete the repair on his own.

Four South was unusually quiet as David stepped off the elevator and started down the corridor toward Room 412. A burst of laughter from the nurses' lounge suggested that it was coffee break time—at least for some of the staff. He thought about Christine Beall, half hoping that she might step out of one of the rooms as he was passing.

Just the image was enough to rekindle an uneasy warmth. So, she's interesting looking and has strange eyes, David thought. Lauren is beautiful and has incredible eyes. You're reacting like this because she's away, that's all. Face it, with Lauren you have everything you've ever wanted in a woman—beauty, brains, independence. Right? Right. The logic was all there, black and white and irrefutable. But somewhere in the back of his mind a small voice was saying, "Think again . . . think again . . ."

The lights in Charlotte Thomas's room were off. David stood at the doorway, staring across the darkness toward her bed. The gastrointestinal drainage machine, set for intermittent suction, whirred, stopped, then reassuringly whirred again. Bubbles of oxygen tinkled through the water of the safety bottle on the wall. He debated whether or not to disrupt her sleep in order to check findings he knew would be unchanged at best. Finally he stepped across the room and turned on the fluorescent light over her bed.

Charlotte was lying on her back, a tranquil half-smile on her face. It took David several seconds to realize that she was not breathing.

Instinctively, he reached across her neck and checked for a carotid pulse. For an instant he thought he felt one, but then knew that it was his own heart, pounding through his fingertips. With both fists he delivered a sharp blow to the center of Charlotte's chest. Then he gave two deep mouth-to-mouth breaths and several quick compressions to her breastbone. Another carotid check showed nothing still.

He raced to the doorway. "Code Ninety-nine four-twelve," he screamed down the deserted corridor. "Code Ninety-nine four-twelve." He ran back inside and resumed his one-man resuscitation.

Thirty seconds passed in what seemed like a year before Winnie Edgerly burst into the room pushing the emergency crash cart. At the same instant the page operator, alerted from the nurses' station, announced, "Code Ninety-nine, Four South. Code Ninety-nine, Four South. Code Ninety-nine, Four South."

Seconds later, Room 412 began to fill with people and machines. Edgerly inserted a short oral airway into Charlotte's mouth and began providing respirations as best she could with a breathing bag. David continued the external cardiac compression. An aide rushed in, then wandered meekly to one side of the room, waiting for someone to tell her what to do. Two more nurses raced in, followed by Christine, pushing an electrocardiograph machine. Leads from the machine were strapped tightly to Charlotte's wrists and ankles.

A resident appeared, then another, and finally the anesthesiologist, a huge Oriental who introduced himself as Dr. Kim. He replaced Edgerly at the head of the bed and looked over at David, who had turned the job of cardiac massage over to one of the residents and had moved to man the cardiograph.

"Tube her?" Dr. Kim asked. David nodded his answer.

As the room filled with still more people, including the inhalation and laboratory technicians, Kim set about his task. He picked up a steel laryngoscope and inserted its right-angle, lighted blade deeply into Charlotte's throat, lifting up against the base of her tongue to expose the delicate silver half-moons of her vocal cords.

"Give me a seven-point-five tube," he said to the nurse assisting at his side. The clear plastic tube, with a diameter of three quarters of an inch, had a deflated plastic balloon wrapped just above the tip. Skillfully, the giant slipped the tube between Charlotte's vocal cords and down into her trachea. He used a syringe to blow up the balloon, sealing the area around the tube against air leaks. Next he attached the black Ambu breathing bag to the outside end of the tube, connected oxygen to the bag, and began supplying Charlotte with breaths at a rate of thirty per minute.

Christine stood just to David's right and watched as he tried to center the needle on the cardiograph. All at once, her eyes riveted on the slashing up-and-down strokes of the stylus. There was a rhythm—a persistent, regular rhythm. *Oh, my God, he's bringing her back!* Her thoughts screamed the words. The one possibility she had never considered, and now it was happening. With every beat a new horrifying image occurred to her. Charlotte, hooked to a respirator. More tubes. Day

111

upon endless day of wondering if the woman's oxygen-deprived brain would awaken. *What had she done?*

The finely lined paper flowed from the machine like lava, forming a jumbled pile at David's feet. The rhythmic bursts continued.

"Hold it for a second!" David called for the resident to halt his thrusting cardiac compressions in order to get a true reading from the machine.

Instantly the pulsing jumps of the needle disappeared, replaced by only a fine quiver. The pattern had been artificial—a response to the efforts of the resident.

Christine had misinterpreted the cardiograph. She felt near collapse.

"Her rhythm looks like fine fibrillation. Please resume pumping." David's voice was firm but calm. Christine sensed a measure of control return. "Christine, please get set to give her four hundred joules."

The order registered slowly. Too slowly.

"Miss Beall!" David snapped the words.

"Oh, yes, Doctor. Right away." Christine rushed to the defibrillator machine. Was everyone staring at her? She couldn't bring herself to look up. Turning the dial on the machine to 400, she squirted contact jelly on the two steel paddles and handed them to David.

David motioned the resident away. Then he quickly pressed one paddle along the inside of Charlotte's left breast and the other one six inches below her left armpit.

"Everyone away from the bed," he called out. "Ready? Now!"

He depressed the red button on the top of the right-hand paddle. A dull thunk sounded as 400 joules of electricity shot through Charlotte's chest and on through the rest of her body. Like a marionette's, her arms flipped toward the ceiling, then dropped limply to the bed. Her body arched rigidly for an instant, then was still. The cardiograph tracing showed no change.

The resident resumed his pumping, but soon motioned to the medical student standing nearby that he was tiring. The two made a smooth change.

Immediately David began ordering medications to be given through Charlotte's intravenous lines. Bicarbonate to counteract the mounting lactic acid in her blood and tissues, Adrenalin to stimulate cardiac activity, even glucose on the chance that her sugar may have dropped too low for some reason. No change. Another Adrenalin injection followed closely by two more 400-joule countershocks. Still nothing. Calcium, more bicarbonate, a fourth shock. The cardiogram now showed a straight line. Even the fine fibrillation was gone. The resident again took his place over from the student and the pumping continued. At the head of the bed, the mountainous anesthesiologist stood implacably squeezing the Ambu bag, which seemed like little more than a pliant black softball in his thick hands.

"Hook an amp of Adrenalin to a cardiac needle, please," David ordered. Although an injection through the subclavian intravenous line should end up in the heart, perhaps the tip had somehow become dislodged. He put his hand along the left side of Charlotte's breastbone and used his fingers to count down four rib spaces. Holding the ampule of Adrenalin in his other hand, he plunged the four-and-one-half-inch needle attached to it straight down into Charlotte's chest. Almost immediately, a plume of dark blood jetted into the ampule. A direct hit. The needle was lodged in some part of the heart. Behind him, Christine held her breath and looked away.

David shot in the Adrenalin. For a moment the cardiograph needle began jumping, and with it his own pulse. Then he noticed that the medical student was

113

rocking back and forth, inadvertently bumping into Charlotte's left arm each time. He motioned the student away from the bed. Instantly the tracing was again a flat line.

Christine felt the tension in the room begin to dissolve. She stared at the floor. It was almost over.

David looked at the anesthesiologist with a shrug that asked, "Any ideas?"

Dr. Kim stared back placidly and said, "Will you open her chest?"

For a few seconds David actually entertained the thought. "How are her pupils?" He was stalling, he knew it.

"Fixed and dilated," Kim replied.

David gazed off into one corner of the room. His eyes closed tightly, then opened. Finally he reached over and flicked off the cardiograph. "That's it. Thank you, everybody." It was all he could manage.

The room began to empty. David stood there for a time looking down at Charlotte's lifeless form. Despite the tubes and the bruises and the circular electrical burns on her chest, there was something beautifully peaceful about the woman.

At last, peaceful.

All at once, some of the impact of what had happened began to register. His hands and armpits became cold and damp with sweat.

As he walked out of Room 412 to call Wallace Huttner, David was shaking. Deep inside him was the chilly feeling that somehow he had just struck the tip of a nightmare. He glanced at the wall clock. How long had they worked on her? Forty-five minutes? An hour? "What the hell difference does it make," he muttered as he sat down at the nurses' station to write a death note in Charlotte Thomas's chart.

"You all right?" Christine asked softly as she set a cup of muddy coffee in front of him.

114

"Huh? Oh, yeah, I'm okay. Thanks," David said, resting his chin on the counter and studying the Styrofoam cup at close range. "Thanks for the coffee."

"I'm sorry she didn't make it through for you," she said.

David continued staring at the cup, as if searching for the answer to some kind of cosmic mystery.

"Potassium!" he exclaimed suddenly.

Christine, who had moved to leave the uncomfortable silence, turned back to him. "What about potassium?"

He looked up. "Something wasn't right in there, Christine. I mean over and above the obvious. I'm probably wrong, but I can't remember handling a cardiac arrest where I couldn't get a flicker of cardiac activity back—even when quite a bit of time had elapsed between the arrest and the Code Ninety-nine. Shit! I wish there had been time to get a potassium level on her. Potassium, calcium—I don't know what, but something felt like it was out of whack."

"Can't you get a potassium level done now?" Christine asked.

"Sure, but it won't be much help. During the resuscitation and after death potassium is released into the bloodstream from the tissues, so the levels are usually high anyway." He clenched his fists in frustration.

Christine felt an ache building inside her. "How could her potassium level have gotten out of line in the first place?"

"Lots of ways." David was too distracted to notice the change in her expression. "Sudden kidney failure, a blood clot, even a medication error. It makes no difference now. I'm probably way off base anyway. Dead is dead." He realized the anguish that she was feeling. "I . . . I'm sorry," he said. "I didn't mean that. I'm afraid the pleasant task of calling Dr. Huttner on the Cape has me a little rattled. I don't think this is the sort of news he'd be too happy about having me save until he gets back. Look, maybe sometime we can sit and talk about Mrs. Thomas. Okay?"

Christine looked away. "Maybe sometime . . ." she whispered to herself.

David fished out the number Huttner had given him. After the usual hassles with the hospital switchboard operator, his call was put through. Huttner's hello left no doubt that he had been asleep.

"Great start," David muttered, looking upward for some kind of celestial help. "Dr. Huttner, this is David Shelton," he said into the receiver.

"Yes, what is it, David?" Even his first words held an edge of impatience.

At that moment David knew that he should have waited until the next day to call. "It's Charlotte, Dr. Huttner, Charlotte Thomas." He felt as though his tongue was swelling rapidly and had already reached grapefruit size.

"Well, what about her?"

"About an hour and a half ago she was found pulseless in her bed. We worked on her, a full Code Ninety-nine for nearly an hour, but nothing. She's dead, Dr. Huttner."

"What do you mean you worked on her? What in the hell happened, man? I checked on her before I left this morning and she seemed stable enough."

David had not anticipated an easy time of it with Huttner, but neither had he expected a war. His tongue passed grapefruit and headed toward watermelon.

"I . . . I don't know what happened," he said. "Maybe hyperkalemia. She had a brief period of fine fibrillation on her cardiogram, then nothing. Flat line. No matter what. Absolutely nothing."

116

"Hyperkalemia?" Huttner's tone was now more one of bewilderment than anger. "She's never had problems with her potassium in the past."

"Do you want me to call Mr. Thomas?" David asked finally.

"No, leave that to me. It's what he wanted anyway." Huttner's voice drifted away, then picked up with renewed intensity. "What you can do for me is to get in touch with Ahmed Hadawi, the chief of pathology. Tell him there's going to be a postmortem on this woman tomorrow. I want to know exactly what happened. If for some reason Thomas won't consent, I'll notify Hadawi myself that it's off. You tell him we'll be at the Autopsy Suite tomorrow morning at eight sharp with a signed permission from Peter Thomas. Good night."

"Good night," David said a minute or so after Huttner had hung up. He set the receiver down, then added, "Good grief."

The nurses' station was quiet—deserted except for David and a ward secretary who was painfully trying not to notice him. Eyes closed, he sat, rubbing his temples, struggling to sort out the unpleasant emotions swirling within him. Confusion? Sure, that was understandable. Depression? A little, perhaps. He had just lost a patient. Loneliness? Dammit, he wished Lauren were home.

But there was something else. It was hazy and diffuse. Difficult to focus on. But there *was* something, some other feeling. Several minutes passed before David began to understand. Underlying all his reactions, all his emotions, was a vague nebula of fear. Trembling for reasons that were not at all clear to him, he dialed Lauren's number, hanging up only after the tenth ring. Even though he had unfinished business in the hospital, he felt the urgent need to get out. He would call Hadawi from home, he decided.

117

* * *

Christine leaned against a doorway and watched David leave. She had no qualms about the rightness of what she had done, but his discouragement was painful for her.

Later, she excused herself from shift report and walked down the deserted corridor to the pay phone. The number she dialed was different from the one she had used the previous day. God, had it only been a day? No voice answered this time—only a click and a tone.

"This is Christine Beall of Boston Doctors Hospital," she said in a measured monotone. "In the name of compassionate medical care and on instructions of The Sisterhood of Life, I have, on October second, helped to end the hopeless pain and suffering of Mrs. Charlotte Thomas with an intravenous injection of morphine sulfate. The prolongation of unnecessary human suffering is to be despised and to be terminated wherever possible. The dignity of human life and human death are to be preserved at all costs. End of report."

She hung up, then on an irrepressible impulse picked up the receiver and dialed Jerry Crosswaite's number. With the sound of his voice, the impulse vanished.

"Hello," he said. "Hello . . . Hello?"

Christine gently set the receiver back.

In the shadows at the far end of the hall, Janet Poulos observed Christine as she left report and made the call that Janet felt certain was her case report on Charlotte Thomas.

"Sound her out about The Garden," Dahlia had urged. "Be careful what you say, but sound her out."

Janet countered with her belief that Beall was far too new in The Sisterhood to be ready for The Garden, but Dahlia insisted.

"Just remember," she said, "what would have happened to you three years ago had I decided *you* weren't ready. As I recall, you were thinking about taking your own life before I phoned."

In fact, Janet had passed beyond the thinking stage. At the moment of Dahlia's call she had more than a hundred sleeping pills laid out on her bedspread. Self-loathing and a profound sense of impotence had pushed her to the brink of suicide.

For years she had lived on hatred—hatred toward physicians in general and one in particular. She had joined The Sisterhood to use the organization in order to put certain M.D.'s in their place. Where necessary, she had even manufactured data on patients to get the Regional Screening Committee's approval and recommendations.

However, after six years and nearly two dozen cases, what little sustenance she had gained from such activities had disappeared.

Then, with a single phone call, everything had changed. Somehow, Dahlia knew about the falsified laboratory and X-ray reports, about Janet's hatred for physicians and their power, about many intimate details of her life. She knew, but she didn't care.

In the course of the year after she joined The Garden Janet was brought along slowly. Every few weeks Dahlia would transmit the name of a patient in the northeast who had been approved by The Sisterhood for euthanasia. Janet would arrange a meeting with the distraught family of the patient and offer a merciful death for their loved one in exchange for a substantial payment. The contract, once made, was then unwittingly honored by The Sisterhood nurse who had initially proposed the case.

It was a wonderful, lucrative diversion, but The Garden had much, much more in store for Hyacinth. Other flowers blossomed within Doctors Hospital. One of them,

119

Lily, was transplanted from the ranks of The Sisterhood by Janet herself. Soon both women were given other responsibilities, primarily in the area Dahlia referred to as "direct patient contact." They were no longer bound to Sisterhood cases—euthanasia was not a concern; the new cases had proven more rewarding in every sense. John Chapman and Carl Perry were just two of them.

As Christine rang off, Janet moved toward her. Dahlia had reasoned that after handling a case as traumatic as Charlotte Thomas's, Beall might be ready. Hyacinth still had strong doubts. She would talk with the woman, but only until her own suspicions were confirmed. Beall would need a few more years of tongue lashings from physicians who, as often as not, were deadly weapons in their own right. She would need a few more thankless Sisterhood cases.

Then she might be ready.

Christine spotted Janet coming and waited.

"It's done?" Janet asked solemnly. Christine nodded. "Talk for a few minutes?" Again a nod. In silence they walked to the visitors' lounge. Christine dropped onto the sofa and this time Janet sat next to her.

"It's never easy, is it?" Janet folded one leg beneath her and watched as Christine picked at a sliver on the edge of the coffee table.

"I'm okay, Janet. Really. I know what I did—what we're doing—is right. I know how badly Charlotte wanted it to end. Cancer throughout her liver, and Dr. Huttner wanted to keep sticking tubes in her. It was right." Her voice was strained but under control.

"You'll get no arguments from me, kid," Janet said, reaching over and squeezing her hand reassuringly. Christine squeezed back. "It's just too bad that we're the ones who have to shoulder all the darn responsibility, that's all." Christine responded with a nod and a rueful shrug.

Perhaps Dahlia was right. Janet elected to push a bit further. "All that responsibility, and what do we have to show for it? Nothing."

Christine spun toward her, eyes flashing. "Janet! What on earth do you mean, nothing?"

Time to retreat, Janet decided. For once in her life, at least, Dahlia had misjudged. Beall's naive, idealistic flame had not yet been doused. She took pains to meet Christine's gaze levelly. "I mean that after all these years, after all the hundreds, and now I guess thousands, of Sisterhood recruits, nothing has changed in the attitude of the medical profession."

"Oh." Christine relaxed.

"So until things change, we do what we have to do. Right?"

"Right."

"Listen, Christine. Let's have dinner sometime soon. We have a lot in common, you and I, but this is hardly the place to discuss our mutual interests. Check your schedule and I'll check mine. We'll set something up in the next few days. Okay?"

"Okay. And, Janet, thanks for your concern. I'm sorry I snapped at you. This day's been a bitch, that's all."

Janet smiled warmly. "If you can't snap at your sister, who can you snap at? Right?"

"Right."

Janet rose. "I've got to get Charlotte taken care of. Her husband left word he won't be coming in to see her. Call me at home anytime you need to talk." With a wave she left. At least Dahlia would know she had tried. Beall simply wasn't ready. Too bad.

Christine returned in time for the end of report. Restless and saturated with nursing and with Boston Doctors Hospital, she stood against a wall until the final patient had been discussed, then left before any of the

121

others. Ahead of her, waiting for the elevator, were Janet and an orderly. Between them, on a litter, lay the sheet-covered body of Charlotte Thomas.

Held fast by the scene and her reflections on it, Christine watched as the litter was maneuvered onto the elevator. Not until the doors had closed was she able to move again.

CHAPTER X

Fox's Golden Laws of Medicine defined *pathologist* as "The specialist who learns all by cutting corners to get straight to the heart of the matter, leaving no stone unturned (gall or kidney)."

As usual, the recollection of one of Gerald Fox's immortal definitions forced a smile out of David. This despite his discomfort at the prospect of having to observe the autopsy on Charlotte Thomas.

He was already ten minutes late, but he knew that nothing would be completed except perhaps the preparation of Charlotte's body and the first incision. Although Fox's observations were usually right on the mark, David had never felt that his cynical maxim about pathologists was totally accurate. He thought back to his first exposure to forensic pathology, a lecture given by the county coroner just before David's group of second-year medical students was ushered in to view their first autopsy.

"Cause of death, ladies and gentlemen," the old pathologist had said, "that is what we in forensic medicine are asked to determine for our medical and legal colleagues. In fact, nobody other than God himself knows what causes a person to die. Nobody. Rather what we can determine is the condition of each organ in a patient's body at the time of his or her death. From this knowledge, we can deduce with some accuracy the reason for cessation of cardiac, cerebral, or pulmonary function—the only true causes of death.

"For example. If a patient is killed by a gunshot wound through the heart, we may say quite safely that death was due to cardiac standstill from a penetrating wound to the heart muscle itself. But what of the patient with a disease like cancer? We might be able to locate cancerous tissue in the liver, brain, lungs, or other organs and certainly, in one respect, may say that cancer is the cause of death. Determining the immediate cause, however, is nigh impossible. Did the heart stop because it was poisoned by some as yet unknown substance secreted by the cancerous cells? Or did lack of sufficient fluid volume, for reasons perhaps unrelated to the cancer itself, cause such an impairment in circulation that the heart could no longer function and simply stopped?

"You must keep this in mind whenever you read such diagnoses as 'cancer,' or 'emphysema,' or 'arteriosclerosis' as the cause of a patient's death. They may have been a cause leading to death, but as to the direct cause of death—that, my friends, remains a mystery in the vast majority of cases."

A mystery. David hesitated outside the two opaque glass doors labeled AUTOPSY SUITE in gold-leaf letters. A sleepless night and chaotic morning had left him tense and uneasy. The prospect of Charlotte's autopsy only aggravated those feelings.

Then there was Huttner. Cape Cod was only seventy miles away, close enough for him to make the drive up that morning without much difficulty. Whether or not he would choose to return there after witnessing the autopsy was a different story. David bet himself a long-overdue and much-feared trip to the dentist that Huttner would elect to stay in Boston and resume control of his practice. He had given some thought to turning the bet around so that at least he wouldn't have to face the Novocain and drill if he lost the last two days of his adventure. In the end, however, he decided that if he lost he would be able to submerge the misery of a visit to the tooth merchant in other, more substantial miseries.

Needles of formalin vapor jabbed deep into his nostrils as he entered the suite. It was a long room, nearly twenty-five yards from end to end. High ceilings and an excess of fluorescent light obscured, in part, the fact that there were no windows. Seven steel autopsy tables, each fitted with a water hose and drainage system, were evenly spaced across the ivory-colored linoleum floor. In addition to the hose, used for cleaning organs during an autopsy and the table afterward, every station had its own sink, blackboard, and suspended scale. A large red number, from 1 to 7, inlaid in the floor, was the only characteristic individual to each one. That is, except for Station 4.

On either side of that table six tiers of wooden risers had been built, identical to those in high school gymnasiums. At certain times the risers were filled with students in various stages of distress or fascination. At other times the stands held groups of residents in pathology or surgery, craning to study the dissecting skills of a senior pathologist. Station 4 was the center court of the Doctors Hospital Autopsy Suite.

At 8:15 on the morning of October 3, Stations 1, 4, and 6 were in operation, and a sheet-wrapped body rested on the table at Station 2. Wallace Huttner was standing, arms folded, at Station 4. The risers were empty but for a resident scheduled to post the body on table 2 and three medical students. As David approached, he caught sight of Charlotte's open-mouthed, chalk-colored face. He bit at his lower lip, swallowed a jet of bile, and decided that it would be best to concentrate on the rest of her anatomy. He could deal reasonably well with autopsies as long as he viewed them as examinations of parts of a body. The nearer he allowed himself to get to the human aspect, the more unpleasant the procedure became for him.

Ahmed Hadawi, a quick, dark little man with disproportionately huge hands, had made his initial incision and was elbow-deep in the chest cavity, busily separating the chest and abdominal organs from their attachments to the neck and body wall. He made a soft clucking noise with his tongue as he worked, but otherwise seemed without emotion or expression. Occasionally he bent over and murmured a few words into a pedal-operated Dictaphone.

Huttner nodded coolly in response to David's greeting. His stance and manner bore no hint of the relaxed, interested, almost fatherly physician who had sat with David in the surgeons' lounge just thirty-six hours before. After the nod, he returned his attention to the dissection, carefully avoiding further eye contact. David looked at the man helplessly. Then, as so ˙en happened in difficult situations, the macabre poi. ᴐn of his humor took over. If he hugs himself any tighter, he thought, maybe he'll just break into little pieces and I can cover his practice until someone glues him back together.

At that moment he caught another glimpse of Charlotte's face. "Stop it, Shelton!" he screamed at himself. "This isn't funny. Just stop it!" The mental slap was enough. He shifted his weight several times from side to side, then settled down, his attention focused on the pathologist.

"Now, then, we are ready to take a look at some things," Hadawi said. The resident stepped down from the risers to get a better view and Huttner tightened his autoembrace a notch as the pathologist began pointing out the anatomical status of each of Charlotte's organs as they existed at the instant of her death.

"The heart," he began, "is moderately enlarged, with thickening of the muscle and dilatation of all chambers. There is a small, fresh puncture wound through the anterior left ventricle, which I assume is the result of Dr. Shelton's commendably accurate intracardiac injection."

David thought that the moment might be right for a modest smile and nod, but then realized that no one was looking at him. He smiled and nodded anyway.

The little pathologist continued speaking as he dissected. "There is fairly advanced narrowing of all coronary arteries, although there is no gross evidence of recent damage such as might be caused by a myocardial infarction." Margaret Armstrong's interpretation of Charlotte's electrocardiogram had been right on the button, David noted. "Keep in mind," Hadawi added, "that evidence of an acute infarction—say, less than twenty-four hours old—is often seen only in microscopic examination of the heart muscle itself, and then only if we happen to catch just the right section."

"I want to be notified as soon as those slides have been examined," Huttner ordered, more, it seemed, to David, out of a need to make some kind of statement than anything else. Hadawi glanced up at him and, with no more acknowledgment than that, turned his attention to the lungs. Immediately his stock as reflected in David's eyes rose several points. Both lungs were more than half consolidated by the heavy fluid of infection. Even if there had been no other problems, it seemed entirely possible that Charlotte would have been unable to survive her extensive pneumonia.

The remainder of the examination was impressive mainly for what it did not show. Pending, of course, microscopic examination of the abdominal lymph nodes, Hadawi announced that he was unable to find any evidence of residual cancer in the woman's body. The liver cysts, which had been misdiagnosed by the radiologist,

127

Rybicki, were scattered throughout the organ, and similar fluid-filled sacs were found in both kidneys. "Polycystic involvement of hepatic and renal parenchyma," Hadawi said into his Dictaphone.

Finally the pathologist stepped away from the table. "I have a few remaining things to do on this body," he said, "but they will have no bearing on my findings. To all intents and purposes, Wally, we are done. Most significant of what I have to tell you is that this woman's pressure sore was extending beneath her skin to the point where I doubt that even with multiple grafts it ever would have healed. Infection of the sacral bones had already begun and would have been almost impossible to treat.

"She has enough coronary arteriosclerosis so that I feel her final event was probably a cardiac one. I intend to sign her out as cardiovascular collapse secondary to her pulmonary and bedsore infections. An additional stress undoubtedly came from her partial small bowel obstruction, which, as you saw, was due to adhesions from her recent surgery."

David said, "Dr. Hadawi, Dr. Huttner, if we could sit down over here, there are a few questions that I have." He could not bear the thought of having to discuss Charlotte's case over her dissected body. Hadawi responded with a brief, understanding grin and took a seat on one of the risers. Huttner, who still held his arms around himself, followed reluctantly. David gauged the expression on his face as somewhere between disgust and fury. Nowhere in his eyes or manner was there a hint of disappointment or sympathy. Regardless of her underlying disease, Charlotte Thomas had walked into the hospital as Huttner's patient, had been operated on, and had died. That made her a postoperative mortality. Her operation and the many complications that ensued would be discussed in depth at Surgical Death Rounds. Hardly a prospect that would sit well

128

with this man, David realized. He was far more accustomed to asking the questions than to answering them.

"Now, David," Hadawi said, "just what is it that troubles you about what you have seen?"

"Well, most of my concern centers about her heart, which seemed so unresponsive to everything that I tried during her Code Ninety-nine. It may have been simply that too much time elapsed between the moment of her cardiac arrest and the time I started working on her, but it just doesn't feel like that. I wonder if perhaps her potassium could somehow have risen too high and caused a fatal cardiac arrhythmia."

"That is always a possibility," Hadawi said patiently. "I've saved several vials of blood. I'll be happy to have her potassium level checked. However, you must keep in mind the limits of accuracy of such a measurement done in a postmortem patient—especially one who has received prolonged external cardiac compression."

Finally Huttner spoke. It was no surprise to David that he was unwilling to surrender without a fight. "Look, Ahmed," he said. His second and third fingers bobbed up and down at the man, but Hadawi showed no outward hint of being offended by the gesture. "I'm not totally satisfied with all this. Dr. Shelton here has a point. Since there's nothing obvious on gross exam to explain this woman's sudden death, then we should look further before signing her out as something so nonspecific as cardiovascular collapse. Maybe some nurse made a medication error on her and caused an allergic, anaphylactic reaction of some kind. She was known to be allergic to penicillin."

Hadawi was obviously used to dealing with Huttner's ego. He merely shrugged and said, "If you wish, I shall be happy to order a penicillin level on her blood. Is there anything else you would like?"

Huttner seized the chance to avoid a Surgical Death Rounds presentation as a drowning sailor might grasp a passing chunk of driftwood. A medication error would provide him with instant absolution.

"Yes, there are some other things I think should be done," Huttner said with a professorial tone that included several significant pauses. He seemed actually to be savoring his own words. "I think she should have a complete chemical screen. Antibiotic levels, electrolytes, toxins—the works."

"With no specific idea of what we're searching for, that will be quite expensive," Hadawi said softly, as if anticipating the eruption that would follow even this mild objection.

"Damn the money, man," Huttner fired, his fingers jabbing even faster than before. "This is a human life we're talking about here. You just do the damn tests and get me the results."

"As you wish, Wally."

Huttner nodded his satisfaction, then started to leave. As he passed David, he snapped his fingers. "I almost forgot, David," he said over his shoulder. "The Cape Vascular Conference really wasn't all that it was cut out to be. I've decided not to go back. Thank you for your help yesterday. I think there's a meeting in January I might want to attend. Perhaps we can work out another coverage arrangement then."

His voice, David thought, held every bit as much sincerity as Don Juan saying, "Of course I'll respect you in the morning."

CHAPTER XI

In his selection of a hospital, as in all the other affairs in his life, Senator Richard Cormier was his own man. While many Washington politicians considered it a status symbol to be cared for at Bethesda Naval or Walter Reed, Cormier overruled the objections of his aides and insisted that he be operated on by Dr. Louis Ketchem at Boston Doctors. "Always trust your own kind," he said. "Louie's an old war-horse just like me. Either he does the cutting or I don't get cut."

The walls of Cormier's room were covered top to bottom with cards, and cartons containing several hundred more were stacked neatly in one corner. In addition to a nurse and the senator, the presence of a secretary and two aides helped to create an atmosphere almost as chaotic as that perpetually found in his Washington office.

"Senator Cormier, I must give you your preop meds, and these people will have to leave your room." The nurse, an ample matron named Fuller, projected just the right amount of authority to get the senator to comply with the request.

Cormier ran his fingers through his thick, silver hair and squinted up at the nurse. "Ten more minutes."

"Two," she said firmly.

"Five." The bargaining brought a sparkle to his eyes.

"All right, five," she said. "But one minute longer and I use the square needle to give you this medication." She bustled out of the room, turning at the doorway to give Cormier a glare that said she was serious. The senator winked at her.

"Okay, Beth, time to get packed up," he said to his secretary. "Remember, I want a thank-you sent to everyone who put a return address on his card. I signed what seemed like a thousand of them yesterday, but if you run out, have some more printed up and I'll sign them after the operation. Gary, call Lionel Herbert and tell him to fly up here for a meeting the day after tomorrow. Tell him to be prepared to make some concessions on that energy package or, by God, it's back to the drawing board again for his boss and those oil people he's so damn friendly with. Bobby, call my niece and tell her I'm fine, not to worry, and, most of all, not to be upset that she couldn't leave the kids to fly here. I'll call her myself as soon as they let me back near my phone. Oh, and Bobby, have you got all the names of people who sent flowers? I want to send each of them a personal note. Do you think it would hurt anyone's feelings if I told them to send candy next time? This place looks like a funeral parlor and smells like a bordello."

Bobby Crisp, a young lawyer as sharp and eager as his name, smiled over at his boss. "You must be getting more confidence in me, Senator," he said. "This is only the fourth time you've told me to do the same thing. Back when I first started working for you, it was seven. Everything's taken care of. I'll have the list ready for you as soon as you're ready to write, which will probably be half an hour after you come out of the anesthesia, if I know you. By the way, do you know someone named Camellia?"

"Who?" Cormier asked.

"Camellia. See those pink and white flowers over there on the table? They came this morning with a note that just said 'Thank you for everything. Camellia.' "

"Men," Beth said scornfully. "Those pink and white flowers, as you call them, *are* camellias. Let me see that note." She read it and shrugged. "That's what it says, all right."

"Thanks for checking," Crisp said. "I got low marks in reading throughout law school."

"Now, now, settle down, you two," Cormier said. He rubbed his chin. "Camellia's a strange enough name so that I should remember it. Camellias from Camellia, eh? . . ." His voice drifted off as he tried to connect the name with a person. Finally he shook his head. "Well, I guess a little memory lapse here and there is a small price to pay for the frustration I'm able to cause on The Hill with the rest of my senility. Whoever she is, she'll just have to live without a thank-you note."

At that moment Mrs. Fuller reappeared at the door. "I said five minutes, and it's already more than that," she said. "I swear, Senator, you are the most obstinate, cantankerous patient I've ever had."

"Okay, okay, we're done," Cormier said, waving the other three out of his room. "You know, Mrs. Fuller, if you don't sweeten up soon, you're going to move from the sleek cruiser class into the battle-ax category." He smiled at her and added, "But even then you'll still be my favorite nurse. Go easy with that needle, now."

The nurse swabbed at a place on Cormier's left buttock and gave him the injection of preoperative medication. Fifteen minutes later, his mouth began feeling dry and a warm glow of detachment crept over him. Like the beacon from a lighthouse, the corridor ceiling lights flashed past as he was wheeled to the operating room.

*   *   *

Louis Ketchem was a towering, slope-shouldered veteran of more than twenty-five years as a surgeon. Over that span he had performed hundreds of gall bladder operations. None had ever gone any smoother than Senator Richard Cormier's. The removal of the inflamed, stone-filled sac was uneventful except for the usual amount of bleeding from the adjacent liver. As he had done hundreds of times, Ketchem ordered a unit of blood to be transfused over the last half hour of the operation.

The anesthesiologist, John Singleberry, took the plastic bag of blood from the circulating nurse, a young woman named Jacqueline Miller. He double-checked the number on the bag before attaching it to the intravenous line. To speed the infusion, he slipped an air sleeve around the bag and pumped it up. Cormier, deeply anesthetized and receiving oxygen by a respirator, slept a dreamless sleep as the blood wound down the tubing toward his arm like a crimson serpent.

At the instant the blood slid beneath the green paper drape, Jacqueline Miller turned away. The drug she had been instructed to use, the drug she had injected into the plastic bag, was ouabain, the fastest acting and most powerful form of digitalis—a drug so rapidly cleared from the bloodstream, so difficult to find on chemical analysis, that even the massive doses she had used were virtually undetectable. Three minutes were all the ouabain required.

Without warning the cardiac monitor pattern leapt from slow and regular to totally chaotic. John Singleberry glanced at the golden light slashing up and down on the screen overhead and spent several seconds staring at it in disbelief.

"Holy shit, Louis," Singleberry screamed. "He's fibrillating!"

Ketchem, who had not encountered a cardiac arrest

134

in the operating room in years, stood paralyzed, both hands still inside Cormier's abdomen. His orders, when he was finally able to give them, were inadequate. But for the work of the nurses, including Jacqueline Miller, several minutes might have passed with no definitive action. Sterile drapes were quickly stuffed into the incision and two unsuccessful countershocks were given. Seconds later, the monitor pattern showed a straight line.

Without warning Ketchem grabbed a scalpel, extended his incision, and slashed an opening through the bottom of Cormier's diaphragm. Reaching through the opening, he grasped the man's heart and began rhythmically squeezing. A nurse ran for help, but everyone in the operating room already knew it was over. Ketchem pumped, then stopped and checked the monitor. Straight line. He pumped some more.

For twenty minutes he pumped, with absolutely no effect on the golden light. Finally he stopped. For more than a minute no one in the room moved. Ketchem bit down on his lower lip and peered over his mask at the body of his friend. Then two nurses took him by the arms and helped him move away from the operating table, back to the surgeons' lounge.

Off to one side, Jacqueline Miller closed her eyes, fearing they might reflect the excited smile beneath her mask. The greatest adventure in her life was ending in triumph. Oh, Dahlia had told her where to go and what to say, but *she* had been the one to actually pull it off. Little Jackie Miller, ordering around one of the richest, most powerful oilmen in the world.

She tingled at the irony of it all: from girlhood in a squalid tenement to a secret meeting in Oklahoma with the president of Beecher Oil. What would Mr. Jed Beecher have said if he knew that the woman who was giving him instructions, the woman who was taking his quarter of a million dollars, the woman who was dictat-

135

ing his every move had just taken her first airplane flight.

Jacqueline silently cheered the good fortune that had brought Dahlia and The Garden into her life. She still knew little about either of them, but for the present she really didn't care. When Dahlia was ready to disclose her identity, she would, and that was all there was to that. As long as the excitement and the monthly payments were there, Camellia would do what she was asked and keep her eyes and ears open for cases that might be of interest to The Garden. As for The Sisterhood of Life, they would simply have to survive without any further participation from Jackie Miller. No more free rides.

Mexico. Jamaica. Greece. Paris. Jacqueline ticked the places off in her mind. One more case like this one, and she would be able to see all of them. The prospects were dizzying.

Behind her on the narrow operating table, covered to the neck by a sheet, Senator Richard Cormier looked as he had throughout his operation. But his dreamless sleep would last forever

CHAPTER XII

"Ladies and gentlemen, if you would all find seats, we can get started and hopefully make it through this inquiry in a reasonable amount of time."

Like an aging movie queen, the Morris Tweedy Amphitheater of Boston Doctors Hospital had handled the inexorable pressure of passing years with grace and style. Although undeniably frayed around the edges, the cozy, domed lecture hall still held its place proudly atop the thrice-renovated West Wing. There was a time when the seventy-five steeply banked seats of "The Amphi" had accommodated nearly the entire hospital staff—nurses, physicians, and students. However, in 1929, after almost fifty years of service, it had been replaced as the hospital's major lecture and demonstration hall by a considerably larger amphitheater constructed in the Southeast Wing basement.

Hours upon hours of heated argument on the pros and cons of demolishing the jaded siren ended abruptly in 1952 when the state legislature designated the structure an historic landmark. Her stained glass skylights, severe wooden seats, and bas-relief sculptures depict-

ing significant events in medical history were thus preserved for new generations of eager physicians-in-training.

But, despite a century of continuous service, never
had the Morris Tweedy Amphitheater entertained a
session such as the one for which this milling group of
fifty men and women was assembled. It was eight o'clock
on the evening of Sunday, October 5—two days after
the postmortem examination on Charlotte Thomas.

As hospital chief of staff, Dr. Margaret Armstrong sat
behind a heavy oak table facing the arc of seats. Beside
her, attempting to bring some order to the room, was
Detective Lieutenant John Dockerty. Dockerty was a
thin, rumpled man in his late forties. He wore a gabar-
dine suit that appeared large for him by at least two
sizes. His limp green eyes scanned the hall, then turned
to a sheaf of papers on the table in front of him. As he
looked down, an errant wisp of thinning, reddish brown
hair dropped over one eye. He absently swept the
strands back in place, only to repeat the ritual moments
later.

His languid, almost distracted air suggested he had
encountered most of what there was in life to see. In
fact, he had spent more than fifteen years on the Boston
police force carefully cultivating that demeanor and learning how best to utilize it.

He looked over the hall again, then spoke to Margaret Armstrong out of the corner of his mouth. "This
group is obviously much more adept at giving orders
than they are at taking them."

Armstrong laughed her agreement, then banged a
notebook on the table several times. "Would you all
please sit down," she called out. "If we can't show
Lieutenant Dockerty cooperation, at least we can show
him manners." In less than a minute, everyone had
found a place.

The hospital administrator sat to one side of the hall
surrounded by his assistants. He was a paunchy, fop-

138

pish man who had run away from his Brooklyn home at age seventeen and changed his name from Isaac Lifshitz to Edward Lipton III. For years he had kept his job by pitting his enemies against one another in a way so skillful that none of them ever had the unified backing needed to push for his ouster.

On the other side of the room were clustered the men and women who comprised the hospital board of trustees. The men, a homogeneous, patrician lot, were vastly more concerned with the impact that their trustee position might have on their Who's Who listings than with the influence that they might have on Boston Doctors Hospital. The token black on the board was distinguishable from the others only by color, and the four women were not distinguishable at all. The inquiry marked the first time in recent memory that the entire twenty-four-member board was present for a meeting.

Midway up the center aisle, Wallace Huttner sat with Ahmed Hadawi and the other members of the Medical Staff Executive Committee. Joining that group, occupying the chair just to Huttner's right, was Peter Thomas.

The back of the amphitheater was the domain of the nurses. Eight of them, all in street clothes, formed a rosette around Dotty Dalrymple, who appeared volcanic in a plain black dress. Janet Poulos was there, along with Christine Beall, Winnie Edgerly, and several other nurses from Four South, including Angela Martin.

On the right-hand side of the hall, several rows behind Edward Lipton III, sat David. He sat alone until the very last minute, when Howard Kim, the anesthesiologist who had helped with Charlotte's unsuccessful resuscitation, lumbered down the stairs and squeezed into the chair next to him.

John Dockerty had drawn up the guest list for the evening. Dr. Armstrong had made the arrangements.

139

"I want to thank you all for coming," Dockerty began. "You must believe me that inquiries such as the one I have requested tonight occur much more frequently on *Columbo* and in Agatha Christie novels than they do in actual police work. However, I want to move forward as quickly as possible on the matter of Charlotte Thomas, a matter involving all of you in one way or another. Theatrics have never been my bag, so to speak, but this meeting seemed like the most effective way for me to gather the preliminary information I need, while at the same time keeping all interested parties informed. In the next few days I'll be contacting some of you for individual questioning." He looked down at Margaret Armstrong, who nodded her approval of his opening remarks. Then, sweeping his hair back in place, Dockerty called Ahmed Hadawi and motioned him to a seat angled across from the oak table, so that the pathologist could look at him without completely turning his back to the audience.

"Dr. Hadawi, will you please review for us your involvement in the case of Charlotte Thomas?" Dockerty asked.

Hadawi spread a few sheets of notes in front of him, then said, "On October third I performed a postmortem examination on the woman in question. The gross examination showed that she had a deep pressure sore over her sacrum, moderately advanced coronary artery narrowing, and an extensive pneumonia. It was my initial impression that she had died from sudden cardiac arrest caused by her infections and the generally debilitated condition resulting from her two operations."

"Dr. Hadawi, is that your impression now?" Dockerty asked.

"No, it is not. The patient's physicians, Dr. Wallace Huttner and Dr. David Shelton, were present at the autopsy. They requested a detailed chemical analysis of her blood."

"Help me out here, Dr. Hadawi," Dockerty cut in. "Don't you do these chemical analyses routinely on each—er—patient?"

Hadawi smiled sardonically and folded his hands on the table. "I wish that were possible," he said. "Unfortunately, the cost of postmortem examinations must be borne by the institution involved, and it is hardly an inexpensive proposition, what with sophisticated tissue stains, clerical help, and all else that is required. While we would never knowingly omit a critical stain or test, we of the pathology department must nevertheless temper our zeal with judgment that will enable us to stay within our budget." He paused for a moment and gave a prolonged, hostile look at Edward Lipton III.

"Please proceed," Dockerty said, scribbling a few words on the pad in front of him.

Hadawi referred to his notes. "Of the many chemical analyses that were done, two came back with abnormally high levels. The first of these, potassium, was seven-point-four, where the upper limit of normal is five-point-zero. The second was her blood morphine level, which was elevated far above that found in a patient receiving the usual doses of morphine sulfate for pain."

"Dr. Hadawi, would you please give us your impression of these findings?" Dockerty's voice was free of even the slightest hint of tension.

"Well, my impression of the potassium elevation—and please keep in mind that it is an opinion—is that it is artificially high, a reflection of events occurring in the tissues during and just after the cardiac arrest. The morphine elevation is an entirely different story. Without question, the level measured in this woman was critically high. Easily, although not necessarily, high enough to have caused cessation of respiration and, ultimately, death."

Dockerty spent a few seconds distractedly combing

141

his hair with his fingers. "Doctor, you imply that death was caused by an overdosage of morphine." Hadawi nodded. "Tell me, do you think an overdose of this magnitude could have been accidental?"

Hadawi drew in a short breath, looked at the detective, then shook his head. "No," he said. "No, I do not believe that is possible."

There was not a whisper or movement in the amphitheater. For several seconds Dockerty allowed the eerie silence to hold sway. Then he said softly, "That, ladies and gentlemen, makes Charlotte Thomas's death murder. And her murder is why we are assembled here." Again silence. This time, Hadawi shifted uncomfortably in his seat, anxious to be done with his part.

"Thank you for your help, Doctor," Dockerty said to him. As Hadawi stood to go, the detective added, "Oh, one more small thing. You mentioned that the chemical tests were ordered by Mrs. Thomas's doctors, ah"—he glanced at his notes—"Dr. Huttner and Dr. Shelton. Do you remember specifically which one of them actually asked for the tests?"

Hadawi's dark eyes narrowed as he searched Dockerty's face for some hint of the significance in his question. Finally, with a bewildered shrug, he said, "Well, as I recall, Dr. Shelton requested the potassium level. The rest of the tests were ordered by Dr. Huttner."

Dockerty nodded the pathologist back to his row, whispering another "Thank you" at the same time. He searched the hall for a moment and was facing away from David when he said, "Dr. Shelton?"

Howard Kim reached up a massive paw and patted David on the back as he inched sideways past the giant and into the aisle. David had known for a day about the abnormal blood tests, had even heard the wildfire rumor around the wards that some kind of police investigation was under way. Although Dr. Armstrong had not told

142

him that he would be asked to make a statement, he was not at all surprised to be called by the detective.

Dockerty smiled, shook his hand firmly, motioned him to the seat vacated by Hadawi, and then, seeming at times disinterested, led him minute by minute through the events that followed Charlotte Thomas's cardiac arrest. Gradually David's statements became free-flowing and animated. Dockerty's style made it easy for him to talk. Soon he was sharing information with the disheveled lieutenant in the relaxed manner of two friends in an alehouse. Then, without changing the pace or tone of their conversation, Dockerty said, "Tell me, Dr. Shelton. I understand that shortly before Mrs. Thomas was found by you to be without pulse or respiration, you had a discussion about her and about seriously ill patients in general with Dr. Armstrong here and some of the nurses—namely, ah"—he consulted his notes—"nurses Edgerly, Gold, and Beall. Do you mind telling me what you had to say in that discussion?"

For five seconds, ten, fifteen, David was unable to speak. The question didn't fit. It made no sense unless . . . His mind began spinning through the implications of Dockerty's question to Hadawi as to which doctor had actually ordered the test that had disclosed the high morphine level. The indefinable sense of fear, so vague among his feelings that night on Four South, now thundered through him. His temples began to throb. His hands grew stiff and numb. *Holy shit, he's going after me! He's going after me!*

At that moment he realized that Dockerty's eyes had changed from liquid to steel and were locked on him, probing, gauging, boring in. David knew it had already taken him too long—far too long—to react to the question. He inhaled deeply and fought the panic. Loosen up and stop reading so much into this, he thought. Just tell the man what he wants to know.

"Dr. Shelton, do you recall the incident I'm asking

143

about?" The elaborate patience in Dockerty's voice had a cutting edge.

Even before he answered, David sensed that his words would be stammered and clumsy. They were. Expressing his thoughts around "er's" and "ah's," he said, "I simply told them . . . that a patient who is . . . in great pain with little hope of surviving his illness might . . . might be treated with some temperance. Especially if the therapy planned is . . . particularly painful or . . . dehumanizing . . . such as being put on a respirator." He battled back the urge to say more, consciously avoiding the panicked talking that comes with trying to explain an explanation.

Dockerty ran his tongue slowly over his teeth. He bounced the eraser end of his pencil on the table. He scratched his head. "Dr. Shelton," he said finally, "don't you think that withholding treatment from a sick patient is a form of mercy killing? Of euthanasia?"

"No, I don't think it's a form of any kind of killing." Molten drops of anger began to smolder beneath his fear. His voice grew strained. His words came too rapidly. "It is good, sensitive clinical judgment. It is what being a doctor is all about. For God's sake, I've never advocated shutting off a respirator or giving anything lethal to a patient."

"Never?" Dockerty delivered the spark softly.

David exploded. "Dammit, Lieutenant, I've had more than enough of your insinuations!" He was totally oblivious now to all the others in the amphitheater. "If you have an accusation to make, then make it. And while you're at it, explain why I was the one who kept saying that something wasn't right during the resuscitation. Why I was the one who requested the potass . . ." The word froze in his mouth. He realized even before Dockerty spoke, what the detective was driving at. "Damn," he hissed his frustration.

"I have had the chance, Dr. Shelton, to speak briefly

with some of the other physicians and nurses who were with you in Charlotte Thomas's room. Like you, several of them were concerned that something was not completely right. Apparently the problem was obvious enough for others besides you to pick up on it. Whether or not they would have gone so far as to ask for blood tests on this woman, we'll never know because you did. At least, for the potassium you did."

"And you're trying to say I did that to cover myself and to insure that nobody thought about anything like morphine?" Dockerty shrugged. "This is ridiculous! I mean this is really crazy," David cried.

"Dr. Shelton," Dockerty said calmly. "Please get hold of yourself. I am not accusing you or anyone else of anything."

"Yet," David spat out.

"Excuse me?"

"Nothing. Are you finished with me?"

"Yes, thank you." Once again Dockerty appeared as mechanical as he had throughout most of the inquiry. As David stalked back to his seat, he noticed that halfway up the center aisle Wallace Huttner sat staring at him with icy, metallic eyes. Involuntarily, he shuddered.

Dockerty whispered with Dr. Armstrong for several seconds, then called Dorothy Dalrymple. The nursing director extracted herself from her seat with the side-to-side movements of a cork coming free from its bottle. Once released from her chair, she glided down the aisle steps with paradoxical grace. A feminine handshake with Dockerty, then she adjusted herself on the oak chair and smiled that she was ready.

Dockerty led her through a description of Charlotte Thomas's appearance over the day prior to her death as summarized in the nurses' notes. "The nurses' notes are generally written at the end of each shift," Dalrymple explained. "Therefore, the notes from the October second evening shift were not done until after the patient's death. However, the nurse who cared for Mrs. Thomas that night, Miss Christine Beall, saw her at seven o'clock, approximately two hours before her death. Her excellent note states that the patient was—and I quote now—'alert, oriented, and somewhat less depressed than she has been recently.' Miss Beall further writes that her vital signs—pulse, respiration, temperature, and blood pressure—were all stable." Dalrymple swung her massive shoulders and head toward the audience and peered up to where the nurses were grouped. "Miss Beall," she called out, "do you have anything to add to what I have told the lieutenant?"

Christine, who had been totally depressed and distracted since David's outburst, was not paying attention. She had learned about the discovery of morphine in Charlotte's body less than twenty-four hours before. The information had come via a telephone call from Peg, the nurse who had asked her to evaluate Charlotte Thomas in the first place. "Christine, I want to keep you abreast of as much as we know of what is going on here without worrying you unduly," the woman had said. "There is going to be some kind of inquiry on the case tomorrow night, I've been told. A policeman will be there. However, your Sister, Janet Poulos, has reviewed your notes in the patient's chart. There is nothing there, she feels, that will in any way implicate you. It is our belief that the investigation will be a short-lived and fruitless one, and that Charlotte Thomas's death will be attributed to the work of an individual whose name and motives will never be discovered. All Sisterhood operations at your hospital will be curtailed indefinitely, and before long the entire matter should just blow over. You are in no danger whatsoever, Christine—please believe that."

Christine, lips pressed tightly together, was staring

146

up into the blue and gold dome when Dalrymple addressed her.

Several seats away, Janet Poulos watched helplessly, every muscle tensed by the prospect of Christine leaping to her feet, shouting her confession to the hall, then crying out the only other Sisterhood name she knew: Janet's. God, she wished there had been enough warning to call Dahlia. Dahlia would have known exactly how to handle things.

Janet's gaze moved past Christine to where Angela Martin sat, cool blue eyes fixed on the scene below, golden hair immaculately in place. The woman was absolutely nerveless. Even if it had been her name that Christine Beall knew, Janet doubted that Angela would have been ruffled. Almost ten years as members of The Sisterhood and they had never even known one another. Now they were best friends, sharing the excitement and rewards of The Garden and speculating about the mysterious woman who had brought them together.

Janet scanned the hall and wondered if Dahlia had eyes and ears present other than Lily's and Hyacinth's. Quite possibly, she acknowledged. The woman remained only a whispered voice on the telephone, but time and again Janet had been impressed with her cold logic and endless sources of information. Because of her The Garden was growing steadily—in other hospitals as well as in Boston Doctors. Anywhere there was a Sisterhood of Life member, there was a potential flower. Dahlia believed that more than anything else. The bottom line of both movements was the same: nurse and patient alone in a room. She had, perhaps, been hasty about Beall, but she remained a woman of near-perfect judgment whom Janet wanted desperately to know.

Powerless for the moment, Janet slid back in her seat and watched.

"Miss Beall?" Dalrymple called again. Winnie Edgerly

147

nudged Christine. "I asked if you had anything to add to what I have told the lieutenant."

Christine swallowed. Once, then again. Still, when she tried to speak only a sandpaper rasp emerged. She cleared her throat and tightened her grip on the arms of her seat.

"I'm sorry," she managed. "No, I have nothing to add."

Janet sighed relief and closed her eyes. Beall had come through.

Christine looked down to where David sat, head resting on one hand, staring vacantly at Dalrymple and Dockerty. She could feel as much as see his isolation. In fact, she realized, she too was isolated. Despite the calls from Peg, despite the words from Janet and the knowledge that the vast Sisterhood of Life was behind her, Christine felt marooned. At that moment she wanted to run to him and somehow reassure him. To tell him that she, above all people, knew he had nothing to do with Charlotte's death. "Everything will be all right," she told herself over and over again. "Just leave things alone and they will be all right." She forced her concentration back to the scene being played out below her.

"Miss Dalrymple," Dockerty continued, "you have a list of the medications given to Mrs. Thomas?"

Dalrymple nodded. "She was receiving chloramphenicol, which is an antibiotic, and Demerol, which is an analgesic."

"No morphine?"

"No morphine," she echoed, shaking her head for emphasis.

"No morphine . . ." Dockerty let the word drift away, but his voice was nonetheless loud enough for all those present to hear. "Tell me," he said, "is it possible for one of the nurses or other hospital personnel to have gotten his hands on morphine sulfate in the quantities Dr. Hadawi has suggested were given Mrs. Thomas?"

148

Dalrymple thought the question through before answering. "The answer to your question is, of course, that anyone can get his hands on any drug if he has enough money and is willing to go outside the legal channels to do so. However, I can state that it would be virtually impossible for one of my nurses—or anyone else for that matter—to get away with more than a tiny quantity of narcotics from the hospital. You see, only a small amount of injectable narcotic is kept on each floor, and that is rigidly counted by two nurses at each shift change—one from the group that is leaving and one from the group that is coming on. The night nursing supervisor has access to the hospital pharmacy, but even there the narcotics are locked up securely and only the hospital pharmacists have keys.

"So," she concluded, shifting her bulk in the chair and folding her hands in a large, puffy ball, "assuming a legal source, only a pharmacist or a physician could obtain a sizable amount of morphine at a single time."

Dockerty nodded and again conferred in whispers with Dr. Armstrong. "Miss Dalrymple," he said finally, "do the nurses' notes indicate whether or not there were any visitors to Charlotte Thomas's room on the night of her death?"

"Visitors to a patient's room, other than physicians, are not usually recorded in nurses' notes. However, I can tell you that none were mentioned."

"Not even the physician who found Mrs. Thomas without pulse or respiration?" Dockerty asked.

Dalrymple's expression suggested that she did not at all approve of the detective's oblique reference. "No," she said deliberately. "There was no mention of Dr. Shelton entering the patient's room. However, I hasten to add that most of the nurses were on break at the time of the cardiac arrest. There was no one on the floor at the time to see him arrive."

Dockerty seemed to ignore her last point. "That will

149

be all, thank you very much," he said. As he nodded the woman back to her seat, David again ignited.

"Lieutenant, I've had just about enough of this!" He stumbled to his feet and braced himself against the seat back in front of him. To his left Howard Kim's moonface looked up at him impassively. "I don't understand why you think what you do or even what you are driving at, but let me state here and now that I would never administer a drug or any treatment to a patient for the express purpose of harming him in any way." In the seconds that followed David heard his tiny mental voice telling him that, once again, he was sailing on his own words toward a maelstrom.

"Sit down, for Christ's sake," the voice kept saying. "He can't hurt you, dummy. Only *you* can hurt you. Sit down and shut up!"

Mounting rage and panic snuffed out the voice. His words were strangled. "Why me? Surely there are others—her husband, relatives, friends who were in that room before I was. Why are you accusing me?"

"Dr. Shelton," Dockerty said evenly, "I have not accused you of anything. I said that before. But since you brought it up, Professor Thomas was teaching a seminar that evening. Twenty-three students. Seven to ten P.M. And, as far as he knows, no other visitors were scheduled to see his wife. Now, if I've answered your questions, we can proceed with—"

"No!" David shouted. "This whole inquiry is a sham. Some kind of perverse kangaroo court. A first-year law student could conduct a more impartial hearing than this. If you want to railroad me into something, then do it in court, where at least you have to answer to a judge." He stopped, grasping for some morsel of self-control. Inside him, the voice resumed. "Don't you see, dummy, this whole inquiry was a setup to get you to do exactly what you have gone and done. I tried to tell you to keep cool, but you don't even know how, do you?"

"Very well," Dockerty said. "I think we've heard enough for now. I'll be contacting some of you individually in the near future. Thank you all for coming." He whispered some final words to Dr. Armstrong, then packed his notes together and left the hall without so much as a glance at the pale statue that was David.

By the time David had calmed enough to release the wooden seat back and look around, the Morris Tweedy Amphitheater was nearly empty. Christine and the other nurses had gone. So had Howard Kim. As he scanned the back of the hall, his gaze met Wallace Huttner's. The tall surgeon's eyes narrowed. Then, with a derisive shake of his head, he turned and strode out, arm in arm with Peter Thomas.

David stood alone, staring up at the glowing red EXIT sign over the rear door, when a hand touched his shoulder. He whirled and met the concerned, blue eyes of Margaret Armstrong.

"Are you all right?" she asked.

"Yeah, sure, great." He made no attempt to clear the huskiness in his voice.

"David, I am so sorry for what just happened here. If I had known how heavily Lieutenant Dockerty was going to pounce on you, I never would have allowed the whole thing to happen. He said he wanted to check the spontaneous reactions of several people. You were just one of them. All of a sudden you erupted, and there wasn't even a chance for me to . . ." She gave up trying to explain. "Look, David," she went on finally, "I like you very much. Have since the day you got here. Just give me the benefit of a hearing. After what's just happened to you, I know that won't be easy, but please try. I want to help."

David looked at her, then bit back his anger and nodded.

"How about an hour or so at Popeye's?" Her smile was warm and sincere.

"Popeye's it is," David said, picking up his jacket. Together the new allies left the hospital.

Popeye's, a local landmark, had seen nearly thirty years of doctors and nurses bringing their problems and their lives to its tables. Outside the tavern an animated neon sign, the pride and joy of the management, depicted characters from the comic strip chasing Wimpy and his armload of hamburgers across the building. As they entered, David caught sight of four of the nurses who had been at the inquiry. Neither Dotty Dalrymple nor Christine was among them.

"I haven't been here in years," Dr. Armstrong said after they had settled at a rear table. "My husband and I courted in some of these booths. Nothing has really changed except for that garish sign outside."

David noted that she wore no wedding ring. "Is your husband living?" he asked.

"Arne? No, he died eight, no, nine years ago."

"Oh, yes, how stupid of me," David said, remembering that he, like everyone else at Doctors Hospital, knew she was the widow of Arne Armstrong, a world famous neurophysiologist and a possible Nobel laureate, had he lived long enough to complete his work. "I'm sorry."

"Don't be silly . . ." Dr. Armstrong said, stopping in midsentence as a shapely blonde in a black miniskirt and skintight red sweater arrived to take their order. "I'll have a beer, a draft. And my date here?" She smiled over at David.

"Coke," he said. "Extra large, lots of ice."

The waitress left and Armstrong looked at David. "Not even with all that's happened to you tonight?"

She knew. Of course she knew. Everyone did. But she wasn't testing him. There was, David realized, admiration in her voice.

"It's been nearly eight years since I touched a drop of

alcohol. Or a pill," he added. "It's going to take a hell of a lot more than Dockerty could ever dish out to get me back there. Even though I'm sure my teeth will finally vaporize from all the cola I consume." His voice drifted away. Thoughts of John Dockerty staring placidly through him were followed by images of other confrontations he had been forced to endure over the years since Ginny and Becky were killed.

As if reading his thoughts, Armstrong said, "David, you know that I'm aware of much that has happened to you in the past." He nodded. "You should be aware, then, that Lieutenant Dockerty also knows. I am not sure how he learned so much so quickly, but he is very good at his job, I think. And you know what a giant glass house a hospital is. Everybody's life is everybody else's business and what people can't gossip about with certainty, they usually contrive simply to fill in the gaps."

David gave a single, rueful laugh. "I've been the center of hospital rumor before," he said. "I know exactly what you mean. This time, though, it's not just harmless speculation. I would never set out to hurt anyone, let alone murder him."

"No need to tell me," she said. "I'm already a believer. As I said before, I think Lieutenant Dockerty is very thorough and very good at his job. I'm sure that will be in your favor. He just doesn't seem the type who will stop until his case is airtight."

Their drinks arrived, and David welcomed the chance to break from the conversation for a few minutes. "Maybe I should voluntarily take myself off the staff until this whole thing blows over," he said at last.

Armstrong slammed her stein on the table, splashing some of its contents and startling the couple in the next booth. "Dammit, young man," she said, "never in all my days have I run into anyone who was more his own worst enemy than you are. Based on what I heard

153

tonight and what I believe to be true, our lieutenant friend had better come up with a great deal more in the way of incriminating evidence before I'll allow anyone, including you, to move for your suspension. And if you don't think I have that kind of power around here, then just watch."

David's smile came more easily than it had all evening. "Thank you," he said. "Thank you very much."

"Well, now." She glanced at her watch. "This old bird has a full day at the office tomorrow, so I suggest we call it quits for the night. We'll talk again. Meanwhile, you've got to make yourself relax. Be patient. People like Lieutenant Dockerty, and also your friend Wallace Huttner, can't be told much of anything. They have to find out for themselves." She smoothed a five-dollar bill on the table and, without waiting for change, walked with him to her car.

As she got in and rolled down the window, David said, "I've repeated myself so many times, I feel like a broken record, but . . . thank you. I guess there just aren't any better words. Thank you."

"Just take care of yourself, David," she said, "and get through this in good shape. That will be all the thanks I need."

He watched until her car had disappeared around the corner, then walked numbly to the adjacent lot where his was parked. The car, a yellow Saab he had owned for less than a year, rested on its rims. All four tires had been viciously slashed. Across the driver's side, in crudely sprayed red paint, was the word MURDERER.

"A big glass house," David muttered as he stared at the sloppy cruelty. "You said it, lady. A big, fucking, animal of a glass house."

154

CHAPTER XIII

Barbara Littlejohn had waited outside the TWA terminal only a minute before a cab arrived. That was long enough for the raw New England evening to penetrate her clothing, stiffen her joints, and draw her skin so tightly that it hurt. The flight from L.A. had been punishing enough, she thought, but this . . . She was still shivering when the cab passed through the toll booth and inched down, in heavy traffic, into the Sumner Tunnel—the dank, exhaust-filled tube connecting East Boston with Boston proper. By the time they broke free on the downtown side it had begun to rain.

Barbara insisted the driver work his way as close as possible to the entrance of the Copley Plaza. She dashed into the lobby wondering how she could once have thought New England weather whimsical and charming.

She was an attractive woman in her late forties, tall, tanned, and nearly as thin as in the days when she'd worked her way through nursing school as a fashion model. The desk clerk, though at least ten years her junior, undressed her with his eyes.

"I'm with the Donald Knight Clinton Foundation,"

she said, ignoring his leer. "We have a board-of-directors meeting here?"

"Oh, yes, ma'am. Eight o'clock, room one thirty-three. Across the lobby to the elevators, one floor up." He glanced at her overnight bag. "Will you be registering with us tonight?" Again the leer.

"No, thank you. I'll be staying with friends." She walked away, leaving the man with his fantasies.

Two women, one from Dallas and the other from Chicago, spotted Barbara as they entered the lobby and caught up with her at the elevator. A brief but warm exchange, then the three rode up together.

It was Monday, not yet twenty-four hours after the inquiry at Boston Doctors Hospital. The women, sixteen of them in all, had hastily rearranged their schedules and traveled to the Copley meeting from all parts of the country—New York, Philadelphia, San Francisco, Miami. They came because Peggy Donner had sent for them and because of their commitment as regional directors of The Sisterhood of Life.

Room 133 was plush—forest green crushed-velvet wall covering, lithographs of elongated horses at the Punchestown Races of 1862, conference table in the center, serving table to one side, and an overstuffed green leather couch beneath the lone window.

Barbara shook hands with the earlier arrivals and made a quick count. Twelve. The four from Boston, including Peg, were late. "No coffee?" she asked no one in particular as she opened her briefcase, extracted a thick folder marked "Clinton Foundation," and set it at the head of the glossy walnut table.

"The chief orderly was just here," one of the women answered. "He said the crash cart would be up shortly." Her humor dented the tension in the room, but only transiently. The emergency meeting was unprecedented, and of those present only Barbara knew its purpose in detail. She checked her watch. Eight ten. Their

156

regular quarterly meetings seldom started late. But this was Boston's show, and although she had some other business to transact, she would wait.

Around the room, in small groups and muted voices, the women shared news of their families, their nursing services, and their institutions. They had come together from worlds where each of them held title, power, and influence. Susan Berger, nursing coordinator for the Hospital Consortium of San Francisco, chatted with June Ullrich, field investigations administrator for the largest pharmaceutical house in the country. They knew, as did all the others, that their lofty positions were due, in part, to their involvement with The Sisterhood of Life. Functioning through its visible arm, the Donald Knight Clinton Foundation, the movement published a monthly newsletter updating the status of various philanthropic Sisterhood projects and outlining available upper-echelon nursing positions for which members would receive special consideration.

As coordinating director of The Sisterhood, Barbara Littlejohn was also administrator of the Clinton Foundation and of half a million dollars in voluntary contributions made each year by Sisterhood nurses. Although the titles were hers, the influence and much of the power still rested with Peggy Donner. Barbara checked the time again and spread her notes on the table. Five more minutes and she would begin, with or without Peg.

At that moment the bell captain, a ferretlike man with petroleum hair, marched in with the coffee cart. He floated a tablecloth over the serving table and arranged the cups, sterling, and coffee urn with a flourish. As a finale, he stepped outside the room, returned with a large floral centerpiece, and ceremoniously placed it between the neat rows of cups.

"Flowers," Susan Berger remarked. "Now this is a

first. Peggy must be softening us up for another of her schemes. God, but they're lovely."

The bell captain smiled, as if taking the compliment personally. He spent a few, final center-stage moments straightening the arrangement, then backed out of the room, still smiling. Despite his efforts, the vase still seemed to be overflowing with dahlias. The Garden would be watching and listening, they warned; the offspring appraising the parent. It was a warning that only one at the meeting would understand.

Ruth Serafini, the robust, dynamic dean of the nursing school at White Memorial Hospital, was the first of the Boston group to arrive. Peggy Donner had spawned the movement in Boston, and although it had spread rapidly to hospitals throughout the country, the Boston representation was still by far the largest. Three directors, including Ruth, were needed to oversee activities in the New England states. Peggy herself was no longer involved with day-to-day operations.

"Are the rest coming soon?" Barbara asked after a brief handshake.

"No idea. I got caught in traffic." Ruth poured a cup of coffee, then took a place at the table.

"Sorry for the delay, everyone," Barbara said finally. "I think we should start and get through the Foundation business. It's only been six weeks, so there won't be a financial report tonight." Those standing took seats. Barbara surveyed the group one at a time and smiled. How far they had come from the small cadre of nurses who had once met in Peggy's basement to share their visions and ideals and to form The Sisterhood. As she moved to begin, the final two arrived. The first, Sara Duhey, was a striking young black woman who held a master's and Ph.D. in critical-care nursing. The second was Dotty Dalrymple.

"Welcome," Barbara said warmly. "Nothing like being twenty minutes late for your own party."

"Not ours, Barb," Dalrymple said. "Peggy's. She'll be here soon. Wants you to go ahead with whatever business you have."

"Very well." Barbara glanced at her agenda. "Meeting's in order. First, we've gotten progress reports from our rural health centers. Patient visits are up almost one hundred percent in both the Kentucky and West Virginia clinics. The nurses administering them assure us that within the year both places will be flying on their own." The directors applauded the news, and the two seated closest to Tania Worth of Cincinnati patted her on the back. The centers had been her brainchild and had been approved largely because of her commitment to them. Tania beamed.

Discussion moved quickly through other projects: day-care centers for children of actively working nurses, modern equipment for underfinanced hospitals, scholarships for work toward advanced degrees in nursing, efforts to upgrade the function and image of hospital nurses. Susan Berger gave a brief report on efforts around the country to establish living wills, giving each person the right, ahead of time, to limit the life-preserving measures employed on him. To date the efforts, conceived long ago by Peggy Donner, had met with little success.

"Last but not least," Barbara said, "we've gotten a letter from Karen. Some of you never met her, but she was on the board for several years before her husband received an appointment to the American Embassy in Paris. She sends love and hopes that we're all well. In less than two years she's made it all the way up to assistant director of nursing at her hospital." Several of the older women applauded the news. Barbara smiled. "It seems," she went on, "that Karen has located five Sisterhood members from a list I sent her of those who

159

have moved to Europe. She says they are close to organizing a screening committee, but can't agree on whether the European branch should name itself in English, French, Dutch, or German."

"Perhaps we should find out what Sisterhood of Life would be in Esperanto," one woman offered.

The directors were laughing at her suggestion when Peggy Donner entered. Instantly the room quieted.

In the silence Peggy made deliberate, individual eye contact with each woman. Almost grudgingly, it seemed, the gravity in her expression yielded to pride. These were the most beloved of her several thousand children.

"Seeing you all once again lifts my spirit as nothing else ever could. I'm sorry to be late." She moved toward the head of the table, but stopped by the huge spray of dahlias. Her lips bowed in an enigmatic smile. Then she lifted a pure, regal white blossom and cradled it pensively in her hands. Finally, with a glance at Barbara, who confirmed that it was time, Peggy took over the meeting.

"It has been nearly forty years—*forty years*—since four other nurses and I formed the secret society that was to grow into our Sisterhood." Her voice was hypnotic. "Recently one of those four nurses, Charlotte Thomas, died at Boston Doctors Hospital. She was Charlotte Winthrop when we first met—only a senior nursing student—but so vital, so very special. She remained active in our movement for only a decade or so, but during that time she was responsible, as much as anyone, for our remarkable growth.

"She had a terminal illness, complicated by a cavernous bedsore, and expressed to me her desperate desire for the freedom of death. She expressed that wish to her physician as well, but as too often happens in his profession, he turned a deaf ear and was using the most aggressive methods to prolong her hopeless agony.

"Several days ago, I called an exceptional young nurse

160

in our Sisterhood, Christine Beall, and asked her to evaluate Charlotte for presentation to our Regional Screening Committee. For many reasons, personal and professional, it was impossible for me to do so myself. The Committee approved and recommended intravenous morphine. Through a series of unforeseeable and unfortunate circumstances, an unusually thorough autopsy was performed and a critically high blood morphine level was found."

The nurses sat in stunned silence as Peggy outlined the investigation that followed and John Dockerty's session in the Tweedy Amphitheater. She paced as she talked, absently using the flower as a prop. Her tone was even and calm, her presentation purest fact. Only when she discussed David Shelton did emotion appear in her words. She described his background in great detail, stressing the difficulties he had encountered through his use of alcohol and drugs. There was disgust in her face and her voice. "A disturbed young man," she said categorically. "One who would be doing the medical profession a great service by leaving it."

Peggy's pacing became more rapid as she searched for words. "My sisters," she said gravely, "it has been over twenty years since our system of Regional Screening Committees was established. Over those years more than thirty-five hundred cases have been handled without the slightest hint of our—or anyone's—involvement. There is every reason to believe that the situation that has developed in Boston will never occur again. Unfortunately, it has this once. I have been close to Lieutenant Dockerty since the very beginning of his investigation. Although he suspects this Shelton is guilty of Charlotte's death, he is not convinced. More and more, he is learning of a special relationship that existed between Christine Beall and Charlotte. He has even mentioned the possibility of requesting her to submit to a polygraph test. I will not allow that to happen!"

For the first time several at the table exchanged concerned glances. None had ever seen her so close to losing control. The atmosphere in the room became increasingly uncomfortable.

Peggy continued. "We are a Sisterhood. Our bond is as sacred and immutable as if it were blood. When one of us suffers, we must all share her pain. When one of us is threatened with exposure, as Christine is now, we must all fly to her aid. I, and each of you, should expect as much from our sisters. We must protect her!" The woman's voice had risen to a strangled, desperate stridency. For a time there was silence, save for pulses of leaden rain clattering across the window behind her. Around the room uneasiness gave way to strain and, for some, an icy foreboding. Petals dropped from the flower, mangled in Peggy's hands.

Barbara Littlejohn moved to reestablish control. "Peggy, thank you," she said, struggling to blunt the tension in her voice. "You know that we all feel as you do about the movement. We are certainly committed to giving Christine Beall all the support we can." She hoped against hope that her reassurance would have some impact on what she knew Peggy was about to demand. The woman's vacant stare told her otherwise.

"I want that man found guilty." Peggy's words, barely audible, were spoken through clenched teeth.

The women gaped at her in disbelief. Dotty Dalrymple buried her face in her hands.

"What are you talking about?" Susan Berger was the first to react. There was incredulity and some anger in her voice.

Peggy glared at her, but Susan did not look away. "Susan, I want the pressure off Christine Beall. There is no telling what might happen to her or to our Sisterhood if the police try to break her down. I've worked too hard to allow anything like that to happen. Our work is too important. I want the Board's approval to

162

take whatever steps are necessary to protect Christine and our interests. With a little ingenuity, I'm sure we can convince the police of Dr. Shelton's guilt. Considering his background, the most that would happen to him is a few months in some hospital and a year or two away from medicine. That seems a small price to pay for—"

"Peggy, I can't go along with this." Ruth Serafini spoke up. "I don't care what this Shelton has done. Something like this works against the dignity of a man's life, against everything we stand for." Her plea brought mutters of agreement and support from several others. Serafini glanced around the table. Of the fifteen women, seven would support Peggy no matter what she asked of them. The others? A vote would be very close. Ruth pushed forward. "What if we just let things be and see what happens? If necessary, we can supply Christine Beall with money, lawyers, anything she needs. At this point it's not even a certainty that—"

"No!" The word was a slap. Ruth Serafini backed away from Peggy's eyes as if they were lances against her chest. Peggy pressed her assault. "Don't you understand? A piece at a time, no matter how hard she resists, Christine will tell them about us.

"Can't you see the distortions that would appear in the press? It would ruin us. It would end forever our dream. I will never allow that to happen!" She hurled the mutilated flower on the table and turned to the window. Her shoulders heaved with each rapid breath. For a time the only sounds were her breathing and the eerie music of the autumn storm. Yet when she turned back Peggy was smiling. Her voice was soft. "My sisters, a year ago I presented a plan by which I felt we could at last inform the public of our existence and of the holy task we have undertaken. With several thousand taped case reports from the finest, most respected nurses in the world, I felt we could mount a campaign for acceptance so intense that those opposed to our beliefs would have no choice but to acquiesce. It would have been the culmination of a life's work, for me and for all of you.

"As is our way, I submitted my belief to a vote. I was defeated. As is my way, I accepted the wishes of our Sisterhood. I promise you now that if we do not act tonight to protect this woman from the threats against her, I shall move ahead with that plan rather than risk a debasing, distorted, sensationalist disclosure by the police and the press. I will release the tapes. I have them—all of them—and *I will do it*."

Looks darted from one to another around the table. The reports were the blood oath that bound them together. Once given—once the first report was completed by a nurse—there could be no turning back from her commitment to the movement. Since the very beginning it had been that way. Reports at first in writing and later by voice. All of those present had made them—some many times—and now Peggy would make them public. What defiance remained among the directors melted.

Peggy turned to Barbara Littlejohn. "Barbara, I would like a vote giving me authority to do whatever is necessary to insure the guilt of Dr. David Shelton and to protect the interests of Christine Beall and The Sisterhood of Life."

Barbara knew that further argument was fruitless. The expressions around the table echoed her feelings. With a shrug she called the question. To her left, Sara Duhey slowly lifted her hand. In order Barbara's eyes called on each one, and like a ripple their hands came up. The vote of support was unanimous.

Breaking the silence that followed, Dotty Dalrymple cleared her throat and spoke for the first time. "Peggy, as you well know, Christine Beall is a nurse on my service. I have come to know her fairly well, although I have not yet chosen to tell her of my commitment to

The Sisterhood. She is, as you have described, a remarkable nurse, devoted to the ideals we all share. Can we be certain she'll allow this man to answer for what she has done, regardless of our decision here tonight?"

The question had been on everyone's mind.

"That, Dorothy, must be our responsibility—yours and mine. When the time is right, you must go to her. Explain the situation as only you can. I know that you will make her understand. You may have to share your secret with her, but I think she has earned that confidence. If necessary, I and the rest of those here will share our secret with her as well. Is that acceptable to you?"

Dalrymple smiled. "I've known you far too long and too well to ask if I have a choice. I'll talk to her."

Peggy nodded and returned the smile.

Dorothy Dalrymple did indeed know Peggy well. From the beginning Dotty had followed her rise—had even been party to her decision to enter medical school at a time when it was difficult enough for a woman, let alone a nurse, to do so. She had followed Peg's astounding success in the field of cardiology and her marriage to one of the most famous scientists and human rights advocates in the world. She had watched her assume the leadership of the medical staff of one of the largest hospitals in the country.

She knew, as surely as she knew sunrise, that Margaret Donner Armstrong could accomplish anything. The sentence they had voted for David Shelton was as good as carried out.

With a few parting words Barbara Littlejohn dismissed the meeting. As she said her good-byes, Dotty paused by the lavish bouquet, bending to inhale its strong perfume and briefly touch a feathery petal. Then, with a final glance at Peggy, she left.

The room emptied quickly. Soon only two remained—Peggy Donner, gazing serenely out the window, and

165

Sara Duhey, who paused outside the doorway, then returned. She was still ten feet away when, without turning, Peggy said, "Sara, how nice of you to stay. We so seldom get a chance to talk."

The willowy black woman froze, then noticed her own reflection in the glass.

"So this is how Peggy Donner earns the reputation for having eyes in the back of her head."

"One of the ways." Margaret Armstrong turned and smiled warmly. Sara had been a personal recruit of hers. "I see a troubled look in those beautiful eyes of yours, Sara. Are you concerned about what happened here tonight?"

"A little. But that's not what I stayed to talk to you about."

"Oh?"

"Peggy, a few days ago Johnny Chapman died at your hospital of a massive allergic reaction—probably to some medicine, they're saying. Had you heard of him and the work he's done?" Armstrong nodded. "Well, I've known Johnny for years. Served on so many committees with him I've lost count."

"And?"

"Well, I've talked to a few people about his death— you know, people from my community. At least one of them felt there was nothing accidental about it. You can probably guess that Johnny's been a thorn in the side of a lot of important people over the years."

"My dear, every time an important or influential person dies, someone has a theory about why it couldn't have been a natural or accidental occurrence. Invariably their theories are nonsense."

"I understand," Sara said, "and I hope you're right in this case. We'll never know for certain, because Johnny's church forbids autopsies. His wife told me that. She had it written in big red letters on the front of his chart, along with a list of the things he was allergic to."

166

Armstrong shifted uncomfortably. "Just what is it you're driving at?"

"Peggy, this man told me he had heard ahead of time that Johnny Chapman would not leave Doctors Hospital alive. He didn't. Then, two days after Johnny suddenly goes into anaphylaxis and dies, Senator Cormier has a fatal cardiac arrest on the operating table. The papers said it was a heart attack, but they also said that because the attack was instantly fatal there was no definite cardiac damage on his autopsy."

"Sara, I still don't see what—"

"Peggy, two of the cases I have handled through The Sisterhood involved intravenous ouabain. Both of them looked like heart attacks. The drug is impossible to detect. Isn't it possible that someone could be—"

"Young lady, I think I've heard enough. Your insinuations are in poor taste and way off base. Worse than that. They come at a time when our movement needs total unity."

Sara Duhey stiffened. "Peggy, please. Don't lash out at me. I don't want to stir up any hornet's nest. All I'm asking is whether it's possible that someone in your hospital is using our methods. There are still more Sisterhood members on the staff of Boston Doctors than at any other single hospital."

"And I know every one of them personally," Armstrong said. "They are all superb nurses and completely honorable human beings. Now, unless you have something much more concrete than what you have presented me here, I would suggest—no, I will insist—that you keep your farfetched notions to yourself. We have much more pressing concerns, you and I, starting with the man who is posing a threat to our entire movement." Armstrong sensed the impact of her outburst and softened. "Sara, after this Shelton business is cleared up, we can discuss your concerns in more detail. All right?"

Sara Duhey studied the older woman, then nodded. "All right."

"Thank you," Armstrong whispered.

The two women left Room 133 together. Outside, the storm had intensified and wind gusted with a fury that shook buildings.

CHAPTER XIV

"A crack that had the habit of looking like a rabbit
. . ." David repeated the words over and over as he
studied the series of thin lines that gerrymandered his
living room ceiling.

". . . had the *funny* habit of looking like a rabbit."
Where had he read that? What were the exact words?
No matter, he decided. None of the cracks looked
anything like a rabbit. Besides, the super had promised
they would be plastered over, so it was a fruitless
exercise anyhow.

He rolled to one side, tucked an arm under his head
and stared out the window. The outlines of buildings
across the alley undulated through a cold, driving rain.

It had been nearly two days since the nightmarish
session with Dockerty. The morning after the inquiry
David had tried to conduct his affairs at the hospital as
usual. It was like working in an ice box. No virus could
have spread through the wards faster than news of the
tacit indictment brought against him. Most of the nurses
and medical staff took special pains to avoid him. Some
whispered as he walked past and one nurse actually
pointed. Those few who spoke to him picked their

words with the deliberateness of soldiers traversing a mine field.

By early afternoon he could take no more. Aldous Butterworth and Edwina Burroughs were the only two patients he had in the hospital. Butterworth was essentially Dr. Armstrong's problem again. The circulation in his operated leg was better than in his other one. Edwina Burroughs was anxious to go home and probably as ready for discharge now as she would be in the morning. David wrote a note in Butterworth's chart instructing Dr. Armstrong to arrange for his sutures to be removed in three days; then he made out a list of directions for Edwina Burroughs and sent her home.

He was walking, head down, toward the main exit when he collided with Dotty Dalrymple. They exchanged apologies, then Dalrymple said, "Heading to the office?"

David fought the impulse to brush aside her courtesy with a lie. "No," he said. "I've canceled the rest of the day. Actually, I'm going home."

He was surprised at the interest and concern in her eyes. Although the two of them were acquainted, they had never talked at length.

"Dr. Shelton, I want you to know how distressed I am about last night." She was, David realized, the first person all day who had openly said anything to him about the session.

"Me too," he muttered.

"We haven't had the chance to get to know one another very well, but I've heard a great deal about your work from my nurses—all of it highly complimentary." David's face tightened in a half-smile. "My praise plus a dime gets you a phone call. That's what you are thinking, isn't it?" she said. David's smile became more open and relaxed. Dalrymple rested a fleshy arm against the wall. "Well, I'm afraid I don't have much in the way of cheery news for you, but I can tell you that Lieutenant Dockerty was in to see me this morning. Your name came up only briefly and, for what it's worth, I think he is not at all convinced of your guilt despite that circus last night."

"From the reaction around the wards this morning, Miss Dalrymple, I'd say that if that's the case he's in a tiny minority. All of a sudden, I feel about as much control over my life as a laboratory mouse. At the moment Lieutenant Dockerty is very low on my list of favorite people."

"I guess if I were in your position I'd probably be feeling the same way," Dalrymple said. She paused, as if searching for words to prolong their conversation. Finally she shrugged, nodded a "Good day," and headed off.

She was several steps down the hall when David started after her. "Miss Dalrymple, please," he called out. "If you can spare another minute, there is something you might be able to help with." The nursing director slowed, then came about like a schooner, smiling expectantly. "You had Charlotte Thomas's chart last evening," David said. "If it would be possible, I'd like to borrow it for a day. I have no idea what to look for, but maybe there's something in there that won't read just right to me."

Dalrymple's expression darkened. "I'm sorry, Dr. Shelton," she said. "The chart I had last night was only a copy. The lieutenant has the original." She hesitated. "Now, I don't even have the copy." David looked at her quizzically. He felt uneasy with the way she was weighing each word. "I . . . ah . . . gave it away, Doctor . . . this morning . . . Wallace Huttner and the woman's husband . . . and a lawyer. They came to me with a court order for my copy of the chart. Apparently it was the only one the lieutenant would allow to be made."

David's hands went cold. A damp chill spread from them throughout his body. He had little doubt as to what they were doing: malpractice. No other explanation made sense. He carried a million dollars in liability. Peter Thomas wanted to be prepared to move as soon as any action was taken against him. David shuddered. On top of everything else, Thomas was going to sue him for malpractice. And his own chief of surgery was helping him do it.

Dalrymple reached out to touch his shoulder and then seemed to change her mind. "I'm sorry, Doctor," she said coolly. "I wish I could make it better for you, but I can't."

David tightened his lips against any outburst. "Thanks," he mumbled, then hurried toward the exit.

By the time he arrived home his emotions were blanketed by a pall of total frustration. He paced the apartment several times. Then, overwhelmed by feelings of impotence, he threw himself across his bed and grabbed the telephone. He would call Dr. Armstrong, or Dockerty, or even Peter Thomas. Anyone, as long as it felt as though he was doing something. Indecision kept him from dialing. His address book lay on the bedside table. He opened it and flipped through the pages, hoping halfheartedly that someone's name would leap out at him. Anyone's who might help.

Most of the pages were blank.

His brothers were listed—one in California and one in Chicago. But even if they were next door, he wouldn't have called them. After the accident, after the alcohol and the pills and, finally, the hospital, they had quietly separated him from their lives. Christmas cards and a call every six months or so were all that remained.

A few associates from his days at White Memorial were listed. From time to time over the past eight years some of them even invited him to parties. He was fun to be around . . . as long as he was fun to be around. The more he had chanced talking about the course his life had taken, the fewer the invitations had become. There would be no real help from any of them.

In a doctor's life, fragmented by college and medical school and internship and residency and marriage and children and setting up a practice, firm friendships were rare enough. For David, having to retrace so many steps had made close ties impossible.

The shroud of isolation grew heavier. There was no one. No one except Lauren, and she was five hundred miles away, probably having lunch with some congressman and . . . Wait! There *was* somebody. There was Rosetti. For ten years, whenever he was down or needed advice, there had always been Joey Rosetti. Joey, and Terry, too. Over the months with Lauren he hadn't seen them very much, but Joey was the kind of friend to whom that really didn't matter.

Excited, David looked up the number of Joey's Northside Tavern and dialed. Even if Rosetti didn't have any advice—which was doubtful, since he had advice for everything—he would have encouragement, probably even a new story or two. Just the prospect of talking with him was cheering.

A curt, gravelly voice at the Northside Tavern informed David that Mr. Rosetti was not available. The cheer immediately vanished.

"This is Dr. Shelton, Dr. David Shelton." David emphasized the title in the manner he reserved only for making dinner and hotel reservations or for working his way past the switchboard operator at an unfamiliar hospital. "I'm a close friend of Mr. Rosetti's. Could you tell me when he'll be back or where I can reach him?"

The voice called someone without bothering to cover the mouthpiece. "Hey, some doctor's on the phone. Says he's a friend of Mr. Rosetti's. Can I tell 'im where he's gone?"

In a few moments it spoke to David. "Ah, sir, Mr.

173

Rosetti and his wife've gone to their house on the North Shore. They'll be back late tonight."

David heard the voice ask, "Any message?" but he was already hanging up. In less than a minute the silence and inaction were intolerable. Purely out of desperation, he called Wallace Huttner. When the ringing began, he fought the urge to hang up by pressing the receiver tightly against his ear. The ear was throbbing by the time Huttner came on.

"Yes, Dr. Shelton, what is it?" The distance in the man's voice could have been measured in light-years.

"Dr. Huttner, I'm very concerned and upset about what happened last night and with some things I've learned today," David managed. "I . . . I wondered if I might talk to you about them for a few minutes?"

Huttner said, "Well, actually I'm quite far behind in the office and—"

"Please!" David cut in. "I'm sorry for raising my voice, but, please, just hear me out." He paused for a moment, then sighed relief when Huttner made no further objection. Struggling to keep his words slow and his tone more composed, he said, "Dr. Huttner, I know that you helped Mr. Thomas and his lawyer get a copy of Charlotte's chart. Somehow you must believe that I had nothing to do with her murder. I may have given you and some of the others the impression that I favor mercy killing, but I don't. I . . . I need your help—someone's help—to convince Peter Thomas and the lieutenant of that. I . . ." At that instant David realized how ill conceived his call had been. He really had no clear idea of what he wanted to say or ask. Huttner sensed the same thing.

"Dr. Shelton," he said with cool condescension, "please understand. In no way have I judged your guilt or innocence. I assisted Peter this morning as a favor to a distraught old friend. Nothing more."

Old friend? David nearly laughed out loud. A few

174

days ago Peter Thomas had made it clear they barely knew one another. Now they were old friends. He clenched the receiver more tightly and forced himself to listen as Huttner continued. "The lieutenant was by to see me earlier today, and it seems as if he's conducting a most thorough inquiry into the whole matter. Let us just wait and see what direction his investigation takes. If, as you say, you had nothing to do with Charlotte's death, I'm sure the lieutenant will be able to prove it. Now if you've no further questions . . ."

David hung up without responding.

When he awoke still dressed at five thirty the next morning, the muscles in his jaw were aching.

David amused himself for nearly an hour by counting the seconds between a flash of lightning in the alley and the subsequent clap of thunder. Three calculations in a row agreed exactly—the electrical discharge was a mile and a half away. Measured against the disappointments of the past two days, his mathematical triumph was like winning an Olympic medal. Fifteen minutes reading a mindless paperback. Two with the weights. Another few with the book. They were, he realized, the random, anxious movements of someone with no place to go. The same sort of restlessness that had characterized his first few weeks of hospitalization in the Briggs Institute.

He stared at the phone and considered trying Lauren again. He had tried earlier in the day—her home number and even the hotels in Washington where she usually stayed. She'll be here soon, he told himself. If not today then tomorrow. Their only contact after she had left had been a brief conversation just before the hideous session with Dockerty in the Amphi. Lauren had called to explain that she would be on the move, covering reaction to the death of Senator Cormier. In fact, she confessed, her main reason for calling (other than

175

"just to say hi," she said) was to see if David could talk to people at his hospital and get some inside information on the sudden tragedy. At the time he'd felt certain he could learn something. Of course, there had been no way of knowing that within a few hours he would become a pariah at Boston Doctors.

David went to the kitchen for some water, then to the bathroom for some more.

She'd said she'd be in Springfield today covering the funeral. Possibly for a day or two after that. Perhaps she would call and they could meet in Springfield. Maybe they could even drive to New York or . . . or maybe up to Montreal.

Random movements, random thoughts.

He reopened the mystery novel, read for a time, then discovered that the last ten pages of the tattered paperback were missing. He barely reacted—just shrugged—and shuffled off to take a shower—his second of the day. As he turned on the water, the telephone rang.

David skidded into the hallw.y and raced to the bedroom. "Hey, where have you been?" he panted. "I've been worried. I didn't even know for sure what city you were in."

"David, it's Dr. Armstrong. Are you all right?"

"Huh?" Oh, damn. "I'm sorry, Dr. Armstrong. No, I'm fine. I was expecting a call from Lauren and . . . uh . . . she's a woman that I . . ."

"David? Take a minute and relax. Do you want me to call back?"

"No, no, I'm fine. Really." He stretched the phone cord to reach his bureau and pulled on a pair of scrub pants. Then he sighed and sank to the bed. "Actually, I'm not fine. I've been sitting around here all day. Half the time I wait, and the other half I try to figure out what I'm waiting for."

"But you haven't . . . ?" She let the question drift.

"No, not even close," he said, forcing a laugh. "Not a pill or a drop of anything. I told you the other night that nothing was going to get me back there." Actually, the urge had been there several times—fleeting, but unmistakable. It never lasted long enough to pose a major threat, but after so many years, any sense of it at all was frightening.

"Good. I'm glad to hear it," Armstrong said. "I'm truly sorry to have taken so long to get back to you."

"I understand." He cut in, hoping to spare her any uncomfortable explanations of the turmoil he knew was surrounding him—and her—at the hospital. "Any news?"

"Not really. Our friend the lieutenant has been present on and off since Sunday. He checks in with me or Ed Lipton to let us know he's around, but that's about it."

"Well, I bumped into Miss Dalrymple yesterday and asked for her copy of Charlotte Thomas's chart. I thought perhaps I could get some brainstorm from studying it."

"And did Miss Dalrymple give it to you?"

David missed the chord of heightened interest in her voice. "No. I think she would have, but she didn't have it anymore." Briefly, he reviewed the conversation with Dotty Dalrymple and his subsequent call to Huttner.

"So," she said after a moment's pause, "the buzzards circle."

David smiled ruefully at the image. "Circle and wait," he said. "I feel so damn helpless. I want to do something to show them all I'm still alive and fighting, but I can't even find a stick to wave."

"I understand," she said. "If I were you, I would just sit tight and see what develops."

"You're probably right, Dr. Armstrong, but unfortunately passivity has never been one of my strong suits. If I don't do something to sort this whole mess out, who will?"

"I will, David."

"What?"

"I told you the other night I would do what I could."

"I remember."

"Well, I have a friend in personnel who's checking the hospital computer for any former mental patients or drug problems or prison records. That sort of thing."

David became excited. "That's a great idea. How about past employment at Charlotte Thomas's nursing agency?"

"We could try that."

"And graduates of her nursing school. And . . . and activists supporting patients' rights, living wills, things like that. And . . ."

"Whoa! Slow down, David. First things first. You just stay where I can get in touch with you, and fight that self-destruct impulse of yours. I'll do the rest—don't worry. Are you coming back to work?"

"Tomorrow. I thought I'd try tomorrow. Anything would be better than sitting around like this waiting for the other shoe to drop. Thanks to you, it'll be much easier to concentrate on my job knowing at least that something's being done."

"Something's being done," Armstrong echoed.

Margaret Armstrong set the receiver down and glanced through her partially open office door at the patients in her waiting room—half a dozen complex problems that she would, almost certainly, unravel and deal with. Even after so many years, her own capabilities awed her.

"Mama, please. Tell me what I can do to help."

She understood now. She had the knowledge and the power and she understood. But how could she have been expected to know then what was right? She had been still a girl, barely fifteen years old.

"Kill me! For God's sake, please kill me."

"Mama, please. You don't know what you're saying.

178

Let me get you something for the pain. When you feel better, you'll stop saying such things. I know you will."

"No, baby. It doesn't help. Nothing has helped the pain for days. Only you can help me. You must help me."

"Mama, I'm frightened. I can't think straight. That lady down the hall keeps screaming and I can't think straight. I'm so frightened. I . . . I hate this place."

"The pillow. Just set it over my face and lean on it as hard as you can. It won't take long."

"Mama, please. I can't do that. There must be another way. Something. Please help me to understand. Help me to know what to do. . . ."

Margaret Armstrong's receptionist buzzed several times on the intercom, then crossed to the office door and knocked. "Dr. Armstrong?"

The door swung open and the receptionist knew immediately that she should have been more patient. It was just one of those times when the cardiac chief was totally lost in thought. One of those times when she sat fingering a small strip of linen, staring across the room. They came infrequently and never lasted long.

The receptionist eased the door closed and returned to her desk. Minutes later, her intercom buzzed.

The talk with Margaret Armstrong and their plan of action, however ragtag, injected a note of optimism into David's day. Some Bach organ music and twenty minutes of hard, almost vicious lifting nurtured the mood. He was showered, dressed, and stretched out, thumbing through a journal, when a key clicked in the front door. He charged down the hall and was almost to the door when Lauren entered. She was carrying her raincoat and a floppy hat, but otherwise looked as if she had just come in from a garden party. Her light blue dress clung to her body, more out of will, it seemed, than design. A thin gold necklace glowed on the autumn brown of her chest.

In those first few moments, standing there, looking at her, nothing else mattered. Then, as he focused on her face, she looked away. Suddenly David felt frightened even to touch her. "Welcome home," he said uncertainly, reaching a tentative hand toward her. She took it and moved to him, but there was no warmth in her embrace. Her coolness and the scent of her perfume—the same fragrance she had worn the morning she left—filled him with a sense of emptiness and apprehension. "I had no idea when you'd be coming back," he said, hoping that something in her response would dispel the feelings.

"I told you when I called the other day that I'd be tied up with the Cormier story," she said, settling into an easy chair in the living room. David noted that she had avoided the couch. "What a shitty thing to have happen," she went on. "Of all the people I ever interviewed in Washington, Dick Cormier was the only one I really trusted. Everyone did. His funeral was very moving. The President spoke, and the Chief Justice, and . . ."

David could no longer stand the tension inside him and in her nervous chatter. "Lauren," he said. "There's more, isn't there? I mean it's not just the senator. Something else is eating at you. Please talk to me. I'm . . . I'm very uncomfortable with the feeling in this room right now. There's a lot I have to tell you, but first we've got to clear the air a little." Another man, he thought. Lauren's met another man. There was nothing in her face to discourage that notion. She stared out the window, biting at her lower lip. For a moment David thought she was about to cry, but when she finally spoke, her voice held far more irritation than sadness.

"David," she said, "a policeman was waiting for me when I arrived home. I spent more than two hours at

180

the police station answering questions from Lieutenant Dockerty—some of them very personal—about you, and about us."

"Did Dockerty tell you what it was all about?" he asked, relieved that he'd been wrong about another man.

Lauren shook her head. "Only briefly. He was nice enough at first, but his questions got more and more pointed—more and more offensive. Finally I just stalked out and told him I wouldn't talk to him again without a lawyer. He made it sound like you were really sick and I was protecting you in some way. David, I can't have—"

"Damn that man!" David shouted. "When this is all over, he's going to answer for this shit. I've had about all I can take." His fists were white and tight against his thighs. "Lauren, this is a nightmare. The man's on some kind of vendetta. Ever since he came on the scene he's gone after me like he had blinders on. I didn't do anything. He's taken a pile of circumstantial horseshit, and he's been trying to mold it into some kind of case against me." His control was disappearing. He sensed it, but was unable to back off. One after another, his words tumbled out, each louder and higher pitched than the last. "I could handle the crap he's been laying down at the hospital. That I could handle. But hauling you in . . . The bastard's gone too far." He was pacing now, thumping his fist against his side.

"David, please!" Lauren screamed. "You're acting crazy. Please get hold of yourself. It frightens me to see you like this."

He stopped in his tracks and forced his hands open. A deep breath, then he said, "I'm sorry, babe. I am. First it's too much joking, then too much crazy." He managed a thin smile. "I guess I'm just . . . too much, huh?" He sank numbly into the couch. "Lauren, could you hold me for a minute?" he asked, reaching his hands to her.

181

Lauren's lips tightened. She looked at the floor and shook her head. "David, we've got to talk."

"So talk." He folded his hands in his lap.

"My wire service has people all over, David. Including the police department here. Business like this—being questioned at the police station and all—my boss is very straight and very conservative. If he gets wind of this—"

"Jesus Christ!" David exploded. "You make it sound as if I'm doing all this to give you a black eye. Can't you understand that I haven't done anything? My God, here I am being harassed up and down by some monomaniac, in danger of losing my career—or worse—and my girl friend is worried about being embarrassed in front of her bureau chief. This is insane. Absolutely insane!"

"David"—Lauren's voice was low and measured with anger—"I've told you over and over again how much I dislike the label 'girl friend.' Now please calm down, and try to understand my position in this thing, too."

Speechless, David could only look at her and shake his head. Lauren straightened her dress, sat rigidly upright, and met his incredulity with defiance. "I know you'll be pleased to hear," she said, "that of all the things you have to worry about, having to endure the Art Society dinner dance Thursday will not be one of them. After the lieutenant brought me home, Elliot May called and asked if I was planning on going. I knew how little you were looking forward to the affair, so I took the opportunity of relieving you of the burden." The wildness in his eyes was frightening. She forced her lips into a proud pout and turned toward the window.

He rose and took a step toward her. In that frozen, terrifying moment, he sensed his self-control slipping away. Fists clenched, he took another step.

Suddenly, the buzzer from the downstairs foyer sounded. David whirled and half stalked, half stumbled to the intercom in the hall.

"Yes?" he shouted.

"It's Lieutenant Dockerty, Dr. Shelton." The policeman's voice crackled from four floors below. "May I come up, please?"

"Do I have a choice?" David said as he pressed the door release.

For the next half-minute the only sound was David's breathing—bitter, frantic gulps, gradually slowing as he fought for composure. He had been expecting a visit from Dockerty for the past two days. Typical of the man to pick a time like this to show up. He heard the clank as the gears of the rickety elevator engaged. Standing by the door, he shook his head disdainfully at the groan from the straining cables. The antiquated box took more than a minute to make the four-floor trip. A second clank, and the rattle of the automatic inside gate signaled its arrival. David stepped from his apartment just as Dockerty pushed open the heavy outside door of the elevator. He was accompanied by a tall uniformed officer.

"Dr. Shelton, this is Officer Kolb," Dockerty said. "May we come in, please?" It was an order. David thought for a moment about Lauren, then shrugged and led them into the living room.

"Miss Nichols." Dockerty nodded, but made no move to introduce Kolb to her.

Lauren stood and picked up her raincoat. "If you'll excuse me," she said formally, "I was just leaving."

She had taken one step toward the door when Dockerty said, "I think perhaps you had better stay, Miss Nichols." Lauren's eyes narrowed at him. She stiffened, then strode back to her chair.

Inside David confusion and panic began to build.

Dockerty stared at the floor for a few silent seconds, then reached into his coat pocket and produced a manilla-covered pad. The forms inside it were green. "Dr.

Shelton," he said, handing the pad to David, "do you recognize these?"

David flipped through the sheets, then stammered, "Yes, they're my C two-twenty-two order forms. But I don't see what . . ."

"For ordering narcotics?" Dockerty asked.

"Yes, but . . ."

"They're preprinted with your name, aren't they?"

"Enough!" The word shot out. "I've had enough of this. Would you tell me what you want, or . . . or leave." He was nearly screaming. Inside his gut, inside his chest huge knots formed and began to tighten.

"Dr. Shelton, I sent notice to all the pharmacies in the city, asking for the names of everyone who purchased injectable morphine in the last month." He produced a single green form from his breast pocket. "This form C two-twenty-two was used to purchase three vials of morphine sulfate from the Quigg Pharmacy in West Roxbury. It's dated October second, the day Charlotte Thomas was murdered. It's your form, Dr. Shelton. There's your name printed right on it."

David snatched the form away. "That's not my signature," he said automatically. He stared at the writing, then closed his eyes. For years he had been kidded—had himself made jokes—about the scrawl that was his signature. "An unscrupulous chimp could prescribe for my patients," he had once quipped. The signature on the C222 would have passed his desk without a second notice.

"Perhaps," Dockerty responded tonelessly. "But I suspect that it is. You see, Doctor, there's more. The warrant I obtained to search your office allowed me to remove not only your forms, but this." He reached in his pocket again and produced a small, gold-framed photo. "Mr. Quigg at the pharmacy has positively identified you from this photo as the one who purchased the morphine from him."

David stared down at the picture. It was one he had never been able to put away. The whole family—David, Ginny, and three-year-old Becky—posing by the swan boats in Boston's Public Garden. It had been taken only two months before the accident.

For a time Dockerty seemed unable to speak. Finally he shook his head. "David Shelton, I am placing you under arrest for the murder of Charlotte Thomas."

The words fell on David like hammers. An uncomfortable, high-pitched buzzing noise began swelling in his head. He tried to shake the sound loose as the tall policeman read him his rights from a frayed, cardboard card. The man's words seemed jumbled and slurred. David watched, a detached observer, as uniformed arms reached out and handcuffed his wrists behind him. Dockerty's apology for having to use the restraints was nearly lost in the mounting buzz.

David was disoriented, frightened almost beyond functioning. He tried to pull away. Without a flicker of expression, the patrolman tightened his grip.

Bewildered and mortified, Lauren backed away as David, needing support to stand, was led out the door.

Dockerty moved to follow, then turned to her. "He's going to need a lawyer, Miss Nichols," he said grimly. "If I were you, I'd make sure it was a damn good one." With a nod, he headed down the corridor.

The wind had died off, but a cold, heavy rain was still falling. Dockerty threw a windbreaker around David's shoulders and zipped it up the front. Even so, by the time they dragged him the short distance to the squad car he was soaked to the skin. Through bizarre, disconnected scenes, David watched the events of his own arrest. The eerie blue light, a strobe atop the squad car . . . tiny, perfect diamond shapes in the metal screen . . . pedestrians bundled against the downpour, frozen

185

through the screen and the front windshield. David saw them all in stop-action. A grotesque slide show.

The station house . . . the lights . . . the uniforms. Then it was the voices. "Empty your pockets . . ." ". . . son, can you hear me? Son? . . ." ". . . here's his wallet. Get the shit you need from his license . . ." "Give me your right hand, thumb first . . ." "Over here, stand over here . . ." ". . . the other hand now . . ." "Look, fella, it's just a number. Let it hang there . . ." "Face straight ahead . . . now turn . . . no, this way, this way . . ." "Three's empty. Put him in there . . ."

Next it was the noises. Scraping of metal on metal . . . a loud clang—the elevator?—no, not here. Can't be the elevator . . . music . . . from where? . . . where is the music coming from? . . . More voices . . . ". . . here, boss, over here . . ." ". . . a light, I need another light. My fucking cigarette's soggy . . ." "When the fuck's dinner? Don't we even get fed here? . . ."

Finally, the wide, blurry bands . . . up and down in front of him. Gradually the blurs narrowed and darkened. . . . Bars! They were bars!

Again the buzzing crescendo. Images of other bars, other screens exploded through his mind.

"No! Please, God, no!" he screamed. He whirled and dropped to his knees by the toilet, retching uncontrollably into water already murky with disinfectant.

Barely aware of the bile singeing his nose and throat, David crawled across the stone floor and pulled himself onto a metal-framed cot. He descended into a cold, unnatural sleep long before his sobs had faded.

CHAPTER XV

"Time to move out, son. There's some Listerine in this cup. Splash some cold water on your face and swish this stuff around in your mouth for a minute. It'll help you wake up."

David worked his eyes open a crack. His first sight of the morning was the same as his last the night before. Bars. This time the narrow blue and white bars of the sweat-stained pillow beneath his face.

The officer was a plethoric man, fifty or so, with a belly that hung several inches over his belt. He leaned against the doorframe of the cell and watched patiently while David pulled himself up and wiped sooty sleep from his eyes. "Are you able to talk, son?" he asked.

David nodded, squinted at the man, then took the mouthwash. The officer seemed in no great hurry, so David took a minute to stretch the ache from the muscles in his neck and back, trying at the same time to get some sense of himself. For the moment, at least, the terror and confusion of the past night were gone. In their place was a strange but quite comfortable feeling of well-being. Knees locked, he bent forward and put the tips of all ten fingers on the floor. Peaceful, he thought.

This shithole, all the madness, and here I am feeling peaceful.

Then he remembered. It was at summer camp. He was eleven—no, twelve—years old. A sudden stomach cramp while swimming far from the raft. In an instant he was on the bottom, pain strangling his gut and water forcing its way into his lungs. Then, as suddenly as it had started, the pain and the terror had vanished. In their place, the same detached peace. He was dying—then and now—helpless and dying.

The sergeant's radish cheeks puffed in a grin. "Glad to see you're feelin' better," he said. "The night boys were worried. Said you weren't even able to hold a dime, much less make the phone call they tried to give you." When David didn't answer, he added, "You are feelin' better, aren't you?"

"Oh, yeah, I'm okay, thanks," David said distantly, still testing his body and his feelings for pain. "Wh . . . where am I, anyway?"

"District One," the man answered. He looked at David with renewed concern. "You're in the jail at District One in Boston. Do you understand that?" David nodded. "We have to go now. You've got to go to court. The judge and the people at the court will help you. Don't you worry."

David watched with bemused curiosity as the policeman clicked a handcuff on his right wrist and led him out of the cell. He smiled politely at the black, silver-haired prisoner who was snapped into the other cuff. Calmly, fuguelike, he focused on the manacled hands—black and white—and followed them into the back seat of a squad car.

"Name's Lyons," the black man said as the car pulled away. "Reggie Lyons." His wise face held countless thin lines, etched by years of hard living, and several thicker ones, clearly carved by more tangible items.

"David. I'm David," he answered.

"You ain't never been this route before, David, have you?" Lyons asked. David shrugged, looked out the window, and shook his head. "Well, you is in for *a* treat. The tank at Suffolk is the worst, man. I mean the pits." David stared at a motorcycle cruising next to them and nodded. "Hey, you all right? Well, it don't matter much one way or tuther. Crazy's prob'ly better. You just stick close to ol' Reggie. He'll take care of you."

The tank was, in fact, a cage. The holding room for prisoners awaiting court appearances. Twenty men, all "presumed innocent" were packed inside—rapists, drunks, vagrants, murderers, flashers. Around the outside, half a dozen lawyers were vying to be heard over one another and over the din inside. "Perkins, which one of you is Perkins? . . ." "Frankly, Arnold, I don't give a flying fuck if the kid is guilty or innocent. He either cops the first charge and saves us a trial or he ends up going down for both and spending three to five in Walpole . . ." "Look, kid, I know what you've seen on *Perry Mason*, but that just ain't the way it works. Today we don't talk guilty or not guilty. Today we talk money. If you have some or can get some, we bail you out. Otherwise you wait for your trial in Charles Street. Nobody cares about your story today. This is just for bail. Understand? Just for bail . . ."

David wedged himself in one corner of the tank and stared through the chain link at a high window that was opaque with grime. Bit by bit, reality—and the terror—was returning. He thought about the hospital. The operating rooms would already be on their second cases of the day.

"Hey, David, you got a lawyer?" Reggie Lyons stood next to him, leaning against the cage. A cigarette, wrinkled and bent, popped up and down at the corner of his mouth as he spoke.

"Ah, no, Reggie, I don't," David said absently. "At

189

least, not that I know of." An uncomfortable pressure
grew beneath his breast bone. He tried to remember
when he had last eaten. When he had last run by the
river. He looked about the cage, awareness growing
every second and with it an abysmal despair.

"Shelton? David Shelton. Which one of you is Shelton?" The bailiff was a dumpy man in his late fifties.
There was an air about him—a look in his eyes—that
suggested his favorite pastime outside of court might be
pulling the wings off insects.

Reggie Lyons leaned over and whispered, "David,
don't you be scared now. Jes' go in there an' think
about the beach or your favorite broad or somethin'. All
the uniforms an' robes is jes' dress-up. A game they
play to impress one another an' scare the shit out of
us."

David turned and looked at Reggie's aged, ageless
face. "Thanks," he said hoarsely. "Thanks a lot."

The man stared at him curiously, then took one of
David's hands in both of his. His palms were thick with
calluses. "Good luck, man," he whispered. "Don't give
in to 'em."

The paunchy bailiff snapped handcuffs on David as
he stepped out of the tank. Moments later, he was
seated in the prisoners' dock. The three-foot-high, four-
foot-square pen was a wooden island, separating him
from the rest of the courtroom. Told to stand, he braced
his legs against one low panel as new words, new voices
and scenes worked their way into his nightmare.

The clerk who read the charges was a spinsterish
woman who looked as if she had been born into the
ornate old courtroom.

"As to complaint number three one nine four seven,
your complainant, John Dockerty, respectfully repre-
sents that in the City of Boston in the County of Suffolk
in behalf of said Commonwealth, David Edward Shelton of Boston in the County of Suffolk on the second

day of October, in violation of the General Laws, chapter two six five, section one, did wrongfully murder one Charlotte Winthrop Thomas with intent to murder her by injecting into her body a quantity of morphine sulfate.

"The court has entered a plea for the defendant of not guilty."

David leaned more heavily against the panel as the district attorney, a slick young man with two rings on each hand, briefly outlined the case against him. Disconnected words and phrases were all that registered. ". . . premeditated . . . unconscionable misuse of his skill and knowledge . . . clandestine injection . . . positively identified as . . . murder, as heinous as any committed in passion. . . ."

"Dr. Shelton, do you understand the charges that have been brought against you?" the judge said mechanically. David nodded. "Speak up, please. Do you understand the charges?"

"Yes," David managed.

"And do you have a lawyer?"

For several seconds there was total silence in the room. Then a voice called out from the last row of seats. "Yes, yes, he does, Your Honor." A thin man, dressed in a three-piece pinstripe suit, rose and walked briskly down the aisle toward the judge.

"You're representing this man, Mr. Glass?"

"Yes, Your Honor."

"Let the record show the defendant is represented by Mr. Benjamin Glass."

David's eyes narrowed as he studied the man who had come forward to champion him. Black hair . . . thinning . . . strands combed carefully across the top . . . scuffed brown leather briefcase . . . broad gold wedding band, intricately carved.

Glass walked to him and smiled encouragement. "You okay?" he asked softly. David managed a nod. "You're white as a ghost. Do you need to see a doctor or

191

anything?" This time a shake. The lawyer's face was dark, nearly olive colored—unlined and youthful, yet at the same time seasoned and assured. Dark circles underscored the intensity in his eyes. "Sorry I'm late. Lauren didn't connect with me until this morning. Let me get you out of here, then we'll talk."

Ben Glass approached the judge. "Your Honor, I would like to move for bail and petition for a probable-cause hearing." He looked slight to David, almost frail. But his stance, the tilt of his head exuded confidence.

It was his world, David realized, his operating room. "Thank you, Lauren," he whispered. For the first time the flicker of hope appeared in his nightmare.

"On what grounds?" the judge said.

"Your Honor, Dr. Shelton is a respected surgeon with no criminal record and no recent history that would suggest the need for psychiatric observation and evaluation."

"Very well. Fifty thousand dollars cash."

"Your Honor," Glass said with just the right incredulity, "this man may be an M.D., but I assure you, he is no millionaire. Please save us a trip this afternoon for review by a supreme court justice. Make it a hundred thousand, but let me pay a bondsman."

The judge tapped his fingertips together for a few seconds, then said, "All right, Mr. Glass. One hundred thousand dollars bail it is."

"Thank you, Your Honor."

Ben took David by the arm and, with the bailiff close behind, led him from the courtroom. "You're almost home, David," he said. "My friend the bondsman will want ten thousand dollars. Have you got it?"

"I . . . don't think so," David said.

"Family. Can you get it from your parents or someplace?"

"My parents are dead. I . . . I have two brothers and

192

. . . a . . . oh, an aunt who might help. What if I can't come up with the money?"

"Believe me, you don't want to have that happen. The place you stayed last night is a palace compared to Charles Street, where they'll send you now. Tell you what. Maury Kaufman, the bondsman, has gotten so fat off my clients that he owes me. He'll agree to cuff this one for a day rather than risk losing my trade. Today is Wednesday. I'll get you until Friday morning to come up with the cash. Okay?"

"Okay," David said as the bailiff removed his handcuffs and motioned him back into the tank. "And Mr. Glass—thank you."

"David, I hope this doesn't shake your confidence too much, but while you were taking Godliness one-oh-one in medical school, I was one of those hippie weirdo flower children getting pushed around at antiwar demonstrations. It's Ben. You can only call me Mr. Glass if it makes it easier for you to come to grips with the fee you're going to have to pay me." He turned and headed down the hall as the bailiff clanged the tank door shut.

"Hey, David, is that Glass dude your lawyer?" A toothpick had replaced the cigarette in the corner of Reggie Lyons's mouth.

"I . . . I guess he is," David said, pleased with the bit of animation that had returned to his voice.

"Well, then. I guess I can stop gettin' all worked up 'n' worried about you. He don't look like much, but I seen him prancin' around in court a few times. The dude's a tiger. I mean he is *the* man."

"Thanks for telling me, Reggie. It helps." David actually grinned. "You've really been great to me. Say, what are you here for anyway?"

Lyons smiled and winked. "Jes' bein', pal," he said. "I is here jes' for bein'."

* * *

The sign over the bar said, "Paddy O'Brien's Delicatessen: Home of the world's best chopped liver, and the most famous Irish Jew since Mayor Briscoe."

"I've never even heard of this place." David smiled as he slid onto the wooden bench across from Ben. Shamrocks and Stars of David were everywhere. On the wall over their booth the photograph of a ragamuffin group of Irish revolutionaries hung side by side with one of a spit-and-polish Israeli tank unit.

"Are you Jewish?" Ben asked.

"No."

"Are you Irish?"

"No."

"I rest my case. It's no wonder you've never found your way here. Sooner or later, though, most people do. And here you are."

"Thanks to you."

"It's what I do," Ben answered matter-of-factly. "If my appendix bursts someday, then I might end up here savoring the chopped liver, thanks to *you*. That's the way it all works, right?"

"Right," David said. He knew that the easy talk they'd shared since leaving the courtroom had been as carefully orchestrated by Ben as his choice of this gritty, vibrant restaurant. He also knew they were wise choices. Bit by bit, he was relaxing. Bit by bit, he sensed the resurgence of hope.

Ben ordered a "sampler of delights" that easily could have fed ten. They ate in silence for a while, then he said, "It's probably unfair to have waited until after you've eaten to discuss my fee, but it is how the wee ones at home get fed. It's ten thousand dollars, David."

David startled momentarily, then shrugged and took a sip of water. Suddenly finding himself $20,000 in debt was little more than a gnat on his nightmare. "I don't have it," he said flatly.

"I'm a bit more lenient in my payment schedule than

Maury the Bondsman," Ben said, "but I expect to get paid."

David's lips tightened. "I guess that after being accused of murder and spending the night in a cell, there's really not much place for false pride. I'm sure I could borrow the money if I can just sit on my vanity long enough to ask. My brothers would probably be willing to help. And I have this friend who owns the Northside Tavern—"

"Rosetti?"

"You know Joey?"

"Not well, but enough to know that he's a good kind of friend to have. Somehow Rosetti's always been able to straddle the fence between the North End boys and the establishment without falling off on either side. If he's your friend, I say give him a call."

"If it comes to that, I will."

"Well, like I said, I expect to get paid." David nodded. "We're in business, then," Ben said, reaching over to shake his hand. "Now I can tell you what you get for your money—and what you have to do to keep me. You get everything I can give you, David. Time, friends, influence, sweat—whatever you need. In exchange I want only one thing from you—besides the fee, that is." He paused for emphasis. "Honesty. I mean total, no-crap, no-bullshit honesty. There are no second chances. If I catch you in even a tiny fib, you find yourself another lawyer. There are enough unpleasant surprises in this job as is without constantly worrying about whether I'm going to get one from my client."

"We're still in business," David said.

"Fine. Why don't you start by giving me some background on yourself. Assume I don't know anything."

At that moment a sprightly little man with freckles and graying red hair bounced over and leaned on the table. He wore a grease-stained apron with a large green Star-of-David on the front. His high-pitched brogue made every word a song. "Benjy, me boy. Openin' the annex to your office again, I see."

"Hi, Paddy. It's been a while." Ben shook his hand. "Place looks good. Listen, this is my friend, David. He's a surgeon, so you'd best keep this rowdy crowd quiet while we're working or I'll have him graft your precious parts to your dart board."

Paddy O'Brien laughed and patted David on the shoulder. "Go ahead, if it'll make 'em work any better. Benjy here's the best there is at lawyerin' *and* at bummin' the check, so watch out. You boys go on about your business. I'll have two pints sent over—courtesy of the house."

"Make that one, Paddy," Ben said. His eyes met David's for an instant. "For me."

"One pint and one Coke comin' up," the little man said without batting an eye.

"So, assume you don't know anything, huh?" David was smiling.

"I was late this morning because I was talking to John Dockerty," Ben explained. "I didn't stay long enough to learn too much, but I will tell you he hasn't put this thing in a drawer. Please, humor me and just assume I know nothing, okay?"

"Okay." David shrugged. "How far back?"

"It's your story," Ben said.

"My story . . ." For a moment David's voice drifted away as pieces of events, bits of people flashed through his thoughts. "Began innocently enough, I guess." He shrugged. "Two older brothers. Decent, loving parents. White picket fence. The works. When I was about fourteen, the whole thing unraveled. Mother got cancer. It was in her brain before anyone even knew she had it. Even so, she lived for almost eight pitiful months. My dad owned a small store. Appliances. He ended up selling it so he could nurse mother—in between her hospitalizations, that is. A few weeks before she died,

196

he had a coronary. Dead before he hit the floor, they told me.

"I'm still not sure why, but from that time on all I wanted to be was a doctor. A surgeon, too. Even back then."

It had been years since David had sat and gone through the whole thing. He felt surprise at how easily the words came. "Is this the kind of stuff you want to know?" he asked. Ben nodded.

"My aunt and uncle took care of me until college, then I was essentially on my own. I was never any great genius, but I knew what I wanted and I clawed and scraped to get it. Scholarships and jobs all the way through medical school. I'd find what I thought was my limit, then I'd push myself past it. By the middle of my internship it was starting to get to me. I was sort of a wunderkind in the hospital, but outside I was coming unglued. Smoking too many cigarettes, sleepless nights, depressions that didn't want to go away. I fought the problem the only way I knew how. I pushed myself even harder at work. Looking back, I feel sure that if it weren't for a stop sign some kids had stolen, I would have gone off the deep end."

Ben startled at the strange association, then he smiled. "A woman?"

David nodded. "Ginny. Her car and mine smacked together at an intersection. The sign her way was missing. The irony is still really painful. I met her through an auto accident, then . . ." For the first time, words became difficult.

Ben raised a hand. "David, if this is too hard for you right now, we can do it another time. Sooner or later, though, they are things I have to know."

David toyed with his glass, then said, "Nope, I'm okay. Just stop me if it gets too maudlin—or too boring." Ben grinned and waved him on. "We got married six months later. She was an interior decorator. A rare and gentle person. My whole life changed just by having her there. Over the next four years there was magic in everything I did. The head of the surgical department at White Memorial asked me to stay on an extra year as chief resident. That job is about the only way a surgeon can get a staff appointment at WMH. So it was all there. For a little while at least.

"We had a little girl, Becky. I finished the residency and started in practice. Then there was the accident. I was driving. I . . . well, I guess the details aren't important. Becky and Ginny were dead. Just like that. I had scrapes and cuts, but really nothing. Except that in my own way I died too. I never really got back to work. I went from being a social drinker—almost a teetotaler— to being a drunk. One long bender. Thank God, I had enough sense to stay away from the operating room.

"I tried seeing minor cases at the office, though. That's when the pill cycle started. My version of changing seats on the *Titanic*. Ups to get started, downs to sleep. You know the story. At first my associates were tolerant. Helpful, even. One at a time, though, I managed to work over their faith brutally enough to drive them away. It went on like that for almost a year. In the end, I was removed from the staff. I didn't even know it had happened because I was lost in another bender."

"It's a bitch of a cycle to break out of," Ben said.

"Alone it is. That's for sure. Well, one morning I woke up in a cage. My last friend couldn't stand it anymore. Actually, it was a hospital he brought me to. Briggs Institute?" Ben nodded that he knew the place. "It turned out to be a great place for me, but not those first few weeks. No handle on the door. Bars on the windows. The whole scene . . . Are you still awake?"

Ben managed a short laugh. "I got snatches of your story from Lauren and Dockerty," he said, shaking his head, "but not like this. Getting locked up last night like you did . . ."

David shuddered. "I don't have classic claustrophobia. At least, I don't think I do. It's just that ever since those early weeks at Briggs the thought of being locked up or trapped in a small place gives me this awful, gnawing sensation in my gut, and sometimes a chill that . . ." He stopped and managed a smile. "It really does sound like claustrophobia, doesn't it?"

"I don't like labels," Ben said.

"Well, no matter." David swallowed against the dusty dryness in his mouth, then drank half a glass of water. "Let's see. . . . There's not much left to tell. Several months at the institute and I was ready to go back to medicine. But not to surgery. I spent almost three years as a G.P. in one of the inner-city clinics, then went back and repeated the last two years of my surgical residency. I made the staff at Boston Doctors nearly two years ago. It hasn't been easy, but things have been picking up. At least until a week ago they were."

"David, this is much more than I ever hoped you would be able to tell me at this point," Ben said. "I'm grateful to you for doing it. Makes my job much easier."

David looked at him quizzically. "I'm curious," he said. "Why is it you haven't asked me whether or not I'm guilty of murder?"

Ben grinned and set his chin in his hands. "I have, my friend. A dozen different times in a dozen different ways. You've hauled yourself too far for me not to move hell and earth to keep you from getting bloodied anymore."

"Thank you." David whispered the words. "Ben, when you talked to Lauren, did she . . . ? Well, what I mean is we had a fight and . . ."

"David, I don't want to get in the middle of anything like this, but I do have something to say. I've known Lauren Nichols for years. She's a bright, incredibly beautiful woman who, by choice or circumstance, has not had to face too much adversity in her life. She . . . ah . . . she asked me to give you this." He pulled out a pink envelope—Lauren's stationery—and handed it to David.

"Not much doubt what it says, is there?" David folded the envelope and stuffed it in his pocket as he spoke.

"No, I guess not," Ben answered softly. "Are you all right to go home? I mean, if you need a place to stay for the night . . ."

"No thanks, Ben. I'll be okay. Really."

"I'll call you tomorrow," Ben said.

"Tomorrow," David echoed.

The steely afternoon sky was threatening, but the steady rain of the past several days had let up. The walk from Paddy O'Brien's to his apartment was about two miles and, with nothing to hurry home for, David forced a leisurely pace, stopping once to wander through the old cemetery where Paul Revere was buried. He reasoned that the graveyard would be an appropriate place to read Lauren's letter.

He needn't, he decided afterward, have bothered. The note was what he expected—semiformal—one-third thank-you-for-everything and two-thirds just-doesn't-seem-like-things-will-work-out-for-us. "I guess she took me for better or for better," David said as he tore the note into tiny pieces and ceremoniously tossed the pink petals over an ancient grave. He was surprised at how little hurt he felt. Perhaps it was because the loss of the relationship was just another brick in the wall that was closing him off from life. Then, as he trudged toward Boston Common, he began to realize that he had rarely been totally at ease around Lauren. It was largely his fault for trying to force her into the spaces Ginny had filled in his life. Even before it had started, he had doomed the relationship with his hopes.

The advance unit of the rush home had begun filling the walkways of the Common. Haggard businessmen, giggling groups of secretaries, and stylish career women— all crossing the grassy park on the way from their day to their evening. For a while David amused himself by trying to make eye contact with each person who passed. In the first few minutes the score was zero connections for twenty-five or thirty tries. He looked down at the pavement wondering if perhaps there was something there he was simply missing. Finally he bet himself that if one absolute, unquestionable eye contact could be made before he arrived home, the nightmare that followed the death of Charlotte Thomas would soon end.

By the time he reached Commonwealth Avenue, a light, misty rain had started falling again. He squinted upward and picked up his pace.

A block ahead of him a thin, elderly gentleman sat on a bench reading the early evening edition of the *Boston Globe*. He gauged the rain with an outstretched palm, and decided there was time to finish the last paragraphs of the article about the mercy killing at Doctors Hospital.

It was on page three, a two column spread describing in some detail David's arrest and arraignment. Unable to find a picture of him in time, the court reporter had resurrected one of Ben Glass from the newspaper's morgue.

The dapper little man finished the article, folded his paper beneath his arm, and started his walk home. Lost in thoughts of the story he had just read, the man failed to notice David's attempt at eye contact.

CHAPTER XVI

"Chrissy, check the bathroom out. Does it look okay?" Lisa called out as she pulled on a skirt and zipped it up the side.

"Lisa, the bathroom looks fine. I told you, don't worry about the place. I've got an hour before she's due. That's plenty of time to clean up." Christine dropped a record into its jacket and replaced it on the shelf, taking a moment to straighten the row of albums. She had felt increasingly jittery and apprehensive since Dotty Dalrymple's late-afternoon call and now wished her roommates would head off for the evening so she could have some time to herself before the woman arrived.

The nursing director had given no hint as to why she wanted to stop over, but it was hard for Christine to believe the visit related to anything other than the death of Charlotte Thomas. She had given thought to calling the Regional Screening Committee for advice on how to handle the situation, but decided it was foolish when she wasn't at all certain of what, exactly, the situation was.

Lisa popped into the living room naked from the waist up. "Carole, bra or no bra for this guy?"

"He's a *blind* date, Lisa," Carole shouted from her room. "Just don't let him touch you and he'll never be able to tell whether you have one on or not."

"What do you think, Chrissy? Bra or no bra?"

Christine appraised her for a moment. "It's been a dull season," she said. "I think you should go for it." Her voice held far less cheer than she intended.

Lisa shrugged and slipped on a blouse. "You seem tight as a drum. Anything you want to talk about?"

"Believe me," Christine said, "if I had something to talk about, I would. I've never had Miss Dalrymple visit like this, that's all. She could want to promote me, she could want to fire me. I just have no idea. Listen, you guys have fun. I hope he's nice. And thanks for helping me tidy up the place."

"Ooh, wait a minute!" Lisa snapped her fingers and dashed to her room, talking as she ran. "These came earlier this afternoon. I guess while you were out." She returned with a vase of flowers. "I think they'll be the perfect touch over here by the window . . . no, on the table . . . no, I think perhaps over the . . ."

"Lisa, those are lovely. Who sent them?"

"The mantel. Yes. They're perfect for the mantel."

"Lisa, *who*?"

"Oh, they're from Arnold. Arnold Ringer, the office heartthrob. The fool believes these are a shortcut to my body. And you know what?"

"He's right!" The two of them said the words in unison, then laughed.

Christine was straightening the kitchen when the doorbell rang. Moments later, Carole and Lisa called their good-byes and she was alone.

Her solitude lasted a sigh and one pace to the living room and back. With a purely symbolic knock Ida Fine slipped in the back door. Folded under her arm was a copy of the evening *Globe*. She started talking before Christine could explain that her visit was ill-timed.

"So where are my other two? Gone for the evening? So why not you?" Ida seldom asked a question without answering it herself or at least following it with another, often unrelated query.

"They've got dates, Ida," Christine said, hoping that the flatness in her voice would get the message across without being offensive.

"And you, the prettiest of the three, have none? You're sick, is that it? You're not feeling well. I have some soup upstairs. I know you nurses are too sophisticated to believe in such things, but . . ."

"No, Ida, I'm fine." There was no stopping the woman short of a frontal assault. "I'm just busy tonight. My nursing supervisor is coming over soon, so I've got to get ready. Maybe tomorrow or even later tonight we can talk, okay?"

Ida slapped the newspaper on the table. "I'll bet it's about that doctor who murdered the woman at your hospital," she said. "A doctor yet. My mother always wanted me to marry a doctor, but no, I had to be pigheaded and marry my husband, God rest his soul . . ."

Christine's eyes widened and fixed on Ida, who just kept talking. ". . . not that Harry was a bad man, mind you. He was a very good man. But sometimes—"

"Ida, what are you talking about?"

"The murder. David somebody. Must be Jewish. No, he can't be Jewish. A Jewish boy murdering a patient? I can't—"

"Ida, please!" Christine's shout produced instant silence. "What on earth are you talking about?"

"It's right here. In the *Globe*. I thought you knew. Here, keep the paper. Just leave me the TV section. I forgot to get a *TV Guide* while I was at the market."

She talked on, but Christine no longer heard her. The newspaper rustled in her hands even after she had folded back the page. "SURGEON CHARGED WITH MERCY KILLING; RELEASED ON BAIL," she read.

204

Color flashed in her cheeks, then drained. "Oh, my God," she said softly as she read the account of David's arrest and arraignment. "Oh, my God . . ."

Ida's verbal onslaught continued for another minute, then slowed and finally stopped. Christine read the article one word at a time, unaware that her landlady's gaze was now riveted on her.

Ida brought a chair from the kitchen table and Christine sank down numbly as she read the last few lines.

> Reliable Globe sources report that Shelton filled prescriptions for large quantities of morphine on the day of Mrs. Thomas's death. Attorney Glass declined comment on the evidence, but reasserted his confidence in the innocence of his client. "When all the facts are in," he said, "I am sure the truth will be learned and my client will be vindicated." Dr. Shelton has been released on $100,000 bail. No date for trial has been set.

Ida rushed to the sink, wet a washcloth, and rubbed the cold compress over Christine's forehead. For almost a minute Christine made no move to stop her. Finally she nodded and gently pushed Ida's hand away.

"I guess you hadn't heard?" Ida said. "You know this David?" Miraculously, she stopped at two questions.

"Yes. I . . . know him," Christine said. David Shelton had been in and out of her thoughts since the day they'd first met on Four South. Nothing persistent or overwhelming—or even well defined—but he was there. Dockerty's inquiry had given her reason to talk about him with other nurses without seeming too obvious or interested.

Ida Fine rubbed her hands together anxiously. "Chrissy, your face is the color of my Swedish ivy. You want me to help you to bed or . . . or to call a doctor?"

Christine shook her head. "Ida, I'm all right. Really. But I have got to be alone for a while. Please?"

"Okay, I'm going. I'm going," Ida said. The pout invaded her voice more by reflex than by intention. "If you need me, I'm right upstairs. Also food, if you need food . . . keep the paper . . ." She was still talking as she backed out the door.

Christine read the article a second time, then wrote Ben Glass's name and law firm in her address book. Why had David purchased so much morphine? And on the day Charlotte died. A coincidence? Perhaps, but certainly not an easy one to accept. Maybe the hospital rumors were true this time. Maybe he does use drugs. Or deal them. Possibly both. But her sense of the man, however hazy, would not permit her to believe that was true.

She pressed her fingers against her temples as a dull, pulsing ache began accompanying each heartbeat. It really made no difference, she realized, why David had purchased morphine. She knew what she had done with the vials left her by The Sisterhood, and there was simply no way she could allow him to suffer for that. It had seemed so right, she thought. Damn it, it *was* right. Charlotte wanted it. The Committee approved. She hadn't acted alone. She closed her eyes tightly against the pulses, which had become hammers. Every tiny movement of her head made the pounding worse.

"Lie down," she told herself. "Find some aspirin, some Valium—something—and lie down." She blinked at the kitchen light, which had suddenly grown sun bright, then pulled herself to her feet. At that instant the doorbell rang.

She moved awkwardly to the stove. Tea, must make her some tea, she thought. The bell sounded again, more insistently.

With a groan Christine turned and raced through the hallway to the front door.

Dotty Dalrymple, wearing a purple overcoat, looked more imposing than usual. She smiled warmly from beneath a broad-brimmed purple rainhat and stepped inside. "This is wet," she said, holding her black umbrella like a baton. "Is there somewhere I can store it?" She seemed totally at ease.

The pounding in Christine's head began to recede as she set the umbrella by the door and hung up the tent-sized coat. "Tea," she said, forgetting to invite the woman in. "Would you like some tea?"

"Tea would be fine, Christine." Dalrymple's smile broadened as she motioned at the hallway. "In the living room?"

Christine calmed down a bit more. "Oh, I'm sorry, Miss Dalrymple," she said. "I didn't mean to be so impolite. Come in. I . . . I'm sorry for the mess the place is in but . . ."

"Nonsense." The director cut her off. "It's a lovely apartment. Please, Christine, relax. I promise not to bite you." She surveyed the living room briefly, selected an armless, upholstered chair across from the couch, and set herself down. "You mentioned tea?"

"Oh, yes, there's water on the stove. Let me heat it up."

"Lemon, if you have it," Dalrymple called out. "Otherwise plain."

"It'll only be a minute," Christine said, bustling about the kitchen. She bit into a biscuit from the only box she could find. "Damn," she hissed, spitting the stale cookie into the trash.

In the few minutes it took to arrange two cups of tea and some lemon slices on a tray, Christine singed her forearm and put a thin cut in the corner of one thumb. Two steps into the living room she froze, barely preventing the cups from toppling over. Dotty Dalrymple had a copy of the evening *Globe* unfolded on her lap.

"I assume from your reaction that you have read this evening's paper," Dalrymple said.

Christine closed her eyes and inhaled sharply. If her nursing director had made the connection between her and Charlotte, something was very wrong. Now she wished she had called The Sisterhood Screening Committee for advice. "I . . . my landlady showed it to me a little while ago," she stammered. "It's awful."

"Do you know Dr. Shelton well?" Dalrymple asked, motioning her to the couch.

"No, not really. We've barely even talked. I . . . I just met him for the first time last week." Too many words, she thought. What could she want?

"Do you know his background?"

His background? The question caught Christine off guard. Why would Dalrymple ask about that? Does she suspect? Was she trying to cover for her somehow? Christine decided to continue the verbal joust until the woman's purpose was clearer. "His background? Well, not much really. No more than some hospital rumors."

"The man is a known drug addict and probably an alcoholic," Dalrymple cut in bluntly. "Did you know that?" Christine was too shaken by the nursing director's statement to answer. After a moment the woman continued. "Several years ago he was removed from the staff at White Memorial. His appointment to the staff of our hospital was made over the loud protests of many of the other physicians. David Shelton is not a credit to his profession."

David's face formed in Christine's thoughts—gentle and intense, with kind, honest eyes. Dalrymple's words made no sense next to that picture. "I . . . I don't know what to say."

Dalrymple leaned forward in her chair and stared at her intently. "Obviously I am here sharing these facts with you for a reason." Her voice held a strange, mystical quality. "Christine, we are sisters, you and I. Sis-

208

ters." Christine gasped. "I wanted so much to tell you that afternoon on Four South, but our rules forbid it. I have been part of The Sisterhood of Life since my earliest days in nursing. In fact, I represent the Northeast on our board of directors."

"I never would have thought . . . what I mean is, I never suspected . . ."

Dalrymple laughed. "There are several thousand of us, Christine. All over the country. The very best nursing has to offer. Joined by ideals and our pledge to forward the cause of human dignity."

"Then you know about Charlotte?"

"Yes, my dear, I know. All the directors know—the New England Screening Committee knows—and, of course, Peggy knows. I am here representing all of them. I am here to help."

"Help me?"

"Yes."

Christine shook her head. "Who's going to help Dr. Shelton?" she asked sullenly.

"My dear, you don't seem to have understood what I said." Dalrymple leaned forward for emphasis. "The man is a . . ."

Christine cut her off with a raised hand and a finger to her lips. She stared toward the side of the house. Dalrymple looked at her quizzically, then followed the line of her sight to the spot.

"I heard something," Christine whispered. "Out there by the window."

Dalrymple cocked her head to one side and listened. "Nothing," she said softly.

Christine wasn't convinced. She tiptoed to the side of the window and peered out at the night. The driveway and as much of the street as she could see were quiet. She stood there pressed against the wall for several minutes. Still nothing. Finally, with a shrug, she pulled the blinds and returned to the couch. "There was a noise out there," she said. "Some kind of a thunk."

"Probably a cat," Dalrymple said.

"Probably." There was little certainty in her voice. Dalrymple sipped patiently at her tea, waiting for Christine's concentration to return enough to continue their discussion.

"I'm . . . I'm sorry," Christine said at last.

Dalrymple smiled. "I understand what you're going through, dear," she said. "We all do, even though a situation such as yours has never before arisen and probably never will again. Ours is not an easy task. Everywhere along the way there are choices to make, and few if any of them are painless." There was an edge in her voice that Christine found unsettling.

"Just what are you suggesting I do?" she asked.

"Why nothing, dear," Dalrymple said. "Nothing at all."

Christine stared at her with disbelief. "Miss Dalrymple, I can't let that man suffer for something I've done. I could never live with myself."

Dalrymple looked back impassively and shook her head. "I'm afraid, Christine, that many more would suffer if you made any attempt to clear him."

Foreboding tightened in Christine's gut. "Wh . . . what do you mean?"

"Peg—the woman you spoke to—is Peggy Donner. Almost forty years ago, she founded The Sisterhood of Life. She has dedicated her entire life to its growth."

"And?"

"Christine, she will not allow you or any other sister to be hurt for doing what is right. She fears that your exposure will sooner or later lead to the exposure of the entire movement."

"But that's not true!" Christine cried. "I would never disclose anything about . . ."

"Please. What matters is not what you think would

happen, but what Peggy thinks would happen. You see, before she would risk having the public learn of us through a sordid police investigation and sensationalist press, she will move to inform them herself." Dalrymple's expression was grave. "She has our tapes, Christine. All of them. If you move to go to the police, she has promised the board of directors that she will make them public in her own fashion. For several years now she has wanted to do so anyway. Only pressure from the rest of us has kept her in check. We did not feel it was time."

The throbbing in Christine's head began anew. "This . . . this can't be happening," she murmured. "It just can't."

"But it is, Christine. And the careers of all those in The Sisterhood hang by the thread that you hold. I'm not at all happy with the situation, despite my personal dislike for degenerate physicians such as Dr. Shelton. However, you must believe me, as one who has known Peggy for many years. She will do it."

Christine could only shake her head.

"We would like you to take a vacation from the hospital," Dalrymple continued softly. "I'll have no trouble granting you a leave for, say, three or four weeks. When you return, a shift supervisor's slot will be waiting for you. Perhaps Greece? The islands are beautiful this time of year. A month in the sun for you and the whole matter will have blown over."

"I . . . I don't think I could do that."

"For all our sakes, Christine, you must. Please believe me, Peggy's threat is not an idle one. With our number and the positive image she would project, she feels certain that The Sisterhood can now withstand exposure. If you go to the authorities, nothing, no one will be able to stop her. She may even be right, but I for one do not wish to risk my career and life on that chance."

211

"There would be chaos," Christine said.

"At least."

"I need time. Some time to think."

"The sooner you take your trip, the better," Dalrymple said. "I promise that getting away from this city will make the whole process much easier on you." She stood up, withdrew an envelope from her purse, and handed it to Christine. "This should help you do what you must. Please call me if I can be of any further help. It is a difficult situation, Christine, having to hurt one to avoid hurting many. But the choice is clear."

Christine followed her to the hallway and stood numbly to one side as she put on her coat. "Your sisters," Dalrymple said, "all of us, are grateful for what you are doing." She reached out and squeezed Christine's hand, then turned and let herself out.

The blue sedan, parked in an islet of darkness between two streetlights, was virtually invisible. Slouched behind the wheel, Leonard Vincent kept his attention fixed on the house as he struggled to catch his breath. The close call beneath the window and his dash to the car had left him winded and, despite the chill night air, soaked with sweat. On his lap his right hand moved in continuous circles, working the blade of a knife over a whetstone with the loving strokes of a concert violinist. The blade was eight inches long, tapered and slightly curved at the tip. The handle, carved bone, was nearly lost in his thick fist. The knife was Leonard Vincent's pride—the perfect instrument for close work.

The front door opened. Vincent snickered at the sight of the huge woman maneuvering herself down the concrete front steps. As she crossed the street to her car, he amused himself by planning the description he would use in his report. "At precisely five thirty a blimp floated into the house." Vincent's sallow face bunched in a mirthless grin. "She rolled out of the house and bounced down the stairs to her car. At precisely six fifteen she started getting behind the wheel. At six thirty she made it."

Distracted by his own wit, Vincent was slow to react when the woman made a sudden U-turn and came toward him. An instant before her headlights flashed by, he dove across the front seat, striking his forehead on the passenger door handle. He cursed the handle, then the door, and then the fat bitch who had made him hit it. But mostly he cursed himself for taking a job without knowing exactly who was hiring him or even what he was expected to do.

It had started with a call from a bartender friend. "Leonard," he had said, "I think I may have something for you. There's this broad in here askin' me if I know of anyone who's interested in makin' some big bucks. She says that whoever it is will have to be able to keep his mouth shut and do what he's told. I tried to find out some details, but she just gives me this fucking look, shoves a fifty across the counter, and says that there'll be more if I can get her someone who asks less questions than I do. You interested? I'll tell you, Leonard, the broad's weird, but I think she's on the level. Also, she's got great tits."

Right away, Vincent hadn't liked her or the setup. The name she had given him, Hyacinth, was a phony, he was sure of that. But no matter. Except for setting up the job, all she would do is deliver the money.

So he had ended up with twenty-five hundred bucks up front, a phone number, and a name—Dahlia. Another phony.

Vincent rubbed at the egg that had started forming over his left eye. He cursed Dahlia, who was responsible for his sitting out in a hurricane, bumping his head on a goddamn door. "Face it, Leonard," he told himself, "you've really hit bottom this time, no matter how good the fucking money is."

213

He watched the house until he was reasonably sure Christine Beall was not coming out, then he shoved the knife into a hand-tooled leather case and drove around the corner to a phone booth. A woman answered on the second ring.

"Yes?"

"This is Leonard." His voice was a toneless rasp.

"Yes?"

"You wanted a report on everyone who talks to this Christine."

"And?"

"Well, a big fat woman just left. She got here about forty-five minutes ago."

"Mr. Vincent, your instructions were to call as soon as she met with someone, not to wait until they had left."

"Hey, you don't sound like Dahlia. Is this Dahlia?"

"Mr. Vincent, please. When Hyacinth paid you, she told you to call this number and report. Now you will either do exactly as instructed or I promise you trouble. Big trouble. Is that clear?"

The threat was effective. Leonard Vincent feared nothing that he could see, but an icy, disembodied voice was something else. He cursed himself again for taking the job. "Yeah, it's clear," he said.

"All right. How long did you watch the house after the woman left?"

"Ten, fifteen minutes. I don't know exactly. Long enough, though. She's staying put."

"Very well. Return to your post, please."

"What about sleep?"

"You are being paid, and paid well, to watch that woman and report on her movements, Mr. Vincent. Now return to your post. And remember, we wish to know the minute she talks with anyone—not after they have already left. Call this number at two o'clock, and we shall discuss your sleep. Oh, one last thing. Before

214

she paid your advance money, the woman who hired you did some checking around. She learned of your tendency to hurt people, sometimes without provocation. No one is to be touched without our say-so. Is *that* clear?"

Vincent shrugged. "Like you said, it's your money." He hung up the phone, stared at it for a moment, then spat on the receiver. A reflex check of the coin return and he drove back to watch the house.

The only lights in the apartment shone through the blinds of the living room window. Every few minutes Christine's silhouette appeared, then vanished. Leonard Vincent picked up his whetstone and began clucking a one-note melody as he withdrew another knife from the glove compartment.

Christine had been unable to sit since Dotty Dalrymple's departure. She paced from room to room, tapping the unopened envelope against her palm. Suddenly she looked down, as if noticing it for the first time. Then she tore it open.

Inside were five neatly banded packets of hundred dollar bills—ten in each.

"The choice is clear," she said out loud, testing her nursing director's words. Again the image of David's face formed in her mind. She stared at the packets, then threw them on her bureau.

"The choice *is* clear," she whispered.

CHAPTER XVII

On Thursday, the ninth of October, as on the previous three days, Boston forecasters predicted an end to the tenacious low pressure system and the rain. For the fourth straight day, they were wrong.

In Huddleston, New Hampshire, ninety minutes north of the city, a one-hundred-fifty-year-old covered bridge washed away before Crystal Brook—little more than a trickle in August.

Accidents on frenetic Route 128, never a rarity, more than tripled.

On David Shelton, however, as on most in the area, the effects of the unrelenting downpour were even more insidious. It was more than a mile from his apartment to the financial district and the law offices of Wellman, MacConnell, Enright, and Glass. Irritable and frustrated by inactivity, he chose to defy the storm and walk to his appointment with Ben. Within a block he was soaked beyond the consideration of turning back. "Wet is wet," he pronounced testily, trudging head down into the wind.

The suite of offices occupied most of the twenty-third floor of a mirror-glass building whose name and address were both One Bay State Square. "No wonder he charges $10,000," David muttered as he approached the reception area. Three women were handling traffic with practiced calm in a space nearly as big as David's whole office.

He looked and felt like a drowned rodent. For a moment he thought of asking the severe receptionist for some towels and a change of clothes, but nothing in her expression encouraged that kind of frivolity. "Mr. Glass," he said meekly, "I have an appointment with Mr. Glass?" The woman, struggling to mask her amusement, motioned him to a bank of leather easy chairs. Discreet chimes sounded, signaling Ben.

Whatever the goals of the interior decorators, David decided, making clients who looked like drowned rodents feel less conspicuous was not one of them. The sterile opulence featured thick gold carpeting, original oils on the walls, and a jungle of bamboo palms and huge ferns. A well-stocked library was prominently displayed behind glass walls. Even more impressive to him was the fact that several people were actually using it.

Ben popped around a corner, smiled at David's appearance, then extended both hands. "Either you walked over or this is autumn's answer to the Blizzard of Seventy-eight," he said.

"Both." He took the lawyer's hands in his and squeezed them tightly. Ben was a thin break in the clouds—an island in the madness and confusion.

"Had lunch yet?" he asked as they walked to his office.

"Yesterday. But please, nothing for me. You go ahead if you want."

"Meatloaf à la Amy?" He produced a brown bag from his desk. "There's plenty here. You sure?"

David shook his head. "No thanks. Really." He looked around the room. Ben's cluttered office was in sharp contrast to the rest of the austere suite. Books and

217

journals were everywhere, many of them open or marked with folded sheets of legal paper. The walls were overhung with framed photographs and pen-and-ink drawings. "Your partners let you get away with all this earthiness?" he asked, gesturing at the disarray.

"They think I'm camp." Ben grinned. "One of my partners once called my office 'funky.' A thousand a month just for this room and he calls it funky." He took a bite of sandwich, then spoke around chews. "Even soaked, you look better than yesterday. Are you holding up all right?"

David shrugged. "I got suspended from the staff at the hospital," he said flatly.

"What?"

"Suspended. I had a visit this morning from Dr. Armstrong—she's the chief of staff and the only one at that place who really seems to give a shit about what happens to me. Anyhow, she called and asked to stop by. I knew what she had to say and suggested she tell me over the phone, but she insisted on doing it in person. That's the kind of woman she is."

"So?"

"So, last night the executive committee voted, over her objection, to ask me to voluntarily suspend my staff and O.R. privileges until this whole business is cleared up."

Ben shook his head. "Not ones to waste any time, this executive committee of yours."

"According to Dr. Armstrong, Wallace Huttner, the chief of surgery, led the push. He's also helping the murdered woman's husband put together a malpractice case against me. If I'm found guilty, they want to be ready to move right in and sue. Dr. Armstrong said they made my suspension voluntary as a favor to me—to keep me from having an enforced suspension on my record. I think they did it because it's less paperwork for them."

"Shit," Ben muttered.

"It's probably just as well. Even before I was arrested the place became instant iceberg the minute I set foot in the door. It's all crazy. I . . . I don't know what the hell to do. I'd fight back if I had even a faint idea of who or what I was fighting, but . . ."

"Hey, easy," Ben urged. "The fight's just starting. For now *I'll* throw the punches, but you'll get your chance. This afternoon we share ideas about who and why. Tomorrow we'll start planning what to do. Somewhere out there is an answer. Just be patient and don't do anything rash or crazy. We'll find it."

David nodded and managed a tense smile. "Hey, I almost forgot this." He pulled a soggy envelope from his pants pocket. "Good thing pencil doesn't run," he said, passing it over. "Dr. Armstrong didn't want me to get into any more trouble at the hospital, so in exchange for my promise to stay put, she did some checking for me. There are four names on the sheet inside. She got them from the hospital personnel computer. Two orderlies with prison records, a nurse with a drug-use history, and another nurse who is pressuring the hospital to post a Patient's Bill of Rights. I don't know any of them. It's not much, but Dr. Armstrong said she would get the names to Lieutenant Dockerty."

Ben cut him off. "She already has, David."

"What?"

"The lieutenant called a short time ago. I talked to him for half an hour. He wants you—and Dr. Armstrong— to quit playing Holmes and Watson and let him do his work."

"Do his work?" David's voice was incredulous. "Ben, the man has spent almost a week tar-and-feathering me. He's the other side. He's one we should be fighting."

Ben shook his head. "No, pal, he's not," he said firmly. "He's a damn good cop. I've known him for as long as I've been in practice. Whether you believe it or not, he doesn't want to see you fall."

219

"Then why the fuck did he arrest me?"

"Had to." Ben shrugged. "Pressure from all sides and a ton of circumstantial evidence. Motive, opportunity, weapon—you know all that."

David clenched his fists. "I also know that I didn't kill that woman," he said.

"Well, John Dockerty's not one hundred percent convinced you did either. Otherwise he wouldn't be trying to work on Marcus Quigg, the pharmacist who—"

"Dockerty told me who he is," David broke in. "But, Ben, I never met the man. Why would he want to do this to me?"

"One of the big three," Ben said. "Vengeance, fear, money."

David shook his head. "Ben, until Dockerty said his name, I'm sure I never heard it before. Marcus Quigg isn't exactly John Jones, you know. If I took care of a Quigg . . . no, vengeance doesn't make any sense at all."

"Unless it was a sister or daughter," Ben said. "Different name."

"I guess." David slapped the desk in exasperation. "But there are just too many unpredictable events to believe anyone could have planned to frame me. Way too many."

"David, right now it can't do anything but harm to try and overthink this thing. There simply isn't enough information . . . yet." Ben paused, twisting his wedding band as he searched for words. "David," he said finally, "I wasn't going to bring this up today, but maybe it's best that I do. I told you yesterday that I wanted complete honesty from you, yes?" David nodded. "You didn't mention to me that you were once accused of deliberately overmedicating a cancer patient of yours. Is that true?"

David stiffened. Disbelief widened his eyes. "Ben, I . . . this is crazy," he stammered. "That was at least nine years ago. I was completely exonerated. I . . . how do you know about it?"

"Lieutenant Dockerty knows. I don't know who, but someone tipped him off."

"The nurse, it must have been that goddamn nurse. How in the hell . . . ?"

"What happened?"

"It was nothing. Really. I ordered pain medicine on a dying old lady—every four hours as needed. And believe me, she had plenty of pain. Well, I found that this one nurse was too damn lazy to check on whether she needed it. So I changed the order to every two hours, lowered the dose, and took out the 'as needed' part so the woman had to receive it. The next day the nurse reported me. There was an inquiry and I think *she* ended up getting censured."

"Well, now it seems she's getting even," Ben said. "Listen, David, you must tell me everything. No matter how insignificant it might seem to you. Everything. This nurse coming forward after nine years may be yet another coincidence. There *was* the article in last night's paper. But if someone put her up to it, we've got even more problems than we realized. And maybe, just maybe, you have the answer inside you without even knowing it."

"Maybe . . ." David's voice drifted off. For a few seconds he squinted and scratched above one ear.

"What? What is it? Do you remember something?"

David shook his head. "I could swear something popped in and out of my mind. Something someone said about Charlotte Thomas. I . . ." He shrugged. "Whatever it was—*if* it was—is gone."

"Well, go home and take it easy, pal. We'll meet again tomorrow. Same time?"

"Same time," David said weakly.

"Say, listen, if you're free tomorrow night, why don't you plan on coming here at four. We can talk, then you can come home and have dinner with us. You can meet Amy and the kids and get a good meal in the bargain. She'd love to get to know you. Would even if I hadn't told her you were paying for little Barry's orthodontia."

"Sounds fine," David said with little enthusiasm.

"Do you good," Ben added. "Besides, Amy has this sister . . ." He smiled, then suddenly the two of them were laughing. David couldn't remember the last time he had.

"You're losing it, Shelton," David said as he paced through the apartment. "You're losing it and you know it." The two hours following his departure from Ben's office had seemed like ten.

Outside, the steady rain continued, punctuated now and then by the muted timpani of distant thunder. One minute the three rooms felt like an empty coliseum, the next like a cage. It was becoming harder and harder to sit, more and more difficult to concentrate—to focus in on anything. Call someone, he thought. Call someone or else ignore the rain and go run. But stop pacing. He picked up his running shoes and stepped to the window. Sheets of rain blurred the somber afternoon sky. Then, as if in warning, a lightning flash colored the room an eerie blue-white. Seconds later, a soft rumble crescendoed and exploded, reverberating through the apartment. He threw the shoes in his closet.

This is how it felt; he recognized it. After the accident. This is how it all started. Still the restlessness increased.

Is there anything in the medicine chest? Didn't Lauren always keep something here for her headaches? Just in case the pacing won't stop. In case the loneliness gets too bad. You don't need anything, but just in case. In case the sleep doesn't come. In case the night won't end.

He paced from one end of the hall to the other, then

back. Each time he paused by the bathroom door. Just in case . . .

All at once he was there, reaching for the mirrored door of the medicine chest. Reaching, he suddenly realized, toward himself. He froze as his outstretched hand touched its reflection. His eyes, glazed with fear and isolation, locked on themselves and held. A minute passed. Then another. Gradually, the trembling in his lips began to subside. His breathing slowed and deepened. "You're not alone," he told himself softly. "You have a friend who has learned over eight hard years to love you—no matter what. You have yourself. Open that door, touch one fucking pill, and lose him. All those years, and he'll be just . . . gone. Then you *will* be alone."

His hand dropped away from the mirror. Resolve tightened across his face, then pulled at the corners of his mouth until he was smiling. He nodded at himself— once, then again. Faster and faster. He saw the strength, the determination grow in his eyes.

"You're not alone," he said as he turned from the mirror and walked to the living room. "You're not alone," he said again as he stretched out on the sofa. "You're not . . ."

Twenty minutes later, when the phone rang, David was still on the sofa. He skimmed over the last few lines of the Frost poem he was reading, then rolled over and picked up the receiver.

"David, I was afraid you hadn't gotten home yet." It was Ben.

"Oh, no, I'm here," David said. He smiled, then added, "I'm very much here."

"Well, enjoy your free time while you have it," Ben said excitedly, "because I think within a day or two you'll be back to work."

David felt an instant surge. "Ben, what's happened? Talk slowly so it registers."

"I just received a call, David, from a nurse at your hospital. She said that she can positively clear you of the murder of Charlotte Thomas. I'm meeting her at a coffee shop in a couple of hours. I think she's for real, pal, and if I'm right, the nightmare's over."

David glanced down the hall in the direction of the bathroom. "Thank God," he said, half to the phone and half to himself. "Ben, can I come? Shouldn't I be there?"

"Until I know what this woman has to say, I don't want you involved. Tell you what. Expect me at your place at nine—no, make that nine thirty—tonight. I'll fill you in then. With luck, our dinner tomorrow night will turn out to be a celebration."

"That would be wonderful," David said wistfully. "Tell me, who's the nurse?"

"Oh, she said she's met you. Her name's Beall. Christine Beall."

At the mention of her name David felt another momentary surge. "Ben, that's what I was trying to think of in your office. Remember? When something popped in and out of my head?"

"I remember."

"Well it was something *she* said. Christine Beall. Right after I shot my mouth off to Charlotte's husband. She whispered to me that she was proud of the way I stood up to Huttner, and . . . and then she said, 'Don't worry. Things have a way of working out.' Then all of a sudden she was gone. Ben, do you think . . . ?"

"Listen, pal, do us both a favor if you can. Try not to project. A few hours, then we'll know. Okay?"

"Okay," David said. "But you know I will anyway, don't you?"

"Yeah, I know," Ben said. "Nine thirty."

"Right." David checked his watch. "Will you at least

synchronize with me so I don't go too nuts waiting for you?"

Ben laughed. "Five of five, pal. I have five of five."

"Four fifty-five it is," David sang. He set down the receiver.

His elation was brief. Over the past few days, conscious thoughts of Christine had been submerged in the nightmare. At that moment David realized they had never been far from the surface.

"It wasn't you, was it?" he said softly. "You know who did it, but it wasn't you."

His concern for Christine faded quickly as the impact of Ben's call settled in. He clenched his fists and pumped them up and down. A grin spread over his face, then a giggle, then a laugh. He rushed to his record collection. Seconds later he was bouncing through the living room, throwing jabs and uppercuts at the air. The music from *Rocky* filled the apartment.

Fanfare still in his ears, he walked down the hall and into the bathroom. He stood before the medicine cabinet and looked at himself. "You made it, buddy," he said to his reflection. "Stronger than ever now. I'm proud of you. Really."

Out of curiosity, not need, he reached up and pulled open the door.

The shelves were empty.

A shower and long-overdue letters to his brothers killed an hour and a half. Feasting on spaghetti with Ragu sauce did in another thirty minutes. The seven o'clock news made it two hours until Ben.

David paced impatiently for a while, then pulled his chess set from the closet along with his copy of *Chess Openings Made Simple*. Within a short time he gave up. Renewed thoughts of Christine made it impossible to concentrate. Somehow, in the short time they had talked, in their brief contacts, she had touched him deeply. There was a disarming, innocent intensity about her—an energy he had seldom seen survive the years in medical or nursing school. Then, too, there were her eyes—wide and warm, inviting and exploring one moment, flashing with anger the next. More and more, he found himself hoping, even praying, that she had no direct involvement in the death of Charlotte Thomas. By nine o'clock he had convinced himself that there was no way she could have.

For a time he entertained himself by measuring what he knew of the woman against Lauren. Quickly he realized that, as typically happened, he was attributing qualities to Christine that he *wanted* to be there. "When are you going to learn, Shelton?" He chastised himself loudly, then returned to the chessboard.

By nine fifteen he was pacing again. Once he heard the elevator gears engage and raced out into the hall. Then he remembered that he would have to buzz Ben through the downstairs foyer door. Still, he waited out there just in case. The elevator stopped one floor below.

He returned to the apartment and spent five minutes playing out a conversation with Wallace Huttner in which the surgical chief apologized for jumping to such misguided conclusions and suggested that they might explore the possibilities of a partnership. David practiced a refusal speech, then, in case Huttner was truly contrite, one of acceptance.

At precisely nine thirty the downstairs buzzer sounded. David leaped to the intercom.

"Yes?"

"David, it's me." The excitement in Ben's voice was apparent despite the barely functional intercom. "The woman is for real. Sad, but very much for real. It's over, pal, it's over."

The word *sad* stood out from all the others. "Come on up," David said as he pressed the door release. His voice held surprisingly little enthusiasm.

226

Thirty seconds later the elevator clattered into use. Shit, David thought, it *was* her. He stood in the open doorway and listened to the groaning cables. Turning his nightmare over to Christine Beall was not the way he had wanted it to end, no matter what her actions had put him through. He was halfway to the elevator when the car light appeared in the diamond-shaped window of the outside door. A second later, the car crunched to a halt. The automatic inside gate rattled open.

David stopped several feet away and waited for Ben. Five seconds passed. Then another five. He took a tentative step forward. The door remained closed. Finally he peered through the grimy window. Ben stood to one side, leaning calmly against the wall.

"Hey, what's going on?" David asked, swinging open the heavy door. The lawyer's eyes stared at him, moist and vacant. His face was bone white. Suddenly the corners of his mouth crinkled upward in a half-smile.

"Ben, not funny," David said. "Now cut the crap and come on out of there. I wanna hear."

Ben's lips parted as he took a single step forward. Crimson gushed from his mouth and down his chin. David caught him halfway to the floor. The back of Ben's tan raincoat was an expanding circle of blood. Protruding from the center was the carved white handle of a knife.

Sticky, warm life poured over David's hands and clothes as he dragged his friend from the elevator.

"Help!" he screamed. "Someone, please help me!"

He pulled the knife free and threw it on the carpet, then rolled Ben's body face up. The lawyer's dark eyes stared unblinkingly at the ceiling. David checked for a carotid pulse, but knew that the blood, now oozing from one corner of Ben's mouth, was the sign of a fatal wound to the heart or a main artery.

"Please help." David's plea was a whimper. "Please?"

The stairway door at the far end of the hall burst open. Leonard Vincent stood there, his massive frame darkened by the light behind him. Almost casually, he reached to his waistband and withdrew a revolver. The ugly silhouette of a silencer protruded from one end.

"It's your turn, Dr. Shelton," Vincent rasped, certain he was facing the man Dahlia had described. He had followed Christine Beall to a coffee shop and recognized the criminal lawyer with whom she was meeting. Dahlia's response to his call was immediate: Glass first, then Shelton, and later the girl. Now, thanks to the lawyer, he could handle the first two almost at once.

David stumbled backward and tried to straighten up, but his hand, covered with blood, slid off the wall and he spun to the carpet. Inches away was the knife. He grabbed it by the tip and hurled it at the advancing figure. It fell two yards short. Vincent picked it up and calmly wiped the blade on his pants. He was less than fifty feet away. Between them, Ben's lifeless body stretched across the corridor. Light from an overhead bulb caught the huge man's face. He was smiling. His smile broadened as he raised the silenced revolver.

David scrambled backward, his mouth open in a soundless scream. His mind registered a spark from the tip of the silencer at the instant the doorjamb beside his ear exploded.

He dove head first into his apartment, flailing with his feet to close the solid wood door. The latch clicked shut moments before a soft crunch and the instantaneous appearance of two dime-sized holes by the knob.

David looked wildly about, then clawed himself upright. He raced to the living room. The fire escape! Opening the window, he looked down at his stockinged feet. For a moment he thought about the closet and his running shoes. No chance, he decided. With a groan of resignation, he stepped out onto the metal landing. There was a crash from inside the apartment as the front door burst open. An instant later David was racing down toward the alley, four flights below.

The night was tar black and cold. The metal steps, slippery in the driving downpour, hurt his feet, but the discomfort barely registered. Just beyond the third floor, his heel caught the edge of a step and shot out from under him. He fell hard, tumbling down half a flight. Several inches of skin ripped from his right forearm. Above him, there was a loud clank as Leonard Vincent stepped onto the fourth-floor landing. At that moment David had the absurd notion that he should have opened the window to the fire escape, then hidden in the closet.

I'll bet it would've worked, he thought, as he scrambled, panting, toward the second-floor landing. He slipped again, electricity pulsing up his spine as he slid the final few stairs. Through the metal slats overhead, he saw the man, a faint dark shadow moving against the night sky.

On his hands and knees, David struggled to release the ladder from the second-floor landing to the alley. Through his soaked shirt needles of rain stung his back. The metal slats dug into his knees. The ladder release would not budge.

With a glance above him, David grabbed the side of the landing and rolled off. He hung there for a moment, trying to judge the distance to the pavement, then dropped. He felt and heard the crunch in his left ankle as he hit. The leg gave way instantly. He screamed, then bit down on the edge of a finger so hard that he drew blood.

Lying on the wet pavement, he heard the clanging footsteps and grunting breaths of the man overhead. The killer was nearing the second landing.

David stumbled to one foot, then hesitated. If the ankle were sprained, there would be discomfort, but he could move. If it was broken, he was about to die.

Teeth clenched, he set his left foot down. Pain seared through the ankle, but it held—once, then again and again. Suddenly he was running.

At the end of the alley he looked back. The man had lowered the ladder and was calmly stepping off the bottom rung.

Clarendon Street was nearly deserted. David paused uncertainly, then decided to try for heavily trafficked Boylston Street. At that instant he saw a figure half a block from him walking in the opposite direction toward the river. Instinctively he ran that way. His gait was awkward. Every other stride was agony. Still, he closed on the figure.

"Help," he called out. "Please help." His cry was instantly swallowed by the night storm. "Please help me."

He was ten feet away when the figure lurched around to face him. It was an old man—toothless, unshaven, and drunk. Water dripped from the brim of his tattered hat. David started to speak, but could only shake his head. Gasping, he supported himself against a parked car. Without sound or warning, the rear window of the car shattered. David spun around. Through the gloom and the rain he saw his pursuer's shadow, down on one knee in position to fire once more. He was running when flame spit from the silencer. Running when the bullet meant for him slammed into the old man, spinning him to the pavement.

He pushed himself forward, through the pain and the downpour. Pushed himself harder than ever in his life. His heels slammed down on small stones, sending dagger thrusts up each leg. Still he ran—across Marlborough Street, across Beacon Street, and on toward the river. It was his route, his run—the path he had jogged so many promising sunlit mornings. Now he was running from his death. Behind him, the huge killer gained ground with every stride.

Traffic on Storrow Drive was light. David splashed across without slowing down—onto the stone footbridge and over the reflecting basin. Ahead of him, the lights of Cambridge shimmered through the rain and danced on the pitch-black Charles.

Double back, he thought. Double back and help Ben. Maybe he needs you. Maybe he's not really dead. For God's sake, *do something*.

He risked a glance over his shoulder. The man, delayed by several cars on Storrow Drive, had lost some ground, but not enough. David knew the chase was almost over. With fear his only rhythm and flailing strides, he was near collapse. He scanned the deserted esplanade for somewhere to hide. The killer was too close. His only hope was the river. Stones along the bank tore away what was left of his socks as he scrambled over them and plunged into the frigid oily water.

He had little capacity left for more pain, yet icy stilettos found what places remained and bore in. Behind him, Leonard Vincent crossed the footbridge and neared the bank. As deeply as he could manage, David sucked in air and dropped below the surface. He was twenty feet from shore, pushing himself along the muddy bottom. His clothes became leaden, at first helping him stay down, then threatening to hold him there. He broke once for air. Then again. Still he drove himself. The water stung his eyes and made it impossible to see. Its taste, acrid and repugnant despite years of waste- and pollution-control, filled his nose and mouth.

All at once his head struck something solid. Dazed and near blind, he explored the obstacle with his hands. It was a dock—a floating wooden **T**, laid on the river to tether some of the dozens of small sailboats that spent the warm months darting over reflections of the city.

For a minute, two, all was silent save for the spattering of rain on the dock and on the river. David crouched by the dock in four feet of water, rubbing at the silt in his eyes. His feet and legs were numb. Then he heard footsteps—careful, measured thumps. The killer was on the dock! David pressed the side of his face against the coarse slimy wood. The footsteps grew louder, closer. He slid his hand under the dock. Did it break water? Was there room enough to breathe? If he ducked under he might be trapped without air. If he didn't . . .

He inhaled slowly, deeply, realizing the breath might be his last. Eyes closed tightly, he pulled himself beneath the dock. His head immediately hit wood. Terror shot through him. He was trapped, his lungs near empty. Pawing desperately overhead, his hands struck the side of a beam. An undersupport! He pushed to one side and instantly his face popped free of the water. There were four inches of air. A thin smile tightened across his lips, then vanished. The footsteps were directly over his face. Through the narrow slits between timbers he could have touched the bottoms of the man's shoes, now inches from his eyes. The pacing stopped. David bent his neck back as far as he could and pressed his forehead against the bottom of the dock. Through pursed lips, he sucked in air slowly, soundlessly.

Above his face, the shoes scraped, first one way and then another, as Vincent scanned the river. Then, with agonizing slowness, the man headed toward the other arm of the T.

In the icy water David began to shake. He clenched down with all his strength to keep from chattering and wedged himself more tightly between the river bottom and the dock. All feeling from his neck down was gone. The footsteps receded further and further, then disappeared. The closed space began to exert its own ghastly terror. Is he just sitting up there? David wondered. Sitting and waiting? How long? *How much longer can I stay like this?*

He counted. To one hundred, then back to zero. He sang songs to himself—silly little songs from his childhood. Gradually, inexorably, he lost control over the soft staccato of his teeth. Still he did not move. "... This old man he played two, he played knick-knack on my shoe ..." "... I knew a man with seven wives and seven cats and seven lives ..." "... Red Sox, White Sox, Yankees, Dodgers, Phillies, Pirates ..."

The chill reached deep inside him. He could no longer stop the shaking. How long had it been? His legs seemed paralyzed. Would they even move? "... Red Rover, Red Rover, come over, come over ..." "... I'll bet you can't catch me, betcha can't betcha can't ..."

"I'll bet ... I'll bet ... I'll bet I'm going to die."

CHAPTER XVIII

Joey Rosetti closed his eyes and breathed in the fragrance of Terry's excitement. That scent, her taste, the way her dark nipples grew firm beneath his hand—even after twelve years the sensations were as fresh and arousing as they were warm and comfortable.

He rubbed his cheeks against the silky skin between her thighs, then drew his tongue upward between her moist folds.

"It's good, Joey So good," Terry moaned, drawing his face more tightly against her. She smiled down at him and dug her fingers through the jet-black waves of his hair.

Shuddering, she brought his mouth to hers. Her heels slid around his body as the hunger in their kiss grew. He entered her with slow, deepening thrusts.

"Joey, I love you," Terry whispered. "I love you so much."

She sucked on his lips and caressed the fold between his buttocks. The heavy muscles tensed as her fingers worked deeper.

Joey's thrusts grew quicker, more forceful. It would be soon, they knew, for both of them.

Suddenly, the telephone on the bedside table began ringing. "No," Terry groaned. "Let it ring." But already she felt a let-up in Joey's intensity. "Let it ring," she begged again. Six times, seven—the intrusive jangling was not going to stop. The pressure inside her lessened. An eighth ring, then a ninth.

"Damn," Joey snarled, popping free of her as he rolled over. "This better not be a fucking wrong number." He mumbled a greeting, listened for half a minute, then said the single word, "Where?" A moment later, he kicked the covers off and scrambled out of bed.

"Terry, it's the doc," he said. "Doc Shelton. He's hurt and he needs help." He flicked on the bedside light and raced to the closet.

"I'm coming with you," Terry demanded, pulling herself upright.

"No, honey. Please." He held up a hand. "He's like crazy. I could barely understand him. But he did say there was trouble. I don't want you there. Call the tavern. See if Rudy Fisher's still working. If he is, tell him to get his ass over to the esplanade by the Charles River. The Hatch Shell. I'll meet him there."

"Joey, can't you call someone else? You know how I feel about that m—"

"Look, I don't have time to debate. Rudy's been with me longer than y—for a long time. If there's trouble, I want him around."

Twelve years had taught Terry the uselessness of arguing with her husband over such matters. Still, his insistence on Rudy Fisher, a giant who doted on violence, frightened her. "Joey, please," she urged. "Just be careful. No rough stuff. Please promise me. If he's hurt, then just get him to a hospital and come home."

"Baby, the man saved my life," he said, pulling on a pair of pants. "Whatever he needs from me he gets."

"But you promised . . ."

"Listen," Joey snapped, "I'll be careful. Don't worry." He forced a more relaxed tone. "I'm a businessman now, you know that. If he's hurt, I'll get him to the hospital. Don't worry. Just do what I asked you to." He grabbed a shirt from the closet.

Terry sat on the edge of the bed, admiring him as he dressed. At forty-two he still had the cleanly chiseled features and sinewy body of a matinee idol. There was a calm, unflappable air about him that gave no hint of the deadly situations he had survived in his life. Reminders were there, though, in the burgundy scars that criss-crossed his abdomen. One, an eighteen-inch crescent around his left flank, was a memento from his days as a youth gang leader in Boston's North End. Intersecting it just above his navel was another scar—ten years old—the result of a gunshot wound sustained while thwarting a holdup at the Northside.

Rosetti had been one of David's first private patients at White Memorial—a twelve-hour procedure that some of the operating room staff still spoke of reverently. During Joey's convalescence, a friendship had developed between the two men.

"Terry, will you stop gawking and make that call," Joey said tersely as he stepped into a pair of black loafers. He waited until her back was turned, then snatched his revolver and shoulder holster from beneath the sweaters on his closet shelf.

He was headed toward the door when Terry said, "Joey, don't use it, please."

Rosetti walked back and kissed her gently. "I won't, honey. Unless I absolutely have to, I won't. Promise."

Terry Rosetti waited until the door slammed shut, then sighed and picked up the phone.

David sat on the ground of the esplanade, hanging on to the dangling pay phone receiver to keep from falling over. He shook uncontrollably, fading in and out of awareness as the driving rain splattered him with mud. Squinting through the downpour, he could see the Hatch Shell Amphitheater. The mountainous half-dome, looming several hundred yards away, was the only landmark he'd been able to think of to give Joey.

Slowly, painfully, he released the phone, rolled over in the muddy puddle, and began crawling toward a night-light at one side of the dome. For ten minutes, fifteen, he clawed his way over the sodden ground. The tiny bulb, at first a beacon, soon became his entire world. It seemed farther away with each agonizing inch. Again and again he tried to stand, only to crumple beneath the pain in his ankle and the overwhelming chill throughout his body. Each time he got to his hands and knees and pushed on. Twice he doubled over as spasms knotted his gut, forcing fetid river water and bile out of his nose and mouth. The taunting light grew dimmer, more distant.

"It can't end like this." David said the words over and over, using them as a cadence to force one hand, then one knee in front of the other. "It can't end like this . . ."

Suddenly the grass turned to concrete, then to smooth slick marble. He was on the stairs at the base of the Shell. His shivering gave way to paroxysmal twitches of his hands, shoulders, and neck—the harbingers of a full-blown seizure. Blood dribbled from the corner of his mouth as his teeth, chattering like jackhammers, minced the edges of his tongue. Overhead, the night light flickered for a moment, then went black. David felt the incongruous peace of dying settling within him. He fought the sensation with what little strength, what little concentration, he had left. Christine knows, he thought. She knows why Ben is dead and now she'll die, too. Must hang on. Hang on and help her. It can't end like this. . . . It can't.

* * *

237

The emptiness had set in only minutes after Christine had declined Ben's offer of a ride and started home. It was as if a tap had opened, draining from her every ounce of emotion and feeling. She had abandoned her attempt to shelter herself beneath the overhangs of buildings and wandered along the center of the sidewalk, oblivious to the downpour.

The session with Ben had been easy—at least, easier than she had anticipated. In his comfortable, nonjudgmental manner, he had assured her again and again that her decision to confess was the right thing, the *only* thing to do. He had accepted the explanation she chose to give—one in which she, acting alone, had honored the wishes of a close, special friend who was dying painfully. The most difficult moment had come when he brought up the forged C222 order form.

"The what?" Christine asked, stalling for even a little time.

"The form. The one Quigg, the pharmacist, claimed Dr. Shelton filled at his store."

Christine's mind raced. Clearly, Miss Dalrymple or one of the others had used the form to protect her. With no forewarning of what had transpired, she had no ready response. "I . . . I used it and . . . and then I bribed the pharmacist."

"How did you come by it in the first place?" Ben asked. There was no trace of disbelief in his face.

"I . . . I'd rather not say just yet." Christine held her breath, hoping the lawyer would push no further. With a few days she could think of something. If Miss Dalrymple still wished to protect The Sisterhood, she would have to do whatever she could to insure that the pharmacist did not contradict her. She would also have to convince Peggy that Christine was determined to keep the movement out of her confession.

Ben studied her for a moment, then nodded. "Very

238

well, then," he said. "Let's talk about how I believe you should handle things. That is, if you want my advice."

"I'd like more than that, Mr. Gl . . . I mean, Ben. If it's possible, I would like you to represent me."

"I'll have to think it over, Christine. Just to be sure there wouldn't be any conflict of interest involved." He smiled. "But off hand, I don't think there would be. You meet me Monday morning at my office. Nine o'clock. I'll see to it that Lieutenant Dockerty is there. Don't worry. I'll tell you ahead of time exactly what to say to him. Monday, okay?"

Christine nodded.

Monday. Christine repeated the word over and over again as she scuffed through the rain. Three days before her life would, to all intents, come to an end. Hell, she realized, it had ended already. A bus careened past, spraying her boots and trench coat with muddy street water. She did not even break stride. In a rush of images, she pictured what was to follow for her: the arrest . . . the judge . . . Miss Dalrymple . . . her brothers and sisters . . . the newspapers . . . her father, already confined to a nursing home . . . the nicknames— Death Angel, Mercy Murderer . . . her roommates and their families. . . . But most punishing of all, perhaps, were the images of David and the hatred she knew he would feel for her.

She walked past the turnoff for her street. Little by little, the great black hole within her grew. The relief and the peace she had felt while talking with Ben were gone. Tears of rain supplanted the tears she was too empty to cry. Monday.

Unseeing, she studied the windows of shops and stores as she passed. All at once, she was standing in front of a pharmacy—her pharmacy. The elderly pharmacist knew her, knew all three roommates, in fact, and liked them all. Dreamlike, she entered, exchanged a few forced pleasantries, then asked the man for a refill of the Darvon she occasionally took for cramps. Her last prescription, filled six months ago, was at home in her bureau, the vial still nearly full. After a brief check of her file, the man refilled it for her.

On the walk home Christine began to compose the note she would write.

"Rudy, he's up here!" Joey cried out. "Mother of God, what a mess! I think he's dead."

David's motionless form lay face down in a puddle to one side of the amphitheater steps. He had crawled up the stairs and wedged himself behind a marble slab, hidden from the sidewalk below. Gently Joey rolled his friend over to his back. The driving rain splattered filth and blood from David's face. At that instant, he moaned, a soft whine, nearly lost in the night wind.

"Jesus, go get a blanket!" Joey screamed. "He's breathing!" He cradled David's head in one hand and began patting his cheek—faster and harder. "Doc, it's Joey. Can you hear me? You're gonna be all right. Doc? . . ."

"Christine . . ." David's first word was an almost indistinct gurgle. "Christine . . . must find Christine." His eyes fluttered open for a moment, strained to focus on Joey's face, then closed. Rosetti set a hand on David's chest. He nodded excitedly at its shallow, rhythmic rise and fall.

"Hang on," he said. "We'll get you to the hospital. You're gonna be all right, Doc. Just hang on." He looked up and muttered a curse at the downpour. In moments the wind died off. The heavy rain gave way to a light, misty spray. Joey stared overhead in amazement, then nodded his approval.

"First thing in the morning You get a raise in pay." He grinned.

David heard Rosetti's voice, but understood only the word *hospital*. No, he thought. Not the hospital. He struggled to hang on to the thought, to put it into

240

words, but his consciousness weakened, then let go, and he plunged into darkness.

Five minutes later, he was bundled in a blanket, propped against Joey on the back seat of Rudy Fisher's Chrysler. His uncontrollable shaking continued but, moment by moment, he was regaining consciousness. Joey ordered Fisher to the Doctors Hospital emergency ward. Like echoes down a long tunnel, David heard his own words—disconnected, tinny whimpers. "Ben is dead . . . Christine is dead. No hospital, please . . . Must find Christine. . . . I'm cold . . . so cold. Please help me get warm . . ."

Several ambulances were lined up in front of the emergency entrance, their lights flashing in hypnotic counterpoint. Joey jumped out and returned moments later with a wheelchair.

"Place is a fucking zoo," he said as they eased David out of the car. "Must be the rain. Looks like a scene from some war movie. Rudy, wait for me in that space over there. You all right, Doc?"

David tried to nod, but the lights and the signs and the faces spun into a nauseating blur. He was retching as Joey pushed him through the gliding doors into the artificial brilliance of the reception area. The atmosphere and action were reminiscent of a battleground infirmary. A constant stream of patients—some bleeding, some doubled over in pain—flowed in through several doors. Litters were everywhere. Joey took in the scene, then pushed his way through the crowd surrounding the triage nurse.

The woman, a trim brunette in only her second month of screening duty, listened to him incredulously and then rushed over to David. He was moaning softly, his head rolling from side to side as he struggled to steady it. "My God, he's cold as ice," she said, holding a hand beneath his chin. "Keep his head still while I get an orderly. What happened to him?" She rushed away

241

before Joey could answer. A matronly intake clerk, clipboard in hand, arrived seconds later and began firing questions at him.

"Name?"

"Joseph Rosetti."

She looked at David. "That's not Joseph Rosetti, that's Dr. Shelton."

"Oh, I thought you meant my name. If you already know his, why did you ask?"

The clerk flashed him an ugly look and tore off the top sheet on her clipboard. "Name?" she said in the identical voice as before.

Joey fished out David's soggy wallet and found some of the information the woman requested. He came near to losing control several times, but held his temper for fear that she would rip off another sheet and start over again. In answer to "Name and address of next of kin," he was about to say he had no idea, but thought about the chaos his answer might cause and gave his own.

"Religion of preference?" the woman asked blandly.

Joey looked down at David, whose skin now had a pea-green cast. "Look," he snapped, "this man is hurt. Can't the questions wait until a doctor sees him?"

"I'm sorry, sir," she bristled, "I don't make hospital policies, I only carry them out. Religion of preference?"

Joey fought the impulse to grab the woman by the throat. The dark-haired nurse returned at that moment with an orderly, sparing him a final decision. "I've emptied out Trauma Twelve," she said. "Take Dr. Shelton there. Sir, if you'll finish signing him in, you can wait in one of those seats. I'll let you know as soon as someone has evaluated him." She looked at Joey's face and realized for the first time how very handsome he was. Her smile broadened. "Any questions?"

"No," Joey said. "But could you tell this—ah—nice lady here that I do not possess the knowledge of Dr. Shelton's religion of preference?" He winked at the

242

young nurse, whose cheeks reddened instantly, then took the intake worker by the arm and led her back to the reception desk.

In the feverish emergency ward only one pair of eyes followed attentively as the orderly wheeled David away. They belonged to Janet Poulos. Only her ears heard and understood the single word he moaned: "Christine."

With multiple accidents and two gunshot wounds tying up personnel, Janet had agreed to work overtime until the crush of patients lessened. Now, she realized, that decision might be paying off in unexpected ways. Her mind raced as she tried to sort out the significance of what she had just witnessed and heard.

Leonard Vincent had been hired by The Garden to watch Christine Beall and to intervene only if it looked to Dahlia as if the woman had decided to confess and expose The Sisterhood. That much Janet knew. Dahlia had made the decision to protect The Garden at all costs; and every flower was also a member of The Sisterhood, whether they were active in that movement or not.

Beall and Shelton must have connected, Janet reasoned. She must have gone to him. Must have spoken with him about The Sisterhood. Why else would he be here in this condition calling out her name? Dahlia had turned Leonard Vincent loose, but Shelton had somehow escaped. It was the only explanation that made any sense. If it were true, then it was Hyacinth's good fortune to be in just the right place at just the right time. Janet began to tremble with the excitement of it all. The opportunity had been laid in her lap. If she handled things well, made the proper decisions, Dahlia might see fit to involve her in the innermost workings of The Garden. The rewards would be enormous.

Janet glanced about. The police, always present in the emergency ward, were occupied with the gunshot and accident victims. She sensed she could move through

243

the chaos unnoticed, but only if she moved quickly. Was there time to call Dahlia? She checked the hallway to Trauma Room 12. The area outside the room was deserted. There might not be another chance.

Adrenalin. Potassium. Insulin. Digitalis. Pancuronium. Janet ticked off the possibilities as she hurried to the nurses' station. She wondered about Christine Beall. Had Vincent already accounted for her? No matter, she decided. The only problem she could do anything about at the moment was waiting for her in Trauma 12.

"Dr. Shelton, my name is Clifford. Can you lift up your bum so I can pull these pants off you?" The pudgy orderly was past thirty, but looked like he had yet to shave for the first time.

David grunted his reply but, with consummate effort, was actually able to do what the man/boy requested. Gradually, ripples of warmth washed over the deep chill inside him. As his awareness grew, so did the throbbing pain in his ankle and arm, along with lesser aches above his right ear and on the soles of his feet.

"You look like you've had quite a time of it," Clifford said cheerfully, spreading David's sodden pants over the back of a chair.

"The river . . . I . . . was in the river." David's voice was distant and flat. "Ben is dead . . ."

"Can you hold this under your tongue?" the orderly asked, shoving a thermometer into David's mouth. "Who's Ben?" David mumbled and struggled to reach the thermometer. "No, no, don't touch that," Clifford scolded. "Doctor will be in shortly to check you over. You just keep that under your tongue until I get back."

Never take an oral temp on someone who's freezing to death, idiot! The unspoken disapproval flashed in David's eyes as the corpulent orderly left the room. Then his lips tightened in a half-smile. He was coming around. Bit by bit his random thoughts were connecting. Suddenly Ben's face appeared in his mind, blood pouring from his mouth. Renewed terror took hold. Desperately, he pulled himself up, first on one elbow, then to an outstretched hand. "Christine," he gasped, spitting the thermometer out. "I've got to get to her." As his head came upright, the walls began to turn, slowly at first, but with rapidly building speed.

David fought the spinning and the nausea, and forced himself to a sitting position. Sweat poured from his forehead and dripped down his sides. The floor blurred beneath him. As he leaned forward, the room began to dim, and he knew that he was falling. For an incredible moment he was weightless, floating in a sea of brilliant light. Then there was nothing.

Janet Poulos caught David by the shoulders as he toppled forward and eased him back onto the litter. His respirations were rapid and shallow, the pulse at his wrist thready. Briefly she thought about sitting him up again. The precipitous blood-pressure drop from such a maneuver might well remove the need for the syringe full of Adrenalin in her pocket. Too chancy, she decided, pulling his feet up on the litter. She made a final check of the corridor. There was a crisis of some sort several rooms away and the crash cart was being rushed in. Perfect, she thought, stepping back into the room and closing the door behind her. Everyone just stay where you are for a little while.

"Dr. Shelton, can you hear me?" she asked. "I'm going to put a tourniquet on your arm to draw some blood. It will only take a minute."

David moaned and pulled his arm away as she looped the rubber tubing around it. "Now, now, David," she said sweetly. "Just hold still. This isn't going to hurt a bit." She slapped the skin over the crook of his elbow and looked for a vein. The area was blanched and cold, every skin vessel constricted to the maximum. Janet groaned and slapped more frantically, cursing herself

245

for forgetting about the body's response to hypothermia and shock.

David's head lolled back and forth as his consciousness began to return. Panicked, Janet jammed the needle into his arm, hoping for a chance hit in a vein. At that instant Clifford burst into the room. The syringe popped free and slipped from her hand as Janet whirled to the sound. A drop of blood appeared at the puncture site.

"Well, Doctor, I'm back. Sorry to have . . ." Clifford stopped short, confronted by Janet's withering glare.

"Damn you," she hissed, ripping off the tourniquet and quickly retrieving the syringe. Shielding Clifford from view, she squirted the Adrenalin beneath the litter, then turned back to him. "Don't you know to knock when doors are closed? I was in the middle of drawing blood on this man and you just screwed it up."

"I . . . I'm sorry." The orderly shifted nervously from one foot to the other and stared at the floor.

"You'll be hearing from me about this," she spat. Her mind was swirling with thoughts of what to do next. Then she froze. Harry Weiss, the surgical resident, was standing in the doorway.

"Is everything all right?" he asked calmly.

Janet nodded. "I . . . I didn't know when someone was going to get in to see Dr. Shelton, here, so I thought I'd draw some bloods on him just to get things started."

"Thank you. That was good thinking." Weiss smiled. "If you haven't drawn them yet, why don't you wait until I've finished taking a look at him."

"Very well, Doctor." Janet managed another icy glance at Clifford, then walked from the room before racing to the telephone.

"Dr. Shelton, it's me, Harry Weiss." The hawk-nosed resident David had guided through the difficult hand case looked at him anxiously. David's eyes were open, but he was having obvious difficulty focusing. Weiss leaned closer. "Can you see me all right?"

David squinted, then nodded. Moments later he was struggling to sit up. "Christine. Let me call Christine," he heard himself say. The dizziness began anew, but he battled it, flailing with both hands.

Harry Weiss grabbed his wrists and pushed him back. "Please, Dr. Shelton, I don't want to have to tie you down," he begged. He looked about for Clifford as David's thrashing increased, but the man had left. "Nurse," he called out, "would someone please get an orderly and a set of four-point restraints in here on the double."

In less than a minute David was lashed to the litter by leather arm and ankle cuffs. His efforts weakened, giving way to sobs. "Please . . . just let me find her . . . just let me call." His words were unintelligible.

Weiss looked down at him and shook his head sadly. "I think we're all right now," he said to the small group who had rushed in to help. "Leave us alone so I can examine him. Call the lab and tell them I want a complete screen and CBC. Have them do a scan for drugs of abuse as well. When I'm finished, start an I.V.—normal saline at three hundred cc's an hour—at least until we know what's going on. One of you find out who's on for psych tonight and let me know. If it's a good one, we might call him down. If it's one of those turkeys who's sicker than the patients, we probably won't." The group smiled at his remark, but only the orderly laughed out loud. Harry Weiss shot him a momentary glare, picked up a piece of the shattered thermometer, then said, "And Clifford, when are you going to learn that we never take oral temperatures on someone with hypothermia. It's too inaccurate. Rectal temps only. I don't want to hear of your doing that

247

again." He nodded that his orders were complete and the room quickly emptied.

"Atta boy, Harry," David wanted to say, but he was unable to get words out. The terror, shock, and hypothermia were taking their toll. Even had the orderly used a rectal thermometer, David's temperature would not have registered. Still, his eyes were open. He watched as the tall resident began examining him. Tell the man, David thought. Sit up and tell him that you don't need a fucking shrink. Tell him that Ben is dead. Tell him that you must find Christine. That she might already be dead. Tell him you're not crazy. But . . . but maybe you *are* crazy. Maybe this is how it is. How it feels. There he is, poking and grabbing all over you, and you can't even talk to him. Maybe this is what crazy is. I mean people don't suddenly have a neon sign appear on their chests saying, "THIS PERSON HAS LOST HIS MIND: THIS PERSON IS MAD." Where the hell is Joey? Joey was here a while ago. Where the hell is he now?

Pain shot up his leg from where Weiss was examining his ankle. David groaned and fought to sit up. The leather restraints held fast. "Sorry," Weiss said gently. "I didn't mean to hurt you. Dr. Shelton, can you understand me? Can you tell me what happened?"

Yes, yes, David thought. I can tell you. Just give me a minute. Don't rush me. I can tell you everything.

Harry Weiss saw him nod and waited for more of a response. Finally he said, "Well, you're beginning to feel warmer. I've ordered some tests. We're going to get X-rays of your ankle, your arm, and, just in case, a set of skull films. I think everything's okay, but I can't say for sure about your ankle. Understand?"

"Joey," David said. "Where is my friend Joey?" For a moment he was unsure of whether he had actually said the words or only thought that he had said them.

The resident's face brightened. "Joey? Is he the one

who brought you here?" David nodded. "Great, well, it sounds like you may be coming around. I'll go talk to your friend. Then I'll send him in to stay with you until X-ray is ready. We're very busy tonight, so there'll probably be a bit of a wait. I'm going to turn off the overhead light. Try to get some rest and don't shake this blanket off."

"Thank you," David whispered. "Thank you." Weiss looked down at him briefly, shook his head, and left the room, flipping the light off on his way.

David tested the restraints one at a time. No chance. He took a deep breath, exhaled slowly, then settled back. The shaking had stopped and much of the deep chill had disappeared. There was something soothing about the dim quiet of the room and the familiar clamor from outside. "Time to rest," he told himself. "Rest and get your strength back. When Joey gets here we'll go after Christine. When Joey gets here . . ." Slowly his eyes closed. His breathing became more shallow and regular.

Through a peaceful, twilight sleep David heard his friend enter the room. Don't wake me up, Joey, David thought. Give me another minute or two, then we'll get going. Well, okay, I know you're worried about me. I can sleep later. His eyes blinked open an instant before Leonard Vincent's massive hand clamped down over his mouth, pinning him roughly against the litter.

Dressed in the orderly's whites Hyacinth had provided, Vincent had encountered no problem in making his way from a rear entrance to Trauma 12. He grudgingly acknowledged Dahlia's wisdom in ordering him to wait by a phone near Doctors Hospital. "A hunch," she had called it. He had balked at the prospect of strolling into the emergency ward, but assurances that the emergency ward police were all occupied and the promise of a bonus had convinced him to try. Now he silently applauded himself for the decision.

"You've been a great pain in the ass, Dr. Shelton," he growled. "I have half a mind to make this hurt more than it should. But because at least you tried, I'm gonna make it quick and easy."

David watched helplessly, his eyes spheres of terror as Vincent raised a knife over his face, giving him a clear view of the ugly tapered blade.

With his hand still pressed over David's mouth, the killer hooked two thick fingers beneath his chin and pulled up. "One slice, just like a surgeon," he whispered, drawing the dull side of the blade slowly across David's exposed neck.

"For God's sake, wait! I didn't do anything," was all David could think of in that final moment. Eyes closed, he listened for his own death scream. Instead, he heard a loud thud and the clatter of Vincent's knife on the floor. His eyes opened in time to see the killer's body lurch sideways, then crumple over. Behind him, Joey Rosetti lifted the heavy revolver he had used as a club, preparing, if necessary, for another blow.

"Nice place you run here, Doc," Joey said, quickly undoing the restraints. "If I ever need another operation, remind me to go back to White Memorial."

"He's the man," David blurted excitedly. "The man who killed Ben. He . . . he was going to . . ."

"I know what he was going to do," Joey said, unbuckling the restraints. "Leonard an' me have met before. He does it for a living. The shit. If he's after you, my friend, then you are into some serious business."

David sat up. This time the dizziness was bearable. Instinctively he rubbed his hand over his throat. The rush of terror had done more to bring him around than had anything else. "Joey, get me out of here," he begged. "Shoot that animal, then get me out of here. We've got to find Christine."

Joey glanced at Vincent, who was lying on one side, his face contorted by the tiled floor. "We'll let the cops take care of Leonard," he said. "I promised Terry I wouldn't use my gun—at least, the other end of it—unless I had to. Someone will find him here. Can you walk? Where the hell are your pants?"

"There, over there on the chair. I . . . I think I can walk with a little help." David slipped off the table and steadied himself against Joey's arm. His ankle throbbed but held weight as he wriggled into his damp, muddy jeans. "Joey, there's this woman, Christine Beall. She's the only one who can straighten out the mess I'm in. We've got to find her." He sighed relief at the realization that, at last, his thoughts were coming out intelligibly.

"Okay," Joey said, "but first we've got to drift out of this place with as little commotion as possible. I saw this gorilla here dressed up like a doctor or something heading for your room. Nobody else even looked twice at him. I figured he wasn't going in to give you a check-up. Now listen—my manager's parked by the front door. Let me get a wheelchair. We'll go as far as we can with that, then run like hell. It's a red car, an Olds or Chrysler or some ox like that. Do you remember it?"

David shook his head. "I'll find it, Joey, don't worry. Let's just get the hell out of here."

Rosetti helped him into a wheelchair, then casually pushed it down the trauma wing corridor and across the reception area. As the electronic front doors slid open, a woman's voice behind them called out, "Hey, you two, where are you going?"

David scrambled out of the chair and hung on to Joey's arm as they raced the last few yards to the Chrysler. "No rubber," Joey panted as they dove into the back seat.

Rudy Fisher nodded and eased past two parked cruisers down the sweeping circular driveway and off toward Boston's North End.

Janet Poulos stood helplessly to one side of the reception area and watched them go. She had told Dahlia nothing of her abortive attempt to handle matters. Now she had another decision to make—whether or not to see if Leonard Vincent was alive and needed help. Since she was the only person the man could identify if he were arrested, the decision was not difficult.

She stopped by the crash cart, took several ampules of pancuronium, and dropped them into her pocket. The respiratory paralysis caused by the drug helped maintain respirator patients. Well, now it would help her, too, provided she had the chance to use it. If not, she would have to find a way to help the man escape. Perhaps she could still salvage some heightened prestige in Dahlia's eyes.

Janet cursed her rotten luck and David Shelton for causing her so much difficulty. Then she stalked down the hall to Trauma 12, hoping she would find Leonard Vincent dead.

"Ouch! What is that stuff?" David winced as Terry Rosetti scrubbed at the dirt embedded in the deep gouge along his arm.

"Just something I use to clean the windows," she said. "Now sit still and let me finish."

The Rosettis' North End apartment was old, but spacious and newly renovated. Terry had decorated the place with grace, making full use of a collection of family furniture that would have been welcome in any of the posh antique shops on Newbury Street.

David lay stretched out on the large oak guest bed, savoring the smell and texture of fresh linen and wondering if he would ever feel warm again. He was weak, lightheaded, and aching in a half-dozen different places. Still, he could sense his concentration improving as the mental fog brought on by his hypothermia began to lift.

He silently thanked Joey for reasoning him out of an immediate search for Christine in favor of a hot shower.

Terry Rosetti, a full-breasted, vibrant beauty, expertly wrapped his arm in gauze. "Fettuccini and first aid," David said. "You are truly the complete woman."

Terry's smile lit up the room. "Tell that to your friend out there. I think he's starting to take me for granted. Do you know he was actually able to stop in the middle of making love to me to answer the phone when you called?"

"No wonder it seemed to be ringing forever," he said. "I almost hung up."

"It's a lucky thing you didn't," Terry said. "David, Joey didn't *kill* that man, did he?"

The fear in her eyes left no doubt of the importance his answer held for her. "I wanted him to pull the trigger back there, Terry. I really did. That animal killed my friend. But Joey said he'd promised you and backed off."

Terry Rosetti swallowed at the lump in her throat.

At that moment, Joey marched into the room, carrying a load of clothes, a pair of crutches, and the Boston phone book. "I think this must be the woman," he said. "C. Beall, 391 Belknap, Brookline. I checked the other books and this is the only name that fits. By the way, the clothes and shit are courtesy of the North End Businessman's Association."

"What's that?" asked David.

"Oh, just some simple business types like me who like to help poor, unfortunate folks that get chased into the river by a gorilla." Joey smiled conspiratorially at Terry and winked. He failed to notice her lack of reaction. "You feel up to traveling, Doc?" he asked.

"Yeah, sure. What time is it anyway?"

"Twelve thirty. It's a new day."

"Three hours." David shook his head in amazement. "It's only been three hours . . ."

"What?"

"Nothing, hand me the phone, please. I only hope she's all right."

Joey squinted down at him. "You positive *you're* all right?" he asked.

"Sure, why?"

"Well, you're the one with the education an' the degrees an' shit. All I got goin' for me is my street smarts. Just the same, I can think of at least six or seven good reasons why we would want to tell this C. Beall what we have to tell her face to face, not over the phone. Remember, you've already been arrested for murder. Right now that woman's your only hope of gettin' off."

David understood instantly. If Christine had nothing to do with Ben's death, the news could panic her into a hasty, possibly fatal move. If she was somehow involved or had knowledge of who might have hired Leonard Vincent . . . He wouldn't allow himself to complete the thought. "When this is all over," he said, "I'm going to write my medical school and tell them to bring you in as a guest lecturer. You could teach medical students about making it in the real world. Let's go find her."

Ten minutes later, they were back in Rudy Fisher's car headed toward Brookline. "Don't push it too hard, Rudy," Rosetti ordered. "We don't want to get stopped. If Vincent already got paper for the woman, all the fancy driving in the world isn't gonna help." David grimaced and looked out the window.

After a mile of silence, Joey said, "Doc, there's somethin' I want to tell you. Call it a lesson if you want, since you're gonna make me a teacher."

David turned toward his friend, expecting to see the wry glint that usually accompanied one of his stories. Joey's eyes were narrowed, dark, and deadly serious. "Go on," David said.

"Leonard Vincent may not be the slickest operator in

254

the world, but he is a pro. And as long as he or someone like him's in the picture, you're gonna be playing by his rules. Understand?" David nodded. "Well, we don't have much time, so I'm gonna make the lesson simple for you. There's only one rule you gotta know. One main rule for survival in Vincent's game. I didn't follow it back there in the hospital because Terry made me promise not to. But you got no Terry, so you pay attention and do what I say. If you even think someone's gonna do it to you, you damn well better do it to him first. Understand?" He slipped his gun into David's pocket. "Here. Whatever happens, I got a feelin' you're gonna need this more than me. Terry'll make you something real special when she hears you got it away from me."

John Dockerty knelt by the door to David's apartment and watched as the medical examiner's team finished working around Ben's body and wheeled it into the elevator. He looked up at the patrolman who had been making inquiries in the other apartments on the floor. The man shrugged and shook his head. "Nothing," he mouthed.

The news came as no surprise to Dockerty. Survival in the city meant hearing, seeing, and reporting as little as possible. He picked at the bullet holes in the doorjamb, then retraced the steps it seemed the action had taken. There was blood smeared on the hallway floor and wall of David's apartment and along the bottom of the open bedroom window. He made a note to check David's military and health records for mention of his blood type.

A fatal knife wound, bullet holes, blood all over, an old drunk shot to death two blocks away, and not one witness. Dockerty rubbed at the fatigue stinging his eyes and tried to re-create the scenario. There were several possibilities, none of which looked good for Shelton. He had little doubt the man was dead.

At that moment David's phone began ringing. Dockerty hesitated, then answered it.

"Hello?"

"Lieutenant Dockerty, please."

"This is Dockerty."

"Lieutenant, it's Sergeant McIlroy at the Fourth. We just got a call from one of our people at Doctors Hospital. Apparently this David Shelton—you know, the one you busted for that mercy killing?"

"Yeah, I know, I know."

"Well, this Shelton showed up a little while ago on the emergency ward all smashed up. I called your precinct and they said you'd want to know about it right away."

"Tell your people to hold him at the hospital," Dockerty said.

"Can't. He's gone. Took off with some guy a few minutes after he arrived. No one realized it until too late. Our men were off taking statements from two assholes who had a shoot-out at the High Five Bar."

"Who the hell was the guy?" Dockerty's head began to throb.

"Don't know."

"Well, isn't it on Shelton's emergency sheet?"

"That's just it. There is no emergency sheet. The clerk swears she typed one out, but now no one can find it."

"Jesus Christ. What in the hell is going on?"

"Don't know, sir."

"Well, tell the men at the hospital I'll be right over. They're not to let anyone leave who saw Shelton. No one. Got that?"

"Yes, sir."

"Jesus Christ." Dockerty dropped the receiver in

place and swept some strands of hair off his eyes and back under his hat. It was going to be a long goddamn night.

Rudy Fisher made three passes along Christine's street before Rosetti felt certain there were no "surprises." He directed the giant to wait half a block away, then helped David up the concrete steps to the house. "Old Leonard's probably having a time of it right now." Joey laughed. "I can just imagine him trying to weasel his way out of that situation in the hospital with the only ten or twelve words that he knows."

David braced himself on his crutches and peered through the row of small panes paralleling the door. He moved gingerly, but even a slight turn or drop of his head brought renewed dizziness and nausea. The prolonged hypothermia, he realized, had somehow impaired his balance center or perhaps his body's ability to make quick blood-pressure adjustments.

The house was dark, save for a dim light coming from a room on the right—the living room, David guessed. He glanced at his watch. Nearly 1:00 A.M.

"I guess we ring the bell, huh?" David asked nervously.

"Well, Doc, given the options, I'd say that was your best bet. I'm glad you're not this tense in the operating room."

David managed a laugh at himself, then pressed the bell. They waited, listening for a response. Nothing. David shivered and knew that the chill reflected more than the fine, wind-driven mist. He rang again. Ten seconds passed. Then twenty.

"Do we break in?" he asked.

"We may have to, but I'd suggest trying the back door first." Joey walked to the street and motioned to Rudy Fisher that they were going around to the back. David gave the button a final press, then fought through a wave of queasiness and followed.

It was that third ring that woke Christine. She was stretched across her bed, careening through one grisly dream after another. On the floor, shards of torn notepaper were strewn about two pill bottles. Both of them were full.

"Wait a minute, I'm coming," she called out. Could both her roommates have forgotten their keys? Knowing them, a likely possibility. She pushed herself off the bed, then stared at the floor. The shredded note, the bottles of gray-and-orange death—how close she had come. She threw the pills into a drawer, then swept up the scraps with her hands and dropped them in the basket. By the end of the terrible dark hour that had followed her return home, Christine had resolved that nothing ever would make her take her own life. Nothing, except perhaps a situation such as Charlotte Thomas's. She would face whatever she had to face.

Again the doorbell sounded. This time it was the buzzer from the back door. "I'm coming, I'm coming." She rushed through the kitchen and was halfway down the short back staircase when she stopped dead. It was him, David, propped on crutches and peering through the window. She reached down and flipped on the outside light; then she gasped. His face was drawn and cadaverous, his eyes totally lost in wide, dark hollows. A second man, his back turned, was standing behind him. Christine's pulse quickened as first confusion, then mounting apprehension gripped her.

"Christine, it's me, David Shelton." His voice sounded weak and distant.

"Yes . . . yes, I know. What do you want?" She felt frightened, unable to move.

"Please, Christine, I must talk to you. Something has happened. Something terrible . . ."

Joey grabbed his arm. "Are you crazy?" he whispered, working his way in front of the window. "Miss Beall," he said calmly, "my name is Joseph Rosetti. I'm a close

258

friend of the Doc's. He's been hurt." He paused, gauging Christine's expression to see if any further explanation was necessary before she let them in.

Christine hesitated, then descended the final two stairs and undid the double lock. "I . . . I'm sorry," she said as they entered the hallway. "You took me by surprise and . . . Please, come up to the living room. Can you make it all right? Are you badly hurt?"

For the next fifteen minutes she did not say another word as the two men recounted the events of the night. With each detail a new emotion flashed in her eyes.

Surprise, astonishment, terror, pain, emptiness. David studied them as they appeared. He wondered if she were even capable of a successful lie. Whatever she might have done, he was now certain that in no way was she responsible for Ben's murder.

Still, she was somehow involved. That reality pulled David's attention from her face. "Christine, what did you tell Ben?" She seemed unable to speak. "Please, tell me what you said to him." There was a note of urgency and anger in his voice.

"I . . . I told him that it was me. That I was the one who . . . who gave the morphine to Charlotte."

David's heart pounded. His arrest, the filth and degradation of his night in jail, the unraveling of everything he had regained in his career, Ben Glass's death—*she was responsible*. "And the forged prescription?" There was bitterness in his words now. "Were you responsible for that, too?"

"No! . . . I mean, I don't know." The muscles in her face tensed. Her lips quivered. The only explanation she could think to give him was the truth; but what was the truth? The Sisterhood had sacrificed David to protect her, she felt certain of that. But why Ben? It was hard enough to accept that they would choose to send an innocent man to prison, but murder? "Oh, my God," she stammered. "I'm so confused. I don't know what's happening. I don't understand."

"What?" David demanded. "What don't you understand?" His eyes flashed at her from their craters.

Christine began to cry. "I don't understand," she sobbed. "So much is happening and nothing makes sense. It's horrible. The pain I've caused you. And Ben—they've killed Ben. Why? Why? I . . . I need time. Time to sort this all out. It's crazy. Why would they do it?"

"Who're *they*?" David asked. Christine didn't answer. "Dammit," he screamed, "what are you talking about? Who're they?"

"Now just hold it a minute." Joey put up a hand to each of them. "You're both gonna have to calm down or we could all find ourselves in trouble. Leonard Vincent's probably out of the picture, but there's no guarantee he was working alone. The longer you two spend goin' at one another like this, the more chance there is that some goon's gonna crash in here and do it good to all three of us." He paused, allowing the thought to sink in, and watched until he sensed an easing in the tension. "Okay. Now, Miss Beall, I don't know you, but I do know the doc here, and I know the shit he's been through. The way I see it, you're both in hot water until this whole business is straightened out. I can see that the news we've brought has shaken you, but this man here deserves an explanation."

"I . . . I don't know what to say." She spoke the words softly, as much to herself as to them.

Joey could see that she was coming apart. He glanced at David, whose expression suggested that he sensed the same thing. "Look," Joey said finally, "maybe what we should do is just call the cops and—"

"No!" Christine blurted. "Please no. Not yet. There's so much I don't understand. A lot of innocent people could be hurt if I do the wrong thing." She stopped and breathed deeply. When she continued, there was a new calm in her voice. "Please, you must believe me. I had nothing to do with Ben's death. I liked him very much. He was going to help me."

David leaned forward and buried his face in his hands. "Okay." He looked up slowly. "No police . . . yet. What do you want?"

"Some time," she said. "Just a little time to work this whole thing through. I'll tell you everything I know. I promise."

David sensed himself soften before the sadness in her eyes and turned away.

"Look, Doc," Rosetti said impatiently, "I meant what I said before. We're just not smart stayin' here any longer than we have to. If it's no police, then it's no police. If it's some time to talk, then it's some time to talk. Only not here."

David heard the urgency in Rosetti's voice and saw, for the first time, a flash of fear in his eyes. "Okay, we'll get out," he said. "But where? Where can we go? Certainly not my apartment. How about the tavern . . . or your place? Do you think Terry would be upset if we went there?"

"I have a better idea. Terry and me have this little hideaway up on the North Shore. I think if you two can keep from rippin' each other apart without me for a referee it would be a perfect place. Doc, you can't see yourself, but let me tell you, you look about ready for an embalmer. Why don't you go on up there tonight and get some sleep. Tomorrow you can take all the time you need to talk things out." David started to protest, but Rosetti stopped him. "This ain't the time for arguin', pal. You're my friend. Terry's friend too. So I know you'll understand that I don't want her mixed up in anything this messy. It's the North Shore or you're both on your own. Now what do you say?"

David looked over at Christine. She was slumped in

her chair, staring at the floor. There was an innocence about her—a defenselessness—that was difficult to reconcile with his pain and the hell she had caused him to live through. Who are you? he thought. Exactly what is it you've done? And why?

"I . . . I guess if it's okay with Christine, it's okay with me," he said finally.

Christine tightened her lips and nodded.

"It's decided, then," Joey announced. "There's food in the house. This time of year, there's not too many folks on Rocky Point, so you shouldn't be bothered. I'll draw you a map. Take Christine's car. We'll follow you to the highway just in case. It's nice up there. Especially if the rain is through for good. There's an old clunker jeep in the garage. The keys are in the toolbox by the back wall. Use it if you want. Okay?"

"Give me a minute to pack a couple of things," Christine said. "And to leave a note for my roommates that I won't be home tonight."

"Okay, but not too long," Joey replied. "And, Christine? Tell your friends to keep the door locked—just in case."

"Mr. Vincent, you have bungled things badly. Possibly beyond repair. Hyacinth took a great risk helping you escape that mess in the hospital, but never again. This time I want results. The girl first, then Dr. Shelton. Understand?"

"Yeah, yeah, I understand." Leonard Vincent slammed the receiver down, then rubbed at the thin mat of dried blood that had formed over the stitches in his head. That twit Hyacinth wasn't his type, but for being cool in a crunch he had to hand it to her. After regaining consciousness, he had been unable to keep his feet. He remembered her helping him to a stretcher. Seconds later, a doctor arrived. It was then that the woman really put on her show, explaining how this poor orderly

262

had slipped and smacked his head on the floor, and how she would take care of all the paperwork if the guy would just throw some stitches into the gash.

Yes, sir, Vincent thought, he certainly did have to hand it to ol' Hyacinth. Then he remembered the way she had looked at him just before she sent him out of the hospital—the hatred in her eyes. "You asshole," she had said. "You absolute asshole."

The memory triggered a flush of nausea and another siege of dry heaves—his third since leaving the hospital. Vincent held on to a tree until his retching subsided. "People are gonna die," he spat, fighting the frustration and the pain with the only weapon he knew. "People are gonna fuckin' die."

Carefully, he eased himself behind the wheel of his car and drove to Brookline, He turned onto Belknap Street just as another car, heading away from him, neared the corner at the far end. Vincent tensed as he peered through the darkness, trying to focus on the car before it disappeared around the corner. It was red—bright red. The killer relaxed and settled back into the seat. He stopped across from Christine's house and scanned the driveway. The blue Mustang was gone.

Muttering an obscenity, he reached inside the glove compartment and pulled out the envelope Hyacinth had given him. "Well, Dahlia, whoever the fuck you are," he said, "I guess you get the doctor first whether you want it that way or not."

He tore open the envelope and spread David's emergency sheet on the passenger seat. Across the space marked "Physician's Report" the words ELOPED WITHOUT TREATMENT were printed in red. The information boxes at the top were all neatly typed in. With an unsteady hand, Vincent drew a circle around the line of type identifying next of kin.

CHAPTER XIX

The wharf was dark, quiet, and even more eerie than usual. John Dockerty backed inside a doorway and listened until the echo of his footsteps had been absorbed by the heavy night. It took several minutes to sort out the random sounds that surrounded him. Clinking mooring chains. Gulls caterwauling over a midnight feast. The lap of harbor swells against thick pilings. The reassuring drone of a foghorn.

Gradually the tension in his neck relaxed. He was alone on the pier.

Through the silver-black mist he scanned along the row of warehouses, ghostly sentinels guarding the inner harbor. Then he crossed the narrow strip of pavement and ducked into a small alley. At the far end a slit of dim light glowed from beneath an unmarked warehouse door. Dockerty knocked softly and waited.

"Come in, Dock, it's open." Ted Ulansky's voice boomed in the silence.

Dockerty slipped inside, closing the heavy metal door quickly behind him. "Christ, Ted," he said. "I spend twenty fucking minutes sneaking around to be sure I'm not followed, and you bellow at me louder than the foghorn out there."

"Just goes to show what confidence I have in you, Dock. Come on over and park your duff." Ulansky pumped Dockerty's hand, then motioned him to a high-backed oak chair beside his desk. He was an expansive man with a physique that bore only a faint resemblance to the All-American linebacker he had been at Boston College two and a half decades before.

"Nice place," Dockerty said sarcastically, looking around the large, poorly lit office. "Is this it?"

"This is it," answered Ulansky with mock pride. "The fabled Massachusetts Drug Investigation Force headquarters. Want a tour?"

"No, thanks. I think I can manage to take it all in from here."

In fact, the MDIF, while not publicized, had gained an almost fabled reputation for quiet efficiency and airtight arrests. Ulansky, as head of the unit, was gradually acquiring a superhuman reputation of his own. The office, however, was hardly the stuff of which legends are made. It was stark and cold. Bare cement walls were lined with filing cabinets—more than two dozen of them—all olive-green standard government issue. Inside the metal drawers, Dockerty knew, was virtually every piece of information available on illegal drug traffic in the state.

In one corner of the room, partially covered by Ulansky's carelessly thrown suit coat, was a computer terminal connected through Washington with drug-investigation and -enforcement agencies throughout the country.

Ulansky lowered himself into his desk chair. "A drink? Some coffee?" Dockerty shook his head. "Must be serious business for you to come out here in this rat's-ass weather, then refuse a drink."

"I guess," Dockerty said distractedly, reopening his

battle with some obstinate strands of hair. "I appreciate your coming out."

Ulansky buried a shot glass of Old Grand-Dad in a single gulp. "Believe me, with the Czernewicz fight on live from the coast tonight, you're about the only one of the precinct boys who could have gotten me out of the house. Jackie Czernewicz, the Pummeling Pole. You follow the fights?"

Dockerty shook his head again. "Too much like a day at the office for me."

Ulansky smiled. "Tell me, then," he said, "what prompts a visit from you to this Hyatt Regency of law enforcement?"

"I'm involved in a really weird case, Ted." Dockerty scratched the tip of his nose. "An old lady got murdered while she was a patient at Boston Doctors Hospital. Morphine. So far I've narrowed the field of suspects down to about three dozen. Even made one arrest."

"Yeah, I read about that," Ulansky said. "A doctor, right?"

"Right. A ton of circumstantial stuff against him, but way too neat, if you know what I mean. The captain, that pillar of justice, got pressure from some fat cat at the hospital and insisted that I bust the doctor. I did it, but I've never been convinced. Now the guy's lawyer has been murdered. Ben Glass. You know him?" Ulansky grimaced and nodded. "Well, he was knifed. Outside the doc's apartment door, no less. There are bullet holes all over, and the apartment door's smashed in. There's blood in the hallway and even on the wall.

"A little while ago the doctor gets brought to the emergency ward at the hospital soaked and freezing and half crazy. Then, before he can get any treatment, he splits with another guy. By the time I hear about it and get to the hospital, there's no record he was ever even there. For all I know he may be dead by now. I've got the usual lines out for him, but I'm at a stone wall with the rest of the case. I feel like the whole fucked-up mess is partly my fault for letting the captain talk me into arresting him."

"How can we help?"

"My only hope of breaking something open is a pharmacist named Quigg. Marcus Quigg. Owns a little drugstore in West Roxbury. He swears that this Dr. Shelton filled a big prescription for morphine the day this woman was OD'ed."

Ulansky's moon face crinkled as he worked the name through his memory. "We've got something on the man someplace," he said. "I'm almost sure of it. What about a C two twenty-two?"

"Quigg's got one. The doctor claims it was stolen from his office, that he never ordered any morphine."

"Signature?"

"Only a maybe from the guys at ident. They tell me Shelton's signature is a scrawl. Easy to duplicate."

"So maybe it *is* his," Ulansky said.

"Maybe." Dockerty shrugged. "My hunches have been wrong before."

"Sure, about as often as a solar eclipse."

Dockerty accepted the compliment with a tired grin. "I need a handle on that pharmacist, Ted," he said. "The man bends, but he won't break. I figure if he'd take a payoff to do something like this, he must have dirtied his hands on something else at one time or another."

"Well," Ulansky offered, "we can go through the files and check the computer for you. I have a feeling something's down on paper about him." He paused, then continued in a softer voice. "Dock, you know that if we can't find anything on him we can easily set something up that will work just as well. Maybe better. You want that?"

Dockerty tensed, then rose and walked slowly to the far side of the room. Ulansky moved to add something,

267

then sat back and let the silence continue. Dockerty rested one arm on a filing cabinet. For more than a minute he studied the blank wall. "You know, Ted," he said finally, "in all these years on the force I've never once purposely set anyone up. If I did it this time, I know it would be to make up for mistakes I've already made." He shook his head and turned back to Ulansky. "I don't want to do it, Ted. No matter what my fuck-ups may have put that doctor through, I don't want to do it." Ulansky nodded his understanding. "Look," Dockerty added, "check everything you can to dig something up on Quigg. Call me first thing tomorrow. If I've got nothing and you've got nothing, we'll talk."

"Don't worry, Dock," Ulansky said stonily. "If Marcus Quigg has so much as pissed on a public toilet seat, I'll find out. Don't worry your ass about that at all."

"That was it, that was the exit. I told you one twenty-seven and you just breezed right past it." David, bundled in an army blanket, sat wedged against the passenger door. He glared at Christine, but turned away before she noticed.

"Sorry," she said flatly. "My mind was on other things." She took the next turnoff and doubled back. Traffic was light, but her difficulty concentrating was such that she kept their speed below fifty. For a time they drove in silence, each aware that the tension between them was building.

Finally Christine could stand no more. She pulled into the dirt parking lot of a boarded-up diner and swung around to face him. "Look, maybe this wasn't a good idea—maybe we should go back."

David stared out the window, struggling to comprehend the existence and the incredible scope of The Sisterhood of Life. Christine had given him only the roughest sketch of the movement, along with the promise of more details in the morning. Still, what she had told him already was awesome. Several thousand nurses! Dorothy Dalrymple one of them! He had listened, his eyes shut, his head close to exploding, as her factual, curiously dispassionate voice divulged secrets that could easily decimate the hospital system to which he had dedicated so much of his life.

Now he felt sick. Tired and angry and sick.

Christine sensed his mood, but could not contain her own growing frustration. "Dammit, David," she said, "I've been trying to explain to you as best as possible what has happened. I didn't expect a reward, but I didn't expect the silent treatment either."

"And just what did you expect?" Irritation sparked in his voice.

"Understanding?" she said softly.

"My God. She kills one of my patients, gets me thrown in jail for it, causes my friend to be murdered almost in my arms, and wants me to understand. And . . . and that Sisterhood of yours. Why of all the presumptuous, insane . . ."

"David, I told you about The Sisterhood of Life because I thought you deserved to know. Back there at my house you seemed willing to listen and at least try to understand. Instead all you've done is pull into a shell and come out every few miles to snap at me. I'll tell you one last time. I did not cause you to be arrested. I didn't even know it had happened until I read it in the papers. I imagine The Sisterhood is responsible, and that sickens me. I joined the movement because of its dedication to mercy. Now I discover it's involved in despicable crimes—against you, against Ben, and God knows whom else. If I had known ahead of time, I would never have allowed any of this to happen. Why else do you think I went to Ben to confess?"

She paused for a response, but David was staring out the window. "I thought you might be able to help me work things out," she continued, "but that was foolish

269

of me. You have every right to be angry. Every right to hate me. I'm going home."

She turned and started the engine. David reached across and shut it off. "Wait, please. I . . . I'm sorry." His speech was halting and thick. "I've been listening to my own bitterness and anger and trying to understand where they're coming from. I thought it was my pain talking, or frustration, or even fear, but I'm starting to know better. I liked you—maybe more than I would allow myself to accept. That's what's doing it. I didn't want to believe you were any part of this. Now you tell me that you *were* part of it, but you ask me to believe you didn't know what your Sisterhood was capable of doing. Well, I want to believe that. I do. It's just that . . ." He gave up fumbling for words. How much of what she had told him had actually sunk in? "Look," he said finally, "I'm absolutely exhausted. I can't seem to hold on to anything. Please. Let's call a truce for the night and just get up to Rosetti's place. We'll see what things are like tomorrow. Okay?"

Christine sighed, then nodded. "Okay, truce." Hesitantly, she extended her hand toward him. He clasped it—first in one, then both of his. The warmth in her touch only added to his confusion. Why did it have to be her? Why? The question floated through his thoughts like a mantra, over and over again, easing his eyes closed and smothering the turmoil within him. He heard the engine engage and felt the Mustang swing onto the roadway in the instant before he surrendered to exhaustion.

"David? . . . I'm sorry, but you have to wake up." Christine pulled the blanket away from his face and waited as he pawed his eyes open. "Are you feeling better?"

"Only if there are degrees of deceased," he mumbled. He pushed the blanket to his lap and peered

270

through the windshield. They were parked on the shoulder of a narrow pitch-black road. "Where are we?"

"We're in lost," she said matter-of-factly.

Her humor, unexpected, nearly slipped past him. He glared at her for a moment, then stammered. "But . . . but we weren't going there. I think we should take the next right, or at least the next left."

"At least . . ." They both laughed.

"What time is it?"

"Two. A little after. We were right where the map said we were supposed to be, then all of a sudden, about fifteen or twenty minutes ago, the landmarks disappeared." She handed him Joey's drawing.

David opened his window and breathed deeply. The air, scrubbed by four days of rain, was cool and sweet with the scents of autumn. An almost invisible mist hung low over the roadway. Within a few breaths he could taste the salt captured in its droplets. Then he heard the sea, like the thrum of an endless train, up through the woods to their right. "Have we passed Gloucester?" he asked.

"Yes, just before I got lost."

He smiled. "You did fine, Christine. The ocean's over there through the trees. It sounds as if we're pretty high above it. I'll bet a Devil Dog we're near this place Joey marked as 'cliffs.' "

"Bet a what?"

"A Devil Dog. You see I . . . never mind. I'll explain tomorrow. Assuming I'm not too foggy to figure out what this map says, and if there are no other roads between us and the ocean, we should be close to the turnoff for Rocky Point. I vote straight ahead."

She eased the Mustang back onto the road and into the darkness.

After a quarter of a mile, the pavement rose sharply to the right. Moments later, they broke free of the woods. The sight below was breathtaking. The steep

271

slope, dotted with trees and boulders, dropped several hundred feet before giving way to the jet black Atlantic. Overhead, a large gap had developed in the clouds, exposing several stars and the white scimitar of a waxing moon. Christine pulled to the side and cut the engine.

"Even if we had no idea where we were, we wouldn't be lost," David said gently. "See that dark mass on the other side of the cove? I think that's Rocky Point."

Christine did not respond. She stepped from the car and walked to the edge of the drop-off. For several minutes she stood there, an ebony statue against the blue black of the sky. When she returned, tears glistened in her eyes. The rest of their drive was made in silence.

The little hideaway, as Joey had called it, was splendid—a hexagonal glass and redwood lodge suspended over the very tip of the point.

"David, it's just beautiful," she said.

"You go ahead and open the place up," David said. "I'll be along."

"Do you need help?"

David shook his head, then realized he was not at all sure he could make it on his own. He pushed himself out of the car and onto the crutches. Immediately the dizziness and nausea took hold. He struggled to the bottom of the short flight of steps leading to the front door. For hours tension and nervous energy had helped him overcome the pain and the aftereffects of his hypothermia. Now, it seemed, he had nothing left. He grabbed the railing, but spun off it and fell heavily. In seconds Christine was beside him, supporting him, guiding him inside.

The huge picture windows and high beamed ceilings were little more than hazy, whirling shapes as she helped him past a large fieldstone fireplace to the bedroom. As she lowered him onto the bed, the telephone in the living room began ringing.

"Go on and answer it, I'll be all right," he said, eyes closed. "It's probably Joey."

He heard her leave, and for several minutes he battled encroaching darkness and waited. By the time she returned, he was losing.

"David, are you awake?" A single nod. "You were right, that was Joey. He wanted to make sure we got here in one piece. Please nod if you understand what I'm saying, okay? Good. He called some friends of his on the police force. David, no one knows anything about Leonard Vincent being picked up tonight. Everyone in Boston is looking for you, but Vincent must have escaped the hospital before he was noticed. Joey said he would keep checking around and call us later today or else Saturday morning. We're okay as long as we're up here, but he said to be careful if we drive back to the city. David?"

This time he did not acknowledge.

Hours later, David's eyes blinked open in misty wakefulness.

He was undressed and under the covers, his torn, swollen ankle propped up on pillows. Nestled beside it was a plastic bag of water—the remains of an improvised ice pack.

He lifted himself to one elbow and looked out through the ceiling-to-floor windows. An endless sea of stars now glittered across the clearing night sky.

A cry came from outside the room. David grabbed his crutches and limped toward the sound. Christine was asleep on the living room couch. She cried out again, more softly this time. David moved to rouse her. Then he stopped. He could wake her for a minute or ten or even an hour, but it would make no difference. He knew the resilience of nightmares.

CHAPTER XX

The sizzle and aroma of frying bacon nudged David from a dreamless sleep and kept his first thoughts of the morning away from the horror of the past night.

Sunlight, isolated from the ocean breeze by the wall-sized windows, bathed him in an almost uncomfortable warmth. Sun! David opened his eyes and squinted into the glare. For nearly a week the world had been a damp, monotonous gray. Now he could almost taste the blue-white sky.

His forearm was throbbing beneath Terry's bulky dressing, but not unbearably so. He dangled his legs over the edge of the bed and flexed his ankle. A numb ache, also tolerable. In fact, he realized, there was a strange, reassuring comfort about the pain—perhaps an affirmation that in order to hurt, in order to feel, he must still be alive. The notion brought with it a fleeting smile. How many times had he encountered patients who seemed to be actually enjoying their pain? Next time he would be more understanding.

He heard Christine moving about the kitchen, then suddenly there was music from a radio. Classical music! Telemann? Absolutely, he decided. A jumbo pizza and six mindless hours of uninterrupted T.V. said it was Telemann. For a time he listened, thinking about the woman and the fantastic story she had told him. Last night he had been furious. As angry and frustrated as he could ever remember. But now, in the sunlight and the music, he realized she was in many ways as innocent, as caught in the nightmare, as he was. True, she had given the morphine to Charlotte Thomas, but in no way could she have anticipated the events to follow. He had to believe that. For his own sanity he had to believe that.

He closed his eyes, savoring a few final seconds of the promise of a new day. Then he picked up one crutch and hobbled out of the bedroom.

The kitchen, separated from the living/dining area by a butcher-block counter, was on the west side of the hexagon. Christine stood by the sink, working a wire beater through a bowl of pancake mix. The sight of her triggered a warm rush through David's body. No afternoon sun could have brightened the room as she did that moment. Her hair, a loose, sandy braid, dangled halfway down her back. A light blue man's shirt, knotted at the bottom, accentuated the curve of her breasts and exposed a band of honeyed skin at her waist. Below that, faded jeans clung to her hips and buttocks.

As he watched, David sensed the hammering in his chest and tried to will it to stop. "Mornin'," he said casually, wondering if he looked more at ease than he felt.

She turned. "I couldn't decide whether to wake you or to wait and risk ruining breakfast, so I took the coward's way out and turned on the radio. Did you get enough sleep?"

David searched her expression. Was she asking for their truce to continue, to be allowed to bring things up in her own time and her own way? "I slept fine," he said. "Thanks for putting me to bed."

275

"I was afraid you'd be upset about my doing that."
Christine set the beater down and walked to him.

"Only that I wasn't conscious when you did," he said.
Her laugh gave him his cue. He would keep things
light until she was ready to talk. "Listen, can I help in
there? I'm a wonderful cook . . . for any type of meal
whose main ingredient is water."

"I think things are under control. You could light a
fire. It's a little chilly on this side of the house. There's
wood already laid in the fireplace. This afternoon, if you
want, you can be in charge of lunch."

"Fair enough." He headed for the hearth.

As Christine returned to the sink she heard him
mumble, "Maybe some Cup-A-Soup and instant mashed
potatoes . . . or perhaps beef jerky in white wine sauce
. . ." Silently she thanked him. A rueful smile tightened across her face as she remembered Dotty Dalrymple's assessment. "A degenerate," she'd called him.
And just what does that make us? Christine wondered.
We who have taken it on ourselves to weigh the value
of a human life. We who can believe so mightily in our
commitment to end it whenever we think appropriate.
What does that make us?

She glanced into the living room. David was sitting
by a low fire, his swollen ankle propped on a hassock.
"Show me how to make it, David," she whispered.
"Show me how you survived the hell I helped put you
through. I know it's a lot to ask, but please, please try."

Joey Rosetti's jeep was antique in body and spirit, if
not in years. From the passenger seat David watched
with admiration as Christine maneuvered the snorting
beast around rocks and muddy puddles on the steep
grade to the ocean.

Talk throughout the morning had been light, with
only oblique references to the horrors that had brought
them together. When Christine suggested a picnic by

276

the water, David started to object—to insist that they confront the issues facing them. Quickly, though, he acknowledged that he too wanted the respite to continue. There would be time enough to talk after lunch.

The stony dirt track they had chosen wound through a tangled fairy-tale forest of beach plum, wild rose, and scrub pine. After several hundred yards, it deteriorated into a series of partly overgrown hairpin turns.

"Maybe we should back up and try to find another road," David said.

"Maybe . . ." She bounced through a vicious loop that he had felt certain would be impassable. "But I'll bet you a . . . a Fruit Pie we make it on this one."

Moments later, the thick brush fell off to either side. A final hairpin and the road spilled onto a sandy oval scarcely thirty yards long, a perfect white-gold medallion resting on the breast of the Atlantic. Christine skidded to a dusty stop. The engine noise faded. They sat, feeling the silence and the colors.

"A penny . . . ?" David asked finally.

"For my thoughts?"

"Uh-huh."

"You'll want change."

"Try me."

"Well, I was just deciding which spot would be best to spread the blanket and set our lunch."

"That's it?"

"That's it." She took the bag of food and the blanket, then kicked off her shoes and hopped onto the sand. "After we eat, we can talk, okay?" He nodded. "Well, are you coming?"

"In a minute. You go ahead."

Concern darkened her face, then vanished. With a delighted whoop, she raced across the beach.

David sank back in his seat, aware of a heavy, husky discomfort across his upper chest. In the minutes that followed the feeling intensified. He struggled to pin it down, to label it. Gradually he understood. He was being drawn into her world, her life. He was caring more almost every minute. Caring for the woman whose actions, whose hubris, had triggered his nightmare and had somehow led to the death of his friend. Caring for a woman who had confessed to murder, for a woman whose situation was . . . hopeless.

This is crazy, he thought. Absolutely insane. This woman is headed nowhere—except possibly to jail. She has no career now. No future beyond the turmoil of an arrest and trial. Lauren had so much—talent, beauty, direction, self-assuredness. What has Christine Beall got?

"David?" Christine's voice startled him, and for a moment he couldn't locate her. Then, through the windshield, he saw her, elbows resting on the hood of the jeep, studying him. "Are you all right?"

"Huh? Oh, sure, I'm fine," he lied.

"Good. I couldn't tell if you were in a trance or just in a snit because I forgot to let you put lunch together. It's ready whenever you are."

David smiled thinly, lowered himself from the jeep, and limped across the sand to the partly shaded niche where she had spread their blanket.

Silence settled in as they picked at the mélange of foods Christine had found—sardines, marinated artichoke hearts, Wheat Thins, boiled eggs, black olives, string cheese, and Portuguese sweet bread.

"That was delicious," David said finally. "Want to flip for rights to that last artichoke?"

"No, thanks, I'm full. You go ahead." She paused, then continued with almost no change in her tone. "Charlotte wasn't dying of cancer, was she?" It was a statement more than a question.

So much for Camelot, David thought. With a deliberateness that he hoped would help him form a response, he set his fork in an empty jar, then swung around to face her.

"You mean the autopsy findings," he said. She swallowed hard and nodded. "Well, then, the simple answer to your question is probably not. On autopsy there was no obvious cancer. For sure it could have popped up again in six months or a year, or even two. But for now that's your answer."

Christine started to reply, then bit at her lip and turned away. Without the slightest warning, even to himself, David snapped at her. "Damn it, Christine, don't do this to yourself. If you're going to work this whole business through—and I think you should—then do it from all sides—not just the ones that will heighten your guilt. Either we take a hard look from every angle or we might as well go back to small talk. Understand?"

Christine nodded. Her eyes were glazed and vacant. "I . . . I just feel so damn lost," she said hoarsely. "So frightened, so . . . so hopeless."

That word again. This time it was David who looked away. He could not shake the feeling that she was right. What *did* she have to look forward to? Then he thought of Lauren. For better or for better. That was how he had described her commitment to him. Now it was his turn to decide.

In that instant he felt a renewed spark of anger. Christine Beall had made choices and because of those choices people had gotten hurt—and killed. Now she was feeling hopeless. Wasn't she getting just what she deserved?

What she deserved. David shook his head. How many of his colleagues thought that getting arrested, then suspended from the Doctors Hospital staff was just what *he* deserved. Did he have any more right to pass judgment than they did?

He reached out and took Christine's hand. Her fingers tightened about his. He could feel her despair.

All at once, he folded his arms in a rigid professorial pose. "Just where do you get off thinking you have the right to make that diagnosis?" he asked haughtily.

"What diagnosis?"

"Hopelessness. Here you are in the presence of perhaps the world's greatest expert on the subject, and you have the temerity to diagnose yourself without asking for a consultation? That is unacceptable. I am taking over this case." The emptiness in her eyes began to lift. "We must take an inventory," he said. "First the basics. I see ten fingers, ten toes, and two of all the parts there are supposed to be two of. Are they all in working order, miss?" She suppressed a giggle and nodded. "So far, this sounds very unhopeless. Are you perchance aware of the classic Zurich study on the subject? They measured hopelessness on a scale of zero to ten in over a thousand subjects, half of them living and half dead. A hopelessness index of ten was considered absolute. Can you guess the outcome of that research?" She was laughing now. "Can't guess? Well, I'll tell you. A marked difference was found between the groups. In fact, those in the deceased group invariably rated ten, the rest invariably zero." He rubbed his chin and eyed her up and down. "I'm sorry, miss. I really am, but I'm afraid that no matter how much you want to be, you are simply not hopeless. Thank you very much for coming. My bill's in the mail. Next?"

She threw her arms around his neck. "Thank you." Her lips brushed his ear as she spoke. "Thank you for the consultation." She drew her head back to look at him. Their kiss simply happened—a gentle, comfortable touching that neither of them wanted to end or change. A minute passed, and then another. Finally she drew away.

"It all went wrong," she said softly. "It seemed so right, and it all just went . . . crazy. Why, David? Tell me. How the hell can I ever trust my feelings again when something I believed in so very much turned out so sour?" She sank down to the sand and stared out at the Atlantic.

"You want to know why?" he said, dropping next to her. "Because you're not perfect, that's why. Because nobody's perfect, that's why. Because every equation involving human beings is insolvable, or at least never solvable the same way twice. I believe in euthanasia just as much as you do. I always have. It's an absolutely right idea as far as I'm concerned. The difference is that somehow I have come to understand that while it is an absolutely right idea, there is simply no way to do it right. Sooner or later, the human element, the unpredictable, uncontrollable X factor rears its ugly head, and *wham*, things come apart."

"And innocent people die," she said.

"Chris, as far as I'm concerned, when it comes to dying, we're all innocent. That's the problem. Someone in your Sisterhood—possibly this Peggy woman—has snatched up the good, honest beliefs of some wonderful, idealistic nurses and has run away with them. Again, the human element. Money, greed, lust, fanaticism. Who knows what will pluck that special string hidden within someone and set him off? You were about to expose The Sisterhood, or at least that's what somebody thought. That string gets plucked and crazy, insane decisions get made.

"There's this riddle I once heard," he continued. "It asks a person what he would do if he was presented with a healthy newborn infant and promised that by slaying that infant he could instantly cure the ills of all mankind. Someone in your Sisterhood has answered that riddle for herself. Ben, you, me—none of us is as important to them as their ideals. The individual sacrificed for the greater good. It happens all the time."

"That's horrible," she said.

"Maybe. But more important, it's human. You can

shoulder the burden of responsibilities for my suffering or even Ben's death, if you want to, but that's being awfully tough on yourself for just doing what you believed in and for trusting that other human beings were just as constant, just as pure in their belief as you were.

"You have decisions to make, Chris. Huge, crunching, God-awful decisions. If you want, I'll help. But don't expect me to stand by holding the matches while you pour gasoline over yourself. I . . . I care too much."

Slowly she turned to him. Her eyes held him as they had during their first moments together. Her hands caressed the sides of his face. Their kiss, this time warm and deep and sweet, carried them to the sand. Moment by moment, as they undressed one another, the world beyond their beach drifted away. David kissed her eyes, then buried his lips in the soft hollow of her neck. Her hands flowed over his body, capturing new excitement for herself as she created it in him.

With every kiss, every touch, the loneliness and fear inside them lessened. With each new discovery the sense of hopelessness ebbed.

Christine's face glowed golden in the late afternoon sun as she pulled herself on top of him. He stroked her firm breasts, first with his hands, then with his tongue.

She was smiling as she reached down and guided him inside her.

"Barbara, just stop fretting and give me the names. I'll take care of it."

"But . . ."

"The names, please." Margaret Armstrong snapped the words, then balled the small piece of fabric in her fist and forced herself to relax.

Barbara Littlejohn hesitated. A throbbing in her head, which had begun during the flight from Los Angeles, intensified. Finally she opened a manilla folder and passed one letter at a time across the cardiologist's desk. "Ruth Serafini," she said. "Resigned from both the board of directors and the movement. Says that she understands you are doing what you think is right, but that she cannot, in all good conscience, go along with it."

"Not even a copy to me," Peggy muttered, scanning the letter, then tossing it aside.

"Susan Berger," Barbara continued. "Says essentially the same thing as Ruth, but goes on to state that until matters are resolved she intends to curtail all Sisterhood operations in northern California. No approval for new cases, and also her recommendation that all contributions to the Clinton Foundation be held up."

Peggy set the letter on top of the other without reading it. "Susan will listen to reason," she said evenly, weighing the possibility of doctoring the half-dozen tapes of Susan's that were locked in her basement vault. Without any reference to The Sisterhood of Life, the tapes would constitute a chilling confession. "She's far too ambitious a woman not to listen to reason." Peggy unraveled the square of linen and absently rubbed it between her fingertips.

Barbara Littlejohn, appearing gray and drawn despite her carefully applied makeup, passed across the third letter. "This is the one that upset me the most," she said. "It's from Sara."

Damn! The expletive was thought more than spoken.

"She says that she will reconsider her resignation if we conduct a careful investigation into involvement of The Sisterhood or its members in the deaths of John Chapman and Senator Cormier—both at this hospital. Peggy, we didn't have anything to do with—"

"Of course not," Peggy said. "John Chapman was a friend of Sara's. She's just upset. Senator Cormier was autopsied and has already been thoroughly discussed at a death conference. I made it a point to attend. He had extensive coronary artery disease and simply had a fatal heart attack during surgery. That's all there is to that."

"I'm glad." There was genuine relief in Barbara's face and voice. "Peggy, I don't know what I would have done if you hadn't been available to discuss this. Everything seemed to be coming apart."

"Nonsense. You're doing a wonderful job. Our Sisterhood has not only survived for forty years, it has grown. A situation like this Shelton business may dent our solidarity, but it won't break it. Just leave these letters with me. By day's end I'll have the whole matter under control."

"Thank you," Barbara said, taking Peggy's hand. "Thank you." She let herself out.

The pillow, baby. Just set it over my face and lean on it as hard as you can. It won't take long. They're trying to destroy me, mama. They're trying to destroy our Sisterhood. Margaret Armstrong's eyes were closed even before the outside door of her office clicked shut behind Barbara. The sense of that evening so many years ago, of the hospital room, of the pain on her mother's face—suddenly they were real once again.

"Mama, I . . . Please, mama. Please don't make me do it."

"I love you. If you love me too, you won't let me hurt so anymore. They all say it's hopeless. . . . Don't let me hurt so anymore. . . ."

"I love you, Mama. I love you." Peggy Donner whispered the words over and over again as Margaret Armstrong watched and listened, the piece of linen gliding continuously across her fingertips.

"I love you, Mama . . ." Peggy said as she placed the pillow over the narrow face and leaned on it with all the strength she could manage.

Margaret watched the movement beneath the sheet lessen, then stop. She was shaking as the girl replaced

284

the pillow and kissed her dead mother's lips. She looked at the square of fabric as if discovering it for the first time.

Once again, the ordeal was over.

John Dockerty paced from one side of the cluttered back room of Marcus Quigg's pharmacy to the other. Off to one side, Ted Ulansky watched, his broad face an expressionless mask. They had been grilling Quigg for nearly two hours, after finding enough improprieties in his records at least to have his license suspended. Dockerty's hunch had been right. There was no need to manufacture evidence against the squirrelly pharmacist. In just a few hours of work, checking his prescriptions and calling a few doctors, they had gained the kind of clout that should have brought Quigg to his knees begging for some kind of a deal. However, the little man had proved surprisingly resistant—or frightened.

"Mr. Quigg," Dockerty said irritably, "let's start all over again." The detective snapped a small stack of Quigg's bogus prescriptions against the palm of his hand. He and Ulansky had agreed ahead of time that Dockerty would assume the role of tough, threatening villain during the interrogation and Ulansky would wait until he felt the tension was right, then ride to Quigg's defense like a knight errant.

"Whatever you say," Quigg mumbled. He was maintaining what composure he had left by chain-smoking and avoiding any eye contact. However, from his vantage point, Ted Ulansky noticed that, for the first time, Quigg's hand was shaking. It would not be long.

"I've laid it all out for you," Dockerty spat. "These prescriptions tell me that you are at least a crook. At worst, you're a fucking dope pusher who is putting bread on his table by dealing pills to kids. Now either you tell us what we want to know, either you tell us who paid you to finger David Shelton, or I'll see to it that your pharmacy license is chopped up and stuffed down your throat as your first prison meal. Got that?"

Quigg bit at his lower lip. The shaking increased.

From the corner of his eye Dockerty saw Ulansky nod. Time for the finale. He tightened his jaw and spoke through clenched teeth. "I want a name, Quigg, and I want it now. Otherwise there's a cell waiting for you at Walpole. And believe me, a cute little fellow like you is dog meat to those guys. After a week, your asshole is going to be so wide from getting screwed that you'll shit in your pants every time you take a step." His voice was booming now. "The name, Quigg—I want the name."

"Enough!" Ulansky cracked the word like a whip. Quigg's ashen face spun toward him. The narcotics investigator inserted himself between the two men like the referee in a prizefight. He put a calming hand on Dockerty's chest, only to have it slapped aside. For an instant he wasn't certain the Irishman was acting. "John, calm down. Just calm down. That temper of yours has gotten you in enough hot water with Internal Affairs as is, so just get a hold of yourself." He turned benevolently to Quigg, noting with satisfaction that a trace of color had returned to the man's cheeks.

"Marcus, I want to help you out, I really do," he said, reassurance flowing from every word. "But you've got to realize what you're up against. You're sitting here balancing your career, your freedom, and your health against a name. Just a name. That's all the lieutenant is asking for. I know you're frightened about what will happen if you give it to us, but just think about what will happen to you if you don't. At least the detective here can offer you some hope. Can the name we want offer you that?"

Ulansky scrutinized the man's face. He saw fear and uncertainty, but not defeat—not the capitulation he had expected by now. He looked at Dockerty and shook his head.

"I . . . I want to speak to my lawyer," Quigg said.

Dockerty shot across the room, grabbed the man by his lapels, and pulled him to his feet. "You get nothing until I get some answers." Reluctantly, he released his grip. "We're taking you with us, Quigg," he said. "I want you to see firsthand what jail is all about. We still have business, you and me. Come on, creep, let's go."

Marcus Quigg felt the knifelike pain beneath his breastbone and thought for a moment that it was all going to end right there. The wafer-thin aneurysm that had replaced much of the muscle of his heart was stretching. He had wanted to tell them at the outset that he was no crook. He wanted to tell them now that the illegal prescriptions were strictly nickel-and-dime stuff—Band-Aids to try and hold together his failing business and his failing health and his wife, terrified of being left alone with four children. He wanted to tell them, but he couldn't.

What difference did it make anyway? He asked himself the question over and over as Dockerty snapped handcuffs on him and led him from the store. So this Shelton was in trouble because of what he was doing. Well, he was in trouble, too. Big trouble. The goddamn balloon in his chest was stretching and his doctor had said it could be a year or a month . . . or an hour. She had said there was nothing that could be done for him. Would Dockerty understand? Would he understand that, after a whole life of trying to do what was right, all he had to show for it was a frightened wife, four kids who needed to eat, and a ball of blood in his chest that could explode at any time?

Quigg felt the knot in his gut and tasted acid percolating in his throat. He wanted to tell them and just go home to his own bed. But he knew what would happen. He knew the money would stop. He knew the additional thousands of dollars he had been promised when the whole mess was over would never come.

As he was shoved into the back seat of the detective's car, Marcus Quigg silently cursed Dr. Margaret Armstrong and the misery she had brought him.

A pot of coffee, a shower together, and suddenly the evening had passed into crystal night. A birch log fire had transformed Joey's living room into a musty womb. Stretched on the couch, David and Christine alternated brief conversation with prolonged gazes at the velvet sky.

"Red silk," David said, fingering the robe he had borrowed from Rosetti's closet. "I never thought of myself as the silk dressing gown type, but it sure do feel fine."

Christine sat up, then pulled an edge of her robe across her lap. "David, I want you to know how much this day has meant to me." His eyes narrowed. "You know I didn't plan it this way, don't you?" He nodded. She saw the tightness in his face and the moist film over his eyes. "All of a sudden I feel . . . sort of selfish— even cruel."

"That's nonsense."

"No, it's not. I've allowed this to happen, knowing every minute it was going to end."

"You haven't exactly been alone," he said huskily.

"No, I guess not. . . ." Her voice trailed away. "David," she said at last, "I'm going back in the morning."

"One more day." His response was so quick that they both knew the thought had already been in his mind.

Christine shook her head. "I don't think that would be fair—to either of us. I know what you're feeling. I've been feeling it too. All day. My mind keeps flip-flopping from fantasies of what I want to have happen to the reality of what I know is going to. Staying here—even another day—will only make it hurt more when I go. I've caused you enough pain already."

"I don't want you to leave." He was battling the truth in what she had said. He knew it. Still, he was unable to stem the torrent of words. "It . . . it just isn't safe. Joey told you that last night. Vincent is loose somewhere in Boston. He's looking for me, and, as likely as not, he's looking for you, too. If we go back, we'd have to go straight to Dockerty. And what would we tell him? We can't go back yet. Hell, Chris, we don't have to go back ever. We could take off. Right now. Tonight. We could go to Canada or . . . or to Mexico. I speak some Spanish. Maybe we could open a little clinic somewhere. Practice together. What good would it possibly do to go back now?"

She kissed him lightly. "It wouldn't work, David. You know that as well as I do. My Sisterhood has done some terrible things. I couldn't live with myself if I didn't try to stop them. I only hope I can find a way to do it without hurting all those nurses like me who believed—"

"Dammit, there must be another way!" David stiffened, then muttered an apology for the outburst and sank into the cushion. She was right. The rational, logical part of him understood that. If their circumstances were reversed, he knew, he would be saying the same things. But at the moment the rational, logical part of him was not controlling his tongue.

"Look," he said, "maybe there is another way. Maybe we could go off somewhere safe and you could send what information you have to Dockerty or . . . or to Dr. Armstrong. Sure, that's it—Dr. Armstrong. She's been a friend and a help to me since this whole nightmare started. If anyone could help us convince the authorities about The Sisterhood's existence, she could." In spite of himself, the idea actually began to take hold. "Chris, the woman would be perfect. You heard it yourself that night on Four South. She's absolutely set against euthanasia. For all we know, if someone of Dr. Armstrong's stature comes out against them, the Sisterhood people might decide it was time to fold up the organization all together. We could write to her and she could—"

"David, please. Don't do this."

"No, wait, hear me out. Just let me finish. Charlotte Thomas wanted to die. As far as we can tell, she was going to die no matter what. Oh, maybe another day of misery or a few agonizing weeks, but she was going to die." Inside, David's mental voice began begging him to listen to the thoughtlessness of what he was saying, to the pressure he was putting on her. The pleas went unheeded. "From what you know of the woman, do you think she would want you, want us, to have our chance together snuffed out because you helped her accomplish what she simply didn't have the strength to do herself? Just another day or two to think things over. That's all I'm asking. We'll find another way, or we'll go back and face things together. At least let's wait until we hear from Joey. Maybe he'll find out Vincent's in jail somewhere after all."

She closed her eyes and held him with all her strength. In the silence that followed, the scene David had started to paint grew in her thoughts. It was a dusty village nestled in a horseshoe of craggy mountains. She even saw their clinic—a white clay building at the end of a sunbaked dirt street. She could feel the warmth and serenity of their life. She sensed the peace that would come from devoting herself to such a place and such a man.

Christine pressed her lips together and nodded. "Okay. Another day. But no promises."

"No promises." He felt only momentary joy at his victory before he began to acknowledge what he had known all along: unless they could find a truly satisfactory option, he would never allow her to run.

They made love in soft, unhurried harmony. For nearly an hour their eyes and mouths and fingertips explored one another. At last, when it felt as if neither of them could tolerate another touch without exploding, he entered her.

Marion Anderson Cooper was tough. Not only a tough cop, although he was that, too. He was tough in ways that only boys growing up on the streets of Roxbury with a feminine-sounding name could be tough. His toughness had been forged by rat bites as he lay on the shabby mattress he shared with his two brothers and tempered by two years in the mud and death of Vietnam. It was tested again and again by situations encountered as one of the first black sergeants assigned to the Little Italy section of Boston—the North End.

In the early morning hours of October 11 Cooper was making his second pass through the largely deserted streets of his patrol. From time to time he stopped the cruiser to shine his light in the window of a store or restaurant where he sensed something out of the ordinary. Each time he identified the source of his uneasiness—a new product display or repositioned table—and moved on.

The purple Fiat, parked inconspicuously by a dumpster in one of the back alleys, had not been there on his earlier swing through the area. Cooper blocked the alley with the patrol car, flashed his spot on the license plate and radioed the dispatcher.

"This is Alpha Nine Twenty-one," he said, "requesting stolen check and listing on a purple Fiat, Massachusetts license number three-five-three, Mike, Whiskey, Quebec. Any backup units available?

"Negative, Alpha Nine Twenty-one. Repeat license, please."

Cooper repeated the number and waited. The car was hot—he felt certain of that. In fact, he was surprised there hadn't been other redistributed vehicles on the first night of decent weather in over a week. If it were stolen, it was kids, not the pros. Had it been the pros, the little Fiat would have already been painted, supplied with new numbers, and on its way to fill an order in Springfield or Fall River or someplace.

The delay seemed longer than usual. Cooper drummed impatiently on the wheel. He flipped on his walkie-talkie and was stepping out of the car when the radio crackled to life.

"Alpha Nine Twenty-one, I have information on nineteen seventy-nine Fiat sedan, Massachusetts license three-five-three, Mike, Whiskey, Quebec." The woman's voice, sensuous and tantalizing, was one Cooper recognized as belonging to a hundred-and-seventy-pound mustachioed mother of five.

"This is Alpha Nine, Gladys," he said. "What have you got?"

"So far the car is clean as your whistle, Alpha Nine—no wants, no warrants. Registered to Joseph Rosetti, twenty-one Damon Street, Apartment C."

"Alpha Nine out," Cooper said. As he entered the alley, he instinctively unsnapped the flap of his service revolver.

The driver's side door of the Fiat was open. Cooper shined his flashlight on the seats, then the floor. Nothing. Suddenly he tensed. The thick, nauseating scent of blood—the perfume of death—filled his nostrils. Wedged behind the seats, covered by a scruffy tan blanket, was a body. He took a quick breath and pulled the blanket aside. At that moment all the toughness, all the gruesome battles in the rice paddies and the jungles and the city streets did not help at all.

Marion Anderson Cooper spun away from the car and puked on the pavement.

Joey's hands and feet were bound. He had been stabbed dozens of times before he died. Arranged neatly on his chest were one of his ears and parts of three fingers. The morning papers would dismiss his grisly death as "a probable gangland slaying."

Twenty miles north of the city, the real reason, a crudely sketched blood-smeared map, extracted after an hour of torture, rested on the passenger seat of Leonard Vincent's sedan.

CHAPTER XXI

Moving soundlessly, Christine set her suitcase by the front door and returned to the bedroom. Through eyes reddened by nearly an hour of crying, she peered across the pale early morning light at David. He was sleeping peacefully, his bushy hair partly buried in the pillow clutched to his face. With a painful glance at the letter wedged alongside the dresser mirror, she tiptoed out of the house.

The morning was chilly and still. Her breath, faintly visible, hung in the air. Far below, a thick mantle of silver covered the ocean as far as she could see. With movements as dreamlike as the world around her she took the key from the jeep, dropped it in an envelope, and walked slowly to her own car. Any moment she expected to hear his voice calling to her from the deck. The sight of him, she knew, would snap her resolve like a dry twig.

Without a backward look, she slid onto the driver's seat of the Mustang and rolled it down the drive before starting the engine. At the end of the turnoff to Rocky Point, a quarter of a mile from the house, she stopped and set the envelope with the key in a small pile of rocks. A final check to be certain David would have no trouble spotting it, then she turned left onto the winding ocean road, heading south to Boston.

The thoughts and feelings whirling inside her made it impossible to concentrate. She took no notice of the dark sedan that cruised past her in the other direction, nor of the huge, featureless man behind the wheel. No notice, that is, until the car suddenly appeared in her rearview mirror only a few yards behind.

Leonard Vincent maneuvered his car close to the smaller Mustang. Christine's momentary anger at being tailgated changed to terror as their bumpers made contact. At first, it was just a scrape, then a crunch. Suddenly Vincent sped inside her on the right and began forcing her across the road. Christine's knuckles whitened on the wheel as she strained to keep from spinning out of control. She searched to her left for an escape route and instantly broke into a terrified, icy sweat.

Not ten feet away was the edge of a drop-off—the high slope of rocks and trees where a thirty-six-hour lifetime ago she had stood and gazed for the first time at Rocky Point. Several hundred feet below stretched the Atlantic.

Another crunch, louder than before. Christine's head spun to the right. The front of Vincent's car was even with her passenger door. Beyond him, a shallow gully, then a sheer wall of sandstone. The Mustang vibrated mercilessly as its tires bounced sideways. Christine slammed on the brake. The acrid smell of burning rubber filled the car.

Leonard Vincent's expression looked bland, almost peaceful as he forced her closer and closer to the drop-off. Less than five feet remained between the Mustang and the edge of the road when Christine released the brake and floored the accelerator. Her car shot forward. Out of the corner of her eye, she saw the sedan slip away. Then the bumpers of the two cars locked.

In an instant they were both out of control, spinning in a wild death dance across the road. Christine fought the wheel with all her strength, but it ripped from her hands. Her right arm slammed down against the gear shift and shattered just above the wrist. At the moment the white-hot pain registered, Christine's car hit the sandstone wall. Her head shot forward, smashing into the windshield just above her left ear. The glass exploded and instantly her world went black.

She did not hear the scream of tearing metal as the two cars separated. She did not see the wide-eyed terror in Leonard Vincent's face as his car snapped free of hers like a whip, then catapulted toward the ocean, hitting nose down on the steep slope and bouncing off trees and boulders over and over again until it disappeared in the thick fog. She did not see her own car ricochet off the rock face, spin full circle, then roll toward the drop-off.

She was unconscious on the seat when the rear wheels of the Mustang dropped over the embankment. The car stopped, its chassis teetering on the soft dirt. Then it slid over the edge.

David felt the emptiness even before he was fully awake. He opened his eyes a slit, then closed them tightly, trying to will what he knew was true not to be so. She's in the living room, sitting quietly, looking out at the ocean. A dollar says she's in the living room. He held his breath. The silence in the house was more than the simple absence of sound. It was a void, a nothingness. There was no movement of air, no sense of energy, no life.

She's gone for a walk, he reasoned desperately. A little morning walk and immediately the great surgeon panics. He rolled toward the window, blinking at the sunless glare. The sky was a thin sheet of pearl—the sort of overcast that would miraculously disappear by midmorning, opening like a curtain on the extravaganza of a new day. A morning walk, that's all.

He pushed himself to one elbow and scanned the room. The realization that her clothes were gone sank in only moments before he saw the envelope wedged alongside the mirror. It was the scene from countless grade B movies, only this time inexorably real. Sadness as flat as the morning sky swept over him.

"Shit," was his first word of the day. Then his second and third. He pulled himself out of bed and walked purposefully past the dresser into the bathroom. He peed, then washed, then shaved. He limped to the kitchen and put on water for coffee. The ankle was stiff and slow, but almost free of pain. His nurse had done her job well.

He tidied the living room and waited for the water to boil. In one final jet of hope he checked the driveway. The Mustang was gone. Christine was gone. Mexico and any chance for a new, unencumbered life together were gone.

Numbly, he shuffled back to the bedroom.

His name was printed in the center of the plain white envelope. He watched his hands tear it open. Another note. The second one in less than a week. This time, though, he felt the anguish in every word—as it was written and as it was read.

Dear David,

I couldn't chance waiting for you to wake up and talk me out of doing this. I tried all night to make myself believe there was another way. God, how I tried. In the end, though, all I could think of was how much pain and sadness I've caused you. It's all so very crazy. Something that seemed so good, so right. And now . . . I am going to see Lt. Dockerty to make a full confession regarding Charlotte. Before I do, I am going to meet with Dr. Armstrong. What you said last night made so much sense. I know she can help me. Despite what has happened, I know in my heart that most of us are only following principles we believe in. With luck, Dr. Armstrong can help put matters to rest with as little public disclosure as possible. I have three names to give her for starters, plus some phone numbers and a few Clinton Foundation newsletters. That's not much, but it's a start. Maybe, we can find a way of getting inside the secrecy. Then there is the matter of who is responsible for hiring Ben's killer. I'll do what I can to find out before involving the police.

Finally, there is you—a special, magic man. In so short a time, you have reached places inside me that I'm not sure I even knew existed. For that, and much more, I owe you. I owe you a life free from running, from constantly looking over my shoulder. I owe you a chance to fulfill the dreams you've worked so hard and endured so much for. If the circumstances were any different, sweet, gentle David—any different—I would have risked it. Gone wherever we decided. I honestly believe you would be worth the gamble.

But circumstances are not different. They are what they are. Don't worry about me. I'll go straight to Dockerty after I see Dr. Armstrong. Just be careful yourself.

Please understand, be strong, and most of all, forgive me for causing you so much hurt.

Love,
Christine

P.S. *The key to the jeep will be at the end of the turn off for Rocky Point. It's in an envelope like this one.*

The jeep. David laughed in spite of himself. From an even start it was doubtful the jeep could stay with Christine's Mustang for more than a few yards. She was certainly determined not to be dissuaded. Well, he would not be dissuaded either. He could not change the situation, so he would simply change his expectations. Whatever she had to face he would face with her, as long as she wanted him there.

David dressed, playing through in his mind the situations the two of them might encounter in the days and weeks ahead. He noticed the bulky sweater he had worn on the ride to Rocky Point. Christine had placed it, neatly folded, on a chair by the bureau. David grinned. Perhaps he could return it to Joey as a contribution toward the wardrobe of the next man chased into the Charles River. As he picked it up, Rosetti's heavy revolver fell out. David had completely forgotten about it. He hefted the revolver in one hand and felt the queasy tension that he had come to expect when handling guns of any kind. He tried to recall when Christine said Joey would call again. Last night? This morning? A moment of reflection and he went to the phone. Rosetti's Boston number was printed on a small card taped to the receiver.

The woman's voice that answered his call was older than Terry's.

"Hello, is this the Rosettis' residence?" he asked.

"Yes. Can I help you?"

"Well, could I speak with Mr. or Mrs. Rosetti, please?" For a time there was silence on the other end.

"Who is this, please?" the woman asked finally. Her voice was ice.

David began to shift nervously from one foot to the other. "My name is David Shelton. I'm a friend of Joey and Terry's, and I'm stay—"

"I know who you are, Dr. Shelton," the woman said flatly. Again there was silence. David felt an awful sinking in his gut. "This is Mrs. D'Ambrosio. Terry's mother. Terry can't come to the phone. The doctor's given her some medicine and . . ." Suddenly the woman began to cry. "Joey's dead . . . murdered," she sobbed.

David dropped to the couch and stared unseeing across the room. "Terry hasn't been able to talk to the police, but she talked to me, and she said it's because Joey helped you that he's dead." She broke down completely, any pretext of anger at him lost in her grief.

"But that's . . . impossible," he mumbled, his mind whirling. It was Leonard Vincent. It had to have been. He pressed his eyes, trying to stop the spinning. First Ben, now Joey . . . and Christine out there somewhere. "When did this happen?" His voice was lifeless.

"Early this morning. They found him in his car, stabbed and cut and . . . Dr. Shelton, I just don't want to talk to you anymore. Joey's funeral is Tuesday. You can speak with my daughter after that."

"But wait . . ." The woman hung up.

For several minutes David sat motionless, oblivious to the bleating of the receiver in his lap. Then he grabbed the sweater and the revolver, along with his crutches, and raced from the house. Hoping against hope, he checked the jeep. There was no key. He threw the gun on the seat and pushed himself down the road in long, swinging arcs. Still, by the time he returned, nearly half an hour had passed. He was soaked with perspiration, gasping for air. His ribs, battered by the unpadded arm supports, screamed as he pulled himself up behind the wheel. Then he stopped.

"Will you calm down," he panted. "She's fine. She's all right." He started the motor. She was probably in Dr. Armstrong's office right now, or even with Dockerty. All he had to do was cool down and get to Boston in one piece.

He glanced over at the revolver and thought about Rosetti's admonition to him. How had he put it? Do it unto others if you even think they're gonna do it unto you? Something like that. David shuddered, then cradled the gun in his hands. Had Joey died because he didn't have the revolver when he needed it? The possibility drained away what little spirit David had left. All that remained was anger. Anger and a consuming hatred. He would find Vincent, or whoever had murdered Joey. He would find them and either kill them or die trying. He clenched one hand, then squeezed it with the other until it hurt. Finally he worked the jeep into reverse and started down the driveway.

Concern for Christine diluted his anger with a sense of urgency. He tried accelerating, but the carburetor, choked on dust and sand, flooded. The idea occurred to him that a perfect thank-you gift for Joey would have been a tune-up and alignment for the jeep.

Would have been. David shook his head helplessly, then glanced at the watch Joey had given him. It was after nine. Above, the frail overcast was showing the first signs of surrender to the autumn sun. He forced himself to loosen up and restarted the engine. By the time he reached the ocean road, he had mastered a rhythm of shifting and acceleration that was acceptable to the relic. His thoughts returned to Christine. Perhaps he should have called the police. If she didn't have too great a start, at least they could detain her long enough for him to catch up. But who—the state police? Would she be upset if he involved them before she was ready? He turned the notion over in his mind. He had decided to stop at the first phone booth when he saw the flashing lights and barriers of a roadblock ahead.

A battered maroon pickup truck in front of him was struggling through a U-turn, its grizzled driver mouthing obscenities. David leaned out of the jeep and called to him.

"Hey, what's going on up there?"

"Eh?" The man stopped the truck obliquely across the road, still several maneuvers from a complete U.

"Up ahead, what's happened?" David tried again, this time shouting.

"Accident. Bad one too, damn it." The old man's

tone left no doubt that he was taking the inconvenience personally. "Two cars over the side. One they just hauled up. One's comin' from way at the bottom. Fifteen, twenty minutes more, they said. Probably be an hour, the way Mac Perkins wc⁻¹ that old tow rig of his."

Uneasiness took hold as David strained to see past the truck. "Did you see either of the cars involved?" he asked too softly.

"Eh?"

David groaned. "The cars," he yelled. "Did you see either . . . Oh, never mind. Could I get by, please?"

"Sure, but you ain't goin' nowhere. An' there's no need for you to go snappin' about it neither." All at once David's questions registered. "The cars, you say? Did I see the cars?" Totally exasperated, David nodded. "Only the little blue one," the man called out. "Smashed to smithereens it is, too."

David's hands knotted on the wheel. A sinking terror deepened inside him. He closed his eyes while the old man worked his pickup out of the way. In that instant the photolike image of another accident appeared in his mind. The rain, the lights, Becky's and Ginny's faces, even their screams. He wanted to open his eyes, to end the horror, but he knew that when he did only a new nightmare awaited. He had no doubt that the blue car the old man had seen was Christine's.

"Mister, road's closed. I'm afraid you'll have to turn around."

David whirled toward the voice. It was a state trooper, tall and thin, with a high schooler's face that made him look slightly ridiculous in his authoritative blue uniform. Before David could respond, his gaze swung past the spot where the truck had been to the cluster of police cars, tow trucks, and ambulances ahead. In the midst of them, resting on flattened tires, was the shattered, twisted wreck of Christine's Mustang.

"Mister? . . ." The young trooper's voice held some concern.

David's face was ashen. "I . . . I know the woman who was driving that car," he said in a remote, hollow voice. "She was my . . . friend."

"Mister, are you all right?" When David did not answer, the trooper called down the road, "Gus, send one of the paramedics over here. I think this guy's gonna pass out or something." He opened the door of the jeep. As he did, David pushed past him and began a hobbling run toward the car, oblivious to the salvos of pain from his ankle. He stumbled the last five yards and hit heavily against the door. Gasping, he stretched his arms across the roof and held on. The car was empty. The windshield was blown out, and the engine had been smashed backward, nearly to the front seat. An ugly brown swatch of blood stood out against the soft blue seat cover.

"God damn it," he cried softly. "God damn it . . . God damn it!" Louder and louder until he was screaming.

Several men rushed toward him just as the trooper took his arm.

"Mister, please calm down," he said in more of a plea than an order. He led David to the side of the road and helped him lean against the trunk of a half-dead birch.

After a minute, David managed to speak. "Wh . . . where's her body?" he stammered.

"What?"

"Her body, damn it," he screamed. "Where have they taken it?"

The young man broke into a relieved grin. "Mister, there isn't any body. No dead one, I mean. Not from this car anyway."

David sank to one knee and stared up at him.

"Passerby found the lady wanderin' down the road," the trooper explained. "Pretty battered up, with a nasty

303

cut or two, and probably a broken arm, but nowheres near dead. Now, can you calm down enough to tell me who you are?"

Kensington Community Hospital, a twenty-minute drive according to the trooper, took thirty-five in the jeep. David had stayed at the accident scene for a short while, learning what he could. Christine's survival was miraculous. A couple had come upon her, bloodied and incoherent, wandering along the road. Later the rescue team found her Mustang wedged upside down against a tree fifty feet down the rocky slope and nearly half a mile from where she was picked up.

David remained long enough to watch with total dispassion as Leonard Vincent's mangled corpse was pried from his car and transferred to an ambulance. He left during the commotion that followed discovery in the wreckage of a silenced revolver and a variety of knives. Throughout his drive to the hospital he sensed renewed hatred building—hatred no longer directed at Leonard Vincent, but at those who had hired him.

The hospital was fairly new and very small—fifty beds or less, David guessed. He paused momentarily inside the front door, trying to develop some feel for the place. The lobby was deserted save for the ubiquitous salmon-coated volunteer behind the desk, rearranging the contents of her purse. To her right an impressive brass board listed the two dozen or so physicians on the hospital staff. Beside each name was a small amber bulb that the physician could switch on when he was "in the house." Only one had a glowing amber light. No one could accuse Kensington Community Hospital of being overstaffed, he thought sardonically.

The emergency wing was labeled with black paste-on letters above a set of automatic doors. As they slid shut behind him, David heard the volunteer say, "Can I

304

help you, sir?" He shook his head without bothering to look back.

The physician on duty, an Indian woman with dark, tired eyes, met him halfway down the corridor. She wore a light orange sari beneath her clinic coat and had a White Memorial Hospital name tag that identified her as Dr. T. Ranganathan.

"Excuse me," David said anxiously, "my name is David Shelton. I'm a surgeon at Boston Doctors. A friend of mine, Christine Beall, was brought in here a short time ago?"

"Ah, yes, the automobile accident," she said in sterile English. "I saw her only briefly before Dr. St. Onge arrived and . . . ah . . . took over the case. She has a fractured wrist and possibly some fractured ribs on the left side. Also two scalp lacerations. However, at the time Dr. St. Onge dismissed me she seemed in no immediate danger. You will find her in there." She pointed at one of the rooms.

In addition to St. Onge, three others were in the room with Christine—an orderly, the lab technician, and a second nurse. David ignored them all and rushed to the examining table. "Dr. St. Onge, I'm Dr. David Shelton," he said looking only at Christine. She was lying on her side, sterile drapes over her head. A large patch of hair had been shaved away from her left ear. The drapes surrounded an ugly, three-inch gash that was nearly sutured shut.

"David?" Christine's voice was the empty whimper of a lost child.

He knelt by the table a safe distance from the sterile field. "Yeah, hon, it's me." The reassurance in his voice belied the anger and sadness inside him. "You're doin' fine. A few dents, but you're doin' just fine."

"We're a pair, aren't we?" she said weakly. The few words were all she could manage.

"And who the hell are you?" St. Onge was obviously

not satisfied with David's introduction. He was a heavy man, barrel-chested with thick hands. His tan was still midsummer dark and his clothes custom made. David guessed him to be about fifty.

"Oh, I'm sorry," he said, backing off a step. "My name is Shelton, David Shelton. I'm on the surgical staff at Boston Doctors. Christine is a . . . close friend."

"Well, right now she's my patient," St. Onge growled. "I'm sure you wouldn't take too kindly to someone barging in on your work. Even if he was a fellow surgeon."

David swallowed what he really wanted to say, backed off another step, and mumbled, "I'm sorry. Could you tell me how she is?"

St. Onge rummaged through his set of instruments, found a needle holder, and returned to the cut.

"She has another gash I've already closed above this one. She's got a busted arm that Stan Keyes will probably have to reduce in the operating room. That is, providing he doesn't capsize and drown in that stupid regatta he's racing in today."

David tightened. "Is he the only orthopedist available?"

"Yup. But don't worry. Fortunately, he's a damn sight better orthopedic surgeon than he is a sailor." St. Onge chuckled. "The arm will keep until he gets back."

David turned his attention to the bank of four X-ray view boxes on the wall across from the litter and studied the views taken of Christine's chest, abdomen, ribs, forearm, and skull. The forearm fracture was a bad one, with multiple fragments, but fortunately did not involve the joint space. The function of her hand would likely be unimpaired. He thought about the superb orthopedic staff at Boston Doctors and began wondering if a transfer there would be possible.

St. Onge finished suturing the laceration as David was snapping the four films of Christine's skull into place. The man whipped off his gloves with a flourish, letting them fall to the floor. "Use one of my standard head-injury order sheets, Tammy," he said. "Keyes will probably want to transfer her to his service anyway when he does the wrist. Any questions, Dr. . . ."

"Shelton," David said icily, brushing past him and kneeling by Christine. The sterile drape had been discarded and David could appreciate for the first time the extent of the battering she had absorbed. Despite some attempt to clean her up, patches of dried, cracking blood still remained over her face and neck. Almost the entire left side of her scalp had been shaved, exposing the two angry gashes. Tiny diamonds of glass sparkled throughout what hair remained. Her upper lip was the size and color of a small plum.

"Christine," he said softly. "How're you holding up?"

"Oh, David . . ." Her words were agonized, tearless sobs. David's fists tightened against his thighs.

"Dr. St. Onge, has a radiologist gone over her films?" He rose with deliberate slowness and turned toward the man.

"Why, no. The radiologist has left for the day. On call, if necessary, but I didn't see any reason to call him in for findings as obvious as . . ."

"Excuse me, miss," David cut in, "could I have an otoscope please. And, while you're at it, an ophthalmoscope." The woman had a bemused expression on her face as she handed the instruments over. St. Onge was speechless.

David slipped the otoscope tip in Christine's left ear. At that moment St. Onge found his tongue. "Now you just wait one goddamn minute," he said. "That woman is still my patient, and if you . . ."

"No!" David snarled the word. "*You* wait one goddamn minute. This woman is being transferred to Boston."

"Why you have your fucking nerve!" St. Onge was

crimson. "I'll have you up before the medical board for this, big city credentials and all."

"Do that, please," David begged. The marginal control he had maintained disappeared completely. "And while we're there, we'll ask why you were too arrogant to call in a radiologist to look at these films. We'll ask why you missed the basilar skull fracture in two of the views. We'll also ask how you overlooked the blood behind her left eardrum caused by that fracture. Okay?" The silence in the room was painful. He lowered his voice and turned to the nurses. "Could one of you call an ambulance for us, please?"

The nurse, Tammy, hesitated, then with an unmistakable glint in her eye said, "Yes, Doctor," and rushed out. St. Onge looked apoplectic.

David turned to the remaining nurse. "I'm going to need some meds and equipment for the trip. I'll send the stuff back with the ambulance. Meanwhile, could you hang a Ringer's lactate I.V., please? Fifty cc's per hour."

"I'll have your ass for this, Shelton." St. Onge hissed each word, then stalked away.

David used the phone at the nurses' station to call Dr. Armstrong. As he was dialing, he heard giggles and a muted cheer from the staff in Christine's room.

"David, I've been worried sick about you," Dr. Armstrong said. "What's going on? Are you all right?"

"I'm fine, Dr. Armstrong. Really," he said. "But Christine Beall isn't. Do you remember her? A nurse on Four South?"

"I think . . . yes, of course I do. A lovely girl. What's wrong?"

"She's had an accident. Automobile. We're at Kensington Community Hospital now, but I'm on my way with her to the Doctors Hospital E.R. Could you meet us there and take over her care? She's got a fractured arm, a basilar skull fracture, and some chest trauma, so

308

you'll probably end up being traffic cop for a three-ring circus of consultants. Will you do it?"

"Of course I'll do it," Dr. Armstrong said. "Are you sure she can handle the trip?"

"Sure enough to try. Any risk is worth taking to get her out of here. Especially with you there waiting for her. I have a lot to talk to you about, but all of it can wait until you get Christine taken care of. We'll be there within an hour."

"That will be fine," Dr. Armstrong said softly. "I'll be waiting."

CHAPTER XXII

At David's instructions the ambulance ride was made at a steady fifty. No lights, no sirens. The fifty-five-minute drive seemed interminable, but what little time they might save by a dramatic dash to the city was hardly worth the catastrophe of an accident.

Throughout the trip Christine slipped in and out of consciousness. David, seated at her right hand, systematically checked her pulse, respiration, blood pressure, and pupil size, looking for changes that might indicate a sudden rise in the pressure against her brain. Any significant increase, either from bleeding or swelling, and he would have only minutes to reverse the process before permanent damage began.

The tension inside him was suffocating. He had acted decisively in dealing with St. Onge, but had he been too hasty? The thought ate away at him. Any crisis in the moving ambulance would be immeasurably more difficult to handle than in the hospital. It was the sort of decision he had spent years in training to be able to make—the sort of decision he had unflinchingly made many times over the years. But this was different.

"Christine?" He squeezed her hand. There was no

response. "Let's go over the equipment again," he said to the paramedic riding alongside him. Out of David's field of vision, the man, a former corpsman in Vietnam, shook his head in exasperation. Granted it was the first time he had ever carried instruments for drilling cranial burr holes, but this was the third check David had asked him to make.

On an off chance Christine could hear, David turned his back to her and whispered the list of instruments and medications. The paramedic held each one up or signaled that he knew exactly where it was. Scalpels, drill bits, anesthetic, laryngoscope, tubes, breathing bag, Adrenalin, cortisone, suction catheters, intracardiac needle—they were prepared for the worst.

Reluctant to take his eyes off Christine again, David began asking their location fifteen miles from the hospital without even trying to digest the information.

"Pulse: one ten and firm; respiration: twenty; B.P.: one sixty over sixty; pupils: four millimeters, equal and reactive." The words became a litany, every two minutes. Dutifully, the paramedic repeated then charted them. There was no banter between the two men. No communication at all, in fact, other than the numbers, every two minutes. Pulse . . . respiration . . . B.P. . . . pupils.

As they entered the outskirts of Boston, the tension grew. David, constantly moving, checking, rechecking, rousing Christine. The paramedic, nervous in spite of himself, fingering the instruments of crisis. The driver, a burly young man with thick brown curls, growled a few words into the two-way radio and toyed with the control switches for the lights and siren. They were close enough now. Any sign of trouble in back and he would make a run for it, doctor's order or not.

Suddenly the trip was over. The ambulance swung a sharp U-turn and backed up to the raised receiving platform. The rear doors flew open. A nurse burst into the ambulance and, with a glance at Christine, went straight for the intravenous bag. Right behind her, an orderly grabbed one side of the collapsible litter. A quick nod from the paramedic and they were gone, the nurse, running to keep up, holding the I.V. bag aloft.

David moved to follow, then sank back on the seat. He caught a brief glimpse of Margaret Armstrong as she met the team halfway across the cement platform and began her examination even before they reached the entrance. Her white clinic coat, unbuttoned, swung behind her like a queen's cape. Her every movement, every expression exuded control and competence.

They had made it. They were home. The decision to move, however hasty, had held up. As relief swept through him, David began to shake.

He weaved his way across the busy receiving and triage area and headed straight for the trauma wing. Real or imagined, it felt as if everyone—staff and patients—was staring at him. Phoenix, rising from the ashes; Lazarus from the dead.

Pausing outside Trauma Room 12, he glanced inside. The room was empty. He shuddered at the memory of Leonard Vincent's knife gliding across his throat. Then he thought about Rosetti. As soon as Christine was out of immediate danger and he had finished speaking with Dr. Armstrong, he would go see Terry.

As David approached Trauma 1, Armstrong emerged and beckoned him inside. Christine was awake. Through a sea of white coats—residents, technicians, and nurses—her eyes—sunken shadows—met his. For a moment all he saw was pain. Then, as he drew closer, he saw the sparkle—the flicker of strength. Her swollen, discolored lips pulled tightly as she tried to smile.

"We made it," she whispered. David nodded. "Now you won't have to do burr holes on me."

David's eyes widened. "You were awake during the trip?"

"Awake enough," she managed. "I . . . I'm glad we're here."

Her eyes closed. A reed-thin surgical resident moved in, swabbed russet antiseptic over her right upper chest, and prepared to insert a subclavian intravenous line. As the man slipped the needle beneath Christine's collarbone, David grimaced and turned away. He came face to face with Margaret Armstrong, who was standing several feet behind him, watching quietly.

"David, I'm so relieved to see that you're all right," she said. "The stories that followed your brief visit here the other night were quite frightening."

"There's some trouble in this hospital—in a lot of hospitals, in fact. I have a great deal to talk about with you, Dr. Armstrong," David said. He glanced over his shoulder at the resident, who was calmly suturing the plastic intravenous catheter in place with a stitch through the skin of Christine's chest. "What about Christine?"

"Well," said Dr. Armstrong, leading him out of the room, "I'll examine her more carefully as soon as the crowd in there has finished. My initial impressions add little to yours. She has a definite skull fracture and some blood behind that drum, but so far she seems neurologically stable. I have both a neurosurgeon and an orthopedic man waiting in the house, but I think we'll hold off on the wrist until we've had a chance to watch her. Ivan Rudnick is the neurosurgeon. Do you know him?" David nodded. Rudnick was the best on the staff, if not in the city. "Well, Ivan will see her and do a CAT scan as soon as possible. If there's no evidence of active bleeding, we'll wait and hope."

"What about her chest trauma?" David asked.

"No problem as far as I can see. EKG shows no cardiac injury pattern. My more extensive exam should help confirm it."

"Dr. Armstrong, I'm really grateful to you for handling this."

"Nonsense," she said. "I can't tell you how flattered—and pleased—I am that you would ask me. By the way," she added, "there is one small problem."

"Oh?" David's eyes narrowed.

"Nothing critical, David, but there are no ICU beds. Not a one. We're checking on one postop patient now, but he's been very unstable and I doubt we'll be able to move him. I've decided we'll be all right putting Christine on a floor. There's a private room available on Four South. I know the girls up there will give her closer attention than she would ever get anywhere else, including the ICU. She'll be moved up there as soon as possible."

"That sounds fine," David said. "If the nurses don't mind, I'll hang around and do what I can to help monitor her. That is, after you and I have had our discussion."

"Yes," said Dr. Armstrong distantly.

"Well, you go ahead and finish. I'll wait in the doctors' lounge until you're free to talk. By the way, which room will she be going to?"

"Excuse me?"

"The room," David said. "What room is she going to?"

"Oh, ah, I have it right here. It's Four twelve. Four South Room Four twelve." The cardiologist smiled, then disappeared into Trauma 1.

Four twelve! David swallowed against the sudden fullness in his throat. Charlotte Thomas's room! Step one on the bloody brick road that had led through one land of madness after another. He fought his sense of superstition and tried instead to focus on the irony. Room 412 would serve as the first command post in their battle to bring The Sisterhood of Life to an end. The exercise worked well enough, at least, to keep him from racing back to Dr. Armstrong to demand a room change. He wandered across the triage area to the

314

doctors' lounge and stretched out with a copy of the monthly periodical *Medical Economics*. The lead article was entitled "Ten Tax Shelters Even Your Accountant May Not Know." Before he had settled into shelter number one, David was asleep.

An hour later, the phone above his head jangled him free of a frightening series of dreams—Charlotte's cardiac arrest and the bizarre events that followed, replayed with all of the characters interchanged—all, that is, except Christine, who died again and again in one grisly manner after another.

His clothes were uncomfortably damp and the sandpaper in his mouth made it difficult to speak.

"On-call room. Shelton here," he said thickly.

"David? It's Margaret Armstrong. Did I wake you?"

"No, I mean yes. I mean I wasn't exactly . . ."

"Well," she cut in, "our Christine is safely in her room. Nothing new for me to add to what we already know. I think she'll be all right."

"Wonderful."

"Yes . . . it is." Armstrong paused. "You said you wanted to talk with me?"

"Oh, yes, I certainly do. That is, if you . . ."

"This would be an excellent time," she interrupted again. "I'm in my office—not the one in the office tower, the one on North Two."

"I know where it is," said David, at last fully awake. "I can be there in five minutes."

The cardiac exercise laboratory doubled as Margaret Armstrong's "in house" office.

David knocked once on the door marked STRESS AND EXERCISE TESTING, then walked in. The small, comfortable waiting room was empty. He hesitated, then called, "Dr. Armstrong? It's me, David."

"David, come in." Armstrong appeared at the door. "I was just making some coffee."

As he passed where she had been standing, David breathed in the distinctive odor of liquor.

Instinctively he checked his watch. It was not yet one. He ran through a number of explanations as to why the chief of cardiology might be drinking under such circumstances, especially at such an hour. None were totally acceptable. Still, the woman seemed quite in control. For the moment, at least, he forced the concern to the back of his mind.

The lab was spacious and well equipped. Several treadmills and Exercycles, each with a set of monitoring instruments, were lined up across the room. The required emergency equipment and defibrillator unit were placed inconspicuously to one side—an effort, David knew, to avoid additional apprehension in patients already nervous over their cardiac testing.

One end of the suite had been set aside as a conference area, with a maple love seat and several hard-backed chairs encircling a low, round coffee table. Armstrong motioned David to the love seat, then brought a percolator and two cups. She seemed more subdued than David could ever remember.

"You seem tired," he said. "If it would be better for us to talk later, I could . . ."

"No, no. This is fine," she said too sharply. "Hospital politics, you know. But for a change I get to sit back and listen. Let me pour us some coffee, then you can fill me in on what has been going on."

She pushed a carton of cream toward him, but he shook his head. "Where to start," he said, using a few sips to sort out his words.

"The beginning?" She encouraged him with a comfortable smile.

"The beginning. Yes. Well, I guess the beginning is that I didn't give the morphine to Charlotte Thomas, Christine did." He sipped some more. "Dr. Armstrong, what I've got to tell you is incredible, potentially explosive stuff. Christine and I have decided to share it with you because . . . well, because we hoped you might use your position and influence to help us."

"David, you know that I'll put myself and whatever influence I have at your disposal." She leaned forward to give him a closer view of the reassurance in her eyes.

In minutes he was totally immersed in the story of Charlotte Thomas and The Sisterhood of Life.

Initially Armstrong encouraged his narrative with a series of nods, gestures, and smiles, interrupting occasionally to clarify a point. Soon, though, her posture grew more rigid, her gaze more impassive. Gradually, subtly, the warm blue invitation in her eyes turned cold. Still, David talked on, relieved at unburdening himself of the awesome secrets that, until now, he was the only outsider to hold. Nearly half an hour passed before he first sensed the change in her.

"Is . . . is something the matter?" he asked.

Without responding, Armstrong rose and walked unsteadily to a telephone resting on a small desk at the opposite end of the lab. After a brief, hushed conversation, she worked her way back and settled heavily into a chair across the table from him. All at once, she seemed frail, and very much older.

"David," she said gravely, "have you discussed all this with anyone other than me?"

"Why, no. I told you that earlier. We were hoping you could help us without involving—"

"I'd like you to start over. There are some points you must clarify for me."

"Chris, are you awake? Can you hear me?"

The voice seemed to be echoing from a great distance. Christine opened her eyes, then blinked several times, straining to focus. She recognized the woman as a nurse, though her features remained uncomfortably blurred. She tried to turn toward the side. Pulses of

317

nausea and an excruciating pressure in her head made it impossible. The room was dark, but even the light from the hallway was unbearable. "I'm awake," she said. "The light hurts my eyes." Slowly she closed them.

"Chris, Dr. Armstrong ordered your pupils to be checked every hour. I'll do it as quickly as I can."

Christine felt the nurse's fingers on her right eye, then a searing pain as the beam from the penlight hit her pupil. A brief respite, then a second stab on the left. She tried to lift her hands, but they would not move. Was she restrained? Her right arm, especially, felt heavy and numb. For a moment, she worried that it was gone. Then she remembered being told by Dr. Armstrong that it was broken. She settled back on the pillow and forced herself to relax.

"Listen, I'm going to let you sleep for a while," the nurse said. "You're due for a new I.V. in about twenty minutes. I'm going to wake you up then and we'll try to get some more of this glass out of your hair. Okay?" Christine nodded as best she could. "Hey, I almost forgot. Only a few hours in the hospital and already you're getting flowers. These were delivered a couple of minutes ago. They're beautiful. I'm going to put them on the table here. I know you can't see them, but maybe by tonight you'll be able to. There's a card. Do you want me to read it?"

"Yes, please," Christine said weakly.

"It says best wishes for a speedy recovery, Dahlia."

Dahlia? The pain and the swelling in her brain made it difficult to concentrate. "But . . . I . . . don't . . . know . . . any . . . Dahlia," she said.

The woman had already left.

"David, this killer, this . . . this Vincent—you must tell me again how you think he found you on the emergency ward and then was able to locate your friend."

David toyed with the cover of a magazine, then dropped it on the coffee table and rubbed at his eyes. What had started as a comfortable, long-awaited unburdening had mutated into a tense interrogation as Dr. Armstrong probed for every possible detail. He felt off balance, bewildered, and threatened by the persistence of her questions and the strain in her voice.

"Look," he said, no longer trying to conceal his mounting apprehension, "I've told you everything I know. Twice. My theories about how Vincent found Ben and me and then Joey are just that—theories. Dr. Armstrong, I know something is going on here. Something that I've said has upset you. I'm not going to tell you any more until you level with me. Now, please, what is the matter?"

The look in her eyes was glacial. "Young man, much of what you have told me is impossible. Preposterous. A series of sick, misguided conclusions that can only cause pain and suffering to many good, innocent people." David stared at her in disbelief. "You are stirring flames of a fire whose scope you do not understand. This so-called killer you have described—it is impossible that he is connected in any way with The Sisterhood of Life."

"But . . ."

"Impossible, I say!" She screamed the words.

"Just what is impossible?" Their heads spun in unison toward the door. Dotty Dalrymple stood calmly watching, her hands buried in the pockets of her uniform. David's skin began to crawl at the sight of her.

"Oh, Dorothy, I'm glad you could make it down this quickly." Armstrong's voice was tense, but composed. "I phoned you because Dr. Shelton here was just telling me a preposterous tale about The Sisterhood of Life and hired killers and—"

"I know what he was telling you," Dalrymple said, her face puffed in a half-smile. "I know very well what

319

he was telling you." She lifted her right hand free. Nearly lost in the fleshy ball of her fist was a snub-nosed revolver.

"The light . . . please turn it off." Christine felt the glare even through tightly closed eyes.

Two women—a nurse and an aide—were picking fragments of glass from her hair with tweezers. "All right, Chris," one of them said. "I guess we've tortured you enough for now. I have to rouse you in forty minutes. We can do a little more then. Okay?" She shut off the overhead light. "Wait a minute. I'm sorry, but I have to turn it back on. Just a few seconds to adjust the flow of your new I.V.

"Prime rib of beef and pheasant under glass were on your little menu sheet, but since you didn't circle anything we decided to serve you the specialty of the house: dextrose and water."

A ten-second explosion and again the room dimmed. Christine tried to ignore the throbbing in her skull.

"By the way," the nurse said. "Ol' Tweedledum was on the floor a few minutes ago. She herded all of us into the conference room just to make it clear that heads would roll if you didn't get first-class service from everyone. As if we would give you anything else. Well . . . see you later."

Christine heard the woman leave. Tweedledum. For a time she wrestled with the name. Then she remembered. Dalrymple! Suddenly bits and pieces of information were swirling about in her head. Dalrymple condemning David. Dalrymple offering a bribe. Her mind, working sluggishly through bruised, swollen tissues, struggled to understand. Deep within her apprehension took hold and fueled the already unbearable pounding in her head. Dalrymple! Could she have been responsible? Nothing made sense. Nothing except that she had to find David. Had to talk to him. She tried to

320

move, to reach the bedside phone. Her free hand touched it, then knocked it, clattering, to the floor.

She searched for the call button. They had pinned it somewhere. Where? Where had they said it was?

From the darkness over her bed drops of intravenous fluid flowed inexorably from the plastic bag, through the tubing, and into her chest.

Christine was fumbling through the bedclothes for the call button when her pain began to lessen. Deep within her an uncomfortable warmth took hold and spread. Thirty seconds alone at the nurses' station were all Dotty Dalrymple had needed.

David . . . call David. Christine battled to maintain her resolve. Her eyelids closed, then refused to open again. So much to do, she thought. David . . . Sisterhood . . . so much to do. Her head sank back on the pillow. Her hand relaxed and fell to her side. Suddenly nothing seemed to matter. Nothing at all.

She listened for a time to the strange hum that filled the room. Then, with an inaudible sigh, she surrendered to the darkness.

Dalrymple motioned Armstrong to the chair next to David. Her brown eyes flashed hatred at both of them. Her sausagelike finger moved nervously against the trigger.

"Dorothy, please," Armstrong begged. "We've come so far. Shared so much. You're just overtired. Perhaps . . ."

"Oh, Peggy, just sit back and shut up," she snapped.

David looked at Armstrong. "Peggy? You? But you're a . . ."

"Doctor?" Armstrong filled in the word. "A few more years of studying, that's all. Believe me, nursing school was easily as difficult." She turned back to Dalrymple. "Dorothy, you know I'm on your side."

"Are you? Are you really on anyone's side but your own? It wasn't you who went to see Beall. It's not your

321

name she associates with The Sisterhood. It's not you whose life goes down the drain as soon as she talks to the police. I have much too much going for me to sit back and let that happen."

"Then . . . then you really did it? You hired a killer?" Dalrymple nodded once. "Dorothy, how could you do a thing like that?"

"Don't start getting high and mighty with me. Killing's our game, isn't it? You taught it to me. Now you draw your line one place and I draw mine another. You were perfectly willing to forge prescriptions and sacrifice Shelton here to save your precious Sisterhood. I'll bet if *you* had gone to see Beall—if it had been your neck on the block—you would have done the same things to protect yourself as I did."

Armstrong started to protest, but Dalrymple silenced her with a flick of the gun. She reached into her pocket and, smiling, withdrew a large syringe, filled to capacity. Then she checked her watch. "Two o'clock," she said. "If my nurses are as efficient at their jobs as I have trained them to be, the I.V. you ordered on young Miss Beall should be up and running."

Christine's death sentence! David stared at Dalrymple with sudden panic. "What did you give her?" He shifted his feet for better leverage and began searching for an opening, however slight.

Dalrymple sensed the change and leveled the revolver at his face. "It would be useless to try anything." She glanced again at her watch. "Besides, it's too late." She set the syringe on the table in front of him. "The two of you will be a murder/suicide," she said calmly. "I really don't care which is which, as long as the police are satisfied there are no loose ends. Doctor, I give you the choice. The needle or a bullet. Astute clinician that you are, I'm sure you can deduce that one will be considerably more painful than the other."

"Dotty, please, you don't know what you're doing,"

Armstrong begged, moving off her chair to grab at Dalrymple's free hand. Before David could react, the nursing director pulled her arm free and swung a full backhand arc, catching the woman flush on the side of the face. With an audible snap, Armstrong's left cheekbone shattered. Her slender body shot across the room and slammed against the wall fifteen feet away.

Her revolver still leveled at a spot between David's eyes, Dalrymple glanced over her shoulder at Armstrong's crumpled form. "I've wanted to do that for so long." She smiled. "Now, Doctor, you have a choice to make." She moved around the table, pushing it back with a trunklike leg to allow herself room. The muzzle of the revolver was only a foot from David's forehead as she offered him the syringe. "Please decide," she urged softly.

David was staring at her face when, out of the corner of his eye, he saw motion. Margaret Armstrong, on hands and knees, was inching across the floor. Desperately David forced his eyes to maintain contact with Dalrymple's.

"Well?" said Dalrymple. "My patience is running thin."

David took the syringe and studied it. "I . . . I don't think I can get this in without a tourniquet," he said, stalling. In the moment Dalrymple looked down he was able to catch another glimpse of Armstrong. The cardiologist was drawing closer. Then he noticed her hands. Each one held a small metal shield. The defibrillator! Armstrong had activated the machine. The paddles, connected to the unit by coiled wires, carried 400 joules.

David rolled up his sleeve and pumped his fist several times. The wires were almost out straight and Armstrong was still ten feet away. Dalrymple's hand tightened on the revolver.

"Now," she demanded.

"Dotty!" Armstrong yelled.

323

Dalrymple spun to the sound at the instant David made his lunge. He threw his shoulder full against her vast chest. The woman stumbled backward, catching the low coffee table just behind her knees. She fell like a giant redwood, shattering the table. As her bulk touched the floor, Armstrong was upon her, jamming one paddle on either side of her face, and, in the same motion, depressing the discharge button.

The muffled pop and spark from the paddles were followed instantly by a puff of smoke. Dalrymple's arms flew upward as her huge body convulsed several inches off the floor. The odor of searing flesh filled the air. Vomit splashed from her mouth as her head snapped back. At the moment of her death the sphincters of her bladder and bowel released.

For several seconds David stood motionless, staring at the two women—one battered, one dead. Then, with resurgent terror, he broke from the room in an awkward, painful dash toward Four South.

Margaret Armstrong, rubber-legged, leaned against the sink, patting cold water on her face. She felt drugged, unable to sharpen the focus of her mind. Behind her lay the mountain of death that had, moments before, been Dorothy Dalrymple.

With great difficulty she forced her concentration to the situation at hand. If Christine were dead, she realized, David Shelton was all that stood against the continuation of her Sisterhood. Could he be eliminated? Should he be? Peggy Armstrong knew she would gladly confess to murder—sacrifice herself—to save the movement. But was she capable of killing an innocent person?

She walked unsteadily toward the door, then turned and looked back in disgust at Dalrymple. If a woman she thought she knew so well, trusted so implicitly, could have tried to buy her own security at such a price, how could she be sure that in a time of crisis there wouldn't be others? Trembling, more from her thoughts than her injury, Armstrong supported herself against a wall. Was it over? After so many years, so many dreams, was it all over?

She slipped out of the office and locked the door. The janitor would not be in until sometime the following morning. Less than twenty-four hours. If she wished to salvage The Sisterhood, she had only that long to plan, to prepare, to act. Questions, one after another, raced through her mind. Was it worth the price of another life? Could she do it? Was there an explanation that would hold up? At that moment the answers were not at all apparent.

CHAPTER XXIII

Using the bannister for leverage, David vaulted down the stairs from North Two to North One. Pulses of adrenaline muffled the screams from his ankle. He exploded through the doorway to the central corridor, scattering a trio of horrified nuns.

The main lobby was in its usual midday chaos. David weaved and bumped his way across it like a halfback in open field, leaving two men sprawled and cursing in his wake.

"Hang on, baby, please hang on," he gasped, scrambling up the stairs in the South Wing. Even two at a time they seemed endless, doubling back on themselves between each landing. "Fight the bitch. Fight her fucking poison. Please . . ."

His feet grew leaden. His legs gave way between the third and fourth floors, then again as he stumbled onto Four South.

The corridor was empty except for one aide struggling to tie an old man safely in his wheelchair. In the seconds she spent staring at the apparition limping toward her, the patient, a stroke victim, squirmed free and fell heavily to the floor. The aide, sensing the emergency, waved him past. "Go on," she urged. "Clarence does this all the time."

David nodded and raced to the nurses' station. "Code Ninety-nine Room Four twelve," he panted. "Call it and get me some help. Code Ninety-nine Room Four twelve."

The astonished ward secretary froze for a moment, then grabbed the phone.

For David the scene in Room 412 was the rerun of a horrible dream. The dim light, the bubbling oxygen, the intravenous setup, the motionless body. He flicked on the lights and raced to the bed. Christine, lying serenely on her back, was the dusky color of death. Through the hallway speaker the page operator began calling with uncharacteristic urgency, "Code Ninety-nine, Four South . . . Code Ninety-nine, Four South . . ."

For a second, two, his fingers worked their way over Christine's neck, searching for a carotid artery pulse. He felt it. The faint, rhythmic tap of life against the pad of his first and second fingers. His own pulse or hers? At that moment, as if in answer to his uncertainty, Christine took a breath—a single, shallow, wonderful whisper of a breath. With the first sound, the first minute rise of her chest, David was in motion. He clamped the intravenous tubing shut, then bent over and gave two deep mouth-to-mouth breaths.

Before he had finished, a nurse burst into the room, pulling the emergency cart behind her. Over the minutes that followed, the two of them, surgeon and nurse, functioned as one. The young woman was a marvel—a controlled whirlwind, providing a needed drug or instrument almost before the words were out of his mouth.

Confronting an unknown poison, David's approach was shotgun: a fresh intravenous solution opened wide to dilute the toxin and support Christine's blood pressure; an oral airway and several breaths from an Ambu

327

bag to maintain ventilation; bicarbonate to counteract lactic acid buildup.

Christine's color darkened even more. He risked a few seconds away from the breathing bag and lifted her eyelids. Her pupils were tiny black dots, nearly lost in the brown rings that constricted them—the pinpoint pupils of a narcotic overdose. God, let it be morphine, David thought. Let it be something reversible like morphine. He ordered naloxone, the highly effective antidote for all narcotic drugs. Within seconds the nurse had injected it.

A few more breaths and David stopped again. This time to recheck Christine's carotid pulse. With a deep sinking sensation he realized there was none.

"Slip a board under her, please," he said, lifting Christine's shoulders free from the bed. "You'll have to forget about the meds and just do closed chest compression until we get some more help. Christ, where is everyone?" His speech was rushed and anxious.

"One nurse went home sick." The woman said the words in rhythm to the downward thrusts of her hands against Christine's breastbone. "Two more are at lunch. They'll be here."

David continued the artificial breathing. "We need someone on the cart," he muttered. "We need someone on the goddamn cart." With the nurse unable to stop her cardiac massage, the trays of critical medications might as well have been on the moon.

An orderly wandered in. David snapped at him to take a blood pressure. The man tried twice. "Nothing," he said.

"Can you do CPR?" David asked, hoping he might free the nurse to return to the emergency cart. The man shook his head and backed away. "Shit!" David hissed.

He looked down at Christine. There were no more spontaneous respirations, no signs of life. Her body was

328

covered with deep blue mottling. Unless he could get help very soon—one more pair of skilled hands—Christine would slip beyond resuscitation. For five seconds, ten, he stood motionless. The young nurse watched him, her eyes narrowed in mounting concern.

Suddenly a woman's voice called out, "Whatever you need, Doctor, just order it."

Margaret Armstrong stood poised by the emergency cart. Her left eye was swollen nearly shut by a huge bruise covering the side of her face. Blood trickled from one nostril. Still she held herself regally, unmindful of the stares from around the room.

David's decisiveness, already dulled by Christine's lack of response, became further blunted by fear and uncertainty. "You . . . you can take over the cardiac massage," he said, wishing the woman were not standing so close to the medication cart. There were any number of drugs there that could serve as lethal weapons.

Armstrong shook her head. "No, no. You're both stronger than I am. Besides, I'm a nurse, and a good one. I'll handle meds. Now, dammit, let's get on with it!"

David hesitated another moment, then shifted into high gear, calling out for antidotes to the substances Dalrymple would have been most likely to use. The crunching blow Armstrong had absorbed had no apparent effect on her reactions or efficiency. She was, as she had claimed, an incredibly good nurse. Adrenalin, concentrated glucose, more naloxone, calcium, more bicarbonate—she drew them up and administered them with speed and total economy of movement.

More help arrived. Another nurse offered to relieve Armstrong, but was directed to the blood pressure cuff.

"She's still not breathing on her own," David said. "I think we should intubate."

Armstrong reached up and pressed her fingers against Christine's groin, searching for a femoral artery pulse.

She looked at David grimly and shook her head. "Nothing," she said.

"All right. Give me a laryngoscope and seven-point-five tube."

"Hold it!" Armstrong's eyes began to smile. "Wait . . . wait . . . It's here, Doctor," she said. "It's here."

Seconds later, the nurse operating the blood pressure cuff sang out, "I've got one! I hear a pressure! Faint at sixty. No, wait, eighty. Getting louder! Getting louder!"

David rechecked Christine's pupils. They were definitely wider. Another fifteen seconds and she began to breathe. The young nurse who had helped from the beginning gave David a thumbs-up sign and pumped her fists exultantly in the air.

The final concern in everyone's mind disappeared when Christine moaned softly, rolled her head from side to side, then fluttered her eyes open. They fixed immediately on David.

"Hi," she whispered.

"Hi, yourself," he answered.

Around the room people congratulated one another.

"I . . . I feel much better. My headache's almost gone." Her expression darkened. "David, Miss Dalrymple. I think she might be the one who . . ."

He silenced her with a finger against her lips. "I know, hon," he said with soft reassurance. "I know everything."

She strained to see inside his words, then calmed perceptibly. "I do feel better. Much better, David. Dr. Armstrong is a miracle worker."

David glanced over at Armstrong. "Yeah," he said stonily, "a miracle worker."

Margaret Armstrong met his gaze and, for a few moments, held it. Then, one at a time, she whispered a thank-you to those in the room and motioned each to leave.

The young nurse was the last to go. Armstrong walked

her into the hall, then said, "You did wonderful work in there. I'm very proud of you."

The nurse flushed. "You . . . you've been hurt. Can I get you anything?"

"I'll be fine," Armstrong said. "You go on along and get back to your patients." Then she turned and reentered Room 412. She knew that at the moment she had stepped to the emergency cart and had drawn up the correct medication, she had sealed the fate of The Sisterhood.

Christine was asleep. Across the room, David had opened the drapes part way and was looking out at the hazy afternoon. His hands hung heavily by his sides, his stance reflecting none of the victory he had just won. Armstrong walked quietly to his side. He would not look at her. For a time the only sounds in the room were the gurgle of oxygen through the safety bottle and the steady sighs of Christine's breathing.

"That's a hell of a bruise you've got," David said, his gaze still fixed on the city below. "I think you should have someone look at it."

"I will," she said. "Later."

"That woman, that . . . that beast lying in your office—she was your creation. Your monster."

"Perhaps. I suppose that in some ways she was. Does it matter that I still truly believe in the good of what The Sisterhood of Life has been doing? Does it matter that the struggle for dignity in human death is just?"

"Sure." David snorted the word. "It matters. Like it matters to the fracture in Christine's skull. Like it matters to the crap she faces when—*if*—she recovers. Like it matters to the fucking judge and the prosecutor and the newspapers who are going to try her for murdering Charlotte Thomas. Like it matters to my friends who are dead just because . . ." His frustration and fury choked off the words.

331

A silent minute passed before Armstrong said, "David, I know how you are feeling. I really do. I know my help with Christine and what I did to Dorothy can't take away the pain you both have suffered. But I also know something else. Something that will do much to soothe your wounds." She hesitated. "I know that Christine will never have to stand trial for murder."

David whirled and stared at her. "What did you say?"

"Christine did not murder Charlotte Thomas." Her eyes leveled at his, her gaze and expression deadly serious.

"How . . . how can you say that?"

"She didn't," Armstrong said flatly, "because I did. And I can prove it."

CHAPTER XXIV

Armstrong closed the door to Room 412 as David first checked Christine's blood pressure, then slowly raised the head of her bed. He had listened to the woman's story for only a minute or two before realizing the importance of having Christine hear it for herself.

Sitting on the edge of the bed, he slipped a hand beneath her head. The room was dark, save for a spattering of pale sunlight through the partially closed drapes. David shook with excitement as he reached up and stroked her bruised, swollen face. "Chris, wake up, honey," he said. "Wake up."

Armstrong pulled a chair by the head of the bed.

Christine opened her eyes, smiled at David, then closed them again. "I'm awake," she said weakly. "It just hurts less with my eyes shut. I'll be okay, though. A few days and I'll be okay."

"You bet you will," he said. "Chris, Dr. Armstrong is here. She has something to tell you. I . . . I thought you would want to hear."

"Christine? Can you hear me? It's Margaret Armstrong." Christine turned toward the voice and again opened her eyes. For several seconds, the women looked at one another. Then Armstrong said softly, "Christine, I am Peg. Peggy Donner."

Christine studied her through the dim light, then reached out and grasped her hand. "The Sisterhood . . . is it over?"

"Not yet, dear. But . . . but soon."

David searched Christine's face for anger, or even surprise, but neither was there. A bond was forming between the two women—a connection that was beyond his understanding. He watched in silent fascination, transfixed by the scene.

"Christine," Armstrong said, forcing each word, "after I leave here, I am going to begin the dissolution of The Sisterhood. It will be done in such a way that none of the members will be hurt. That is, provided you and David can live with the secrets we share. Do you understand?"

Christine managed a nod. "I understand. But the reports—the tapes . . . ?"

"They will all be destroyed. All, that is, except one. That one I shall send to you. It was made by me after I injected Charlotte with a fatal dose of potassium. Christine, the morphine you gave her was not enough. She was stronger, far stronger, than anyone suspected. Charlotte was my friend. She was . . . she was our sister. I had promised her a peaceful death. After you left her room, I went in to say good-bye. One last good-bye. She was breathing easily. I waited, but she only seemed to get stronger. Once she actually opened her eyes. I had promised her. I loved her as . . . I loved her as I did my mother. I . . . ." Armstrong could go no further. For the first time in almost fifty years she wept.

Christine loosened her fingers and brushed them across the older woman's tears. "I love you, Peggy," she said haltingly. "For what you tried to do, I love you."

A minute passed before Armstrong continued. "After

334

I've done what is necessary for our Sisterhood, I'll go to see Lieutenant Dockerty and take full responsibility for Charlotte's death. Believe me, Christine, I *was* the one who did it." She turned to David. "I shall also take responsibility for Dorothy and for the deaths of your friends. I think there would be fewer questions if there is no suggestion of more than one person involved in all this."

David saw the concern in Christine's face at the word *friends*. "I'll explain later, Chris," he said. "Dr. Armstrong, I do appreciate what you did during the resuscitation. For that, I promise that as long as you do what you've said, there will be no interference from me."

"Thank you." Armstrong studied the coldness in his eyes, then bent down and kissed Christine on the forehead. Moments later she was gone.

David knelt by the bed. The scant light in the room glinted off the moisture in Christine's eyes. "When you get out of here," he said, "we're going to take a trip to some dusty little village in Mexico."

"But we get to come back?" There was joy and sadness in her smile.

"We get to come back."

She closed her eyes. For a moment, it seemed she had fallen back to sleep, but as he moved away she grasped his hand. "David, could you tell me one more thing now?" she asked.

"What's that?"

"Do you have vanity plates on your car?"·

John Dockerty gulped at what remained of the stale coffee in his mug and sank back in his chair. It had taken the entire night and most of the morning, but at last Marcus Quigg had broken and had given him the name. The triumph—if that is what it was—felt hollow. Images of the frightened, sick, little man would haunt him possibly forever.

That it was Margaret Armstrong who was responsible for the murders and the mistakes and the pathetic pharmacist only made things worse. She was someone he respected and, even more depressing, someone he had trusted.

"John Dockerty, master sleuth," he said sardonically. "Danced around the barn by a lady who turns out to be another goddamn Ma Barker." Well, at least he had gotten the pleasure of telling the captain—though not in so many words—what an ass the man had been to order the hasty arrest of David Shelton.

Dockerty checked his watch. It had been nearly an hour since the captain had promised to get a magistrate's probable cause warrant for Armstrong's arrest. He rubbed at the stubble on his face and was deciding whether to shave or not when the phone rang.

"Investigations. Dockerty," he said. ". . . Yes, Captain . . . that's fine, sir . . . I'll be down to get it right away. . . .Yes, sir, I know he looked guilty as sin. If I were in your position, I would have made the same decision. . . . Thank you, I'll be down in five minutes. . . . Turkey." Dockerty delivered the last word to the dial tone. He combed his hair with his fingers and pushed himself out of his chair. At that moment, with a soft knock, Margaret Armstrong stepped into his office.

"Lieutenant Dockerty, I have some things to talk with you about," she said.

"Yes," he replied, settling on the edge of his desk, "you certainly do."

Within thirty minutes, Dockerty had heard enough of Armstrong's confession to call in a stenographer. As a final act of defiance, he rang the captain and asked him to witness the proceeding. The man, a silky half-politician, half-policeman with bottle-black hair, listened in dumbfounded silence as Armstrong calmly admitted

responsibility for the murders of Charlotte Thomas and
Dotty Dalrymple, as well as for hiring the killer of Ben
Glass and Joseph Rosetti. It was a story she had rehearsed
carefully before driving to Station 1—an explanation
she hoped would leave Dockerty satisfied that she had
acted totally on her own. It disgusted her to have to
paint Dalrymple as a heroine who had died because she
had stumbled onto the truth, but any hint of a conspiracy would have risked exposure of the movement. She
knew what policemen like Dockerty could do. Besides,
Margaret was sure that up until the end Dotty had
been just as dedicated to The Sisterhood as she was.
The woman was frightened of losing her position and
her influence, that's all.

Armstrong's confession held together well enough,
but there was a vagueness about the details that made
Dockerty uncomfortable. He attempted to pin her down,
but was silenced by the captain, who found his tongue
in time to say, "Now, Lieutenant, I'm sure the doctor
will fill in some of these details in good time. As you
can see, she's had a rather rough go of it."

Armstrong thanked him, adding a look that clearly
made Dockerty an outsider in the exchange between
two people of stature.

Dockerty decided to push his luck. "Just one thing,"
he ventured. "Exactly how did you go about hiring a
killer like Leonard Vincent?"

"I shall cover that in a moment," she said, giving him
her most withering, patrician stare, "but first, if you
would direct me to your ladies' room?"

"If you'll wait," Dockerty said, "I'll get a matron to
go . . ."

"Nonsense," the captain cut in. "Dr. Armstrong has
been officially charged with nothing as yet. The . . . ah
. . . ladies' room is just down the hall to the right. You
can't miss it."

Armstrong again favored the captain with a look and carefully adjusted her skirt before striding from the room.

The ladies' room was a sty. The institutional mosaic floor was stained and cracked. What paper towels there were overflowed the metal wastebasket to one side of the sink. The air reeked of urine and disinfectant.

Margaret Donner Armstrong did not notice the filth. She scanned the room, then went directly to the toilet stall, hooked the plywood door shut, and sat down.

She felt pleased at the way she had manipulated Dockerty and the captain. If David and Christine were true to their word, The Sisterhood of Life would die with dignity. The irony in that realization brought her some solace.

After leaving the hospital, Armstrong had gone home and honored her promise. The tapes—all but one—she had incinerated, stopping now and again to listen to a particular report or to reflect on her friendship with a particular woman. Her dream—her ultimate dream—had nearly been fulfilled. If only Dorothy hadn't come apart.

Barbara Littlejohn had agreed that it was no longer possible for the movement to continue. At times during their telephone conversation the woman had actually sounded relieved. Armstrong wondered if Barbara would have reacted the same way as Dalrymple had her own reputation and career been on the line. The painful fact was that she simply did not know for certain—about Barbara or any of them.

So it had been decided. Barbara would make the calls and write the letters, then do what she could to continue the Clinton Foundation projects. And as the receiver dropped to its cradle, Armstrong knew that, after forty years, it was over.

Now, she sat looking at the sordid messages and primitive drawings on the door in front of her, remembering back fifty years to the last time she had been in such a place. She had felt frightened then. Frightened and dirty. She had feared the detectives and the way they stared at her breasts. She had taken her mind to special hidden places to keep from telling them what they wanted her to say. Hour after hour she had resisted their control, at one point choosing to wet herself rather than ask to leave the room. And in the end she had won. And with her victory had come the chance to strike out on a holy mission—a journey she had come close—oh, so close—to completing.

Now it was time to embark on another.

Armstrong reached inside her blouse to the waistband of her skirt and withdrew the syringe Dotty Dalrymple had almost forced David to use. For a few moments she fingered the deadly cylinder. Then she rolled up one sleeve and skillfully slipped the needle into a vein. She rested her head against the wall and closed her eyes. With a fine, slim finger, she depressed the plunger.

"It's all right, Mama . . . I'm here, Mama," she said.

EPILOGUE

The breeze, which had been little more than a zephyr all day, picked up suddenly, sending noisy flocks of dry leaves swirling about the gray stones.

Dora Dalrymple paused on the narrow path to pull her greatcoat tightly about her. She was, in face, size, manner, and dress, a virtual mirror of her late twin. Her incongruously tiny feet handled the steep downgrade with a sureness born of having taken the same walk each evening for three weeks.

The grave, still a fresh mound of dirt, was encompassed by a ring of pines. In the same grove a small, uncarved block of marble marked the plot where someday she herself would be buried. Ritually, she picked up the metal folding chair she had left there the first day and positioned it next to the dark soil. Then she placed a single flower over the spot where she knew her sister's heart to be.

"It's a mum, Dotty," she said, "sort of rust colored. I know mums aren't one of your favorites, but this one's so pretty and so like autumn. You're not upset by my choice today, are you?" Dora paused, as if listening to her sister's reassuring voice. "Good, I thought you'd understand," she said finally.

"People at the hospital are being very nice to me now. I think they've even stopped calling me Tweedle-dee behind my back . . . yes, I know. Well, it's out of respect for you that they don't, I think. Dotty, you got a call today from Violet in Detroit. I told her you were out for the afternoon and to call back later. I . . . I don't think I can continue The Garden without you. I mean, I helped and all, but you were the one who started it and kept it growing. . . . But The Sisterhood is finished. All of the nurses, including our flowers, have been notified. None of them wants The Garden to die, but to survive we must grow. How will I find new nurses to join us? . . . Perhaps. Perhaps you're right. You always understood human nature better than I did. . . . So, I could cook better than you—what does that prove? It's apples and oranges as far as I'm concerned . . .

"I checked today with Mr. Stevens. Your stone is almost ready. It's beautiful. You'll love it, I know you will. . . . Okay, okay, so I'm changing the subject. I'm frightened of making a wrong decision, that's all. You were always so confident, so decisive . . . . Is that a promise? . . . Good. In that case I think I'll follow your suggestion and ask that lovely Janet to move in with me. . . . Dorothy, are you sure you know what you're saying? Forever is a long time to stand by anyone. . . . Well, all right. I'll call Hyacinth today. But remember, we'll both be counting on you every step of the way."

The conversation over, Dora placed the chair to one side of the grove and returned to her car, oblivious to the light rain that had begun falling.

Inside the Tudor mansion she and Dotty had purchased shortly after the inception of The Garden, she brewed a pot of tea and settled into an oversized easy chair, one of a pair they had designed themselves. Fifteen minutes later, the telephone rang.

"I'm calling Dahlia," the young woman's voice said.

"I'm sorry, but Dahlia is not readily available," Dora said, assuming the whispered tone she had heard Dotty use on so many occasions. "However, this is her sister . . . Chrysanthemum. You may, if you wish, confide in me just as you did in Dahlia."

"Well . . . all right, I guess," the woman said uncertainly. "This is Violet calling again from Detroit. Saint Bart's Hospital. A situation has come up here that I think could use some further research."

"Go on," Dora said reassuringly.

"It's a woman named Agnes Morgan. Her husband is Carter Morgan, one of the executive directors at Ford. She's only forty-two, but is drying out in our hospital for the third time this year. The scuttlebutt has it that her husband's been trying to get a divorce for several years so he could marry his secretary. Apparently Mrs. Morgan won't let him have one without bleeding him dry and doing what she can to ruin his career."

"Sounds very promising," Dora said, doodling the picture of an automobile on a yellow legal pad and overlaying it with an ornately inscribed dollar sign. "I'll do some checking up on the situation and call you. Meanwhile, dig up as much information as you can on this Mr. Morgan and his wife. It sounds like the benefits in this case would be quite substantial, assuming the gentleman decides to do business with us."

"I think he just might," Violet said. "When can I expect to hear from you?"

"Within a day or so, I think," Dora answered. "As you know, we'll take care of any business dealings. You'll have all the help you need."

She replaced the receiver and picked up a gold-framed photo of Dotty from the table. The likeness to herself was such that she might have been holding a looking glass.

"Well, love, we're still in business," she said, resting the picture on her massive lap. "I can't do it without your help, though, so you'd better not forget your promise. Anyhow, that's what sisters are for, aren't they?"

ABOUT THE AUTHOR

MICHAEL PALMER, M.D., is the author of *Miracle Cure, Critical Judgment, Silent Treatment, Natural Causes, Extreme Measures, Flashback, Side Effects,* and *The Sisterhood.* His books have been translated into thirty languages. He trained in internal medicine at Boston City and Massachusetts General Hospitals, spent twenty years as a full-time practitioner of internal and emergency medicine, and is now an associate director of the Massachusetts Medical Society's physician health program.

Turn the page for an exciting preview of
Michael Palmer's medical thriller

MIRACLE CURE

available now in paperback from
Bantam Books

It took every bit of her strength, but Sylvia Vitorelli managed to force a third pillow under her back. She was nearly upright in bed now. Yet she still felt queasy and hungry for air. It was the dampness and the mold, she told herself. If she had been in her apartment in Boston rather than her son's farmhouse in rural upstate New York, this would not be happening. Not that her breathing had been all that great in Boston, either. For months her ankles had been badly puffed and her fingers swollen. And over the past few weeks she had been experiencing increasing trouble catching her breath, especially when she lay down.

Sylvia cursed softly. She should never have agreed to make this trip to Fulbrook. She should have told Ricky that she just wasn't up to it. But she had desperately wanted to come. The ghost of her husband, Angelo, had made living in their apartment a constant sadness. And the dust and noise surrounding construction of Boston's central artery tunnel had made living in their part of the North End most unpleasant. Besides, her daughter-in-law, who had always acted as if her visits were an inconvenience, had actually made the call inviting her to spend almost two weeks away from the city. *The kids ask for you all the time, Mama,* she had said. *And autumn is so beautiful up here.*

Sylvia checked the time. Ricky, Stacey, and the children would be at church for another half hour or so, and then they were going to stop by a friend's. She had begged off going with them, citing a headache. The truth was, she didn't feel she had the strength to get dressed. She should try to get up, maybe make something to eat, watch Mass on TV; but when she tried to move, she suddenly was seized by a violent, racking spasm of coughing, accompanied by a horrible liquidy sound in her chest.

For the first time she began to feel panic. The dreadful gurgling in her lungs persisted. Now she was gasping for breath. Sweat began to pour from her forehead, stinging her eyes. Her purse was right beside her, on the bedside table. She fumbled through it for her pills, with no clear idea of what she would do once she found them. Her fingers were stiff, obscene sausages, bluish and mottled.

The air in the musty room seemed heavy and thick. An extra diuretic pill might help, she thought. Perhaps one of the nitroglycerins too. Desperately, she emptied her purse out onto the bed. Alongside several vials of pills was an appointment card from the clinic at Boston Heart Institute. Drops of perspiration fell from her face onto the ink. Her next appointment was a week from tomorrow. In order to fly to Ricky's, she had had to skip a Vasclear treatment—the first one she had missed in almost six months. But the missed medication couldn't possibly be the reason she was having so much trouble breathing now. She was down to only one treatment every two weeks, and was due to drop to once a month before much longer. Besides, her cardiologist had told her when she called that it was perfectly okay for her to go.

Oh my God, she thought, as she frantically gulped down one pill from each of the medication vials. *Oh my God, what's happening to me?* Suddenly she remembered that the nitroglycerin, which she had not had to take since the early days of her Vasclear treatment, was supposed to be dissolved under her tongue, not swallowed. She tried to get a tablet into place under her tongue, but her hands were shaking so badly, she spilled the tiny pills all over the bed and onto the floor.

Her left ring finger was beginning to throb now. The gold band she had worn for over fifty years was completely buried in her flesh. The finger itself looked dark and violet, almost black in color. *Oh please, God, help me. . . . Help me!*

Drowning now, she struggled to force air through the bubbling in her chest. A boring, squeezing pain had begun to mushroom outward from beneath her breastbone and up into her neck—angina, just like before she began the treatments. She had to try and call Ricky. Or was it better to call 911? She had to do something. Her nightgown was soaked with sweat now. She was breathing and coughing at the same time, getting precious little air into her lungs. There was no telephone in the guest room.

Gamely, she pushed herself off the side of the bed and lurched across to the bureau. Her feet were like water bottles, her toes little more than nubs above the swelling. Another spasm of coughing took away what little breath remained. She clutched the corner of the bureau, barely able to keep herself upright. The cough was merciless now, unremitting. Perspiration was cascading off her. Her head came up just enough for her to see that the mirror was spattered with blood. Behind the scarlet spray was her ashen face. She was a terrifying apparition. Her hair was matted with sweat. Bloody froth covered her lips and chin.

Seized by fear unlike any she had ever known, Sylvia turned away from her reflection, stumbled, and fell heavily to the floor. As she hit, she heard as much as felt the snapping of the bone in her left hip. Sudden, blinding pain exploded from that spot. Her consciousness wavered, then started to fade. The agony in her hip and chest began to let up. *Ricky . . . Barbara . . . Maria . . . Johnny . . .* One by one her children's faces flashed through her thoughts. The last face she saw was her Angelo's. He was smiling . . . beckoning to her.

Two years later

Brian Holbrook squeezed into the ambulance for the short ride from the Back Bay to White Memorial. His father's chest pain was down to a two or three from a ten by the time they left the Towne Deli. Still, throughout the ride, Brian kept a watchful eye on the monitor. The absence of extra beats was a good sign, but the shape of the cardiogram wave pattern strongly suggested an acute coronary.

Jack's cardiologist at Suburban was Gary Gold, one of Brian's former partners—the only one of the four partners who had suggested that Brian's recovery from addiction was the same as recovering from an illness and that he should be readmitted to the practice as soon as he was ready. Silently, Brian cursed himself for not insisting that Gary be more aggressive with Jack in pushing for a repeat cardiac catheterization and surgical evaluation. But then again, with Jack so adamantly against repeat surgery, what was there to do?

White Memorial Hospital was an architectural polyglot of a dozen or more buildings crowding four square blocks along the Charles River. All around, as with most large hospitals, there was construction in progress. Earthmovers and other heavy equipment were as much a part of the scene as were ambulances, and two towering cranes rose above all but the tallest building. A new ambulatory care center, one sign proclaimed. The twenty-story future home of the Hellman research building, boasted another. Like the patients within, the hospital itself was in a constant cycle of disease and healing, decay and repair, death and birth.

The ER was on the southwest side. As they backed into

the ambulance bay, Brian wondered what it would feel like to be back in a hospital for the first time in eighteen months. A mixture of shame and the time pressures of his jobs and his daughters had kept him from attending regular cardiac rounds at Suburban. Instead, he had kept up his continuing education credits through tapes, certified journals, and two in-depth courses, both paid for by Jack.

The vast ER was in noisy but controlled disarray. The two triage nurses were backed up, and the waiting room was full. Brian took in the scene as they rushed Jack to a monitor bed in the back. The drama and energy of the place was palpable to him—his element. Merely walking into the ER made him feel as if he had been breathing oxygen underwater and had suddenly popped through to the surface. He had anticipated heightened emotions at reentering this world, but even so he was surprised by the fullness in his chest and throat and the sudden moisture in his eyes. Not that long ago he had been part of all this, and his own actions had caused it to be taken away. Now there was no telling when, or even *if,* he would ever get it back again.

"How're you doing, Jack?" Brian asked, taking his father's hand as they waited for a clean sheet to be thrown over the narrow gurney in room 6.

"Been better. The pain's gone, though."

"Great."

"Two bucks says I don't get dinner."

Brian glanced at the monitor. The elevation in the ST segment of the cardiographic tracing was less striking—definitely a good omen.

"If this place serves the typical hospital food," he said, "you stand to win twice."

He helped the team transfer Jack to his bed, then stood off to one side as a resident named Ethan Prince began his rapid preliminary evaluation. Brian grudgingly gave the young man high marks for speed and thoroughness. Then he remembered where he was. Suburban was a decent enough hospital, but not one of the interns or residents there would ever get a callback interview at White Memorial. Slip below the top ten percent of your medical school class and you didn't even bother applying.

"You know anybody here?" Jack asked Brian.

The resident, listening through his stethoscope, shushed him.

I hope not, Brian thought.

"I don't think so," he whispered.

As if on cue, he heard his name called and looked over to the doorway. Standing there, hands on hips, was Sherry Gordon, not much older than Brian's thirty-eight but a grandmother several times over. She was also right up there with the sharpest ER nurses Brian had ever worked with.

"Hey, you're a Suburban girl," he said, crossing to her and accepting a warm hug and a kiss on the cheek. "What're you doing here?"

"Cream rises to the top. They've had my application on file for years. Openings don't come too frequently in this place."

"You like it?"

She gestured to the chaos and smiled.

"What do you think?" Her expression darkened. "You okay?"

Brian held her gaze.

"It took three months in a rehab," he replied, softly enough for only her to hear, "and about a billion AA and NA meetings, but, yeah, I'm okay."

"I'm happy to hear that, Brian. Real happy. That's your dad, right? I remember that bypass nightmare he went through at Suburban."

"Six years ago. He's probably having a small MI now."

"Well, he's got a crackerjack resident going over him. Kid reminds me of you."

"I wish."

"Tell him to look into getting your dad put on Vasclear. Everyone around here has started talking about it all of a sudden. Listen, I've got to get back to help Dr. Gianatasio. He's got a real sick lady down the hall."

"Phil Gianatasio?"

"That's right. You know him?"

"From years ago, when we were interns and then residents together. I can't believe it. This is like old home week for me. Please tell him I'm here, Sherry. I'll stop by when I'm certain my pop's stable. Would that be okay?"

"I don't see why not. Got to run. Good luck with your dad."

Vasclear. Brian knew next to nothing about the drug, and most of what he did know he had learned from the newspapers. He wasn't as medically current as in the days when he was attending cardiology rounds twice a week and reading or skimming a dozen different journals. But he had kept up fairly well, and Vasclear, the latest in a long line of experimental drugs aimed at reducing arteriosclerosis, simply hadn't been written about widely.

Ethan Prince freed his stethoscope from his ears, reviewed Jack's EKG again, then passed it over to Brian. Brian accepted it calmly, consciously trying to keep his eagerness and gratitude hidden from the younger physician. There was still a persistent two-millimeter elevation in the ST segment in several of the twelve standard views in the tracing.

"Looks like some persistent anterior injury," Brian said.

"I agree. I'll get the wheels in motion for his admission. Meanwhile, we've got to decide whether to try and melt the blockage. Before we do that, I'll try and get him a cardiologist. Dr. Gianatasio is on first backup, but he's got all he can handle with a very sick woman in four. I'll have to find out who's on second call." He turned to Jack, whose color had improved significantly. "Mr. Holbrook, it appears you're having a very small blockage, and as a result a part of your heart is not getting enough blood."

"A heart attack," Jack said. "It's okay. You can say it."

"Actually, we won't be certain it's a full heart attack until we see some blood tests and another cardiogram."

"Two bucks says it is."

"Pardon?"

"Never mind him," Brian said, taking Jack's hand again. "He was a football lineman in school—offense *and* defense. Too many blows to the helmet."

"I see. . . . Well, I'd better get going. I need to find out who's on cardiology backup and I need to get back in with Dr. Gianatasio."

"Just one quick thing. Sherry Gordon said I should look into Vasclear."

The resident shrugged. "You probably know as much about it as I do. It's a Boston Heart research drug. Rumor has it the results have been really promising."

"Thanks."

"*Anesthesia . . .*" The overhead page sounded. "*Anesthesia to the ER stat . . .*"

"That lady in four must be going down the chute. I guess they're calling Anesthesia to intubate her."

Prince hurried away, leaving the nurse tending to Jack. Brian shifted uncomfortably from one foot to the other, aware of feeling impotent and embarrassed. Just down the hall a cardiac patient was in serious trouble. Brian was another pair of skilled hands, another cardiologist for Phil Gianatasio to bat ideas off of. Yet for all the good he could do anyone at this point, he might as well be a high school dropout.

"Dr. Holbrook?"

The stocky, dark-haired nurse standing by the door had the bearing of someone with authority. Her expression was grim.

"Yes?"

"Dr. Holbrook, I'm Carole Benoit, the head nurse down here. I'm sorry to interrupt, but Dr. Prince told me your father was quite stable. Could I speak with you for a moment?"

"Of course."

"Dr. Holbrook, there's a critically ill woman in room four. Dr. Gianatasio asked if you'd mind going in there."

Brian felt an immediate adrenaline rush.

"I'd be happy to."

He glanced back at Jack, who was resting comfortably, then took a step forward. The head nurse continued to block the doorway. She motioned Brian to a spot in the hall, out of earshot of both Jack and the staff.

"Before you go in there," she said in a stern half-whisper, "I want you to know that I insisted Sherry Gordon tell me who you are and at what hospital you are working. She told me you had lost your license."

"So?"

"And when I pushed her for an explanation, she told me why."

Brian's reaction to the woman had blossomed from a kernel of wariness into full-blown mistrust. He pulled himself up to his full height plus half an inch or so.

"Get to the point," he said.

"I don't want anyone without a valid license practicing medicine on any patient on my emergency ward."

"Frankly, I don't see where sharing my experience and ideas is practicing medicine."

Carole Benoit's eyes were hard.

"I'll be in there watching," she said.

Brian stepped back into the room to reassure Jack that he'd be nearby and would be right back. Then he flexed a bit of tension from his neck and headed over to room 4.

It had been ten years since Brian and Phil Gianatasio had been medical residents together at Eastern Mass Medical Center. They had worked well together during those two years. Phil seemed at ease with Brian's flamboyance and self-confidence, and Brian appreciated that Phil, more steady and meticulous than brilliant, always worked within his limitations and was never afraid to ask for help. After residency, Brian had won a cardiac fellowship at one of the finest hospitals in Chicago, and Phil had temporized his future by enlisting in the service—the army, Brian thought. At first they had exchanged a few letters and calls. But gradually their connection weakened, then vanished.

Phil greeted him from the far side of the gurney. Phil had always been overweight, but since residency he must have gained twenty pounds. His dark hair was yielding to an expanding bald spot on top and was longer in the back than Brian remembered. But one thing that hadn't changed a bit was the warmth and kindness in his face. At this moment, though, Phil looked worried. It was not difficult to see why.

On the gurney, unconscious and clearly toxic, was a disheveled woman with graying red hair, in her late sixties or early seventies. Her grunting respirations were barely moving air, and the paleness around her eyes and mouth was a frightening contrast to the crimson of the rest of her face. Also in the room were Ethan Prince, Sherry and another nurse, the anesthesiologist, and, over in a corner, an older man with a rumpled suit and a stethoscope protruding from his jacket pocket. The woman's private physician, Brian guessed. It was just a snap judgment, but the man seemed ill at ease and out of his element in the face of a crisis. Just inside the doorway, observing more than participating, stood Carole Benoit.

Monitor pattern . . . cardiac rate . . . pulse oximeter reading . . . complexion . . . fingernail bed coloring . . . cooling blanket . . . By the time Brian had gone from the doorway to the bedside, his mind had processed a hundred bits of information. He breathed in the action and the urgency.

"Brian, you're a sight for sore eyes," Phil said. "Like one of those gods in Greek tragedy who pop out of the wall of the theater just when they're needed."

"Hey, careful. I'm through doing the god thing. It ended up causing me nothing but trouble. What's the scoop here?"

"Well, Mrs. Violet Corcoran here is a sixty-eight-year-old patient of Dr. Dixon's. That's Fred Dixon right there. Fred, Brian Holbrook." Brian and the older doctor exchanged nods. "As far as Fred knows, she's never been really sick before this week."

Something in Phil's tone suggested that merely having Dixon as one's physician carried with it certain health risks. But the man *had* come in to see his patient on a Sunday afternoon, and in Brian's mind that negated a certain amount of clinical incompetence.

"He was treating her with some erythro for an upper respiratory infection," Phil went on. "A couple of hours ago her husband called in that she wasn't looking so good. Her temp's one-oh-four. Pulse one-forty. She's got a pretty dense left lower lobe pneumonia. BP was one-sixty. Now it's down to one hundred."

"Septic shock?"

"Probably. But look what she's doing."

Phil indicated the cardiac monitor screen, which now showed a heart rhythm pattern Brian was almost certain was sustained ventricular tachycardia. V. tach of this sort was very unstable in most situations and was often a precursor of full-blown cardiac arrest.

"I read v. tach," Brian said.

"We all agree. She's been in and out of it since she arrived. Short bursts at first. Now more prolonged."

"Treatment?"

"We're working our way through the pharmacy. So far we've tried Xylocaine, bretylium, and Pronestyl, and we're about to give her a hit of digitalis. Nothing's touched it."

"She's going too fast to try and guide her out of it with a pacemaker."

"Exactly."

Brian motioned toward Phil's stethoscope.

"May I?"

Carole Benoit had seen and heard enough.

"Dr. Gianatasio," she cut in, "I'm sorry to have to remind you, but Dr. Holbrook has no license to be treating *or touching* our patients."

For a few seconds there was no movement in the room, no sound save for the soft gurgle of the oxygen bottle. Then Gianatasio slipped his stethoscope from his neck, rounded the gurney, and handed it to the head nurse.

"Okay, then, Ms. Benoit," he said without rancor, "suppose you evaluate this woman and give us *your* considered opinion."

Benoit's face grew pinched and flushed. She pushed the proffered instrument back at Phil and moved away.

"Suit yourself," she said. "But I'm holding you responsible for whatever happens."

"I'll take my chances. Brian, if you don't come up with something we haven't tried, I'm going to have Sule here intubate her and we'll take a crack at shocking her out of this."

Brian took Phil's Littmann stethoscope and moved to the bedside.

"I don't think zapping her with a lightning bolt is going to make any difference," he said. "Not unless we figure out the underlying reason she's *in* that rhythm and do something about *it*."

"It could be just massive infection in a woman with some preexisting heart disease."

"Maybe."

"Whatever it is, be quick, Brian. She's in it again."

Brian first scanned Violet Corcoran, head to feet. There was something about her, something that reminded him of a case he had seen somewhere in his training. *Where? What was it?* He felt over her heart, then her neck, then the arterial pulses at her elbow, wrist, and groin. Finally, he slipped the earpieces of Gianatasio's Littmann into place and worked the diaphragm side of the stethoscope over her heart, chest, and neck. Next he repeated the exam using the bell side.

"Sule, go ahead and intubate her," Phil said. "Then we've got to try shocking her. Damn, this is getting out of hand fast."

Brian didn't respond. He was completely immersed in a sound—a sound coming from the front of Violet's neck. And suddenly he remembered. To his left, the anesthesiologist had slipped in an endotracheal breathing tube so smoothly that Brian had not even realized she was doing it.

"We'll try two hundred joules once, then go right to three-fifty," Phil ordered.

"Wait!" Brian said, indicating a spot on Violet's neck. "Phil, listen to this."

The easily heard humming sound, Brian was nearly certain, was a bruit—the noise of turbulence caused in this case, he believed, by blood rushing through a markedly overactive thyroid gland.

"Pressure's dropping," Sherry Gordon said. "Ninety."

Phil listened for a few seconds.

"I heard that sound when I first examined her, but I thought it was a murmur transmitted up from her heart."

"I don't."

"Thyroid?"

"I'm almost sure of it. I've only seen one case of thyroid storm in my life, but this looks just like it. High temp, wild pulse, coma, increasing stretches of v. tach."

Gianatasio listened to the sound again.

"Could be," he said excitedly. "Dammit all, it just could be. Fred, does this lady have any history of hyperthyroidism?"

Fred Dixon flipped through his office notes and lab reports.

"Eighty," Sherry called out.

"Well," Dixon said, his voice a bit shaky, "I noted a slightly elevated thyroid level at the time of her physical a year ago. But people her age get *underactive* thyroids, not overactive, and besides, I didn't think—"

"Brian, where do we go from here?" Phil cut in.

"Call an endocrinologist. But I would say, in the meantime, massive doses of steroids, high doses of IV propranolol to block the effect of the hormone on her heart, and then some sort of specific chemical blockade of thyroid hormone production as well. The endocrinologist or a book can tell us what and how much."

"Let's go with it," Gianatasio said. "Ms. Benoit, find out who's on for endocrine and get 'em down here or on the phone as quickly as possible. If it's the phone, put Dr. Holbrook on. Then get over to the residents' lounge, please, and get me Harrison's *Principles of Internal Medicine* and the fattest endocrinology textbook you can find. If there's none at least two inches thick, go to the library. The rest of you, listen up, please. We're sailing into some uncharted waters. . . ."